May 1989 ~~~~
March 1990

✓ W9-BKY-410

SAVAGE DESTINY

SWEET PRAIRIE PASSION

BY F. ROSANNE BITTNER

ZEBRA BOOKS
KENSINGTON PUBLISHING CORP.

ZEBRA BOOKS

are published by

KENSINGTON PUBLISHING CORP.
475 Park Avenue South
New York, N.Y. 10016

Fourth printing: April, 1989

Printed in the United States of America

To Otto From Sunshine

My gratitude to Dee Brown, whose compelling book, BURY MY HEART AT WOUNDED KNEE, inspired me to write a series about the Plains Indians. I am also grateful to other authors whose writings have both inspired and aided me in learning about the Indians: Will Henry, THE LAST WARPATH; Donald Berthrong, THE SOUTHERN CHEYENNES; George Bird Grinnell, THE FIGHTING CHEYENNES; Stan Hoig, THE SAND CREEK MASSACRE.

What more can a woman ask than to find her love
when all else is lost?

One

The year was 1845, and for fifteen-year-old Abigail Trent, it was just the beginning of her life. Until that first day she rode into Independence, Missouri, in the back of her father's covered wagon, she had never known anything but the simple and rather quiet life of a Tennessee farm girl. She was hardy and strong from the life she'd led, and she could even use a rifle. However, true danger and daring adventure were unknown to her, and she did not yet know just how brave and stubborn she could be when necessary. She would soon learn.

Abbie and her older sister, LeeAnn, stared out the back of the wagon as it bumped and jostled over the rutted streets of Independence. Their eyes were wide at the sights, their lips speechless, as they gazed at a mixture of Indians and mountain men, trappers headed for St. Louis with fresh furs from their winter hunts. Half-clothed, painted women strolled the boardwalks in front of saloons that were full even in the daytime. Wagons rattled back and forth in the streets, and the general noise and confusion, mingled with the strong odor of horse dung, made Abbie long for the peace and beauty of the Tennessee hills.

Abbie glanced over at LeeAnn and gave the girl a shove when she noticed LeeAnn actually smiling at some of the strange men.

"You looking to get us attacked?" she asked Lee-Ann in a hoarse whisper. "You've heard the tales about the wild men in these parts!"

"Pooh! I'm gonna find me a man before this trip is out, little sister!" the girl tossed back. "And he'll be rich! I'm not going all the way out to that awful, uncivilized western land—not if I can help it! I'm going to be married and be a proper lady!"

"You'll get into trouble, that's what!" Abbie spouted back. "You can't make eyes at men like these!"

"It so happens I know a lot more about men than you do!" LeeAnn snapped. "In a couple of years, you'll be panting after one yourself."

Abbie turned up her nose and crawled to the front of the wagon, yelling out to her recently widowed father, Jason Trent, who walked beside the oxen.

"How much farther, Pa?" she asked.

"Just a little ways," he replied with a grin. "We'll make camp outside of Independence. Tomorrow morning we'll head for Sapling Grove and hold up there till we get organized—maybe find us a scout."

Abbie smiled and watched him with a heavy heart. He had taken her mother's death very hard, and part of the reason for their move was his intention to get away from painfully familiar surroundings. Neither of the girls had really wanted to go, yet neither had had

10

the heart to refuse. Jason Trent had a yearning to go to Oregon and start life over, if that was possible, and he was too lonely already to bear the thought of leaving his daughters behind. Their little brother, Jeremy, was excited and happy about the trip, as would be expected of an active seven-year-old boy. He sat squirming in the wagon seat, and Abbie reached up and tousled the boy's hair, then darted away when Jeremy reached around to tickle her.

Since their mother's death, the responsibilities of motherhood and of taking care of her father had seemed to fall automatically into Abbie's lap, even though LeeAnn was older. LeeAnn had a lot of looks, but little sense, and seemed the frail sort, weak and scatterbrained. Abbie, on the other hand, had an ability to accept responsibility far beyond her years, and an inner strength and level-headedness that made her a natural for filling the void left by their dead mother. She did most of the cooking and sewing and washing, and she looked after her father and brother, whereas LeeAnn had to be prodded and scolded to lend a hand.

LeeAnn was more interested in her looks and in finding a man. In Abbie's mind, LeeAnn was the pretty one, blond and blue-eyed and nicely shaped, as their mother had always been. Abbie, on the other hand, was dark, like her father. She was pretty in her own way, a lovely child in whom one could already see the promise of a beautiful woman. But in her mind she couldn't hold a candle to LeeAnn in looks. She hadn't yet developed a roundness to her form, and she sometimes wondered if her breasts would ever fill out. Young boys back in Tennessee gathered around Lee-Ann like bees to honey, and LeeAnn in turn fluttered

11

and giggled and flirted with ease, loving the attention. Abbie cared little for the opposite sex, especially the younger boys. And she vowed that when she did fall in love, it would be with a strong, dependable man, who would be brave and honest, a man who could not be controlled by silly giggles and batting eyelashes. He would not be pretty and smooth and fancy, like the kind of man LeeAnn wanted. He would simply be all man.

She reached over and picked up a brush, running it through her long, thick tresses. The fact remained that no man was going to look at Abigail Trent as a woman yet, let alone the kind of man she sometimes day-dreamed about. But she already knew the kind of man she wanted—not some fancy, undependable dude; or some callow young boy who fainted at a smile.

In the surrounding thickets, crickets sang and frogs croaked, while near the campfire Abbie sat beside her father, clapping her hands and tapping her toes to his fiddle music—Tennessee mountain music that warmed her heart. Jason Trent was good with a fid-dle, and her eyes teared a little as she remembered the times her mother had laughed and whirled her skirts to the music while he played. That was before the strange disease had come to claim her—the horrible disease that ate at her until she was a skeleton. Abbie was actually glad when her mother finally died, for at last she was out of her awful misery and pain. It had been a long and cruel death, and Abbie could not help but agree that it was best they leave the old farm and the house that held so many memories of their mother.

Mr. Trent's fiddle was soon joined by a banjo,

played by a handsome, sandy-haired young man who was part of a four-wagon supply train heading West. The boy's name was David Craig, and they had already met him and the three men traveling with him. It was obvious David had an eye for LeeAnn already, and he was glad to be able to use his banjo playing as an excuse to be close to the Trent campfire. But as he eyed her up and down and played, LeeAnn hardly looked twice at him. He wasn't dressed fancily enough for her, and he was most certainly not rich.

David's wagon was one of the four owned by Bentley Kelsoe, a pleasant-looking, strong and solid man about forty years old. Kelsoe's wagons were loaded down with supplies to trade and sell to settlers who'd already gone West, and he hoped to purchase some rare Chinese silks and stones. His other two drivers were Bobby Jones, a quiet and slender seventeen-year-old who often glanced bashfully at Abbie; and Casey Miles, a short, red-headed man who was always full of jokes. Abbie had learned that none of them were married, and that all of them looked forward to the trip as a kind of adventure, while for some it was also a chance to set up a line of trade. David and Bobby had been eager to see new places; they had no intentions of settling out West as Jason Trent planned to do.

Abbie wondered to herself why so many people now seemed intent on going West. Was it all just for the adventure? Surely many were fleeing something in the East, perhaps the law, perhaps a memory. Her own father was running from things too familiar. Perhaps others were going to realize some kind of a dream, to start life anew, or to own a lot of land—some of it free

13

for the taking.

Whatever their reasons, to do it took bravery and strength. Of that she was already certain, for she'd heard many stories about the untamed lands west of the Missouri River. There were terrible thunderstorms and plagues of locusts. The mountains were much higher and colder than those in Tennessee—so high that trees couldn't even grow on top of them. There was no law, and men took what they wanted. And, of course, there were the Indians.

Her feelings about Indians were mixed. She knew that many Cherokees and Chickasaws had been run out of Tennessee and the surrounding states, and she often wondered how fair that was. Abbie's heart was soft and her reasoning logical. Yes, the Indians had done some bad things, but weren't they just fighting back, trying to hang on to what they thought belonged to them? And wouldn't the white man do the same if he were the one being attacked and driven off his land? It was all terribly confusing to her young heart.

She continued to clap her hands to the music, as a few townspeople gathered around to visit, to enjoy the music, and to tell them that more wagons were already waiting at Sapling Grove to see if others would show up. For a trip like the one they were preparing to make, it seemed only logical that there would be more safety in numbers, especially when most of them really didn't know what they were doing in this country or even exactly what route to take. A bigger train had left two weeks earlier, and Abbie wished they had made it in time to travel with it. There was an odd heaviness in her chest that night, an ominous, intangible "something" that made her uneasy. But she did not betray

14

her feelings to her father. He needed her, so she would go with him; and whenever he looked at her, she smiled.

That night, another man with a wagon joined them —a graying man of about fifty who called himself Morris Connely. He, Jason Trent, and Kelsoe and his men entered into a conversation and soon Connely also agreed to travel with them; their little group was growing. LeeAnn and Abbie stood up and, holding hands, whirled around and danced to the music, as David Craig made his banjo come alive again while he sang a song about "Tennessee Annie," the lonesome mountain girl. Friendships were established quickly in such times, and soon they were all laughing and talking and dancing, anxious to establish close relationships they knew would be sorely needed out on the prairies and in the mountains.

But the laughing and talking and dancing quickly diminished when a tall, dark man with long, braided hair stepped into the firelight. He was somber of face, his physique broad and commanding. His dark eyes darted around the little group and quickly surveyed each person. Abbie saw him first, quickly letting go of LeeAnn's hands to stare transfixed, and it was into her own eyes that the quiet stranger looked first. When their gaze held, she felt a chill run down her spine, while at the same time the rest of her body felt hot. He stared at her as though he knew her, then quickly looked away, silently waiting for the group to quiet, looking as though he had something to say but was not about to shout it.

Jason Trent rose, and even though he was a big man, he seemed dwarfed by the dark stranger. There

15

was no doubt that the intruder was Indian, if not all, then most certainly half, but Indian or not, Abigail Trent was sure of one thing. He was the most handsome man she had ever beheld, and no man could have better fit her idea of a real man. She felt, stirring deep inside herself, a feeling she had never before experienced, and for the first time, she cared how she looked to someone of the opposite sex.

"Somethin' you want, mister?" her father asked the man.

"Word is you're looking for a good scout," the man replied in a low, soft voice.

Abbie's eyes widened, for she had expected the man to grunt something in some strange, Indian tongue. But the words, few as they were, were spoken in a Tennessee drawl, and did not fit the dark-skinned man dressed entirely in fringed buckskins that were beautifully decorated with beads. Beneath his worn leather hat he wore a red kerchief as a headband.

"We're looking," Jason Trent replied with a nod. "You volunteering?"

The man scanned the group again; this time his eyes avoided Abbie's. While he wasn't looking at her, she stared at him and found herself in awe of his quiet gracefulness and the many weapons he wore. She knew without a demonstration that this man knew how to use the fancy-handled knives that hung in sheaths at his waist.

A belt of ammunition was draped crosswise over his shoulder and midsection, and a pistol hung at his hip. He was both fascinating and frightening. His eyes displayed subtle humor mixed with a trace of scorn for the whites with whom he spoke. His face was finely

16

chiseled, the cheekbones high and the nose straight and prominent. His lips were nicely shaped, and she wished he would smile, suspecting he was even more beautiful when he was not so silent and sober.

"I've scouted a couple other trains," the man replied. "Did okay. I know my way around from here to Oregon—north or south, prairies and mountains. Went to California with Joe Walker back in 'thirty-three."

"Joe Walker!" David Craig spoke up. "Why . . . he's famous!"

The stranger's eyes shifted to David, but showed no particular emotion.

"You couldn't have been very old," Trent replied.

"Old enough to go, young enough to learn a lot," the man replied. "Thirteen. Been around a lot since then. Been out West several times."

Abbie calculated as quickly as she could. Twenty-five. He was twenty-five years old and had been traveling the West for twelve years! A full-grown man who knew his way.

Jason Trent rubbed his jaw and looked over at Connely, who scowled and turned away, muttering something about Indians. The stranger eyed him darkly, and the look in his eyes put fear into Abbie.

"Like I say," he continued. "I know my way, and I can get you there. I raise horses—Appaloosas—on the Arkansas River. Just finished a deal on a few, and I'm wanting to do a little moving around before I go back. My people will tend the horses, and I need the extra money."

"And by your 'people,' you mean Indians, right?" Connely spoke up, his back turned. He said the word

17

as though it were something detestable. The stranger shifted his feet, and Abbie could sense the anger he was fighting to keep hidden.

"I wasn't talking to you, mister," he replied quietly. The words had a finality to them that kept Connely's mouth shut. The man's attention returned to Jason Trent. "Name's Zeke. Cheyenne Zeke," he told Jason. He scanned the group again, this time catching Abbie's eyes and holding them like a magnet. A softness that surprised her appeared in his own eyes, and he smiled just slightly. She could not help smiling back, even though she felt her father's looking at her and knew he objected. Then Zeke moved on to the others again. "To answer your question, I'm part Cheyenne—on my ma's side. My father was a Tennessee man, like I expect some of you are. Best scout you can have is a half-breed. I know both worlds. I can talk to the Indians. And like I say, I know the land. I'll just step aside, and you can discuss it with the others."

Like a sleek panther, Zeke moved back into the shadows, and Abbie's father stepped aside to talk with Kelsoe and the others. Abbie could vaguely see the side of Cheyenne Zeke's face that was lit faintly by the firelight; yet in spite of the dark, she knew his eyes were on her again. She felt badly because he might think she looked at him disdainfully simply because she was white and he was a half-breed. Abigail Trent had no prejudice in her young heart, and no malice. And for some reason it was important to her that he know that. LeeAnn, afraid of the half-breed, scurried off to the wagon, but Abbie looked in his direction and swallowed.

"Would you . . . like some coffee, Mr. Zeke?" she asked, disgusted by the girlish sound of her voice.

"I'd be obliged," the man replied. From an old iron pot that hung over the fire, she poured some coffee into a tin cup, then walked closer to Zeke and handed it to him.

"Abbie!" her father suddenly barked. She jumped, and some of the coffee spilled. "Why are you still out here?"

She reddened deeply, ignoring the pain of the hot coffee that had splashed onto her hand. She glared at her father, angry with him for the first time in her life. He had interrupted a beautiful, secret moment between herself and this fascinating stranger called Cheyenne Zeke.

"I never knew us Tennessee folks to shun offering a man a cup of coffee!" she replied defiantly. Her father looked angry enough to hit her. But she knew he'd never lay a hand on her, and she felt as though she'd just won a little victory of her own. She looked up at Zeke. "Here's your coffee," she told him, as the others returned to their discussion.

"Perhaps I'd best not take it," the man replied, his eyes making her knees feel weak.

"I have a feeling you are not the type to back down from something you know is right," she replied boldly. "There's no reason why you shouldn't drink this, if you choose."

Now he grinned a little, stirred by this child struggling to act like a woman in front of him. He took the cup from her, his hand touching hers briefly and sending lightning through her bones. "Thank you, ma'am," he told her with a nod.

19

"Abbie, get to the wagon!" her father ordered, this time with less harshness. She glanced over at him, then back at Zeke.

"You'd best do what your pa says, ma'am," Zeke told her. It seemed to make all the difference in the world that it was Zeke telling her and not her father. She nodded and slipped quietly away to the wagon, but rather than climb inside, she stood at the corner to watch and listen.

Jason Trent, Kelsoe and the others walked back in a group to where Zeke stood drinking his coffee.

"We . . . uh . . . we'll seriously consider hiring you, Cheyenne Zeke," Trent spoke up, rubbing his chin again. "But we have a right to know a little more about you—like how you can have a father from Tennessee and a Cheyenne mother. Quite a distance between Tennessee and Cheyenne territory."

"Long story," Zeke replied. "My pa come out to the plains years back, married a Cheyenne woman, then left again. Went back to Tennessee. Took me with him. Guess that's when I learned to talk like a Tennessee man. At any rate, my pa was a wandering man; that's what led him out West to the mountains. When he went back to Tennessee, he married a local girl. I have three half brothers in Tennessee. Lived there myself a lot of years. Had some bad experiences and came back out here to find my real ma. Been out here ever since."

"No family other than that? No wife?" Kelsoe asked.

Zeke just stared at him a moment, looking as though someone had stuck a knife in his chest. Abbie's own heart tightened, for the pain in his eyes was evident. She felt sorry for him in that instant, and then secretly chastised herself, warning her heart that the man she was staring at would probably violate and scalp her in the dark if he got the chance. Why should she feel sorry for a half-breed Indian she'd known five minutes? But no—Cheyenne Zeke would never hurt a woman. Her own intuition told her that. And there was that awful pain in his eyes!

"Had one," he replied quietly. "Wife and son. They're dead. I'm not answering any more questions about it."

"White?" Connely spoke up, suspecting by the previous answer and by the fact that Zeke had lived in Tennessee that he could have married a white girl. The man seemed to detest Indians, and more than that, he seemed to enjoy rubbing them the wrong way. The word "white" was sneered haughtily.

"It's not your business," Zeke replied. "She's dead, so what's the difference? I came here looking for work. Like I said, I'm good. Now do you want a scout or not? I don't have all night!"

Abbie felt like hitting Connely for making Zeke angry. The remark about his dead wife had seemed to cut deeply into the man, but to her own surprise, Abbie found that she was glad Cheyenne Zeke was now unattached. The realization that he was a widower and had lost a son besides only melted her heart even more. Jason Trent turned to the others.

"I say we hire him. Like he says, he knows both sides, and he knows the land. Looks like a good fighting man to me—a brave man. I say we use him. God knows none of us knows his way around out there."

"Well," Kelsoe answered, rubbing his neck doubtfully. "I don't know. Half-breeds can go either way. Folks say you can't trust them."

"Ain't so with this one!" The voice had come from outside the circle. It belonged to a big, burly man dressed in skins and a beaver hat who was making his way closer—a white man, overweight but mostly muscle, with a bearded face. He appeared to be about forty, and he was smiling now and putting out his hand to Cheyenne Zeke. "How are you doin', old friend!"

Now Zeke broke into a full smile, and Abbie's legs felt like water. It was just as she suspected. That smile brought a disturbing handsomeness to his face, and her heart pounded so that she put a hand to her chest.

"Olin!" Zeke replied. "Where in hell have you been?"

"Just about everywhere—same as you," the man replied as they shook hands firmly. The new man turned to Trent. "Mister, I'm Olin Wales," he said, putting out his hand to Trent. "Zeke here—he's a good man. A good man. Saved my life once. You can bet your very lives that he'll be one damned handy man to have along on a train. He knows all about everything out there, including the Indians. He'd never abuse a woman or be dishonest or lead you wrong. I'll vouch for him. I'd stake my life on Cheyenne Zeke. In fact, I wouldn't mind going along myself—give me and Zeke a chance to catch up on old times, and two scouts are always better than one. I've made that trek before, and I've trapped in the Rockies for years. How about it?"

Trent looked relieved, as did Kelsoe. But Connely began to look a little worried. Abbie liked the man less

22

and less, yet she was not sure why. Perhaps it was the way he had of not looking straight at people, as though he had something to hide. At any rate, once it looked as though Zeke might scout for them, Connely lost some of his cockiness and appeared suddenly uneasy.

"All right, Zeke," Trent told the man. "You're hired. By the way, I'm Jason Trent." They shook hands, and Zeke's eyes moved to Abbie again. She felt herself blushing.

"She going along?" he asked. "And that blond girl I saw?"

"They're my daughters," Trent replied warily.

"Risky business," Zeke told him. "Pretty young girls can mean trouble. Best to watch them close."

Abbie's heart pounded even harder. Pretty! He'd called her pretty!

"I keep a good eye on them," Trent replied. "And they're Tennessee bred. They can fend for themselves. And they know how to use rifles."

"I don't doubt that," Zeke replied, the odd pain returning to his eyes. "But the fact remains . . . well . . . a lot of bad things can happen to a woman out there. And it's not Indians I'm talking about. It's your own kind. I've seen what your own kind can do. There's men out there who haven't seen anything prettier than their horse's—" He stopped short. "Just watch them close," he finished. "What about their ma?"

Trent's face clouded. "My woman died last year—some kind of cancer," he told the man. "There's just the two girls—and my son Jeremy. He's asleep. This man here beside me is Mr. Kelsoe, and he's got three other men with him—four wagons in all. The . . . uh

23

. . . older gentleman there is Morris Connely. Don't know his business and haven't asked. It's his affair."

"That's right!" Connely snapped, turning and stalking off to his wagon. Trent shrugged and looked back at Zeke.

"We aren't all like him," he added. "I . . . uh . . . I want you to know I didn't yell at my daughter because you're part Indian. I'd have done the same with any stranger. Abbie's a little too trusting—too young to know the difference, I guess."

Zeke smiled a little and Abbie looked down at the ground, embarrassed.

"I expect there will be more at Sapling Grove when we get there tomorrow," Trent added.

"I expect so. And I understand about your daughters, Mr. Trent. I'd do the same."

To Abbie's relief, her father finally smiled at Zeke. "The one who got you the coffee is Abigail. She's fifteen. The other daughter is LeeAnn. She's seventeen. But it's Abbie who's kind of taken over since their ma died. She's the strong one of the two."

Zeke looked over at Abbie again, seeming pleased with the remark. "I sensed that," he told Trent. Abbie blushed again and turned around to climb into the wagon, where LeeAnn sat in a robe brushing her hair.

"Abigail Trent!" she said right away in a loud whisper. "I was peeking and I saw you hand that coffee to that half-breed! How could you do such a daring thing!"

"I think he's wonderful," Abbie replied, unbuttoning her dress.

"Abbie! Why you don't have any sense at all?" LeeAnn scolded. "You stay away from that one, or

24

he'll be making a woman out of you before you're wanting to *be* one, and he'll have that long hair stuck in his belt!"

"That's hogwash!" Abbie shot back. "He'd do no such thing! I'm not one bit afraid of him!"

"You make eyes at that half-breed, and you'll be sorry; mark my words!" LeeAnn answered. "Besides, he's got no more than the clothes on his back, I'll bet. There's no future in a wandering, penniless half-breed, who's probably twice your age, I might remind you!"

"Twenty-five," Abbie replied with a grin. "I already figured it out."

"You see? He *is* almost twice your age!"

Abbie giggled. "Oh, LeeAnn, a man like him wouldn't look more than once at something like me anyway. But I can still dream. You can have your fancy men. Me, I'm not after fancy, perfumed, ruffled men. When I take a man, he'll be all man, strong and brave, a man who'd die for me in a second if it meant saving my life and my virtue. I'll bet that's the kind of man Zeke is."

"You're talking dumb!" LeeAnn replied. "You don't know beans about men!"

"And what do *you* know!" Abbie shot back, suddenly jealous of her sister's looks.

"A lot more than you do!" the girl replied. "I've been kissed, and that Leonard Brown touched my breasts once."

"LeeAnn!" Abbie chided. "What a brazen thing to let a boy do to you!"

LeeAnn smiled smugly. "A girl has to learn a few things, doesn't she? When the right man comes along, now I'll know how to handle him. A woman has to have a little experience if she's to be able handle a man. I don't intend to be a bumbling nincompoop when my fancy man comes along. I'll be a real woman for him."

"A man of experience would surely understand when a girl hasn't ever had a man before. He wouldn't blame her or laugh at her. If he was really in love with her, he'd be patient and kind with her. And if he was all that experienced, then he wouldn't be in a hurry to rush at her and scare her to death."

LeeAnn's eyebrows went up. "Well, aren't you the big know-it-all. If you think that's how a man like Cheyenne Zeke would be, think twice. Half-breeds are always panting after white women, and don't forget they're part savage! So they'd make love like a savage, and they don't wait around to find out if you're willing or not. They don't give their women any choice!"

"Oh, what do you know?" Abbie said quietly. "So what if you've been kissed and touched," she pouted. "Those were stupid, back-hill boys who don't know what they're about."

LeeAnn giggled and climbed under her quilt. "I declare, Abbie, for a girl who this morning didn't want anything to do with boys, you sure did change your thinking of a sudden! Now quit talking. I want to sleep."

As she snuggled down into the quilt, Abbie sat staring at the lamp.

"I changed my mind because it isn't a boy I'm thinking about," she replied in a near whisper.

"That's a fact," LeeAnn teased. "It's a man—too

26

much man for the likes of you, little sister!" She giggled again, and inside, Abbie felt like crying. LeeAnn was probably right, and she wished with all her heart she could grow up overnight and emerge a full-grown woman from the wagon in the morning. She sighed and, snuggling down under her own quilt, closed her eyes and thought of Zeke. She dreamed she was walking up to him, smiling, and she put out her hand and he took it. She told him he had a friend, and that she didn't hate Indians; and he smiled his handsome smile and was grateful. Then he kissed her cheek and told her he was glad to have a friend, and they walked away together. But then she fell asleep, and that was the end of the dream.

Two

The next day found them at Sapling Grove, but to Abbie's disappointment, Cheyenne Zeke was not there to greet them. She watched for him the rest of the afternoon, as they made camp and met the others who began to congregate and introduce themselves.

The Trents had arrived with the four Kelsoe wagons and the Connely wagon, and among the six wagons there was a total of thirty-two mules, six horses, and four oxen. Most of the mules belonged to Kelsoe, who had six hitched to each of his wagons, plus four extra mules and four horses. Connely's wagon was pulled by four mules, and the Trent wagon was pulled by two oxen, with two spare oxen and two horses along.

Connely still appeared nervous and spoke to hardly anyone, but the rest of them were soon sharing stories of why they were there and what they intended to do in Oregon. David Craig kept watching LeeAnn, but she paid him no heed. For one of the new arrivals at Sapling Grove was a smooth and handsome man named Quentin Robards. LeeAnn could not help but be attracted to him, for in her mind, Robards was just the man she had been seeking. His dark hair was slicked back tidily, and his well-tailored pants and long coat complemented his lean, attractive build. But there was a prettiness about him that Abbie did not like. His skin was too clean, his hands too white, as though he had never worked hard. She guessed his age to be thirty or so, and thought it humorous that just the day before LeeAnn had been warning her about older men. It was possible Robards was even older than he looked, for he had apparently led a soft life and had pampered his looks.

Robards spotted LeeAnn's flirtations immediately, and quickly introduced himself when a group gathered around the Trent campfire. Abbie tried to keep from making a face at the man's perfumed smell, but LeeAnn smiled beautifully and fluttered her eyelids as he gave his name and bowed in a gentlemanly fashion. He spoke well, as though he was educated, but in spite of her youth and inexperience, Abbie suspected he was a ladies' man, who had cared for no woman in particular in his whole life, and who cared mostly about himself. He wore flashy rings, and earlier she had seen him smoking an expensive-looking cigar. She wondered if he was a gambler. She had already heard whispers to that effect, and it angered her to see her scatterbrained sister mooning over the man. Robards had no wagon. Instead he rode alone on a horse, a grand, shiny, black stallion that carried two fancy carpetbags on either side of the saddle.

As Robards smiled prettily and introduced himself to the others, they were joined by another man, sober of face and stern looking, who introduced himself in very pious tones as Wendell Graydon, a preacher. But to Abbie, Preacher Graydon did not seem like a preacher, for in his unattractive face and narrow eyes she could see that the man had no real love for others. He was middle-aged, tall and spindly, with a large, sharp-hooked nose and an extremely white complexion that was already reddening from the day's sun. There was a coldness about him that made her stomach quiver when he shook her hand with his own cool, bony one, and she decided this was not the kind of preacher she would ever turn to for help. He also had no wagon, and rode only a horse with his supplies in his saddle bags, informing the others that all he needed was the Good Book and prayer to get by on. But Abbie suspected he would need more than that.

Her apprehension was relieved by the arrival of another woman, a Mrs. Harriet Hanes, who appeared to be in her late twenties, and who was traveling with her farmer husband, Bradley Hanes, a stocky, blond, and bearded man, who was short, broad-chested, and rather plain looking. They were a friendly couple with three children, which made Abbie's little brother happy, since two of the children were boys: Jeff, who was ten, and Mike, eight. The third child was their six-year-old daughter, Mary. They drove one wagon, pulled by four oxen, with three horses tied to the back.

The last to join the group was a schoolteacher, a man named Winston Harrell and a widower like Abbie's father. He had a ten-year-old son with him, a quiet boy named Philip. Harrell carried a number of books in his wagon, and Abbie wondered if he would get over those high mountains she'd heard about with such a heavy load. They had already been talking

31

about not being able to take along too much weight. Now she grew worried, for her father had brought along her mother's grandfather clock, and Abbie would rather die than to lose the precious heirloom.

And so their group had grown, some of them going to the West for known reasons, and some for unknown reasons. Preacher Graydon spouted off about saving the "heathen" Indians, and Mr. Harrell spoke with sincerity about setting up a school for settlers' children. The Haneses intended to settle in and to farm one of the rich valleys of Oregon they'd heard so much about. Robards was evasive about his intentions, and Abbie suspected that he planned to get rich off gambling. Connely still gave no indication whatsoever of his reasons for heading beyond the Missouri, while Kelsoe was going to set up a trade line to the West. Now their group was big enough to travel, with eight wagons, twelve men, three women—if Abbie and Lee-Ann could be considered women—and five children. There were twelve oxen, fifteen horses, and thirty-three mules.

Abbie felt safer now, knowing that two of the twelve men would be Cheyenne Zeke and Olin Wales. Her father had already told the others they would be their scouts and had explained that Zeke was a half-breed Cheyenne. Some expressed doubts, but the more Jason Trent explained, the more at ease they seemed to be, except for the preacher, who openly protested. He promptly declared that all must remember that Indians were not among "God's children" and could not be trusted; he added that Indians were not a part of the "Manifest Destiny" of America. Abbie recognized that term as one used to claim that the white man was destined to conquer and rule all of America. She detested the preacher for his words, and knew she'd been right in fearing that there would be trouble between Preacher Graydon and Cheyenne Zeke. For Abbie was certain that everyone was equal in God's eyes, including the Indians; and she felt there were probably some Indians who were more "Christian" than the preacher. His comment even seemed to rub some of the others the wrong way, and her heart swelled with love when her father spouted back that a man's worth should be based on his honesty and his actions, not on his race, be that white or Indian. If Cheyenne Zeke could get them where they were going, that was all that was important.

Talk turned to who would be captain of the wagon train. Neither Jason Trent nor Bradley Hanes wanted the job because each had his family to look after. The fancy Quentin Robards didn't know enough about such travel to be a leader, and neither did Connely, who seemed too preoccupied with himself to care anyway. The preacher declared he would tend to God's matters and let someone else do the leading of the train, and the schoolteacher preferred to spend his spare time studying his books instead of thinking about the trail ahead. That left Bentley Kelsoe, who said he'd be glad to take the job, since he had no family and since he had the most wagons and men. They all knew the real leading would be done by Zeke and Olin Wales, but they needed someone from their own group to keep things organized in camp, to settle arguments, and to supervise the mending of broken wagons and such, since much of Zeke and Olin's time would be spent scouting the trail ahead.

On hearing the latter part of this discussion, Abbie realized that must be what those two were doing at that very moment, and that was why they had not yet shown up in camp. The prairies were quite muddy from the spring rains, and Zeke would have to check to see what would be the best route to take that first day to avoid the prairie spring quagmires. The sun began to fade over the western horizon, and Abbie was sure now that she would not see Cheyenne Zeke that day.

LeeAnn pulled her toward a hollow, where there was a big clump of trees, so she could go to the bathroom, and since Abbie had to go also, she went along with her sister.

"Oh, Abbie, did you see that beautiful Quentin Robards?" LeeAnn asked as they walked.

"I saw him, all right. Looks like a smooth one to me, LeeAnn. I'd say that nice-looking David Craig is a better catch."

"He's just a boy! Quentin is a man, and he's got money! You can tell! Oh, he seems so educated and refined!"

"He probably won the money gambling!" Abbie retorted. "Don't forget that a gambler can be rich one day and broke the next. Pa always warned us never to marry a man like that. I'll bet he's going out West just to take advantage of anyone out there who doesn't know he's a card shark. He's probably running from somebody in the East who's after his hide for a gambling debt."

LeeAnn sighed disgustedly. "Abbie, we never do agree on men!" She stopped and grasped her sister's arms. "You *do* agree that he's handsome, though, don't you?"

Abbie shrugged. "I guess." Then she smiled. "So is Cheyenne Zeke. You don't like my kind of man, and I don't like yours; but that doesn't mean we have to fight about it, does it? I hope you find what you want, LeeAnn. I just don't want you to get hurt."

The two girls hugged. "I feel the same about you, Abbie." They hurried on to the hollow, and in later years, Abbie would always remember how pretty and happy LeeAnn was that day.

They ducked down out of sight of the wagons, pulled up their skirts, and pulled down their pantaloons to go to the bathroom. Abbie finished first and pulled up her pants; then she dropped her skirt and froze. Three men sat behind them, astride large horses, watching and wearing big grins at the sight. How they had gotten there without a sound was beyond Abbie, especially considering the fact that they smelled so bad she'd caught a whiff without even having to stand close to them. The odor was that of old blood, which she surmised came from the poorly dried buffalo robes they wore. She swallowed and touched LeeAnn's shoulder.

"Get up!" she squeaked. Turning to look, LeeAnn screamed, jumped up, and pulled on her drawers. She half fell in doing so, and one of the men laughed. In the next moment, he had a rope slung around LeeAnn so that she could not move her arms.

"Well, well! This is the best thing I've trapped all winter!" the man snickered through yellowed teeth. "You got a nice pair of legs, honey, and a real perty ass. Brings an ache to a man's innards, you know? You and me are gonna have us a little fun, blondie."

Almost immediately, a rope was around Abbie, and two of the men had dismounted. One of them quickly crammed a filthy kerchief into LeeAnn's mouth and tied a rope tightly around that. The other tried to do the same with Abbie, but she had more fight in her than the totally frozen LeeAnn, and she let out a loud scream and bit the man's hand as hard as she could. He yelped and hit her hard across the face. It stung, and she tasted blood, then the gag was in her mouth also. Her arms were tied fast, and both ropes were secured to the pommel of the third man's saddle. He backed up his horse a little so that the girls fell down, then he laughed.

"I got them into position for you, boys. All you got to do is spread them little legs and get your piece. The folks out yonder won't even know what's goin' on till it's over and we're gone from here.

One man moved warily toward Abbie, who kicked at him, but LeeAnn just lay still and cried while the other man pushed up her dress, licking his lips. Abbie struggled wildly, giving her attacker a good kick in the shin bone, angering him. He hit her again, and her head reeled. She waited for the horrible hands to rip at her underclothes, trying in vain to scream again, but for some reason the man did not touch her. She blinked her eyes against her dizziness, and when they focused, she saw the two men staring at something. She looked up to see a huge horse, a very fine and strong Appaloosa, the finest horse she had ever seen. And astride the horse was Cheyenne Zeke. Never had she been so happy to see someone, but the look in his eyes frightened even Abbie. For they blazed with fire and vengeance, and all three of her attackers were very obviously afraid of him.

Zeke held his rifle casually on the man still sitting on his horse with the ropes tied to the pommel.

"Let loose of the ropes, Rube," he said in a low growl.

The one called Rube smiled nervously. "Well, if it ain't the half-breed son of a bitch that tried to kill me a couple of years back. You sure do have a way of spoilin' a man's fun, Zeke."

"Cut the rope," Zeke repeated, raising his rifle a little. To Abbie's surprise the gun went off, and Rube's hat went flying. The man's horse jumped and jerked the girls' bodies. "Cut the rope! Now!" Zeke ordered.

"You bastard!" Rube snarled. "These little fillies are *my* catch—like catchin' beaver skins! You got no right stealin' what's mine!"

"Those two don't belong to anybody but their pa," Zeke replied, his jaw twitching with anger. "Now you'd best cut them loose, or I'll start remembering how it felt when your whip cut into my back!"

The words were spit out hatefully, and Abbie was sure that if it weren't for her and LeeAnn's presence, Zeke would have put a hole in the other man's heart right then and there.

"And you put a hole in me and left me for dead!" Rube replied.

"You deserved it! You're a thieving, stinking murderer, Rube Givens! I don't know how you managed to live after I shot you, but I'm kind of glad. Now maybe I'll have the pleasure of killing you all over again. You slipped past me once. It's not likely to happen again! Now let loose of those girls!"

37

"You half-breed skunk! You fixin' to keep them fresh for yourself, Zeke? Huh? Everybody knows how half-breeds like white girls!' "

Zeke's rifle fired again, and Rube Givens cried out as the bullet ripped across his upper arm.

"You son of a bitch!" Givens screamed. He put his hand to the wound, and blood trickled down over his fingers. By then, having heard the gunshots, most of the people from the train had come, and Jason Trent was leading the pack, knowing Abbie and LeeAnn were not at the wagon. Rube Givens was climbing down from his horse to walk over and cut the ropes from the girls, but when Trent saw his daughters lying there, he quickly surmised the situation, and lit into Givens, calling him names and swinging hard. Jason Trent was a good fighter, but not a cutter, and after he'd gotten in a couple of good blows, the smelly trapper whipped out a huge knife from his belt and waved it at Trent, who backed up slightly in surprise.

Abbie moaned with fear for her father as the two men circled. Abbie knew her father didn't have a chance against an experienced knife fighter, but he wouldn't be one to back off from a fight either. She looked pleadingly at Zeke, who was already sliding down from his horse. He stepped up beside Trent and shoved his rifle into Trent's arms, but his eyes were riveted on Rube Givens.

"This is no fight for you to be in," he told the man. "He'll cut you to pieces."

"They're my daughters!" Trent replied angrily.

"And they need you," Zeke replied. "No sense getting yourself sliced up in front of them. Let me take over."

"But I can't—"

Zeke whipped out one knife and held it out to Trent.

"Cut your girls loose," he commanded, as he drew out the other, bigger knife. It was the biggest, ugliest blade Abbie had ever seen, and Givens backed up as Zeke held out his arms for battle.

It was then that the other side of Cheyenne Zeke came alive; his warrior ancestry came to the fore. His eyes flashed with an eagerness to get his blade into Rube Givens, and the fringe of his buckskins danced as the two of them circled and eyed each other. That was the first time Abbie noticed that Cheyenne Zeke had a thin scar on the left side of his face, from the edge of his forehead all the way down to his jawbone, and there was another thin scar across his chin. He looked fierce and mean, and she wondered just how hard life had been for him, being a half-breed.

Trent quickly cut his daughters loose, hustling them to their feet and getting them out of Zeke's way while they pulled the filthy gags from their mouths. Rube Givens' two friends backed off, not daring to help him, since Olin Wales sat nearby on his horse holding a rifle on both of them. Givens' fear was evident and sweat broke out on his forehead. He stood up straighter and put up his hand as though he wanted to call a halt to the fight. He carefully slid his knife back into its sheath, aware that Zeke would not murder a defenseless man in front of the people who stood watching.

"I ain't knife fightin' with you, Zeke. I ain't lettin' you cut me up like your red brothers would do."

Zeke kept hold of his knife warily. "Now you're

showing your true color, Givens!" he snarled. "Yellow!"

"I ain't yellow!" Givens growled, backing toward his horse. "I just happen to know how a Cheyenne can use a blade! Well, you ain't usin' it on me, you half-breed scum! We'll meet again—on other terms—without all these here witnesses!"

"When you can shoot me in the back?" Zeke sneered. "Why not settle it here and now, Givens! It makes no difference! You'll be just as dead either way!"

"I've put my knife away! You kill me now, it's murder!" Givens said confidently.

"The man is right!" Preacher Graydon spoke up. Abbie felt like kicking him.

"I don't care if you *do* kill him!" she spit out in her anger, forcing back tears, as she stood, shaking, next to her father. Givens looked at her and grinned, stepping daringly closer to Zeke as he did so. His eyes moved back to Zeke.

"All these people here heard me say I didn't want to fight," he told Zeke. "You'd best remember it don't take much to get a half-breed hung. And there's somethin' else they get hung for." He eyed the girls again, then looked at Zeke and laughed lightly. "You think I don't know what you saved them two for? Some night they're gonna find a half-breed sneakin' into their wagon and feelin' their—"

Givens did not finish the sentence. Zeke's foot came up into the man's private parts, and Givens gave out a terrible howl. In the next second, Zeke's knee came up into Givens' face when the man bent over, and there was a bone-crunching sound. Givens fell backward, his face covered with blood. Abbie squeezed her eyes shut and looked away; and others gasped and covered their mouths. Zeke picked up Givens' body and threw it over the man's horse, at the same time ordering the other two to mount up.

"You get him out of here!" he growled at Givens' friends. "And when he comes around, you tell him that the next time I see him, I'll split open his hide, stretch him out to dry in the sun, and feed his innards to the wolves! I've had my fill of Rube Givens! He's just goddamned lucky these people were here watching, or he'd not be alive! Seeing little girls abused is something I don't take lightly, and I'm not going to forget today!"

He slapped the rump of Givens' horse and it galloped off, with Givens' body bouncing up and down on it. The other two went riding after it to catch Givens' body before it could fall to the ground. Zeke turned to face Abbie and LeeAnn, and Abbie's heart swelled with pride at how the man could handle himself. Now he'd saved her from being violated, and in her young eyes no greater hero could walk. She wanted to cry, but she held back her tears for fear of looking more like a little girl to him. She wanted to hug him, but she could not. Trent put out his hand to Zeke.

"I want to thank you," he told the man. "I didn't even know there was trouble till I heard the gunshots. I guess it's like you said. They need watching."

Zeke nodded. "Me and Olin saw the girls heading for the hollow, and we was coming here to warn them not to go so far from the wagons when we heard one of them scream. Them being down in the hollow and all, you probably didn't even hear. Givens was counting on that." He looked down at the girls. "You two would do best to stick closer to your pa and the wagon. If you need to tend to personal things, take your pa along."

"Yes, sir," LeeAnn replied sheepishly. Abbie blushed at the thought of the man talking about her lifting her skirts to relieve herself, but he treated it as a simple matter and was already talking to her father again, advising him to stay out of fights with men like Givens. Part of Zeke's job was to protect the people of the train from such things.

Trent shook his head. "I expect I'd have been cut up good if you hadn't stepped in for me," he replied. "But you shouldn't have risked your neck like that."

Olin Wales laughed. "What's the risk?" he joshed. "Mister, you've never seen Cheyenne Zeke in a knife fight. If you did, you'd understand why Givens backed off. Zeke's got a reputation from here to west of the Rockies with that big blade. Nobody comes out on the winnin' end in a knife fight with Cheyenne Zeke."

Abbie stared at Zeke in admiration as the others thanked him, all but the preacher and John Connely. Mrs. Hanes hung back, wary of this half-breed Indian whom she had not yet even met, but she did not look at him with malice, only curiosity.

"Get on back to camp, and I'll be along to explain some things you need to know before we head out to-morrow," Zeke was telling them. The group split up, and Abbie frantically tried to think of a reason to stay behind with Zeke so she could thank him alone. Her mind raced, and finally she asked her father if she could stay and look for a barrette she'd lost in the scuffle. Zeke nodded to Trent to go ahead, that he'd stay and wait. Abbie's heart pounded as she and Zeke gradually became the only ones left in the hollow, and she quickly began searching for the barrette, aware that Cheyenne Zeke was silently watching her. She was sure she was red all over and sweating from nervousness, and again she longed to be an experienced woman.

"I was sure I'd be able to find it," she spoke up, not knowing what else to say. He held his horse's reins and walked closer, searching himself with the eyes of a hawk.

"Don't see anything. What color was it?"

"Red," she replied, bending over and picking up some leaves. "I expect it's gone for good now."

She did not see his knowing grin. Cheyenne Zeke knew women, and he suspected the barrette story had been made up.

"Probably so," he replied. "We'd best go back."

She stood up and faced him, and he reached out with a big hand and gently pushed some hair behind her ear, his eyes holding her own. Pleasant shivers rushed through her limbs. "You look just fine without the barrette," he told her. "Did they hurt you bad?"

"Only my pride," she replied, suddenly at ease, captured by the intensity of his dark eyes. A little smile made one side of his mouth curve up a little.

"You're a real Tennessee scrapper, I can see that."

There was admiration in his eyes, and she was proud then of the way she'd fought her attacker, instead of just whimpering like LeeAnn had done. "I guess I couldn't have done much," she found herself saying, "but no man's going to touch me unless I want him to, not without a fight." She suddenly reddened at her brazen words, and he brushed her cheek with the back of his hand, then brushed some dirt from her hair.

"Well, he'll be a lucky man, now, won't he?" he replied. Abbie could hardly believe the statement, nor the strange, familiar way he looked at her, again as though he knew her. A lucky man, he'd said. Her heart pounded so hard her chest hurt. But then the admiration in his eyes quickly changed to cold aloofness, and he stepped back, as though something had frightened him away from her. "You'd best get on to the wagon now," he told her matter-of-factly. "I apologize for not getting here quicker, Miss Trent."

"Please . . . you may call me Abbie. And you did fine, Mister Zeke."

"Just Zeke," he told her.

"All right, Zeke," she said with a slight smile. "My God, I think I love you!" she wanted to shout. But how could a fifteen-year-old girl say such a thing to a grown man she hardly knew—and a half-breed at that!

"I'll ride you over," he was telling her. He hoisted her up on the big Appaloosa as though she were a feather, and she thought she'd faint at his big, strong hands on her waist. He led the horse back to the wagons, and she sat there watching his wide shoulders and the dark, thick braid of hair that hung down his back. She suddenly realized she didn't care if this man *did* make love like a savage, as LeeAnn had put it. She didn't doubt she'd enjoy lying next to Cheyenne Zeke, *however* he made love.

Jason Trent sat inside the wagon with his daughters, gently sponging their faces and carrying on about how they'd better never go so far from the wagon again. He stressed how lucky they were that Cheyenne Zeke had come along when he did. He hugged each of them, and Abbie hugged him back extra hard, realizing he could have been killed trying to fight with Rube Givens. But at the time, she knew her father had been desperate and angry; the already lonely man would have been devastated if something had happened to his daughters. There had been one good thing that had come out of the attack. Jason Trent had warmed to Cheyenne Zeke, and that gladdened Abbie's heart.

"Brush your hair now and change your dresses and come on out to the meeting," he told them, kissing their foreheads. "You two sure you're okay?"

"Just . . . shook up," LeeAnn whimpered, still dabbing at her tears. Trent looked at Abbie's bruised face and sighed.

"I'm sorry, girls. But you'll like Oregon. I'm sure of it. And I'll make sure you get there safe." He patted their heads and climbed out of the wagon, hoisting little Jeremy up to his shoulders and walking off to the meeting while the two girls quickly changed.

"Well, I guess your Zeke showed his stuff this evening, didn't he?" LeeAnn said as she pulled her dress over her head and began buttoning it.

"*My* Zeke?" Abbie replied.

"Well, he will be before this trip is out. You've got designs on him, I can see that. And you and I both know you didn't have any red barrette in your hair today. But I won't tell pa."

Abbie reddened and quickly pulled on her own dress. "What does it matter? I'm never going to get a man like that to think fond thoughts of me, especially

45

considering my age.''

"Fiddle! Older men like younger girls. Why, look at how it is back in Tennessee! Some girls get married at thirteen and fourteen to men forty or better!''

Abbie's eyes widened at the thought. "They *do*, don't they?''

"Of course they do.''

Abbie brushed her hair and frowned. "You said yesterday that you didn't think it was right for me to be interested in a man twice my age. Why are you talking like this now?''

LeeAnn fussed with her golden hair. "Because now that I've met Mr. Robards, I know how wonderful an older man can be. The only difference is, there's no future in Cheyenne Zeke, but with a man like Jason, I could have a fine home and fancy clothes. I just know it. But like I said, if that Cheyenne Zeke is what you want, I hope you get him, Abbie.''

Abbie brushed off the remark about Zeke, attributing it to LeeAnn's scatterbrained way of looking at things. "There's an awful lot about him I don't know," she replied. "I don't even know his last name, if he has one. Surely his name isn't just Cheyenne Zeke. And perhaps he already has a woman he's interested in. Besides, there's no sense in even sitting here and talking about him. His being interested in me is about as likely as the sun falling out of the sky.''

Someone knocked on the side of the wagon. "Miss Trent?'' LeeAnn's eyes got wide, and she smiled.

"It's him!'' she whispered. "It's Quentin Robards!''

"Miss Trent . . . LeeAnn? I've come to inquire if you're all right,'' the man's voice spoke up.

"I . . . I'm fine," she replied. "Just a moment." She pinched her cheeks, and as she climbed out, Robards took her hand. Abbie watched from the back of the wagon. The man was all smiles, and he boldly put an arm around LeeAnn's shoulders. Abbie still did not like him.

"I'm very sorry I wasn't present when you were attacked, Miss Trent," he was telling her. "I'd have given those men what for!"

Abbie didn't believe a word of it. She was sure he'd have run and left them there.

"Oh, Mr. Robards, I know you'd have helped," LeeAnn was saying, now dabbing at her eyes. "It was so terrible!" She looked up at him and batted her watery eyes.

"It must have been," the man replied, as they stopped to gaze at each other. "After all you're . . . so innocent." His eyes scanned her body, and Abbie felt sick. "Are you sure you're all right?"

"I am now, Mr. Robards."

"Call me Quentin please. May I escort you to the meeting?"

"By all means."

As Robards smiled and led her away, Abbie stuck her tongue out at him before she climbed out of the wagon. He apparently didn't care that she was now alone, nor did LeeAnn. She was reaching inside for her shawl when she noticed Olin Wales walking toward her. She smiled when he stepped closer.

"You okay, Miss Trent?" he asked.

"Please call me Abbie," she told him. "And I'm fine, sir."

"Zeke sent me to check. He noticed everybody was

47

comin' but you and LeeAnn, and now I see LeeAnn's on her way." He said the words with a sour note.

"You don't like Mr. Robards either, do you?" she asked.

"Not especially. Fancy man. Let's go now, Miss Abbie."

Abbie held back. "Did you say . . . Zeke sent you?"

"Yes, ma'am."

"Mr. Wales, would you . . . could you answer a question?"

"I'll try."

"Why does Zeke look at me so strangely, like he knows me?"

Olin studied her eyes a moment, then took off his beaver hat and scratched his graying head. "Well, ma'am, you . . . uh . . . you look an awful lot like his dead wife."

"I *do?*"

"That's what he tells me, ma'am. I didn't know Zeke then—when he was married back in Tennessee. His wife was a white girl, but I never knew her or his little son." He saw the excited look in Abbie's eyes, and he frowned. "Now don't you go tellin' him I told you about that. He'd have my hide. Zeke don't like other folks talkin' about his private life."

"But what happened to his wife and son, Mr. Wales?"

"Call me Olin. And I ain't tellin' you. It's Zeke's affair. I expect if he wants you to know that, maybe sometime he'll tell you. Now let's get goin'."

"Mr. Wales . . . I mean, Olin . . ."

"What now?"

"Zeke, if he told you I looked like his wife . . . then . . . then that means you two were talking about me, doesn't it?"

He saw the hope in her eyes, sighed, and took out some chewing tobacco and poked a piece into his mouth.

"Let me set you straight, little Abbie. Just 'cause Zeke mentioned you look like his wife and just 'cause he saved you back there, that don't mean you need to go gettin' your sites set on that one. Cheyenne Zeke has been to hell and back many a time. He's a man full of hurt and hate, and he ain't lookin' for no settlin' woman, least of all a white one. He figures what happened to his white wife was his fault, and he ain't gonna let himself get hurt like that again—or bring harm to another woman. He's mostly a wanderer now, more Indian than white, and you'd be best to be lookin' at some nice down-home boy. Wherever Cheyenne Zeke goes, there's trouble, and you don't want no part of that."

Abbie gazed over at the group that had gathered around Zeke. "Every man needs a woman," she said longingly.

"Maybe so . . . and woman is right. Not a little girl! Cheyenne Zeke done had his woman and lost her, so for him and me, the loose squaws will do."

Her heart suddenly burned with jealousy at the thought of Cheyenne Zeke holding some squaw in his big, strong arms, hovering over her and being one with her, giving her what Abbie was beginning to want for herself. She could already see that when a woman loved a man she could take a lot of joy in letting that man have his way with her; for men and women were

49

partly designed to give each other pleasure and to fill each other's needs. And she didn't doubt that when a woman filled Cheyenne Zeke's needs, she got a good share of pleasure herself. She'd never been with a man, never even been kissed, but Tennessee girls who grow up on farms know about male and female, enough to know what men and women in love do to get babies. Olin seemed to be reading her thoughts and he put a gentle hand on her shoulder.

"Believe me, you'd best keep your thoughts off of Zeke," he warned. "It would be bad for you—and for Zeke. You don't understand it all. Now let's get to that meetin'."

Abbie sighed and wrapped her shawl tightly around her and they joined the others. "Fort Laramie is about here," Zeke was telling them. He pointed to the drawing he'd made in the dirt with a stick. "It's a good six weeks getting there. I hope all of you have lots of provisions. You have to understand how big the country is out there, and believe me, you'll be damned tired and hungry by the time you reach the Rockies, but your journey won't even be half over. And don't bank too much on having plentiful game to kill, because that doesn't always hold true. When we get to Fort Laramie, we'll hold up a couple of days and stock up some more. Mr. Kelsoe?"

"Yes, sir."

"I expect you can sell some of your goods at Fort Laramie, if you're looking for buyers. The next fort after that will be Fort Bridger, and it's pretty new, so I expect Jim Bridger will be glad to buy some more things from you. We'll be able to buy other useful goods from him in return."

"Do you know Jim Bridger?" the schoolteacher asked. "He's quite a famous man."

"I know him . . . and Joe Walker, and Broken Hand Fitzpatrick and Kit Carson, too. Know them all."

"Wow!" little Jeremy exclaimed. Zeke grinned a little at the boy, then glanced up at Abbie and Olin before turning back down to his drawing.

"Most of the first part of the journey won't be too bad, till we get to the mountains," he went on. "That's where there will be trouble for any of you who have too much weight along. You don't realize how high those mountains are, and the air is thin, so it's a real struggle for the animals."

Abbie looked at her father, and he frowned. "Something wrong?" Zeke asked. Trent shrugged.

"We've got their ma's big clock along. It's kind of special—especially to Abbie. Leaving it behind would be like cutting off her arm. It's all they've got left of their ma, except for a few clothes and whatnots. The clock was brought over from Europe by their grandmother."

Zeke looked at Abbie, his eyes softening again. "Well, we'll worry about that when it gets to be something to worry about," he replied. "Maybe we can work something out." Abbie blinked back tears. She knew Cheyenne Zeke would do his best to get the clock over the mountains.

"What about the Indians?" Kelsoe asked. "Are they a big threat?"

"Why ask him?" the preacher put in. "He *is* an Indian! If those savages attack us, he has no worries!"

Zeke looked up at the man. In the firelight his dark

51

face revealed his Indian side, and his eyes danced with anger. He rose and looked straight at the preacher.

"Mister, when I'm hired to do a job, I do it. And if these folks should be attacked, I'll fight right along side of them! But I'll tell you one thing. If we have trouble with the Indians, it will be because somebody like you starts it! If they pay us a visit, you'd be wise to treat them with respect, because right now there are a hell of a lot more Indians out there than white men. They don't take kindly to being insulted—and it's the same for me!"

The preacher blinked nervously, and Connely quietly dropped back into the shadows, as though he was afraid for Zeke to catch his eyes.

"And will our *women* be safe around the savages?" the preacher sneered, sweating with fear but determined not to back away.

"You know, mister," Zeke hissed, "the trouble with men like you is you think Indians think like the white man—lusting after what's under a woman's skirts! The Indian has a name for men like that, but I won't repeat it in front of these ladies. Most Indian men are plenty satisfied with their squaws, and they don't think about white women the way I can tell *you're* thinking about women right now!"

The preacher's eyes widened with disdain. "How *dare* you speak to me that way! I am a man of God!"

"And *I'm* half Cheyenne, mister, and damned proud of it! There's no finer looking or better fighting Indian in this country! And believe me, I know the white man, from very personal experience! I've seen what he can do—not just to squaws, but to his *own* kind! So don't you stand there and ask me how safe

52

your women will be around the Indians! I'd trust them all to a whole tribe of Cheyenne for a month, before I'd let them spend one night with a white man I didn't know!'"

Everyone was quiet as Zeke knelt back down to his drawing, tense anger emanating from his body. He pulled out a cheroot and stuck it in his mouth.

"His wife!" Abbie thought to herself. *"Perhaps white men raped his own wife! Why else would he get upset so easily about such things?"* Zeke looked up then, at everyone, but he wouldn't look at Abbie. Now she knew why. He'd been thinking of his wife, and Abbie looked like her.

"I'm sorry," he was telling the others. "A man gets tired of being branded because of his heritage. Any of the rest of you don't like having me along, say it out now. I'll leave and you can get a different scout."

"The preacher doesn't speak for all of us," Abbie's father spoke up. "I'm not about to forget what you did a little bit ago for my girls—and for me. That man would have cut me up good."

"We want you with us," Kelsoe added. Preacher Graydon looked at the others with condemning eyes, but kept quiet for the moment. Zeke lit the little cigar and puffed on it, then rose again, his stature commanding and impressive. Those with any sense knew they could count on him and that he was too valuable to turn away. He glanced at the preacher, then back at Trent.

"The Indian doesn't judge a man by his blood," he told Abbie's father. Then his eyes scanned the others. "That's why I came out here to be with my mother's people. Folks back east judged me by my skin. But the

Indian judges a man by his merits and strength, honesty and courage. They respect courage more than anything." His eyes rested on Trent again. "I'm obliged for your confidence. Now, let's get on with our meeting."

"But don't the Indians steal horses and stock when they get the chance?" Bobby Jones spoke up before Zeke could go on. Zeke turned his eyes to the boy, who expected to see anger in them. But Zeke didn't seem upset.

"Yes, boy, they do. It's best to keep an eye on the stock and let them graze inside the camp as much as possible. Stealing horses is hard for the white man to understand, but horses mean power and a higher station to an Indian. They mostly swipe from each other—one tribe against another—that's been going on for hundreds of years. A young buck takes pride in his catch. He thinks it's the same for the white man. Taking a few horses from the white man is a big accomplishment for the brave, and he'd likely trade the horses back for a few trinkets if he got the chance— something pretty to give to his woman and make him a big man in her eyes."

Zeke's eyes rested on Abbie after that remark, and again she felt hot and tingly and could feel herself blushing.

"Taking horses is a game with them," he went on, looking at Bobby again. "They don't understand. Some of my people understand because I've talked with them, tried to help them understand how the white man thinks, told them a white man hangs men for stealing horses and cattle. But theirs is a whole different upbringing, Bobby. The more horses he has, the more important a brave becomes. It's his wealth. It's like you going out and finding gold. You may not understand it, but sometimes you have to try. And there are a lot of beautiful people out there among the Indians. They have a relationship with the land and nature that the white man could learn from, if he'd take the time. And the Indian could learn a lot from the white man. But they're both so different that I have my doubts that will ever happen." His eyes moved to the preacher, who breathed hard with anger at the suggestion that the white man had anything to learn from Indians.

"I'll pray for your heathen soul!" the man told Zeke. "But I doubt there is much hope of your ever reaching heaven, Cheyenne Zeke! You're part savage. It's obvious you've killed men, and I don't doubt you've spent time with whores and loose squaws! And you've insulted a man of God! It will not be easy to pray for you, but I will try."

Zeke actually laughed lightly and shook his head. It was the first time any of them had actually heard him laugh. "Don't waste your time, preacher," he replied. "I have my own personal religion, and if I'm to get to heaven, I'll do it on my own. Maybe I'll just sort of hang in the middle—my Indian half in hell and my white half in heaven—till God makes up his mind which I'm to be." Everyone snickered, and the preacher walked off in a huff.

"We haven't discussed your fee yet, Zeke," Trent put in. Zeke still seemed upset on the inside, and Abbie was sure he was still thinking about his wife. He took out a little flask of whiskey from his belt and uncorked it, drinking a little. Abbie could feel the tension among the others. All had heard rumors of what whiskey does to Indians. Zeke wiped his lips and corked the bottle, sticking it back in his belt.

"How much you got to offer?" he asked Trent.

"The most we can scrape up is two hundred dollars, plus your meals," the man replied.

"Don't need meals most of the time. I take care of myself. And two hundred is good enough for me if it's good enough for Olin here. We'll split fifty-fifty."

"Makes no difference to me, Zeke," Olin replied. "I'm just along for the ride."

"Like hell. I know you, Olin Wales, and you'll do your share." Zeke looked at Trent. "Olin's a good man. If something happens to me, you can depend on him." He looked around at the others, as he puffed on the cheroot. "In the morning all of you check your gear real good and make sure your axles are well greased. I noticed you have only one yoke of oxen, Mr. Harrell," he told the schoolteacher. "You're carrying a lot of books. You'd be best to have two yokes on that wagon. It's risky setting out on this trip with only two oxen. Four's a lot better. Any of you others willing to rotate your spares and loan Harrell a couple of oxen?"

"Right now I'm the only one with spare oxen," Trent spoke up. "Kelsoe's wagons are pulled with mules, and Bradley Hanes needs all four of his oxen. I have six along."

"Then I think I'd best send Olin back to Independence tonight to buy a couple extra for Harrell. It's too dangerous, him setting out with only two, and we can't risk you being without spares." Zeke looked over at Hanes. "You ought to have a couple extra yourself,

Mr. Hanes. It would cost you about fifty bucks. You got that much?"

The man frowned. "I can't spare more than twenty-five."

"Here's a hundred," Harrell said, handing the money to Zeke. Abbie was glad to see that the men were beginning to trust the half-breed. "I want two extra to pull, and two more as spares. I have plenty of money along."

Zeke looked over at Hanes as he took the money from Harrell. "You've got family, Hanes. You'll need your money. Give me twenty bucks. I think Olin can con a man back in Independence into giving us two good oxen for that price. He . . . uh . . . owes a little gambling debt, you might say."

Zeke grinned at Olin and Olin chuckled. "I know who you mean," he told Zeke. "I'll get the oxen."

Hanes looked relieved. He dug out the twenty dollars, walked up, and handed it to Zeke. "I'm real obliged," he said sincerely. "Real obliged."

"I don't mind putting out for good men," Zeke told him. He looked over at Connely and the preacher. "It's the dishonest ones I'd just as soon skin alive." He turned his eyes to Mrs. Hanes. "You'd best get yourself and them little kids to bed. We'll start off early tomorrow. Olin will catch up in a day or two with the oxen. We can't waste any more time. We have a couple thousand miles to go and not much time to do it in. Snow comes early to the Rockies."

He handed the money for the oxen to Olin, who then rode back in the direction of Independence, while the rest of them began preparing to retire.

"Zeke, you come around our wagon in the morning,

57

and the girls will fix up a little extra breakfast for you," Trent told the man. "It's the least we can do."

Zeke looked straight at Abbie. "How's your cooking, little lady?"

"Good as any grown woman's," she replied defensively.

"I expect it probably is," Zeke replied with a little grin. He looked back at Trent. "Much obliged." Then he took out the little bottle of whiskey and walked off into the darkness.

Abbie wondered what kind of memories he'd sleep with that night, and how long it had been since he'd lost his family. She watched him until she couldn't see him anymore, and then when she turned to go to the wagon, the preacher was standing there. Her heart jumped with fear at the look in his eyes.

"You'd best not set your eyes on that heathen, Miss Trent!" the man told her sternly. "If that one gets you alone, you'll lose your virginity and your honor—and your place in heaven! No matter that he saved you this day. Ask yourself what he saved you *for!* It's for himself! And he'll take your sister and whatever other women he can violate! Mark my words!"

Abbie glared back at him angrily. "My woman's intuition tells me *you're* the one to watch out for, Preacher Graydon!" she spat back at him. "You sneak up on me like that again and say those dirty things, and I'll have Cheyenne Zeke split you up the middle! I reckon he'd enjoy it!"

She stalked off to her wagon, hiding her fear of the cold and stony preacher but feeling his eyes on her. The preacher thought hungrily about the twelve-year-old girl from his former congregation—the one whom he had seduced and "cleansed" in a moment of weakness. He had barely gotten out of town with his life when the deed had been discovered. But the delicious time he'd had with her had been worth the risk, and he was certain God would forgive him for his one and only weakness. He would just be careful from now on. It would be much easier preaching to the ignorant Indians. He could "cleanse" all the young Indian maidens, and God would not blame him a bit. After all, they were worthless heathens, and of no use to God whatsoever. At least if they bedded with a man of God, they might have a slight chance of being saved.

Three

Abbie went all out on breakfast, hoping to show Zeke just what a good cook she was. She was secretly proud when he complimented the homemade biscuits and good coffee, mentioning that he didn't often taste that kind of cooking.

"Mostly I eat pemmican and jerky, and whatever fresh berries I can find or fresh meat I can kill," he commented, sipping a third cup of coffee on a full stomach.

"What's pemmican?" Abbie asked, taking his empty plate.

"Oh, it's a kind of dried food the Cheyenne make. It can be pulverized. Dried meat, sometimes berries, or both mixed together with melted fat and bone marrow. It keeps good, and tastes better than it sounds."

"Do you live just like an Indian when you're with them . . . I mean, in a tipi and all?" she asked cautiously. Their eyes held a moment, and he knew what the woman-child was thinking.

"Yes, ma'am," he replied. "Just like an Indian. It's

not an easy life for one not born to it. I was born to it. Lived away from it for a long time, but got back to it real easy. Guess it's in my blood. I learned to eat light from living with them. You don't find too many fat Indians, Miss Abbie. Life is real hard out there. Real hard. And since the white man started coming out, there's been a lot of disease."

She wanted desperately to ask him if he had a squaw back with his people, but that would be far too bold. Zeke rose.

"Thank you again for the meal. It was real good—like being back home eating my stepmother's cooking in Tennessee."

"Don't you miss Tennessee?" she asked.

The pain returned to his eyes, and behind that she could see a flash of vengeance. "No, ma'am," he replied. "You'd best clean up camp now. We have to leave." He shook hands with Abbie's father and walked off, followed by little Jeremy, who began peppering him with questions about Indians. Zeke answered them patiently as Abbie watched him walk toward his horse, a tall, dark, provocative man who had left so many unanswered questions in her mind. She liked the way he walked, with long, graceful strides. They accentuated his slim hips and broad shoulders, and the fringe of his buckskins swayed with his gait. He mounted the big Appaloosa in one swift, easy movement, using no saddle, and rode off into the distance to watch for Olin Wales. But there was no sign of the man. What he did see was two more wagons approaching. Abbie paid no further heed; she continued to clean up camp and pack the wagon.

About a half-hour later Zeke's horse galloped by her

wagon, and she watched the ease with which he rode the stallion, as though he were a part of it. He was puffing a cheroot again and was bedecked with weapons as he had been the first time she saw him; plus he had two fancy-looking Spencer carbines secured on each side of the horse. That was the first time she'd noticed what looked like the arm of a banjo sticking out from his pack, but she thought little of it at the time, being more curious as to why he rode by so fast with such a concerned look on his face.

The wagons that had been approaching earlier came closer now. Zeke, who had stopped and dismounted, was talking with Bentley Kelsoe. Jason Trent left his wagon to go and see what was going on, while Abbie, watching the two new wagons, noticed that a man herded about ten shorthorn cattle alongside them. She turned to see some conversation among the men. Then Zeke mounted up again and rode ahead of the train, while Kelsoe and the others began shouting "Gee's" and "Haw's" and "Giddap's" and the wagons began to roll. Trent came back to his own wagon, and after much lashing and cursing, he got the lazy oxen into motion. Abbie walked along beside him, but LeeAnn preferred to ride inside where it was more comfortable. Jeremy ran ahead, excited and full of energy.

"What's going on, pa?" Abbie asked her father.

"Well, as you can see, we have two more wagons joining us. Tennessee folk, like us. Name of Hadley and Caroline Brown, and their son and daughter-in-law, Willis and Yolanda Brown. They've got a herd of cattle along, and four horses."

"Why's Zeke looking so upset?" she asked. "We've

got more people. Isn't that good?"

"Depends on how you look at it. For one thing, them cattle will take extra watching. There's the Indians to worry about—and storms. Cattle get mighty skittish in storms. The other problem is that Yolanda Brown is pregnant—about five months along—and she's only sixteen. Zeke doesn't think a trip like this is the place for a young, pregnant woman, especially when it's her first. I have to agree she doesn't have any business out here, but she's got her head set and we don't have time to argue about it. Better to let them come with us than to make them go it alone."

The first day's journey was difficult. Most of the people in the train were not yet in shape for such a venture, and soon Abbie's feet hurt so badly that she stopped talking. She turned her thoughts to Zeke to help ease her pain and smiled inwardly at his kind concern for the pregnant girl. She was sure he must be feeling the weight of the responsibility he had undertaken: ten wagons, fourteen men, five women, and five children; let alone the nineteen horses, thirty-three mules, twenty-two oxen, and the cattle. Besides that, Olin would be coming along with six more oxen. Zeke's work was cut out for him.

She thought about the others and wondered just how well they would all get along when the going got rough, which it most certainly would as they progressed farther into untamed territory. It was a strange mixture of people: her own family from Tennessee; Quentin Robards, the gambler from who knew where, except that he had a Virginia accent; the suspicious and nervous Morris Connely, who also claimed to be from Tennessee; Preacher Graydon from Illinois; the Haneses from Kentucky; Kelsoe and Bobby Jones, both from Pennsylvania; David Craig and Casey Miles from Kentucky; the schoolteacher, Winston Harrell, and his son from Georgia; and the newcomers, the Browns from Tennessee. Then, of course, there were Zeke and Olin Wales, whose homes seemed to be everywhere, except that Zeke's had been Tennessee for part of his life. All of them had their stamina and tempers tested that first day, as they were frequently stuck in swollen stream beds and prairie mud. There was little the women could do at those times, and Abbie often trotted off to pick a few wild flowers while the men struggled to unloose each wagon.

The abundant flowers made the prairie a fairyland, and Abbie wished that the weather and landscape could always be that way—except for the mud. For the land was relatively smooth otherwise, and the prairie flowers were magnificent. They made her heart sing as it began to fill more and more with a secret love for the dark half-breed who led them onward.

Zeke seemed to be everywhere at once: first scouting far ahead of them; then beside them, helping someone push out a wagon; then far behind them, looking for Olin Wales. Sometimes he rode a wide circle around them, and Abbie worried that perhaps Rube Givens would follow them and shoot Zeke in the back, as Zeke had accused the man of wanting to do. Her heart froze at the thought of Cheyenne Zeke lying dead, but she knew that even though she'd known him only three days, she would fold up and die herself if anything happened to him.

Two more days passed without a sign of Olin Wales,

and although Zeke made little mention of it, Abbie was sure he was getting worried himself. He seemed to ride backward more than foreward on the third day. Abbie hoped Olin had not been ambushed by Rube Givens, but late that day he finally appeared in the distance. Zeke galloped by then, riding hard to meet him, and Abbie knew that there was a deep and unspoken love and friendship between the two men when she saw the joy and relief on Zeke's face.

During those first several days, Jason Trent made Abbie ride inside the wagon frequently to relieve the cramps in her legs and the sores on her feet. He loved her deeply for showing her devotion to him by walking beside him every day to keep him from feeling lonely, and by scrubbing his clothes and fixing his meals. Abigail Trent would make a man a fine wife some day. But he often worried about LeeAnn. He had to constantly scold her to get her to help, and he could only hope she'd find a man who could provide for her well enough so that she wouldn't have to do too much work. She just didn't seem cut out for it. But he did not like the sleek and suave Quentin Robards who frequently visited their camp in the evenings to talk to LeeAnn. He'd only mentioned his dislike for the man once, and LeeAnn had promptly clammed up and stormed away from him. Jason wished he could be more stern with her, but she looked so much like her mother. And how he had loved her mother!

Zeke ordered the pregnant girl to ride lying down, and whenever he caught her sitting up in the bouncing wagon or doing any hard work, he promptly scolded the girl and then her husband for letting his wife overdo herself. He seemed unusually concerned, and

Abbie wondered if his own wife had once miscarried. At any rate, the young Mister Brown treated the pregnancy casually, arguing with Zeke that surely the Indian women worked hard and did a lot of walking when they were pregnant.

"They're a hardier lot," Zeke argued back, "already accustomed to the elements and the work. But don't kid yourself. Indian women lose plenty of babies—and a lot of the women die, too."

"I was of the opinion that they simply lie with any man and then squat along the trail when their time comes and give birth to the little bastards," Morris Connely spoke up, surprising them all with this ludicrous remark. Zeke's piercing eyes darted in the man's direction, and he studied him a moment as though he were trying to remember something from the past.

"That's an almighty ugly statement from a man who hasn't said two words since we left," he replied. "There's something about you I don't like, Connely, and I've been trying to figure out what it was. Now I know what part of the reason is. It appears you and the preacher over there are of the same opinion on Indians. I've killed men for remarks like that, and you're just lucky you're a part of this train and I've already agreed to get you to Oregon. If I wasn't a man of my word, I'd—"

"Zeke!" Olin interrupted. "Let it go. He's not worth the trouble."

Connely grinned to himself and walked to his wagon, feeling more confident now that they were so far from civilization that his identity and reasons for heading out of Tennessee would not be discovered. But he reminded himself he'd have to watch his mouth about Indians until Cheyenne Zeke got them to their destination. He detested their dark skin and ignorance, but perhaps he'd be wise to continue his silence.

The more insulting remarks Abbie heard people sling at Zeke about Indians, the more she loved him and felt sorry for him. Connely and the preacher seemed the most prejudiced, but the Browns were not far behind with their mumbling about how an Indian, especially a half-breed, which was as bad or worse than being full-blooded, had no right ordering around their personal lives. Abbie hated them for their prejudice and was appalled that they could scorn his concern and be so ungrateful. Cheyenne Zeke had taken on a great responsibility for very little money, and all some of them could do was insult him and complain. She sometimes wondered why Zeke bothered to stay with them at all, struggling to help them push wagons out of mud, out riding the perimeter before sunrise, hunting game for them, keeping watch at night, and teaching them the rules of the trail when only a few of them truly appreciated what he did. She could not comprehend the real reason Zeke stayed on—to be sure that one important person made it to Oregon . . . a little girl who looked so much like the woman he'd loved . . .

Quentin Robards had LeeAnn completely enamored within those first few days. The more Abbie and their father preached to her about the man, the more obstinate she became, puckering up and pouting and not speaking to either of them. In her mind, Quentin Robards was the most wonderful man who'd ever come into her life, and that was that. And it seemed the more the man hung around, the colder LeeAnn grew toward her own family. At night she teased Abbie about Zeke, insulting him and telling Abbie that if she was going to be foolish enough to love a worthless half-breed, then she shouldn't preach to her sister about a fine gentleman like Quentin Robards. What hurt Abbie the most were her remarks that the "wild half-breed" would never see anything in Abbie anyway. "Whores and squaws are more his type, I expect," she told Abbie one night. "I notice he hasn't so much as blinked at you in days."

What she'd said was true, and Abbie quietly cried herself to sleep that night, her heart heavy for the man she knew she could not have, the man she would always have to love secretly. She felt again the weight of the personality conflicts among the people of the train—the fact that some of them hated Zeke—and of the dilemma created by the fancy-smelling Quentin Robards who rode into their camp every night on his grand, black horse, while David Craig watched in the shadows. Abbie felt sorry for David, who tried so often to talk to LeeAnn or to be nice to her, only to be totally ignored. Abbie fell asleep with a heavy heart that night, praying quietly for her sister, for her father, and most of all, for the lonely half-breed called Cheyenne Zeke.

They soon had their first taste of bad luck when Bradley Hanes accidentally shot himself in the foot while cleaning a hand pistol. He let out a yelp and fell to the ground, while Mrs. Hanes screamed. The wagons having circled for the night, the accident interrupted the quiet evening and brought Zeke riding at a gallop from somewhere in the shadows. He dismounted before his horse even came to a halt and ran up to Hanes. who by then had his boot off and was holding his ankle while trying not to break into tears from the pain.

"What happened here!" Zeke demanded as he knelt down beside the man and began examining his foot.

"My gun—it went off!" Hanes groaned. Zeke studied the foot a little longer, then picked up the boot and sighed when he studied the sole.

"Well, at least we won't have to cut into you to get the bullet out. Look here. It went clean through your foot and lodged in the sole of your boot."

Mrs. Hanes sighed with relief and suddenly burst into tears, while Zeke ordered someone to get some warm water. "We'll wash it down good and pour some whiskey over it," he told the others. "Kelsoe?"

"Yes, Zeke."

"There's a creek up ahead a ways, runs by a few cottonwood trees. Ride up there and see if you can find some moss. It has a way of bringing out the poison in a wound. We'll pack the foot in moss before we bandage it."

"Right, Zeke."

Abbie watched, proud at the way Zeke took command of things and always knew what to do. Moss. She'd never heard of such a thing. It must be an old Indian remedy. She admired the Indians for the way in which they could live with the land and the elements and survive. How soft and pampered the whites seemed to be in comparison. Even these brave and hardy ones who ventured West knew so little about survival. Zeke looked up at the others.

"This man won't be able to drive his animals for a few days. He's got to stay off this foot," he told them.

"I'll take over while he's disabled," Robards spoke up, surprising Abbie with his offer to help. It was the first time he'd offered to do anything since they'd started out. He'd seldom even helped push out wagons, not wanting to get his fancy clothes muddied.

"I'm much obliged, Robards," Hanes told the man. Zeke studied Robards a moment, and Abbie could tell he didn't like the man either. But for the moment he kept his feelings to himself.

"All right," he replied. "You sure you know how?"

"I think I can manage," Robards replied, looking proudly over at LeeAnn, who smiled. It was then Abbie realized he'd only offered to make himself appear more manly in LeeAnn's eyes.

"I'm sorry about this," Hanes was telling Zeke. "I guess I shouldn't have messed with that gun."

"I told all of you once to leave sidearms alone," Zeke replied. "Stick to rifles, and only use those when they're really needed. You people are farmers and teachers and so forth—not gunmen. More folks get shot out here from their own guns than from any enemies, believe me."

Someone brought the water, and soon Kelsoe was back with the moss. Hanes screamed with pain when Zeke poured the whiskey over his foot, then groaned as it was packed in moss and wrapped.

"What does the moss do?" Mrs. Hanes asked, warming more to the half-breed of whom she'd been so distrustful at first.

"Old Indian remedy," Zeke replied. "Should help keep the foot from getting infected. I'm not sure how it

71

works, but it does." He saw the concern in her eyes for her husband. All were aware of what could happen if gangrene set in. Hanes would lose his foot, perhaps his whole leg, and still he would most likely die. "Don't you worry, ma'am. He'll be okay. The moss will help a lot."

"Thank you," she replied quietly. "I'm glad you're along. And I'm . . . sorry . . . for the remarks some of the others have made. I hope you'll stay with us."

Zeke nodded gratefully. "I made a deal, ma'am. I'm a man of my word."

Just then Olin Wales rode into camp, and Abbie's heart wrenched with jealousy at the sight of a lovely Indian girl astride the horse in front of him. Part of her legs were exposed where her doeskin dress came up, and Zeke approached Olin and the girl, giving her the once-over with pleasure in his eyes.

"What the hell have you got there?" he asked his friend. "And where have you been all day?"

Olin chuckled and climbed down; then he reached up and helped the girl down. The preacher watched the Indian girl, feeling an ache in his groin at the sight of her slender legs.

"You told me to ride behind again and make sure Rube Givens wasn't followin'," he told Zeke. "Didn't find anything to indicate he was, but I did find this pretty little thing—bought her off a Chippewa brave back there. He was pullin' her along with a rope, headin' for Independence to sell her to a whorehouse."

People gasped, and the Indian girl stood staring at Zeke, holding her head proudly. She was beautiful in shape and face, and was obviously frightened of what her next fate would be.

72

"When I seen how bad that Chip was treatin' her, I felt kind of sorry for her. I powwowed with him, had a smoke, and found out he'd stole her a year or so ago from the Sioux. You know how the Sioux and Chippewa don't get along."

"I know," Zeke replied, folding his arms and walking around the girl to study her, now looking like a proud brave with his captive. The girl watched him, obviously impressed by his stature and looks, promising favors with her eyes if he would help her.

"At any rate, he was plannin' on sellin' her for a prostitute, and I didn't figure you'd go for that. There's been enough of these pretty little things destroyed in the whorehouses, and she looked kind of proud and scared, you know? Come to find out, that Chip was the only man she'd ever been with, and I could tell she had no idea what he planned to do with her. I finally talked him into sellin' her to me instead —convinced him I was payin' him more than he'd make in town. And . . . uh . . . well, I did it partly for you, Zeke. I figured you wouldn't want her taken to Independence."

Zeke walked around to the front of her again, lifting her chin so she had to look up at him. "You did right," he replied.

"Well, I owed you a little from that card game back in Independence, so I'm payin' you off this way. She cost a lot, and she's the . . . uh . . . grateful type, if you know what I mean. Figured since we're headed into Sioux country, we can deliver her back to her own kind. She told me she cries to go home to her people."

Zeke studied the girl's eyes, then spoke softly to her in the Sioux tongue, and Abbie's jealousy raged. The girl answered, then Zeke said more, and she suddenly began crying and hugged him, as though deeply grateful. The preacher watched hungrily, and Morris Connely shook his head sneeringly and went to his wagon. The rest watched with mixed emotions, some feeling sorry for the girl and others considering her loose, Abbie hating her because she was Indian, just like Zeke. His kind—something she herself could never be. But then wasn't he half white, and hadn't he lived in Tennessee? Surely there was enough white in him for her to capture.

"You did right, Olin," Zeke told the man as he patted the Sioux woman's shoulder. "We'll see she gets back to her people."

"Well, in the meantime, she's yours. She'll give you enough pleasure out of gratefulness to make up for what I owe you."

Zeke just chuckled and shook his head, gently pushing the woman away and wiping at her tears as he said something more to her in the Sioux tongue. Abbie fought her own tears of jealousy.

"That slut has to go!" the preacher shouted. "These Christian people cannot mingle with this loose heathen! She will taint the young girls!"

The Indian girl looked frightened, as Zeke whirled on the man. "She stays!" he commanded. "She's been badly abused and she wants to go home, and I'm seeing she gets there. And if you people are really Christian, you'll want the same for the poor girl." He glared at the preacher again. "And I'd better not catch you near her!"

The preacher's eyes widened. "How dare you even suggest such a thing?"

74

"I know your kind better than you think. She's my property now. You remember that! The Indians have a certain understanding in these things, and I won't bother to try to make folks like you understand. But till I get her back to her people, she belongs to me, and what I do with her is nobody's business!"

Others whispered as, to Abbie's bewilderment, Zeke led the Indian girl directly up to her.

"She says her name is Yellow Grass," he told Abbie. "I'd be obliged if you'd let her walk along with you and your pa, and let her help you around camp, Miss Abbie. I've got no time for a squaw, and you're the only one I'd trust to be kind to her. It's not her fault what she's been through."

He seemed to read Abbie's thoughts, and he gave her a little smile. She reddened at the realization that he'd sensed her jealousy, blushing deeply. Cheyenne Zeke had barely given her the time of day the whole trip, yet she'd grown to love him more and more; and the worst part was that she suspected he knew it. That was why he'd stayed away. But then maybe it hurt to look at her because she looked like his wife.

"I'd . . . be glad to help you out, Zeke," she responded faltering as she fought to hide her jealousy of Yellow Grass. "She's . . . very pretty. You should keep her."

Zeke grinned more. "I know what I want to keep and what I don't want to keep," he replied. Her heart leaped at the words, and he vanished into the darkness.

To Abbie's relief, Zeke seemed to have no desire to accept the pleasures of Yellow Grass's gratefulness, nor did he have the time. During the next two weeks, Abbie and the Indian girl managed to set up their own sign language and got along quite well. Abbie began to like the industrious Sioux squaw. She was much more help than LeeAnn, who was now totally absorbed in Quentin Robards. He hung around every night, often eating their food without offering any sort of payment.

The days were hot and the nights cold, and Abbie worried about her father, who slept on the ground under the wagon most of the time. And she worried about Zeke, even though she told herself it was foolish. After all, a man like Zeke had spent most of his life sleeping under the stars. She wished she could be beside him to keep him warm at night; but that was a silly little girl's dream, and her heart ached with unrequited live.

As if the daily heat and insects and monotony were not enough, the friction between Quentin Robards and David Craig grew worse and developed into an open confrontation one evening when David came to ask LeeAnn if she would take a walk with him. Seconds later Robards was right there, looking haughtily at David and telling him that he didn't have any right moving in on another man's woman, especially since he was a boy who wasn't even dry behind the ears yet. LeeAnn's eyes lit up with pleasure at Robards' obvious jealousy, and David Craig exploded with his own, taking a swing at Robards. LeeAnn screamed and jumped back, and David lit into Robards with a strength and skill that surprised them all, including Robards. He did a good job of messing up Robards' face before Zeke came thundering up on his horse from out of the darkness to stop the fight, grabbing

David from behind with powerful arms, while Kelsoe pulled Robards back.

"What's going on!" Zeke growled.

"Looks like we have a little love triangle, Zeke," Hanes replied. "We all know there's a problem here."

Jason Trent came storming up to camp with a bucket of water, quickly added up the situation, and scowled at LeeAnn with shame in his eyes. Zeke let go of David and gave him a little warning shove.

"I want no fighting on this train!" he commanded.

"Then tell that to the *kid!*" Robards replied angrily, wiping at a bloody lip. "He took the first swing!"

"*I* took *all* the swings, you fancy coward!" David hissed proudly. Abbie smiled. "I don't need to stand here and take your insults," the boy continued. "You have no right coming around here every night with your fancy duds and your fancy words and sparkin' with a girl who doesn't realize you're no good!"

LeeAnn stormed up to David, facing him with folded arms. "*I'll* choose my man friends, if you don't mind, mister David Craig!" she spat at him. "I never asked you to come around here, and I'd like you to apologize to Mr. Robards for that remark! You have no way of knowing whether he's good or bad!"

"A man can smell a skunk right easy!" David sneered.

LeeAnn slapped him, and David turned red, his eyes actually tearing.

"I feel sorry for you." he finally stammered. Abbie's heart ached for the boy, and she hated LeeAnn at that moment; for she had changed considerably since spending so much time with Robards. Jason Trent walked up to his daughter and gave her a light shaking.

"That was a damned shameful thing to do!" he told her. LeeAnn, seemingly untouched by the remark, glared haughtily at her father. Trent sighed and, running a hand through his hair, walked to the back of the wagon.

"You two fight again and I'll hogtie both of you to a wagon and drag you a ways to get the orneriness out of you!" Zeke warned David and Robards. His eyes were on Robards, whom he judged to be worthless, just as most others had, except for LeeAnn.

"You just try it!" Robards hissed, brushing off his fancy clothes. Zeke suddenly grabbed the man's tie and jerked him forward, half strangling Robards with the hold. He whipped out a big knife, and LeeAnn's eyes widened with fright as Zeke waved it under the man's nose, while Robards glared back at him, trying to look brave.

"It would be good for your health, Robards, if no harm comes to Miss LeeAnn Trent—neither physical, nor emotional," Zeke hissed. "You understand me?" He made a quick flick with the knife and cut Robards' tie. LeeAnn screamed, and Robards stepped back, beads of sweat on his forehead.

"Your job is to lead this train, not to interfere with peoples' personal matters!" the man growled in reply. He reached inside his fancy jacket, but Zeke was ready. For the rest of her life Abbie would try to remember actually seeing Zeke pull his sidearm, but it had happened too fast. She simply could not remember it happening. All she knew was that the gun was out and cocked and aimed at Robards before Robards' own hidden handgun was pulled all the way out of its hidden holster. Zeke stepped closer and held a big Colt .45 against Robards' forehead.

"I won't fire this gun, Robards, because Miss Trent is standing right here. But you pull a pistol on me again, and you're a *dead* man! *I* know what my job is! *Leading* this train means keeping the *peace* on this train, and I'll do what I have to do to accomplish that! I'll speak with David, too. And I'll advise him to leave you and Miss Trent alone. But like I said, you'd better not bring any harm to that young lady, or you'll answer to *me*—not David Craig!"

Robards swallowed nervously and stepped back. Zeke looked over at Abbie, and seeing the gratefulness in her eyes, he realized how worried she must be about the man's involvement with her scatterbrained sister. He turned to LeeAnn, who looked at him with hatred.

"Your ma must have taught you some common sense," he told the girl. *"Use* it!" He turned and mounted his horse as Yellow Grass watched him admiringly.

LeeAnn immediately began fussing over Robards, telling him to come to the creek with her and she'd wash his bleeding lip and his bruises. "I'm so sorry, Quentin!" she whimpered, as the others dispersed, whispering among themselves. David Craig watched her for a moment, then stalked off.

"You stay here, LeeAnn!" Jason Trent ordered his daughter.

LeeAnn shot a defiant look at her father. "I'm old enough to do what I please!" she clipped. "You can't order me around anymore, pa! You brought me out to this horrible place, and the least you can do is let me pick my friends! I hate it out here! I hate it! It's hot and dirty—and I'm tired! You must not love me very much if you won't even let me be friends with Mr. Robards!" She burst into tears, and Trent turned away, shame and hurt in his eyes, while LeeAnn walked off with Robards. She turned once to face Abbie. "You tell that Cheyenne Zeke to leave my Quentin alone!" she hissed. "He might be good with a knife and a gun, but he's got no education, not one ounce of refinement or manners! He's got no right threatening an intelligent prosperous man like Quentin!"

She turned and walked into the darkness with Robards, and Abbie's heart burned with anger in defense of Zeke. "Cheyenne Zeke's got more brains than Quentin Robards has in his little finger!" she shouted back. "He's ten times the man that fancy gambler will ever be! Go on, LeeAnn! I don't like you anymore since you started hanging around with that no-good! I don't know you anymore!"

The tears came then, and she knew others must have heard her, maybe even Zeke, but she didn't care. She wouldn't have believed her sister could change so much, and she knew it was because of Robards. She sniffed and walked over to hug her father, and for the next few minutes nothing was said between them.

"She's right, Abbie girl," the man finally spoke up. "She's grown up now, and she's not about to listen to her pa anymore. Thank God for you, Abbie. You're a good girl."

"I love you, pa. I'll stick by you," she sobbed.

"I know you will." He sighed and gave her a squeeze. "Abbie, I I know how you're starting to feel about Cheyenne Zeke."

80

She stiffened in his arms. "Pa I—"

"Now, now, it's okay. I think he's a good man, Abbie, a good man. But you'll get hurt feeling like that. For one thing, he's a man . . . and not likely to have those thoughts for a girl child like you. But I think if he did, he'd be honorable enough not to act on them. I want you to know that no matter what happens, I approve of Zeke. It's just . . . it's the others I worry about. Folks look down on a white girl who has eyes for an Indian, especially a half-breed. I don't want any trouble for you, baby, no pain and heartache. That's a dead-end road, and you could get hurt bad. You be careful, Abbie girl. You're giving your feelings away, and maybe it's best you keep them to yourself."

"I know it's silly and hopeless," she whimpered. "Cheyenne Zeke has no eyes for me."

"Well, maybe not . . . and maybe so. I just think he's wise enough to know what harm that could bring you. You tread real careful, Abbie. That's a risky business, falling for a man like that. And you're just a child. It's probably something you'll get over." He gave her a squeeze. "You dry those tears now and get Jeremy to bed."

Down at the stream LeeAnn gently washed Robards' face with cool water. He dabbed it dry with a white handkerchief, then grasped her arms. "You're beautiful, LeeAnn," he said softly. "And I want you. . . . I ache for you."

Her heart pounded and she blushed. He had held her and kissed her before, but she knew he meant something much more intimate now. More than ever, she wanted to be sure to keep him. Perhaps he would get angry about the fight and decide she was not worth the trouble if she didn't please him in this moment of need. And, after all, he'd been in a fight over her, calling her his woman and jealously guarding that claim.

"I—We aren't married, Quentin."

He touched her breast lightly with the back of his hand. "What does it matter? We're already married in thought, aren't we? When we get to civilization, we can have a ceremony. But in the meantime, we're out here in the middle of nowhere, wanting each other."

She met his eyes. "You truly want to marry me?"

"Of course I do, LeeAnn! Maybe we can even find a way to go back East. I thought going to Oregon sounded like a good idea, because I'm a lonely man and I'm searching for something new. I have money, LeeAnn, a lot of money. I was going to Oregon to find a lovely place in the mountains, where I'd use my money to build a beautiful home with all the modern fineries. But if you don't want to go West, we'll find a way to go back. Either way, we'll marry and have a fine home, and you'll wear beautiful clothes and be a grand lady—Mrs. Quentin Robards!"

Her eyes teared. "Oh, Quentin I'd love that!"

He grinned and kissed her lightly. "You've lived the plain life too long, my dear. You're much too beautiful for that. And I didn't think this trip would be so hot and filthy and distasteful. Neither one of us is cut out for this. I don't know yet if we can get back, but whether we go back or go on, let's not deny ourselves the pleasures we both crave any longer."

He kissed her again, this time hungrily, forcing her lips apart and ignoring the pain in his own lip as he grasped her breast and groaned. It had been a long time since he'd left Tina's whorehouse in Illinois. This lovely young virgin would be worth a considerable sum to Tina. Once he broke her in and taught her to like it, then started her on the drugs, she'd make a profitable whore. He envisioned her lying naked and drugged on a bed, clean and covered with sweet oil. How delicious she must taste!

"Oh, Quentin I do so want to be your woman!" she was whispering. "You won't hurt me, will you?"

"How could I hurt such a beautiful woman? Would I hurt someone I intend to marry?" As he opened her dress and tasted her virgin nipples, LeeAnn's breathing quickened. He wished he'd run across her sooner, before they'd gotten this far West. If he'd known this would happen, he wouldn't have left Tina's place. As it was, he owed her a great sum of money, and he'd run off to avoid being murdered by Tina's "collection agents." Now he'd be able to repay her with this voluptuous young girl who would bring in a lot of money. Until he decided for certain whether to continue to Oregon or go back to Illinois, he would taste of LeeAnn's sweet fruit himself. He laughed inwardly at her vulnerability. Yes, he would dress her in fine clothes, but she would most certainly not be his wife. He moved his hand under her dress and groped for her untouched places while she lay whimpering and in ecstasy.

"Oh, Quentin, I love you!" she whispered.

He did not reply as he moved on top of her.

They were two weeks from Fort Laramie, and Bradley Hanes's foot had healed well, thanks to Zeke's moss. Things had smoothed out somewhat among the travelers, except for a couple of remarks exchanged between Zeke and the preacher. David Craig stayed away from LeeAnn, hating her and loving her at the same time. Every morning a few stray cattle and horses had to be rounded up, and there was a little bit of diarrhea among the travelers, along with a lot of mosquito bites and sore feet. Abbie was sure part of the reason things had quieted down was that they all were too hot and tired to care about anything but getting through the day so they could sleep and enjoy the cool of the night.

There had been a couple of violent storms that had made Abbie cover her head with a quilt and shiver with fear, but they'd survived the rains and the accompanying flash floods. And they plodded ever westward, with barely a word exchanged between Abbie and LeeAnn. A wall had been built that would never again be torn down, for LeeAnn was totally convinced that Quentin Robards was the most wonderful man in the world, while Abbie hated him more than ever. And where Cheyenne Zeke was concerned, their feelings were the same, only in reverse. Abbie loved him, but now LeeAnn hated him.

Nonetheless, they settled into a daily routine in which Yellow Grass helped Abbie with the chores, while LeeAnn and Robards walked and talked and often disappeared after camp was set up at night. No one spoke about that, but Abbie knew what the others were thinking, and her heart ached for her father, who felt helpless and ashamed. Abbie saw little of Cheyenne Zeke, who did his job well and was often gone the whole day scouting the trail ahead, while Olin led the way down the trail Zeke had already scouted the day before. Abbie's hope of anything ever coming of her love for Cheyenne Zeke dwindled more every day. That only made the days seem longer and more dreary, and she was beginning to hate this desolate land to which her father had brought them. But never would she tell him.

One typically dreary morning, as they headed into the unchanging horizon, they suddenly heard a child scream farther ahead. Abbie could see Zeke riding toward the sound from another direction, and shortly after he dismounted, she heard a gunshot. Everybody began to run toward the spot, and Abbie arrived about the same time as the others, to see little Mary Hanes lying on the ground, her dress pulled up and her pantaloons ripped open, exposing her right thigh. Zeke was bent over her. The preacher lit into Zeke and pushed him away, shouting something about Zeke putting heathen hands on a small white girl and violating her. Zeke stood up and landed a fist hard into the preacher's middle. The man cried out and vomited. Then Zeke kicked him in the shoulder and sent him sprawling backward.

"The girl's been snake-bit!" he growled at the rest of them. "I was fixing to cut the bite and suck out the venom!" He shouted something to Yellow Grass, and she ran toward the wagons, while the others spotted the dead rattler lying near Mary Hanes. As the girl's parents came running, Abbie saw the ugly fang marks on the little girl's thigh. The child lay crying and shaking, and Mrs. Hanes knelt beside her as soon as she'd learned what had happened.

"She'll die!" Mr. Hanes moaned.

"I can help her, if you don't mind me touching her," Zeke explained to the man. "I have to work fast,

Mr. Hanes, or she *will* die! But I have to have your permission! Time is important!"

Hanes looked with tearing eyes from his daughter to Zeke. "You saved my foot. If you think you can save my daughter, then go ahead. You do whatever you have to do." His voice broke, and he knelt down beside his wife, who was crying, stroking the girl's hair, and telling her to lie still.

Yellow Grass was already making a campfire and throwing something into a black kettle, while Zeke took out a big knife and a flask of whiskey. He poured the whiskey over the knife, ordering the Haneses to hold the little girl still. He quickly cut an *x* over the bite mark, while the child screamed and others gasped and turned away. Then Zeke bent down and sucked on the bite several times, spitting out blood and venom each time.

"Somebody make some strong coffee!" he ordered. "We have to keep her awake. Olin, there's a mud hole up ahead. Go dig it out some! Is Yellow Grass done with that brew yet?"

"I'll check," Kelsoe replied.

Abbie stood and stared admiringly as Zeke again took hold of the situation. He seemed to have a remedy for everything. He picked up little Mary and held her close, speaking softly and tenderly to her and telling her she must be very still and that he was going to play a little game with her and that soon the bite wouldn't hurt anymore.

Yellow Grass finally came running with a tin cup, and Zeke talked soothingly to little Mary while he quickly stripped off her clothes. The others watched in bewilderment as he said something in the Sioux tongue to Yellow Grass. She nodded, and then he dipped his hand into the cup and smeared something green and greasy over the bite on Mary's thigh.

"There now, doesn't that feel better?" he asked. The girl nodded but continued to sniffle. Zeke quickly stood up and started running with her to the hole Olin had dug. He put her down into the hole up to her neck, and as Olin started shoveling the mud back in around her, Mary started screaming with fear.

"What are you doing?" Mrs. Hanes asked anxiously.

"It's the only thing that might work," Zeke told her. "That stuff we put on the bite dulls the pain and draws the poison. The mud will help even more, plus it's cool and will keep her from getting the fever bad. And once she's buried good, it will keep her immobile. It's important she doesn't move, Mrs. Hanes, and important to keep her head up like this. Go ahead and let her cry. At least it means she's awake and alive. We'll hold up the train a day or two till we know which way she's going to go."

"A day or two!" Hanes replied. "You mean you're going to leave her in there like that? Buried to her neck for a day or two?"

"It's better than burying her for good, isn't it?" Zeke replied. "You want her to die?"

Hanes blinked and looked ready to cry. His wife did cry quietly as she watched Olin shovel the mud in around little Mary.

"I'm sorry, Hanes, but this is my remedy," Zeke explained. "If you've got a better one, you can dig her out of there. I know it's no fun for her, but dying is a lot worse."

Hanes ran a hand through his hair. "All right. You've been right about other things. I'll have to trust you on this one."

"I'll stay right here by her," Zeke promised. "We'll take turns filling her with coffee and keeping her awake. She'll urinate right into the mud, but we can clean her up when it's over. It won't hurt her any. I've seen it done with Indian children . . . and it almost always works."

"Almost?" Mrs. Hanes asked through tears.

"Depends on how much venom they take, the size of the child, how long between the bite and the treatment. A little praying doesn't hurt."

"What would you know about praying?" the preacher asked, now standing near them with a bloody mouth. Zeke rose and stepped closer to him.

"A lot more than you think, preacher! You delayed me in helping this little girl, and you'd best not let me set eyes on you if she dies!"

The preacher looked around at the others, who all looked at him scornfully, so he turned in a huff to go back and nurse his lip. Zeke looked down at little Mary; then he knelt and touched her head with a big, strong hand.

"Don't you cry, honey," he told her gently. "We're going to play that game now."

Four

Camp was quiet, and through supper Abbie kept glancing over to Zeke who was still sitting by little Mary as he'd promised. He had not budged since she had been buried in the mud, nor had he eaten. With Yellow Grass's help, Abbie was packing away dishes as Olin Wales approached and handed something to Yellow Grass that looked like a homemade brush. He spoke to her in her own tongue, and the girl's eyes widened with pleasure as she nodded in agreement. Then she turned and hurried off to where Zeke sat. Jealousy returned to Abbie's heart, for Zeke must have asked for Yellow Grass. But she grew curious about why Yellow Grass had left with the brush, so she quickly finished cleanup and took her shawl from the wagon. The sun was disappearing beyond the horizon that had not changed for weeks, and she felt a slight chill as she walked quietly toward the spot where Zeke sat with Mary. Mr. Hanes had built a campfire near his daughter, and the Haneses sat by it with Zeke, while the others on the train left them alone and waited to see if Cheyenne Zeke's remedy was going to work.

Abbie stayed in the shadows, watching with a mixture of jealousy and curiosity as Yellow Grass unbraided Zeke's hair and began brushing it. Abbie's amazement at seeing more of Zeke's Indian side revealed helped block out her jealousy, for now she was interested in just watching and learning. Cheyenne Zeke sat cross-legged behind little Mary, his hands gently rubbing her hair and temples, and the child was calmed and quiet. Zeke was shirtless, and noticing the scars on his back, Abbie remembered Zeke's statement about a whipping by Rube Givens. She wished she knew more about what had happened between the two men, and she wondered if Cheyenne Zeke bore as many scars on the inside as he bore on the outside.

Zeke was all Cheyenne that night, the muscles of his bronze arms and shoulders glowing provocatively in the firelight, his long, black hair being brushed by his squaw and falling to his waist. Abbie looked in awe at his magnificent build and handsome face. Olin approached them, carrying a cup of water and something in a leather pouch. He spoke to Yellow Grass, who handed him the brush and then dipped her fingers in the water, then into the pouch. She leaned around Zeke and with the tips of her fingers she smeared white streaks on his cheeks, then across his chest. Zeke sat silent, his eyes still closed. He seemed lost unto himself, until Olin handed him an odd-looking pipe.

Zeke put the long pipe to his lips, still not speaking. The pipe stem was very long and light colored. It was painted, but Abbie could not decipher from where she stood what the pictures were. The bowl of the pipe was a reddish stone shaped like a tomahawk, with the bowl on the top end and the tomahawk blade pointing downward beneath it. Picking up a burning twig from the fire, Olin dipped it into the bowl, and Zeke puffed. Then Olin stepped back, and Zeke pointed the pipe skyward.

"*Heammawihio*," he said quietly. Then he pointed the pipe at the ground and in all directions, after which he repeated the word, "*Heammawihio*," closed his eyes, and puffed the pipe for several minutes. Then setting the pipe aside, he raised his hands toward the sky and spoke in an odd, clipped tongue. Olin handed something to Yellow Grass, and she in turn handed it to Zeke. Now Abbie could see that it was a feather. Zeke placed it in Mary's hair.

"Now the great spirit of the gray eagle will be with you," he told the child. Yellow Grass sat down beside Zeke and, closing her eyes, began to sing a soft chant as she swayed sideways, while Zeke closed his eyes again and sat silent. The Haneses watched without interference, and Abbie was glad to see they were putting their trust in Zeke.

Olin Wales walked away from the scene and, spotting Abbie, came to stand beside her.

"It's best you stay back and don't try to talk to Zeke," he told the girl. She looked up at him curiously.

"Why?"

"He's prayin'. He has to concentrate."

Abbie stared back at the Tennessee man who was now all Indian. "Who does he pray to?"

"Religion is a real personal thing to the Cheyenne. Zeke's prayer color is white. That's why Yellow Grass put the white paint on him. He prays to what they call The Wise One Above - *Heammawihio*. His God is really no different than our own, perhaps the same God, only with a different name is all. Smokin' the pipe is a prayer offerin'. When he points it different places, he's offerin' love and prayers to all the spirits of the earth and sky and animals that are a part of *Heammawihio*. The most powerful spirit is that of the gray eagle, and that's why he's put the feather of a gray eagle in Mary's hair. He'll stay with her till she's through the crisis, and he'll fast until it's over. Fasting is a form of sacrifice to get prayers answered."

Abbie watched in fascination. How different this man was! He lived in two worlds, and it was not likely she would ever reach him in either one. But she was convinced that a more perfect specimen of man surely could not exist, in outward appearance, inner strength, or power and courage.

"Does he have a Cheyenne name?" she asked.

"Yes, ma'am. It's Lone Eagle. Got it from a vision he had after fasting for several days in the mountains alone . . . after he returned to his people a few years ago. Somethin' happened to him back in Tennessee that brought him back out here, and because of what happened, I expect for the rest of his life Zeke will be a lot more Cheyenne than white. He'll never do much livin' in the white man's world again."

Abbie looked up at Olin again. "What happened to him?" she asked curiously. "How did his wife and son die?"

Olin grinned. "Oh, no you don't. I told you once that was his private matter."

Abbie sighed with disappointment and looked back

92

at Zeke. Others from the train were tending to their chores and preparing for bed. Some approached quietly to watch for a while then left again, whispering about how changed Zeke was with his hair hanging long and his face and chest streaked with paint. "Like the savage people he comes from," some of them said. The young, pregnant Yolanda Brown hurried away, frightened now of the "wild Indian," but Abbie just watched him with total admiration and love. However, when Preacher Graydon approached the scene, she panicked.

"What's going on here?" the man demanded to know, stepping closer to Zeke and little Mary. Zeke did not reply or even look at him, and Olin Wales gave Abbie a warning look to stay back, while he walked over to where the preacher stood. Bradley Hanes rose and faced the preacher angrily.

"Get out of here before you upset my daughter!" the man exclaimed to Preacher Graydon.

"I've come to pray for this child, and I find her being chanted over by heathens!" the preacher shot back. "What kind of a Christian are you, Hanes? Do you want your little girl to go to *hell?*"

Hanes gave the man a shove. "I just want my daughter to *live!*" he replied angrily. "And part of the way to do that is to keep her *still!* I believe Zeke here prays to the same God as you do, mister, and he's sure as hell done a lot more to help her than you have! Now go away! Please!"

The preacher glowered at the man, his breathing heavy. "You're a fool!" he hissed. "Do you really think God is going to save a child being chanted over by these heathens?"

Little Mary started crying, and Olin grasped the preacher around the chest from behind, holding a knife against the preacher's cheek.

"The girl's pa asked you to leave, mister. You've already got the child upset again. I suggest you get the hell back to camp, before I give you more of what Zeke done give you earlier today!" He yanked the man around and gave him a shove, and the preacher looked scornfully at the whole group, his eyes resting last on the beautiful Yellow Grass, whom he had watched hungrily for several days. As he turned and left, little Mary's tears spilled into the mud. Zeke began stroking her temples again.

"Don't cry, Mary," he said gently. "Have you ever heard the story of the crying stones?"

His comment immediately made some of Mary's tears subside because of the curiosity it provoked in her, and Abbie, too, listened for the story to begin, the interest of the child that still dwelled within her changing body aroused.

"No, Mister Zeke," Mary replied, choking on a sob. Mrs. Hanes reached over and wiped the tears from the girl's face.

"The stones can keep you from crying," Zeke told Mary. "You must let them cry for you, so that you can be strong."

"I don't know . . . what you mean," the girl whimpered in her tiny voice.

"Olin, you know where I keep them," Zeke spoke up to his friend.

"I know," Olin replied. The man hurried off, and Abbie stepped closer now, her curiosity and awe compelling her to watch everything Cheyenne Zeke did. She quietly sat down beside the Hanes, and for a moment Zeke's dark eyes met hers. He looked almost frightening, sitting there in the night with the white streaks on his face and body glowing in the firelight. At that moment, he was all Indian, and it was a side of him she knew was worlds apart from anything she had ever known. She felt small and insignificant under his piercing eyes, and she also felt a certain animallike power emanating from his sleek body. It stirred desires in her that she had never before experienced, and the look she returned was suddenly that of a woman and not a child. He quickly looked away when Olin returned with a little leather pouch which Zeke opened, taking out four lovely turquoise colored stones, each one polished smooth. He placed them in front of Mary where she could see them well, and they seemed to glow in the firelight. Each stone was about one inch in diameter, and each shaped differently.

"These are crying stones, Mary," Zeke told the girl.

Utterly fascinated Mary stared at the stones, and it was obvious that whether Zeke's story was true or not, it would at least take her attention away from herself, which was his ultimate aim.

"Look real hard at the stones, Mary," he told her, rubbing her temples again. "They'll cry for you if you concentrate hard enough."

"Cry for me?" the girl asked. Mr. and Mrs. Hanes looked at each other and smiled.

"Yes," Zeke answered. "My people consider it a weakness to cry. That doesn't mean we don't cry, because it's hard not to cry when your child is dying of disease, or you're starving to death or freezing to death, or maybe being attacked for no reason. Everybody cries, Mary. But life is hard, and we have to learn to be strong. And during the times when it's best not to cry—like when you've been snake-bit and have to be still—then we have to give our tears to something else so we can be stronger. You can give your tears to those stones. They're sacred stones, and *Heammawihio* and the gray eagle will let the stones take your tears—and your pain. If you believe hard enough, it will happen. Just keep looking at them and thinking about giving them your tears and pain."

Mary stared wide-eyed at the stones, completely entranced by the story.

"Did *you* ever make them cry for you?" Mary asked.

Abbie waited anxiously for his reply, sensing Zeke's pain at the question. He kept his eyes closed and replied in a strained voice.

"Oh, yes," he said in a near whisper. "For a long time, I sat every night staring at those stones, begging them to take away my tears and the terrible hurt."

"Why were you crying?" the child asked innocently.

Zeke breathed deeply. "Somebody I loved was . . . taken from me," he replied. That was all he said, and the statement was followed by a dead silence, the only sound being the crackling of the campfire. Finally Zeke asked Mary. "Are the stones crying yet?"

"I . . ." The child's face lit up and she actually smiled a little. "They are!" she whispered in awe. Abbie and the Hanes looked at the stones, leaning closer to study them.

"They're just sweating," Hanes remarked.

"It isn't sweat," Zeke replied. "You have to believe

like your daughter here, Mr. Hanes. Those are tears—
Mary's tears. Touch them. Taste the moisture. It will
be salty—just like tears."

Hanes looked at Zeke, whose face was completely
serious. If he was making it all up, no one could have
guessed. Abbie felt a tingle at the realization that he
meant what he was saying. Hanes touched one stone
with his finger and put it to his tongue, then looked
back at Zeke in surprise.

"It *is* salty!" he remarked.

"Give the child some water," Zeke told the girl's
mother. "She needs a lot of water. She's starting to fever up now and sweat. Once the fever leaves her, she'll
be fine."

The woman left, and Zeke's eyes met Abbie's again.
"Do you believe in the stones?" he asked.

She nodded. "I do," she replied quietly.

He studied her a moment longer, and then suddenly
the look in his eyes changed to one of deep concern. "I
see many tears ahead in your own life, Abigail Trent,"
he said. He seemed so sure of it that Abbie became
frightened. "Many tears," he repeated quietly. "I am
sorry. After tonight, you may have the crying stones.
You will need them."

Abbie frowned. "How can you know that?"

"I . . . feel it. The Indian is very spiritual—close to
the elements and the spirit world. The Indian has visions. Often the Great Spirit warns him of things to
come. Now they warn you to be strong, Abigail. First
you will stand alone—completely alone. And then I
see . . ." The words became strained, and he closed
his eyes, breathing harder. "I see . . . someone . . .
standing beside you . . . someone . . . strong and—"

97

He suddenly shook his head. "Go away, Abbie!" he whispered.

She swallowed. "You're scaring me!" she squeaked. "You shouldn't tell me those things!"

He rocked quietly, massaging Mary's temples again. "I did not mean to frighten you." He still breathed hard, as though upset. "You will have an inner strength that will see you through whatever happens to you. It will not fail you. Now, please go!"

As Abbie blinked back her tears and rose, Mrs. Hanes returned with the water.

"Zeke?" Abbie said.

But he did not reply, and she finally walked back to Olin, wiping at a tear. "Why did he tell me that?" she asked. Olin took her arm and urged her back toward her wagon.

"When he looks at you, Miss Abbie, he sees his dead wife. That draws him close to the spirit world. If Zeke says he sees somethin' in your future, he's probably right, and he's just tryin' to prepare you to be strong."

"It scares me," she replied, pulling her shawl closer.

"Don't never be afraid. He said you was a strong girl. Zeke knows."

"But . . . who do you think he saw standing beside me? He got so upset."

Olin stopped walking and turned to face her. "Who do you think?" he asked.

Her eyes widened and lit up with hope. *"Him?"*

"That's my guess. And if I'm right, Cheyenne Zeke is in for one hell of a battle with himself. A vision is somethin' that can't be denied, but for reasons of his own, the last thing Zeke would ever want is to be involved with another white woman. He'll do his best to see beyond that vision—to find another vision that will tell him the first one don't mean what it looks like it means. I know by how upset he got that it was somethin' he'd rather not have happen."

"Why shouldn't it happen?" Abbie replied. "I don't understand any of this."

Olin looked down at her, and she was shocked to see the pain on his face. "Miss Abbie, you have to believe me when I tell you . . . it would be a lot better, for you and Zeke both, if you get your mind off him and just get to Oregon and forget him. Please don't make me explain. And please don't make things hard on Zeke."

"Some things can't *be* avoided," she replied. "And there's some purpose for me and Cheyenne Zeke—I just know it. I felt it the first time he stepped into our camp and I handed him that cup of coffee."

Olin sighed. "You're a child, Abbie. There are a lot of things you don't understand yet."

"Then maybe one day I'll learn from Zeke," she replied with confidence, taking hope in the vision. Her heart raced with anticipation and with visions of her own: visions of one day standing beside Cheyenne Zeke as his woman, of lying with him at night, and of giving him children to replace the son he'd lost. "I guess I'll just have to wait and let things take care of themselves, won't I?" she went on.

Olin sighed and started walking again. "I guess," he said quietly. "Ain't no use arguin' with a love-struck little girl."

"Tell me more about Zeke, Olin," she pleaded. "At least tell me about you and him—how you got to be friends and all. Can't you tell me that much?"

The rotund, bearded man chuckled and shook his head. "Okay. For a cup of coffee I'll share that much with you."

"Oh, thank you!" she replied, walking faster now. When they reached camp she hurriedly poured him a cupful of coffee from a pot still hanging over the fire. LeeAnn and Jeremy lay inside the wagon, already asleep, but Jason Trent greeted Olin and asked how things were going with the child. Abbie excitedly told him about the stones, while Jason studied the love in her eyes with a heavy heart. His little girl was falling for a man she could never have; she was headed for disaster. But he said nothing. "Olin promised to tell me how he met Zeke and all," she told her father. "May I please sit up a while longer, pa?"

The man grinned resignedly. "I suppose so. Me —I'm turning in, little girl. I'm a tired and sore man. And you get yourself to bed before long, you hear?"

"I will, pa," she replied. Trent rose and said his good-nights. He crawled into his bedroll under the wagon and listened to most of what Olin had to tell Abbie, praying at the same time that his child's love for the half-breed would not bring her too much harm.

"Well, I reckon the feud between Zeke and Rube Givens started mostly over me," Olin was saying. He took a sip of coffee, then lit a pipe. "You see, when I met Zeke, I was half dead. Zeke—he saved my life, Miss Abbie. That was about four years ago. I'd been trappin' up in the Tetons. Furs was gettin' real cheap by then, and it took a lot to make any decent money. Seein' as how it was a lean year and everybody needed all they could get to make enough money to live on, I was lucky. I'd had a real good season and was on my way east with them furs when Rube Givens and his men come along and attacked my camp. Filled me full of lead and run off with my furs. Givens, he's one of them trappers that don't bother doin' the work himself. He just takes somebody else's furs whenever he can get away with it. At any rate, they left me for dead and stole my furs. But Zeke, he come along and found me. He didn't know me, but he dug out the lead and then prayed over me, like he's doin' now for little Mary."

He stopped and puffed his pipe again, while Abbie listened attentively.

"I got well, thanks to Zeke. I'd have died for sure if he hadn't come along when he did. And while I was mendin', we got to be pretty good friends—done a lot of talkin'. Then Zeke took me to an Arapaho camp, where he left me to be cared for while he headed out to find Rube Givens. He already knowed who the man was—had met him and knew his reputation. Him and Givens had already had a run-in over a card game. At any rate, Givens had no way of knowin' Zeke knew what he'd done to me, and Zeke promised me he was goin' to look up Givens and somehow get my furs back."

"I'll bet he got them back, didn't he?" Abbie said with an eager smile.

Olin chuckled. "Sure did. He hunted Givens up. Found him down at Jackson Hole and real calmlike joined up in another card game. Ol' Rube—he had five other men with him—told Zeke they never did settle their dispute over the last card game. I guess the both of them was feelin' each other out, each with somethin' to settle. I guess Rube figured him and his men could take Zeke then and there, and Zeke, he figured maybe he could take all six of them. After a while, after both of them did their secret figurin' as to how they was gonna go about it, Rube, he started goadin' Zeke, wantin' him to start the fight he figured him and his men would finish. Zeke, he was winnin' at cards besides, and when Rube run out of money, Zeke, he suggested he put up my furs for collateral. Well, it was then Rube figured out just why Zeke was really there, and he started shoutin' filthy names at Zeke and tellin' him them furs was his and that he didn't have to pay nothin' to Zeke, cause Zeke was gonna die that day anyway. Zeke, he had other plans. Only they got messed up a little when one of Rube's men drawed a gun on Zeke before Rube did. Zeke was hopin' it would be Rube, 'cause that was the man he wanted most of all. Zeke, he's fast himself, like you saw the other day. He pulled out that gun of his and used it on that other man first. By then the others was ready for him, and Zeke ain't fast just with his gun, but with his body, too, bein' part Indian and all. He can duck and whirl and roll and get a man all confused on his aim. I reckon bullets must have flew everywhere. Zeke, he got one graze on his shoulder, but by God he got all four of them others that was left, while ol' Rube, he run like the yellow bastard he is." He chuckled again and puffed on his pipe. "You know, I can just picture Zeke sittin' there real calm and cool, and then the next minute he's duckin' everywhere, pumpin' lead into them men like they was jackrabbits."

Abbie smiled, picturing the scene herself. "Did

Rube Givens get away then?" she asked.

"Yup. Zeke, he had his hands full with them others. He's got a way of chargin' in and gettin' the job done real quicklike, but while all that was goin' on, Givens was runnin'. When the smoke settled, the man was gone, and Zeke, bein' a half-breed, he knew he'd best get out of there quick, 'cause most folks would hang him, even if it wasn't his fault what happened. He'd seen my furs bundled onto a horse out front that was tied with Givens' horse, and when he run out, that there horse was still there. I reckon Givens didn't want to be burdened down with it, for fear Zeke would come after him. I expect he figured if he left the furs, Zeke'd return 'em to me rather than follow Rube, and he did 'cause Zeke had give me his word he'd get them furs back. Next thing I know, here he comes into that Arapaho camp with my furs, and when I was well enough, he went with me as far as the Arkansas down in Colorado Territory, where he lived with his people, and I went on and sold my furs for a good price. Then I went back and visited Zeke, livin' there among the Cheyennes, and the friendship continued."

"Zeke said something to Givens about taking a whipping, and I saw scars on his back."

Olin nodded. "Me and Zeke went out to do more trappin' that fall. We split up, Zeke goin' up by Yellowstone and me farther south by the Green River. We made plans to meet at Jackson Hole. Figured whoever did the best, we'd put our furs together and split the money. But that Givens, he'd been lookin' for Zeke that winter, figured maybe he'd come back around there, and Rube wanted to get even. Well, he did. That S.O.B. found Zeke through word of mouth,

103

snuck up on him in camp alone, and ambushed him. Zeke fought hard; but this time he didn't have his gun on, and there was ten of them. They beat the hell out of Zeke and strapped him to a tree with his shirt off in the cold; then they proceeded to whip him till his back didn't even look human no more. They left him there to die from the cold, and he hung there for two days, more dead than alive. Rube, he took off with Zeke's furs."

"Dear God!" Abbie whispered, her heart aching at the thought. "How did he live?"

"Ol' Zeke, he's a tough bird. It's the stubborn Cheyenne in him. He hung on till, finally, some northern Cheyennes found him. They took him in and nursed him back to health. Zeke, he met me at Jackson Hole like we'd planned and told me what happened. We left there quick, 'cause we was afraid there was still people at Jackson Hole that might want Zeke's hide. We'd heard rumors of Rube Givens bein' at a little town on the Sweetwater in Wyoming Territory. Word travels fast among outlaws and trappers and Indians. We rode there fast as we could ride, and by God we found Givens. We got into a hell of a gunfight with that man and his friends—rode right into that little town and walked into the saloon where people said Givens was, and commenced firin'. Givens, he ducked behind the bar, and I was sure I'd plugged him. Me and Zeke shot the place up pretty good, and most of them men was dead or had run off, and then everything was quiet. We backed up to leave, and all of a sudden Givens popped up from behind that bar, fixin' to surprise us and plug us. Zeke's eagle eye caught the movement before I did, and he fired that .45 of his and put a big hole in Givens' gut. Then he whipped out that big knife of his, fixin' to do one of his special jobs on Givens for the terrible whippin' Rube had given Zeke. But I already seen a mob formin' and headin' for the saloon, and I advised Zeke to get the hell out of there, 'cause that there town had a sheriff and all, and like I say, Zeke bein' a half-breed, they'd like nothin' better than to hang him. So we left and rode fast out of there, takin' Zeke's furs with us. Zeke, he was disappointed that he hadn't got to cut Givens up. He's got a way with a knife like you never saw or ever want to see, Miss Abbie. At any rate, I told him ol' Rube would die from that gunshot, but I turned out to be wrong as you saw back there at Sapling Grove. We figured him for dead, 'cause we never saw no sign of him for them years followin' the shootout. Me and Zeke trapped together one more year after that, sharin' our feelin's and all. Zeke, he told me about Tennessee and what had happened to him there. Since that last year of trappin', Zeke pretty much stayed down on the Arkansas with his ma and her people, raisin' Appaloosas and all. Me, I always stopped there in the summers and stayed on. That's where I was headed when I run into him back there in Independence. Hadn't seen him all the winter before, so I'm glad to be with him again. I give up trappin', so I figured I'd go along on this trip for the money—and to be with Zeke again. Trappin' is gettin' to be a mighty poor way of makin' money and I've got to look to other things now."

"Why didn't Zeke kill Givens back there at Sapling Grove?" Abbie asked. "He must have a pretty big hate for the man by now."

"He does. But you was watchin'. He'd just as soon not shock you with his violent side if he can help it. But before this trip is out, he might have to. Zeke don't generally let men go like that. I guess that shows his respect for you. Zeke, he can split a man open and dress him out in about ten seconds flat with that knife of his. Rube knows it. That's why he backed off when Zeke pulled that knife back there at Sapling Grove. Rube would rather wait till he can ambush a man or shoot him in the back."

"Will he follow us?" Abbie asked.

"Already is."

Abbie's eyes widened. "Are you sure?"

"Yup. Zeke knows it, too, but he can't do nothin' about it, not unless Rube shows his face around here. Zeke has the train to think about. He can always take care of Givens later. But he'll take care of him sooner than that if he bothers anybody on this train, especially you. But if I know Givens, he'll not show unless it's a time when Zeke's at a disadvantage and can't do nothin' about it. He liked to goad Zeke that way."

Abbie rested her chin in her hand. "How did Zeke get that scar on his face?"

Olin puffed the pipe again. "A Crow did that, up in Montana. Crows and Cheyennes never did get along. Them Crow is a wicked lot. Zeke had a run-in with one who decided to prove he was the better man. He managed to get a cut at Zeke's face, but that Crow's insides soon saw daylight, I'll tell you. Zeke split that man right up the middle and—"

"Please!" Abbie interrupted, holding her stomach. "I . . . don't think I want to hear the rest."

Olin grinned. "Sorry. It's just that I ain't never seen

anybody use a knife like that. At any rate, I reckon now you've got a pretty good idea of the kind of wild man you've been havin' romantic thoughts about. He ain't for the likes of you, Miss Abbie."

Abbie blushed and looked over to where Zeke still sat behind Mary. His brawny frame was outlined in the eerie firelight, and he was sitting quietly and praying over little Mary. Abbie felt a strange chill, and wondered if she truly would need the crying stones.

Zeke stayed by Mary all that night and all the next day, while she sweat out a fever and whimpered and cried. He never moved, not even to get up and go to the bathroom. The others used the camp time to mend wagons, to rest the oxen and mules, and to bathe in the Platte River. Some hunted, bringing back a couple of deer and a buffalo, which they quickly dressed out, hanging out the meat to dry and packing some in lard to preserve it. It was hard work, and Abbie helped, all the while glancing over to where Zeke still sat and pondering the extreme diversities of the man's personality.

When they threw out most of the buffalo bones, the odd pieces, and the skin, Yellow Grass, who had come to help, shook her head and carried on in her own tongue, looking very upset. Abbie guessed that an Indian probably had a use for every part of the buffalo, and that Yellow Grass was upset with the waste, but the people in the train didn't know how to use the other parts, only the meat. The Indian girl finally returned to Zeke and Mary, still fretting to herself over the waste.

It was late in the afternoon, the day after the snake

107

bite, when the fever broke. As Abbie was heading over to see how the girl was, Zeke stood up, raising his arms in the air, his shoulders gleaming in the sun and his hair streaming down his back. Abbie thought again what a magnificent specimen of man he was. Suddenly Zeke looked up at the sun and let out a strange sound, like a battle cry. Then he got down on his knees and started digging around Mary with his hands. The Haneses stood up and watched, looking anxious; and people came running to see what was going on. Then Zeke pulled little Mary out of the mud and held her naked body up high in the air toward the sun. She was caked with mud. Zeke laughed.

"*Kse-e, rarutah!*" he said with a big grin.

"What did you say?" Little Mary asked him with a scowl.

"I said, young girl, you are filthy!" Zeke replied. White streaks were still painted on his face and chest. Mary covered her mouth and giggled, and Zeke handed her to her mother, who quickly put a blanket around her. "Wash her. She will be fine," Zeke told Mrs. Hanes. The woman's eyes teared.

"What can we say? How can we thank you?"

"I did nothing. It was our God who saved her. I only prayed and kept her calm," Zeke replied.

"You did more than that," Hanes replied, putting his hand out to Zeke. Their eyes held for a moment, and Abbie suspected this was one of the rare times when Zeke had found a white man who had confidence in him and would shake his hand. He shook Hanes's hand.

"Tonight we will celebrate!" he told Hanes. He turned to Olin, catching Abbie's eyes for a moment and then looking away. "Bring my things, Olin!" he shouted. He turned and put his arm around Yellow Grass and walked to the river with her. Abbie's heart burned with jealousy at the sight of them walking together. And when Zeke and Yellow Grass did not return for quite some time, her insides hurt so bad she thought she might die. When they did, Yellow Grass was smiling, and Abbie was woman enough to put two and two together. Surely, after the long ordeal of praying and fasting and worrying, Cheyenne Zeke had been ready to let loose in more ways than one. And as they had performed prayers and rituals and chants together, a closeness must have developed between himself and the lovely Sioux woman. Perhaps that closeness had become even greater while they were alone together.

Zeke seemed completely changed when he returned, his arm still around a smiling Yellow Grass. Now his serious, sober face was gone, and he was smiling and happy over Mary's recovery. Abbie was sure he'd also been drinking some. He asked if there was anything to eat, and in her gratitude, Mrs. Hanes scrambled to get him something, while Zeke talked to little Mary, who had been scrubbed up and now wore a pink dress. Zeke himself was dressed in his buckskins. His hair, rebraided, hung down his back and he wore a headband with the gray eagle feather in it. This evening he wore no weapons except the one big knife in his belt. The white paint was gone, and he was more talkative than usual as he ate voraciously. When he had finished, he made an announcement.

"Folks, we are going to celebrate little Mary's recovery tonight. No work! We'll celebrate the Tennessee way. Tonight I'll be a Tennessee man with the rest of you. Now you tell me what Tennessee folks and Kentucky folks and other Southern folks do to celebrate."

"Plenty of singing and dancing!" Hanes replied with a laugh.

Zeke picked up little Mary, who hugged him. "Your father is right, *Hohanino-o!*"

"What is that?" the child asked with a giggle.

"That is your Indian name. It means 'Little Rock.' You are a brave little girl, and strong like a rock. So that is my name for you."

The child tried to repeat the name, and everyone laughed.

"Trent, get out your fiddle," Zeke told Abbie's father, as he set Mary down. "David, get your banjo. And I will show some of you doubters that I can be a Tennessee man when I choose to be. Olin, go get my mandolin."

Abbie's eyebrows went up, as did others. Cheyenne Zeke played a mandolin. So, that was what she'd seen sticking out of his supply pack! Zeke took out his flask of whiskey and took a swallow, and the preacher scowled and left the group.

"Mind sharing some of that?" Kelsoe spoke up.

"Don't mind at all," Zeke replied, handing it to the man. Kelsoe took a swallow and handed the flask to Jason Trent, who also took a swig before handing it back to Zeke. Jeremy came running with his father's fiddle, while David Craig hurried over with his banjo, but Quentin Robards watched Zeke with hatred in his eyes. He put his arm around LeeAnn.

"We'll sneak off in a bit," he whispered in her ear.

"They'll all be busy with their hoedown, and Zeke will be with them. No one will know."

He rubbed her back, and LeeAnn felt weak and hot. In the three times they had managed to go off alone, Quentin Robards had shown her things she'd never dreamed men did to women, and it had been exciting and thrilling. She was Quentin's woman now, and soon they would be married—just as soon as they figured out how they could get back to civilization. She did not even ask herself why he didn't marry her then and there. After all, there was a preacher along. But Quentin wouldn't want it to be that way. He would want a fancy wedding, in a proper church. His hand moved down and rubbed across her hips, and she knew she was totally in love.

When David Craig and Jason Trent charged into a fast mountain song, Zeke picked up little Mary and did a Tennessee stomp with her that amazed all of them. He side-stepped in one direction, turned, and side-stepped in another; then he whirled around and around, while little Mary screamed and laughed. The others clapped their hands to the fast beat, and that night, for all intents and purposes, they were all back home again. Abbie ran to her wagon and put on her prettiest dress, a yellow cotton with a ruffled hem. She brushed her hair until it shined, then tied a yellow ribbon in it and came back out, wanting to look pretty and womanly for Cheyenne Zeke that night. Perhaps he would even dance with her.

"How can they let that half-breed hold their daughter and dance with her like that!" Yolanda Brown was commenting to her mother-in-law. "I'd never let him touch a child of mine! Who knows what's going

111

through his mind! He's even drinking whiskey!"

Abbie's blood boiled, and she stepped close to Yolanda and talked low to her. "Cheyenne Zeke saved their little girl's life," she said heatedly. "How can you say such a thing? You've got about as much sense as a muddy pig!"

Yolanda's mouth fell open, and then her eyes narrowed into angry slits. "You'd best watch out, sticking up for a half-breed, Miss Abigail Trent! It could make you look real bad."

"Zeke's never done anything but help all of us!" Abbie shot back. "I might remind you he's been looking out for you, too, making sure you don't lose that baby! Don't you have any feelings of gratefulness when somebody helps you?"

"I don't like him telling me what to do with my own wife!" Yolanda's husband replied proudly.

"Well, it appears he has more concern for her than *you* do!" Abbie shot back. She turned and left before he could reply, going over to sit beside her father. Everyone but the preacher seemed to be having a good time, except when David Craig watched with sad eyes as LeeAnn and Robards quickly disappeared into the darkness.

Olin came back with Zeke's mandolin, and Bobby Jones asked Abbie to dance. Abbie obliged, only because she thought perhaps she could make Zeke a little jealous. She stepped lightly, whirling her skirts and letting her hair fly, trying to look as pretty and tempting as possible. But to her disappointment, Zeke didn't seem to notice. As he walked around talking to others, carrying his mandolin in one hand and a flask of whiskey in the other, he took several more swigs

and also shared the whiskey with the other men; and
the dancing and music continued, with everyone loos-
ening up and forgetting hardships and prejudices.
They all sang some humorous mountain songs; then
Zeke sat down with the mandolin. Everyone quieted,
finding it hard to believe that the "wild Indian" who
had sat with Mary could be so different now, changed
back to a Tennessee man and strumming a mandolin.
They waited curiously to see just how good he was
with the instrument, and his strong but graceful fingers moved over the strings, producing a beautiful,
strange, echoey sound that turned the night to magic.
To top off the amazingly beautiful mandolin music,
Zeke surprised them even more when he began to sing:

> "Oh, give me Tennessee music
> When my heart is feelin' low.
> Take me to the hills again;
> It's there I want to go.

> "Ain't nothin' like the Smokies;
> Good music and moonshine!
> Throw in a pretty Tennessee gal,
> And I'll get along just fine!"

The mandolin music floated over the night air, and
his voice was smooth and mellow. Abbie's heart was
close to bursting with love, for now she knew that
Cheyenne Zeke could also be a part of her white
world, all Tennessee, except for his long hair and dark
skin. And it turned out to be a wonderful evening for
all of them, because Zeke next joined with Trent and
David, and the three of them sang song after song,

harmonizing beautifully. Some of the tunes were funny, toe-tapping songs that had everyone laughing and keeping time.

Abbie forgot about the blue stones and Zeke's vision that she would be alone and that there were many tears ahead for her. It was wonderful to see Zeke having a good time with the others and being all "Tennessee" that night. The music they made floated out over the prairie, and Abbie wondered if Rube Givens was out there somewhere and could hear it. Zeke's fingers flew over the mandolin strings, while Trent fiddled away and David beat the banjo strings, all of them feeling their whiskey. But later in the evening, the whiskey seemed to make Zeke begin to mellow and sadden, and he announced that he had a couple of slower, pretty songs he'd like to sing—songs he'd made up himself. The others readily agreed, pleasantly surprised by Zeke's appealing voice and his talent with the mandolin. Everyone quieted, and the night was warm and still except for a soft breeze. It seemed to Abbie that there were a zillion stars overhead. For a moment, Zeke strummed the strings, trying to find the right tune; then he looked at Abbie, almost longingly, as though she were someone else, and she felt a stirring deep inside herself. When he sang, his beautiful voice and touching words seemed to transmit his inner pain into the atmosphere, and the others listened transfixed and touched.

> "See the mist a-risin',
> Out there upon the hill.
> The mornin' sun's a-comin' up,
> And dawn is bright and still.

"I've lived on this here mountain
Since I was freshly born.
And there ain't nothin' nicer
Than a misty mountain morn.

"Lord, I know heaven's pretty,
And death I do not fear.
But I hope that heaven's mornin's
Are like the ones down here.

"I've lived on this here mountain
Since I was freshly born.
And there ain't nothin' nicer
Than a misty mountain morn."

Abbie and Mrs. Hanes actually got tears in their eyes, and even Yolanda Brown was touched. Most of the people in the train were beginning to miss home badly, and all wondered if the prairies would ever end.

"What are the Rocky Mountains like, Zeke?" Mrs. Hanes asked, dabbing at her eyes. "Are they as nice as the mountains in Tennessee and Kentucky?"

Zeke looked up at her with his dark eyes, and everyone was so quiet Abbie thought they'd hear the sagebrush growing.

"There's nothing like them, ma'am. You've not seen mountains until you've seen what's waiting out there for you. I know it seems like the prairie will never end, but it will. All of a sudden you'll see them way out in the distance, looming up to the clouds stark and gray on the horizon, jagged peaks cut out sharply against the blue sky and reaching up to the heavens like church spires." He closed his eyes. "They're high.

Higher than anything you've ever seen before. Ten thousand, thirteen thousand, fifteen thousand feet high . . . With snow on top that never melts because it never gets warm enough to melt . . . so high nothing will grow there. Pure rock, they are—gray and purple and red. Always the same, yet always changing. I see a lot of change ahead for this country—some good, mostly bad, especially for the Indian. A hundred years from now the red man will be about gone, and most of the country won't be anything like it is now. Man will destroy it. All except the mountains. They'll be the same forever. They'll last through everything, even to the day when this world comes to an end, which it will. Man will see to that somehow. But them mountains, they'll still be there—silent, strong, immovable. Always and forever, there will be the Rockies and the Sierras . . . there'll be the Guadalupes, the Santiagos, the White Mountains, the Wind River Range, and the Tetons. They'll never die, not like people."

He opened his eyes, and they were full of pain. Everyone had listened like little children. Zeke had a way of putting people under his spell, and now no one said a word. The next thing they knew, Zeke was singing again, his voice strained and kind of far away, as though he wasn't really there. He strummed the mandolin softly and sang:

"My lady, she waits at the old oak tree.
Her hair long and soft, she waits there for me.
She's got lips red as roses, and her kisses are free.
Yes, my lady, she waits there for me.

"I can see her there still, at the old oak tree.

116

Her eyes full of love. Yes, sweet love, just for me.
Her skin soft as velvet, what an angel is she!
Yes, my lady, she waits there for me."

He strummed quietly, unable to go on right away,
and Abbie's heart ached for him, for all the sadness
and loneliness she knew lay behind his dark face and
flashing eyes that seemed close to tears.

"But I find that I'm dreamin, when I get to that tree.
'Cause my lady is gone; from this life she did flee.
She's way up in heaven, leavin' poor, lonely me.
And now that is where she's waitin' for me.
Up in heaven is where she's waitin' for me.

"But I see her there still, at the old oak tree.
Her eyes full of love, yes, sweet love, just for me.
Her skin soft as velvet, what an angel is she!
Yes, my lady, she waits—"

He suddenly stopped playing and blinked, then set
down the mandolin and stood up. "Excuse me," he
said in a broken voice before he walked off into the
darkness, and everyone looked confused until Olin
stepped forward, smiled, and tried to liven up the
party again.

"Okay, everybody, just keep on celebratin' like you
was doin'. Zeke's just feelin' a little sad from too much
whiskey, but he'd want you to have a good time on account of little Mary bein' okay, so let's get to it!'"

Trent saw that Olin was right. Starting up a fast
tune on his fiddle, he was soon joined by David, and
they all seemed to come out of the spell under which

117

Zeke had held them.

Abbie stared out into the darkness where Zeke had walked, her young heart crying out for him. She knew he felt extra lonely that night. He was a man torn by the loss of his loved ones, and torn between two worlds, belonging to neither. She started after him, but Olin grabbed her arm.

"Don't you be goin' out there!" he whispered. "Not tonight! You stay away from him tonight!"

Abbie jerked away. "I'm *going!*" she replied determinedly. "And nobody is going to stop me!" She was in tears by then, and she ran off into the darkness. Olin let her go, not wanting to make a scene that would cause harmful talk about Abbie. He shook his head dejectedly.

Five

"Zeke?" Abbie could see his outline in the distance, a tall, dark shadow in the moonlight. She boldly approached him, not caring if it was right to be there, only caring that he'd left the dancing and singing with some terrible memory weighing on his mind. He said nothing when she came closer, and she swallowed, not sure what to say or do and now needing an excuse for being there. "I'm . . . sorry . . . about your wife," she spoke up. "I wish there was something I could—"

"What are you doing out here?" he asked in a gruff whisper.

"I . . . I didn't want you to feel so . . . alone," she replied.

He stepped closer, and her heart pounded with fright and desire when he suddenly reached out and grasped her hair tightly in his hands, working it through his fingers and breathing hard. She could smell whiskey on his breath, but she stood fast and refused to scream or run.

"Her name was . . . Ellen," he told her softly, still

119

grasping her hair. She could feel him trembling, and her own heart pounded so hard she was sure he could tell.

"That's a pretty name," she replied.

He moved his hands to the sides of her face. "So is Abigail," he whispered. He moved his hands to her shoulders. "You shouldn't be out here. How many times does somebody have to tell you something?" He put one hand to the back of her head and grasped her hair again, boldly moving his other hand down over her breast. "Maybe you ought to remind yourself that I'm half savage!" he hissed.

Abbie swallowed.

"You're a liar," she said calmly. "Maybe in a fight you can be a savage, but not with a woman, and especially not with a half-grown woman who's never been with a man. If you think you're scaring me, Cheyenne Zeke, it isn't working. You can stand here and strip me and throw me down if you want, but I wouldn't be afraid, because I don't really think you want to do something that would make me hate you. The trouble is, I couldn't hate you anyway." She blinked back tears. "Even if you used all that strength against me like you're thinking in the back of your mind, I couldn't hate you. I came out here with good intentions, out of my concern for you. But if you want to violate me, then you go ahead! But I won't scream, because I'm not going to be the cause of those people in camp hanging you! I care about you too much, and I think you care about *me!*"

He moved his other hand back to her hair, grasping it so tightly this time that it hurt.

"Damn you! *Damn* you!" he whispered. "I've got

no use for you, Abigail Trent, understand? No *use*, except to maybe take advantage of your youthful stupidity in thinking I care about you! I ought to do just what you said—throw you down and get my piece of you and break you in like you're asking for by coming out here alone! I expect you'd feel right good to a man, being a virgin and all! Yes, ma'am, right good!"

She stood there stiffly, afraid and angry and in love all at the same time.

"But it wouldn't mean *anything!*" he added. "You're *nothing* to me! When are you going to understand that? I try to keep away from you. All these weeks we've been on the trail we've hardly spoken. And do you know why? Because I'm sick and tired of you looking all moon-eyed at me every time I'm around! You hear? Sick of it! You're just a stupid kid with big dreams about a man you don't know anything about—a man who takes his pleasures with *women*, not wet-eyed little *girls!*" He gave her a push. "Get on back to your wagon!"

Abbie clenched her fists, forcing herself not to cry. "I don't believe anything you say!" she told him flatly. "You're making it up! Why is it so important for you to hurt me? You don't mean it! I *know* you don't!"

He grasped her arms and shook her. "Hurting you this way is a whole lot better than seeing you get hurt like you would if you were Cheyenne Zeke's woman! I've *seen* that kind of hurt, Abbie! In the worst way! Terrible! Ugly and terrible! You don't understand how some people think about Indians—and about half-breeds even worse!"

"I'm strong, Zeke! I can take a lot! You even said

121

that yourself when you were talking about the stones. And it was *you* standing next to me in that vision, wasn't it? It was *you,* and that's what you're fighting now. We're *meant* to be together!"

He grasped her face tightly between his hands, squeezing it and speaking in a low hiss. "No! It was *not* me! You get those ideas out of your head!"

"I know I'm right!" she answered stubbornly. "You say this kind of hurt is better than the kind of hurt I'd suffer if I was your woman! But I'm telling you right now that this kind of hurt—not being able to hope you'll even *think* of me as a woman, not being able to . . . to love you—is a hundred times *worse* than any harm that could come to me from being your woman!"

"You don't know the first thing about what you're saying!"

"Don't I? Then why don't you explain it to me?" She grasped his powerful wrists with her hands. "Help me understand what it is about your past that makes you shun me just because I look like your wife!" Her tears started to come then. "Help me understand!"

Some of the anger left his eyes, and his grip on her lightened. "No," he whispered. His face was so close to hers that her whole body felt on fire. "If I told you everything, you'd just feel sorry for me, because that's how that little heart of yours works. It would just make your silly feelings even stronger. It's best you don't know it all. And it's best you hitch up with some nice young man and live a normal life. You're too pretty and too sweet for insults and abuse—just like Ellen was. I thought once, when I was younger, that I could make it work, but I can't. That's why I live with the Cheyenne now."

"But *I* could live with the Cheyenne . . . by your side!" she replied hopefully. He snickered scornfully.

"Don't be a fool!" he groaned.

"But I could! I wouldn't mind!"

He stared at her quietly, his eyes glittering in the moonlight. She could see the outline of his mouth, its lips tempting, not too wide or too narrow, sharply outlined against his handsome face.

"You could never live that way," he said softly. "You weren't born to it."

"I can learn! I'm strong!"

"Abbie, Abbie!" he moaned. "Your youth makes you think you can do anything."

"I *can!* For you, I can! I *love* you, Cheyenne Zeke! Surely you know that! All these weeks I've been watching you, loving you more all the time." Tears streamed down her face now. "I love you."

He closed his eyes and sighed. "Don't say that, Abbie."

"But it's true! Your keeping yourself from me hurts much more than anything else could! And—"

Her words were cut off when he suddenly pressed his mouth to hers, and for the rest of her life she would not forget that first kiss, not from a boy, but from a man. He groaned and forced her lips apart, and her body burned with strange new feelings she did not totally understand. He pulled her tight against him, and she let him, loving the feeling of her breasts pressed against his broad, strong chest. She could feel his hardness through her skirts and her body melted against his. For the next few seconds she was lost in him, under his control, returning the kiss as best she could for all her innocence, glorying in the fact that Cheyenne Zeke wanted her.

His lips left her mouth and moved across her cheek to her neck, and he held her close. It was then she felt a wetness on her neck, and she knew it was his tears.

"That was just good-bye, Abbie girl," he told her quietly. "We both needed that kiss. But there can't ever be anything more than that between us. And if you really love me, you'll keep away from me after tonight and not talk anymore about it. Please, Abbie."

"But I love you!" she gasped, keeping her arms tight around his neck. "And you love me! I know it! I know it!"

"Sometimes love isn't enough," he replied. "I've already learned that very hard lesson, Abbie girl." He forced her away from him. "Besides, maybe it's just the whiskey and me remembering my wife. Go on back, Abbie."

"No." she sobbed.

"Go on! Please!" His voice was expressing anger again. "Go back, Abbie. I'm just feeling my whiskey. I don't love you, you hear? I don't love you!"

"I don't believe—"

"Believe it! And stay away from me! I'm not about to let history repeat itself. Now get yourself back to camp and send Yellow Grass out here! I'll be needing my *squaw* tonight!"

The remark pierced her like a sword, and she bristled, wishing she were big enough to hit him.

"Go ahead!" she spat out. "A man can relieve his frustrations whenever he chooses, can't he? That's just fine! But a woman—a *proper* woman—is expected to suffer! I can just go back and go crazy think-

124

ing about you with her!"

"I'm doing you a favor, little girl! It's you I'm considering when I tell you to stay away, so go on with you!"

She choked on a sob, and they were interrupted by Olin's voice. "Zeke?"

"Over here!" Zeke replied, still glaring at Abbie. Olin came closer and looked from Zeke to Abbie, and back to Zeke.

"I hope this ain't—"

"It's nothing!" Zeke snapped. "Miss Trent was just going back to her wagon! What is it you want, Olin?"

"Yellow Grass. I can't find her nowhere, nor the preacher. Thought maybe we should check things out."

Zeke tore his eyes from Abbie. "That bastard!" he hissed. "I'll wager he's got her someplace! Help me look!" Olin nodded and hurried off, while Zeke grasped Abbie's arm and gave her a gentle push. "Get on back . . . and forget tonight ever happened, understand?"

"But—"

"Get!" he growled. He hurried off, and she stood there shaking and crying, his kiss still burning her lips and her body still hot and trembling. She walked back, every bone and muscle aching for him. Deep inside she felt an agonizing longing to have Cheyenne Zeke for herself. She reached camp just as the music stopped because of Bentley Kelsoe's shout.

"My God, he's killing the preacher!"

Everyone began running in the direction of the man's voice, Abbie with them, and not far from camp

125

they could see Yellow Grass lying on the ground, naked, her hands tied behind her. She was whimpering and crawling out of the way, as Zeke fists and feet landed into the preacher who, under the light of Kelsoe's torch, could be seen to be wearing nothing but his underwear. Abbie saw Olin coming, and she ran to him, tugging on his clothes.

"You've got to stop him, Olin!" she pleaded.

"Yes, stop this!" Kelsoe added. "It's no match! He'll kill the preacher!"

Olin just stood there with vengeance in his own eyes. "It wasn't no match between the preacher and that Indian girl, neither," he snarled. "She wouldn't lay for him without him forcin' her! She belongs to Zeke, and she wouldn't let nobody else touch her now!"

"Hypocrite!" Zeke roared, slamming his fist into the preacher's already bloodied face. Women gasped and turned away, and Abbie ran over and picked up Yellow Grass's buckskin dress, laying it over her so no one could look upon her. Then she ran back to Olin, tears of fear on her face.

"Please stop him!" she pleaded again. "You're the one who talked to me about how whites feel about half-breeds! If Zeke kills that preacher, we don't know how the others will take it! They might want to hang him! Please stop him! Please!"

Olin looked down at her and nodded. "If it had been a white girl that the preacher molested, everybody would let Zeke kill him and think nothin' of it. But it was an Indian woman, who don't count for nothin' in their eyes. Are you beginnin' to understand things better now?"

She hung her head, while the others watched the

fight, but not a man there was brave enough to try to stop Cheyenne Zeke. Zeke pulled out a knife, and women screamed and children began to cry. Abbie thought about what Olin had said Zeke could do with a knife, but just then Olin jumped in, grabbing Zeke from behind, probably the only man who would dare to interfere with Cheyenne Zeke when he was in a fight. The unexpected grab caused Zeke to fall, and the two of them rolled and struggled on the ground, while the preacher lay unconscious nearby.

"That's enough, Zeke!" Olin shouted. "She ain't Ellen! She ain't Ellen!"

Zeke raised up and shook the big, burly Olin Wales off his back as though he were just a bug; then he whirled and faced the man with his knife.

"Since when do you move in on another man's fight?" he snarled, waving the knife. Everyone stood frozen, certain that Zeke was going to use the blade on his own friend. He was full of whiskey and not thinking straight, and Olin knew there was more than just the preacher on his mind.

"He's learned his lesson!" Olin shot back. "There's women and children present! You want little Mary to see you gut out a man? Is *that* what you want?"

Zeke circled the man menacingly.

"Go ahead and use your knife!" Olin growled. "God knows I can't beat you in no knife fight! Use it on me and show these people that what they're thinkin' about half-breeds is true! Show little Mary! Show them all! You want to cut up a man who's tryin' to take your life, that's one thing. But I ain't pullin' no knife on you, my friend, and that preacher there ain't in much shape to do no more harm. Yellow Grass ain't

Ellen, Zeke. And she's okay. You gonna kill me just 'cause I try to stop you from doin' somethin' stupid?"

Zeke's body relaxed some. Then he glanced over at the preacher and around at the others. He straightened and slowly put back the knife. Then looking over at the frightened Yellow Grass, he said something to her in her own tongue, and she hung her head when she replied through tears. Zeke turned to the others.

"The preacher led her out here by confusing her with smiles and gestures," he told them, "as though he had something to show her. She's ignorant and trusting. When he got her out here he bent her arms back and forced her down through pain! That's the kind of *Christian* your preacher is!" he snarled. "She stayed quiet while he stripped her and relieved his filthy, lustful needs with her! She kept quiet because she was afraid he'd tell everyone she was loose—that she induced him to come out here with her! In the Indian world, when a man's squaw is loose, he has the right to disfigure her face or cast her out—or both. She didn't want to shame me! Until I deliver her to her people, she belongs to *me!*"

"And would you have . . . uh . . . disfigured her - if it had turned out that way?" Connely asked snidely.

Zeke glared at the man. "I'm not even going to answer that! All of you can believe what you want, because it's in your grain to always suspect the worst from Indians and half-breeds! I've never hurt a woman in my life, but I wouldn't expect you to believe that!"

"Zeke," Trent spoke up. "Don't hold it against all of us. We appreciate what you've done so far—especially with little Mary. You're the reason for our celebration tonight. Without you, there'd be a small grave on this trail. We apologize for the preacher. He had no right hurting Yellow Grass. Please tell her that."

Zeke's breathing calmed, and he brushed dirt from his clothes. "Sure," he replied disgustedly.

"Zeke, we know the preacher did wrong. But we couldn't let you just murder him," Kelsoe spoke up. "We just don't settle things that way. I hope you don't let what's happened cause you to quit on us."

He looked around at all of them with angry eyes and replied sarcastically. "I won't quit on you," he growled. "An Indian keeps his word!" He walked over to Yellow Grass and picked her up in his arms. She put her head on his shoulder and cried, and he said something to her softly and walked off with her. At that moment, Abbie knew that the woman would be the victim of Cheyenne Zeke's savage fury and his manly needs that night. And she wished she were Yellow Grass.

The next morning found everyone involved in the bustling preparation to move on, anxious now to make up for lost time. Some of the men didn't feel too well after a night of too much whiskey and dancing, including Jason Trent. LeeAnn floated through breakfast, actually offering to help, lost in her own world of happiness over the wonderful night she had had with Quentin Robards. It dawned on Abbie only then that LeeAnn and Robards had not been around for most of the dancing and singing, nor during the fight between Zeke and the preacher. She forced from her mind the terrible hurt she'd felt when she'd pictured Zeke with

Yellow Grass the night before, but jealousy burned at her insides when he finally showed up in camp astride the big Appaloosa with Yellow Grass, looking very happy and sitting straddled behind him, her arms about his waist.

Zeke rode straight up to Abbie, his face showing no emotion. "Morning, Miss Trent," he said rather formally. Their eyes held a moment, and she blushed from the memory of the night before thinking of his lips on hers and his hand touching her breast. It was all like a dream now; yet it was true, and her jealousy burned scorchingly. She could not bring herself to smile or even reply. She just glared back at him with tearing eyes. Zeke slid down off his horse, then reached up and lifted Yellow Grass down.

"Mind if Yellow Grass continues to stay in your camp?" he asked. "I don't trust the others to be kind to her. I know you will."

Abbie could have hit him. By counting on her kindness, he'd put her on the spot. Surely he had to know how she felt about Yellow Grass, but he was relying on Abbie to care more about Zeke's concern for the woman than about her own jealousy. She couldn't turn him down; he knew it. And she almost hated him for the half smile that was on his handsome face.

"Of course," she replied curtly.

"I'm obliged," he returned with a nod.

"Would you . . . like some coffee?" she asked, hoping she wouldn't burst into tears in front of him.

"Had some. But there is something out there a ways I'd like to show you, if your pa doesn't mind." He turned to look at Jason Trent, who suspected something had already occurred between Abbie and Zeke.

130

And because of Abbie's despondent mood, Jason was sure Zeke had told her to turn her thoughts elsewhere. Trent appreciated what the man was trying to do, and he trusted him. "I'd like to show your daughter a rare flower, Mr. Trent," Zeke told the man. "Perhaps you wouldn't mind her walking out there alone with me for a moment?"

Trent read the look in Zeke's eyes. "It's all right. You did save her from that Givens man, you know. Why should I worry if you want to go show her a flower?"

"Nobody knows better than me that people can make something out of it," Zeke replied. "I wouldn't want to bring your daughter any bad talk."

"Let them say it to my face and I'll knock their teeth out!" Trent replied. Zeke grinned and looked down at Abbie. "Will you walk with me?" She pressed her lips tight, wanting to kick him. "Please?" he asked, his eyes full of pain and apology. She wondered how she could ever say no to such a man.

"I'll walk with you," she replied sullenly. Zeke took his horse by the reins and led it along, Abbie walking beside him until they were out of hearing range.

"Well, where's the flower you spoke of?" Abbie asked, trying to sound cold and uncaring.

Zeke sighed. "There's no flower and you know it," he answered. "I just . . . wanted to get you alone for a minute, Abigail. I want to apologize . . . for last night."

She felt her heart going soft again and hated herself for it. But when she stopped and looked up at him, her love again took control.

"Perhaps *I* should apologize," she replied. "Olin

131

told me not to walk out there after you. I did a foolish thing. It was much too bold of me, and I hope you don't think I don't have any morals. I've never done anything so stupid in my life."

Their eyes held. "I don't consider it bold or stupid, Abbie," he replied. "And it wasn't wrong, because of your feelings. You're the nicest girl I ever knew . . . except for my Ellen. You're sweet and innocent and pretty, and I had no right saying what I did to try to scare you, touching you like I did, kissing you. I was drunk and I'm sorry. I took advantage of your feelings, and it was an almighty poor thing to do."

"I don't recall objecting," she replied. "There is nothing to forgive. I asked for it. It was dumb. I know you don't care about me."

"That's not completely true." He sighed. "Abbie, look at me, will you?"

"I . . . can't," she replied, the tears coming again. She turned away from him. "I'm too ashamed. I made a God-awful fool of myself last night, and you must have had a good laugh when you thought about it. I expect you laughed the whole time you were laying with that . . . squaw!"

He stepped close behind her, afraid to touch her for fear people would see. "That isn't so, Abbie girl," he said softly. "I never once laughed, nor would I even think of it." He pulled his horse around to where it would be between them and the wagon train, then gently turned her and lifted her chin with his big hand, forcing her to look at him. "I'm honored you have such feelings for me, Abigail. And I appreciate the concern you felt last night in coming to me. But most of what I told you was right, except when I said I didn't care. It's just that . . . it seemed easier to try to frighten you and make you hate me . . . so you'd leave me alone. Being associated with me can only bring a lot of hurt, Abbie. My mind is made up on that, and I wish you could understand. My mind's been made up for years—ever since I lost my wife and son. If you really care about me, then you'll respect my wishes and take the advice of someone older— someone who knows about things you don't know, who's already been through things you've never experienced. I won't talk to you much after this morning, because it's best that way. But I have to know you understand, or I'll go crazy with worry about you."

She studied his dark eyes and saw his pain and remorse, and she knew she was losing the battle. Even in love, a person couldn't win in a fight with Cheyenne Zeke.

"I understand," she told him, tears running down her cheeks. "But my feelings won't ever change."

"Some day they will . . . with time," he replied. "When you're older, you'll see that everything I said and did was right." He brushed at her tears with his fingers and quickly kissed her forehead. "I have something for you—a gift. I'd be obliged if you'd accept it, and remember me by it. It's something I already promised you."

She sniffed, and her body jerked in a sob. "I'd . . . treasure anything you gave me," she replied.

He pushed some hair behind her ear. "You have to smile first," he told her. She sniffed again and finally forced a smile, and he grinned a little himself as he reached into a leather bag strapped to his horse. He pulled out a small leather pouch, and she recognized it as the one that held the stones. He took her hand and placed them in her palm, squeezing her hand around them with his own huge hand.

"I hope the vision about you needing these won't come true," he told her. "But if it does, you'll have the crying stones."

"And . . . what about . . . the rest of the vision?" she asked.

Their eyes held. "Must have been somebody else," he told her. "You're a fine young girl with a full life ahead of you. There will be plenty of good men who will want you. Some day you'll be married to one, and you'll be telling your children and grandchildren about these stones, and about the crazy half-breed you once knew on the Oregon Trail."

She sniffed and wiped at her eyes. "You mean the crazy half-breed I loved," she replied.

"Perhaps. Just so you say it in the past tense, because it can't be any other way. I'm sure it's my loss, but at least I'll know I did the right thing by you. We'd best get back now."

"Tell me one thing, Zeke," she sniffled. "Tell me . . . you really meant it when you said you . . . didn't love me or want me."

Their eyes held for several long, anxious seconds. "You'd be making me lie, and Indians don't lie," he replied. Her heart pounded with overwhelming love. "But when you're grown up, you learn to face the fact that some things just can't be the way you want them to be, Abbie girl. You're wanting to show me how grown up you are. So show me you can accept what I'm trying to tell you, and show me you're woman enough to do what I ask and let it go. I'd honor your memory a lot more that way."

She nodded. "I'll try," she told him, knowing she'd rather die than let him go. But then she'd never had him after all.

He looked around nervously, and she realized just how much he feared being seen with a white girl. "We've been out here too long," he told her. "Come on, now." He bent down, picked a flower, and stuck it in her hand. "Wouldn't want folks to think I was lying about the flower," he said with a grin.

She smiled at him, quickly wiping at her eyes to get rid of the tears as they started back. When they reached camp, Willis Brown stormed up to Zeke with his pregnant wife beside him. He glowered at Abbie knowingly but did not mention that they'd seen her walk off with Cheyenne Zeke.

"You want to know what happened last night while you were drunk and bedding that squaw?" Brown spoke up bitterly. Zeke bristled, his jaw twitching with anger.

"I expect you're about to tell me, Mr. Brown," he replied, "so get to it."

"Indians! They ran off with two of my cattle!" the man replied. "And three of my horses! And I want to know what you intend to do about it!"

Zeke looked over at Olin, who rode up beside them now. "You seen any sign of Indians, Olin?" he asked.

"I was just comin' to tell you," the man replied calmly. "They're out there, all right. Seen a lot of tracks. Ponies with no shoes. There's a lot of them, and they know we're here."

Yolanda Brown gasped and held her stomach, looking ready to faint, while the others listened with concern.

"No reason to go getting all upset," Zeke told them. "You calm down, Mrs. Brown, or you'll lose that baby. Contrary to the terrible things you're thinking, they aren't after the women. Just food, most likely. It was a lean winter. I suspect they'll show their faces eventually, maybe today or maybe a week from now. It's hard to say. But like I say, they'll be wanting to trade for food." He looked sarcastically at Willis Brown. "Your women are safe. The only men who steal women are *white* men! Which reminds me, where's the preacher?"

"He's in a bad way," Kelsoe spoke up. "He's laid out in one of my wagons."

Zeke lit up a cheroot, his eyes cold. "Good," he replied. "He's lucky he's alive." He scanned the little group of travelers. "If Indians do show up, you make sure that preacher isn't anyplace around. He's just likely to do something stupid and get us all killed. Let me do all the talking."

"You mean they might attack us?" Hanes asked.

Zeke almost laughed, but instead he took his side-arm from around his horse's neck and began strapping it on. "Not likely," he returned. "Let me ask you folks something. You ever been hungry—I mean, *really* hungry—like not eating for days at a time?"

Everyone looked at each other.

"They have," Zeke went on. "I've been that hungry before, and I know how it feels. Those Indians likely took the cattle for food—figuring you whites are real wealthy and you've got plenty more where that came from. They live mostly on buffalo meat and deer and antelope; but game isn't always in abundant supply,

136

and since the white man started coming west of the Missouri, Indians have less and less land to hunt on. And most of them don't have rifles like we do to hunt with in the first place. When you're feeding a few thousand people on what you can find off the land, you don't always succeed, so they took a couple of cattle."

"What about the horses?" Kelsoe asked.

Zeke looked at Olin. "What are they? Sioux?"

"Yup. Camped maybe four miles back of us. Big camp. Maybe eight hundred of them."

"Oh my!" Yolanda paled.

Zeke sighed disgustedly. "Get her to her wagon!" he ordered. "Make her lie down."

"What about my horses? Aren't you going to go after them?" Willis Brown asked, not even taking his wife's arm.

Zeke finished strapping on the gun, then put one arm around his horse's neck and half grinned. "Mr. Brown, do *you* want to ride into a camp of eight hundred Sioux and take your horses back? I might be good, but I'm not *that* good!"

Everyone chuckled a little from nervousness, and Willis Brown turned red in the face.

"You know what I mean!" he growled. "You're their kind!"

"That's right, mister, and I know how they think!" Zeke snapped. "That's why I say we just head out and keep moving and pay them no mind."

"And leave my horses behind? What about my cattle, too?"

"You've got breeders along. You can raise more cattle. A couple of head won't break you. As for the horses, you'll get them back when those Sioux ride in here wanting to trade them for food—flour and salt and the like. And when they do, you'd best trade, Brown! I don't want any trouble! They're just hungry."

Brown looked ready to explode with anger. "Do you mean to tell me we have to trade our *own* supplies for our *own* horses?" he fumed.

"That's *exactly* what I mean!" Zeke replied sternly. "And when and if they show up, all of you stay out of it! I'll be dealing for more than your horses! I've got Yellow Grass to think about. I promised to get her back to her own kind, but I don't intend to just hand her over to just any buck, either. So I'll have some of my own dealing to do to make sure she gets treated right."

Brown spat on the ground. "Horses and women! They're worth about the same in an Indian's eyes!"

Zeke grabbed the man by the shirt front. "Mister, the way you're acting right now, I'd say it's about the same for you! I already told you to tend to your wife, and you're still standing here worried about your damned horses!" He gave the man a shove. "Now get your woman back to your wagon and make her lie down! We've been held up here long enough. If she miscarries, we'll be held up even longer!"

Brown glared at him, then grudgingly took his wife's arm and led her back, grumbling about his animals.

"Why didn't you tell us about the Indians before, Wales?" Connely asked. "Surely you knew before this they were out there."

"No need to get folks all worked up," the man replied. "I figured I'd discuss it with Zeke first and size up the situation. This is the closest they've got so far, probably because of us being held up because of Mary's snake bite. But them Sioux won't give us no trouble, except to maybe want to do a little tradin'."

"How can you be so sure they're not after our women?" the older Mr. Brown asked haughtily. Robards moved over next to LeeAnn, trying to impress her by acting brave and protective. Zeke sighed and shook his head.

"Any of you ever heard yet of a white woman being captured and raped or tortured by a Plains Indian?" he asked.

They all looked around at each other, while Mrs. Hanes blushed.

"But people say—" Bobby Jones started to speak up.

"People *say!*" Zeke replied angrily. "But they don't *know!* Now I'm telling you all they want is a little food. As far as women go"—he pulled Yellow Grass close beside him—"they get all they need from their own squaws in their own tipis. There aren't many bucks who go hungry in that department." Abbie's jealousy flamed again, and some of the men grinned a little. "You've got to stop thinking of Indian men the way you're thinking," Zeke continued. "They're more interested in their strength and honor and bravery in battle than in dwelling on the dirty thoughts a lot of white men dwell on. Capturing and raping a woman isn't exactly honorable, nor does it prove bravery. You have to learn to think the way the Indian thinks, and then you won't be so afraid of them. And like I said, it's your own kind you've got to look out for—men like the preacher!"

Annoyed again, he turned and climbed up on his horse. He looked down haughtily at the older Mr. Brown. "I saw a white woman abused once, mister, real bad—worse than anything you could ever picture. And it was *your* kind that did it. That woman was my *wife!* So don't you ask me about what Indians do to white women!" He turned his horse and rode up the line. "Let's get moving!" he hollered. "Git up there! Let's roll!"

People hurried to their wagons, and the air was filled with the snap of whips, men's curses, and orders shouted to the animals. As the wagons creaked and started moving, they were off again. But Abbie's heart was heavy because of Zeke's last statement about his wife and her realization of the terrible pain and loneliness he suffered. When the Trent wagon began rolling, she looked back over her shoulder, watching for painted faces.

Six

All that day there was no more sign of Indians. One
of Kelsoe's wagons developed a bad squeak, so they
had to stop and grease a wheel; and the school teacher's wagon became stuck in the mud. Later in the day
a storm hit, a fierce prairie storm that made Abbie feel
the world was coming to an end. She huddled under a
quilt with LeeAnn and Jeremy, while their father, undaunted by the fury of the thunder and lightning outside, sat in a corner going over a list of supplies. During the worst of it someone banged on the side of the
wagon, and they all jumped.

"Everybody okay in there?" came Zeke's voice.

Abbie scrambled to the back of the wagon before
anyone else could get there and lifted the canvas
slightly, squinting when rain pelted her face. Zeke sat
there on the big Appaloosa, with nothing but his worn-
out leather hat to protect his head, and an Indian
blanket around his shoulders.

"You'll catch pneumonia!" she called out to him,
yelling so that she could be heard about the torrential

downpour.

"I've been wet before!" he replied. "Everything okay?"

"Yes, sir!" she shouted. "Is Yellow Grass all right? She'd been walking with the Haneses' children."

"She's in the wagon with them," he shouted back. Their eyes held a moment, then he just nodded and rode off into the downpour. Abbie crawled back inside, suddenly unafraid of the storm because she realized Zeke was watching over them. She reached inside her trunk, took out the little leather pouch of blue stones, and held them tightly, thinking to herself that if she could not have Cheyenne Zeke for her man, he was at least her friend, and that was comforting. But that thought only dulled the terrible ache in her young heart; she knew it would never really go away. Until her dying day she would love Cheyenne Zeke.

It was three more days before the Indians appeared. The camp was asleep when Olin Wales came around to each wagon, pounding on the side and telling those within to get dressed fast. Abbie and LeeAnn lifted the canvas and peeked out.

"Oh, my God!" LeeAnn whispered.

"Lord in heaven, we're surrounded!" Abbie added.

They dressed quickly, and Abbie jumped out of the wagon without even putting on her shoes. Sioux were lined up side by side around the train, and she worried about Zeke who would be right in the middle of whatever happened.

Yellow Grass stood by their wagon beside Abbie's father, waiting quietly, and Abbie wondered if the girl was afraid. Zeke would be trying to make a deal to give Yellow Grass back to the Sioux.

When she spotted Zeke, her heart beat with pride and desire at his appearance. His buckskin shirt was off, and instead he wore only a leather vest. His arms were well muscled and powerful looking, his hair unbraided and hanging loose again. His face was painted in black and red and yellow. He rode boldly away from the camp and about halfway out to the Sioux who sat proudly on their mounts, with their women and children behind them. The Sioux were dressed in beautiful colors, and some of the men carried lances with feathers decorating them from one end to the other. The braves also wore feathers in their hair, and their horses, painted from head to tail, had feathers decorating their manes. This sight was both beautiful and frightening to Abbie and the others. Abbie thought to herself that if she lived through this, she would certainly have a story to tell her children. She noticed that Yolanda Brown was not about, and she suspected Zeke had told the girl to stay inside her wagon. The preacher was not visible either, although he'd been up and walking the day before, still limping somewhat from Zeke's beating. Abbie hoped that wherever he was, he was tied and gagged so he wouldn't start any trouble.

A grand looking buck rode forward to greet Zeke, and Abbie knew by his impressive headdress, the mounds of fancy stone jewelry he wore, and the extra feathers in his horse's mane that he must be a leader of some kind, or perhaps one of the better warriors. He spoke with Zeke for a moment in his own tongue, and everyone waited anxiously. Then Zeke nodded his head and turned his horse, heading back to camp.

"Anybody who can spare it, get out some flour and sugar and salt—dried beans if you have any—and some meat," he told them quietly but firmly. "We have plenty from that kill a couple of days ago, and we'll be at Fort Laramie before too long."

"Do you mean we're supposed to hand over our food—just like that?" Willis Brown asked.

"Just like that," Zeke replied, looking as fierce as the Indians who surrounded them. "You want to go out there and argue about it, Mister Brown? Be my guest."

Brown glared at Zeke. "What about my horses?"

"Their leader is bringing some to trade. I expect they'll be yours."

"This is a farce!" Brown exploded. "I'm to trade my own food for my own *horses!*"

"That's right."

"Pay them off, Brown," Connely spoke up sarcastically. "Indians love to trade, and more than that, they love a good joke. They'll have a good laugh on us when they sit around their fires tonight."

The man's remark surprised them, since Connely seldom spoke. Zeke eyed him suspiciously. "And where did you get your knowledge about Indians, Connely?" he asked.

Connely's sneer turned to a regretful expression, as though he'd given something away. "I've had some dealings with them," he mumbled.

Zeke nudged his horse closer to the man. "And I have my doubts you dealt with them fairly," he replied, eying the man closely. "Something about you smells, Connely, but I haven't figured it out yet, except that your name is familiar for some reason. I don't have time to worry about that right now, but you're wrong about this being a joke. Those Sioux are hungry and desperate. It was a bad winter, and they lost a lot of children and old folks to disease and cold— even more to hunger." His eyes scanned Connely's rotund build. "You remind me of one of those government men whose belly gets fat off dirty deals with Indians. I don't suppose you'd know anything about the Trail of Tears, would you?"

Connely would not meet Zeke's eyes. "Everybody knows about that," he replied. "You can't blame that on all white men," he said and turned away, as Zeke watched him with the hate-filled eyes of an Indian.

"My guess is you know a lot more about it than you let on," he told Connely. He looked at the others. "Get the food together," he told them. "I gave my word to the warrior out there that we'd trade, and I don't intend to break it. The faster we get this done, the sooner we can be on our way!"

They all hurried to their wagons, taking out what food they thought they could spare and placing it all onto one blanket. Kelsoe and his three men each took a corner and carried the food out to where the warrior waited. Zeke rode ahead of them. After they set down the food and returned to their wagons, the Sioux warrior turned and went back to the rest of the tribe, returning with Willis Brown's horses. He spoke with Zeke again, and it appeared the deal was going to be made peacefully until Willis Brown interfered. He stormed out to Zeke and the Sioux warrior and grabbed the reins of his horses from the Sioux before Zeke realized what was happening. Then Brown spit a wad of tobacco on the Sioux's leg.

145

"Thieving redskin!" he snarled. "How dare you make a fool of us like this, you ignorant bastard!"

Whether the Sioux understood the words or not did not matter. It was obvious they were not kind, and his eyes lit up like fire.

"Shut up!" Zeke growled at Brown.

"I'll not let this uneducated savage put one over on me!" Brown retorted.

The Sioux warrior looked down his nose at Brown, and his lips curled back in a sneer as he spouted something back to the man in his own tongue. Everyone from the train stood and watched, frozen into place. Zeke barked something back to the warrior, apparently trying to explain that Brown didn't know what he was doing, but the warrior was furious. He angrily flicked the tobacco off his leg, outraged at the insult. Pulling out his lance, he threw it at Brown's feet, and Brown jumped back. Mrs. Hanes screamed from fear, but Abbie watched wide-eyed, worried only about Zeke.

"What's he doing now?" Brown asked Zeke, startled.

"He wants to do battle with you, you stupid son of a bitch! You insulted him! Why didn't you just do like I said and stay out of it! I had everything settled!"

"I'm not taking any dirty deal off an Indian!" Brown retorted.

"Well now *this* one is fixing to *kill* you, you ass!" Zeke replied, backing up his horse. The Sioux warrior dismounted, removed a hatchet from his horse, and started for Brown; but Zeke charged his horse between them and shouted something to the man. The Sioux looked up at Zeke and replied angrily; then

Zeke talked back, even more angrily, dismounted, and removed a hatchet from his own horse. Abbie gasped.

"What are you doing?" Brown asked.

"Your woman is carrying," Zeke replied, his eyes on the Sioux. "She's in no condition to be without a man—not out here. I've got nobody, so I'm filling in for you, you worthless bastard! You don't have a chance against this man!"

Brown just stood there speechless.

"Get going!" Zeke ordered, beginning now to circle the warrior. "It's my fight now! Get out of my way! This man has his honor to defend!"

Brown turned and started running, leading his horses, and if Abbie could have shot the man, she would have. For now Cheyenne Zeke, who was fighting Brown's battle for him, could get himself killed for that cowardly, stupid Willis Brown and his mousy wife.

Her heart pounded with fear as the Sioux took a vicious swipe at Zeke, but Zeke ducked out of the way and took a swipe back. The Sioux got out of the way just in time, then brought his hatchet down again, aiming for Zeke's shoulder, but Zeke kicked up and caught him under his arm. The hatchet cut into Zeke's leg slightly, but the blow from Zeke's foot caused the Sioux to drop it. Zeke quickly kicked it out of the way and stood between the Sioux and his hatchet; then he took another swipe at the Sioux. The warrior caught Zeke's wrist and pushed. Zeke pushed back, and in the next instant they were both falling to the ground and rolling. At first it was difficult to tell who was on top of whom, because Zeke looked so much like an Indian himself, and the dust flew in every direction.

Abbie's eyes filled with frightened tears. When Zeke rolled on top of the Sioux, raising his hatchet over the warrior's head, she held her hands to her chest. She expected the hatchet to come right down into the Sioux's skull, but in a flash the Sioux whipped out a knife and plunged it into Zeke's shoulder.

People gasped, and Abbie whispered his name, her eyes wide with horror. Zeke only grunted. His arm went temporarily useless from the pain, and he dropped the hatchet, and the two of them rolled in the dirt again, this time with Zeke trying to keep the Sioux's knife from plunging into his body. But Zeke managed to throw the man off and get to his feet, blood streaming down the front of him, and quicker than the eye could decipher, he had whipped out his own knife. Abbie remembered what Olin had said about how good Zeke was with a blade, and it gave her hope; still Zeke was wounded.

Zeke slashed out fast, ripping across the front of the Sioux's buckskin shirt and drawing blood instantly. The warrior made no sound, but jumped back, and the two men circled for several long seconds. The other Sioux warriors moved closer, watching silently. The Sioux slashed out, catching Zeke's left arm. Both men were bleeding badly, and Abbie fought the tears that made it difficult for her to see clearly. She hated Willis Brown with every bone in her body, for the fight was all his fault.

The Sioux warrior thrust forward with his knife hand, aiming for Zeke's middle, but Zeke caught the man's arm with his left hand and held it tightly. They stood there struggling, both of their bodies trembling from straining muscle against muscle. Then Zeke's knee suddenly came up into the Sioux's middle, hard, and the Indian grunted and lost his balance momentarily, giving Zeke time to turn slightly, his hand still on the warrior's wrist. He brought his knee up again and snapped the warrior's arm over it. Abbie and the others could hear the terrible crack, as the Sioux screamed out and dropped his knife. The man's scream was followed by a sickening grunt, and blood suddenly poured from the Sioux's lips, as Zeke lunged his own blade deep into the man's belly, then yanked it up almost to the man's throat, splitting him open.

"My God!" LeeAnn whispered. She turned around and vomited. The rest, including Abbie, stood and watched in horror, hardly able to believe their eyes. Now Abbie knew what Olin Wales meant about how Zeke could use a knife.

Zeke pushed the Sioux off his blade, and the warrior's body fell to the ground, horribly mutilated. Zeke bent down and wiped the blood from his knife onto the Indian's buckskins, then he slid his knife back into its sheath. He backed away, bleeding badly and covered with dirt, his breath coming in quick pants. Another Sioux warrior rode forward, this one much older and more grandly dressed than the one who had just died. He spoke to Zeke, while everyone watched, their hearts in their throats because of what the Sioux might do now. Zeke and the old Indian spoke for several minutes, while Abbie worried about how much Zeke was bleeding, then both men nodded and Zeke managed to climb back onto his horse, in obvious pain.

The old warrior turned to face his people, raising his lance and giving out a frightening howl. The other braves returned the call, raising their own lances and hatchets, and for a moment Abbie was sure they would ride down and kill them all. But then the old warrior turned to Zeke and smiled and nodded again.

Zeke rode back to the camp, while the old Indian waited in the distance. Several Sioux women rushed forward to pick up the blanket full of food and carry it off, while two Sioux braves hurried out to pick up the dead warrior's body. As Zeke approached the settlers, he looked mean and menacing, covered as he was with dirt and blood and paint, with his long hair hanging down and his arms bulging with muscle and veins still tense from the fight. He glared at Willis Brown.

"I hope you're glad you have your horses, Mr. Brown!" he sneered. "I had to kill a good man because of your stupidity! He was one of their best warriors!"

"You could have let him live!" Brown retorted.

Zeke looked as though he wanted to spit on the man. "He'd have lived in dishonor," he replied. "His spirit will be happier now, knowing he died bravely, fighting to the end. If I had let him go, he'd have lived in disgrace. He *had* to die! But then I guess a coward like you wouldn't understand that kind of honor. I'd much rather have stuck that knife in you, you stupid white bastard!"

Zeke's whole attitude was that of a vengeful and hate-filled Indian now. Not one thing seemed white about him. Abbie watched, fascinated by him and secretly proud that he had defeated one of the Sioux's best warriors. But it was difficult to picture him as he'd been just a few nights earlier, singing and playing the mandolin—all Tennessee man. She thought of the

150

way his lips had gently tasted hers. Now, although blood poured down from his shoulder, it was already drying on his leg; yet he didn't seem to notice his injuries. He said something to Yellow Grass, and after a short conversation she nodded and hoisted herself up on Zeke's horse behind him. Zeke looked around at the others.

"Yellow Grass has agreed to be part of our payment for insulting their great warrior," Zeke told the others. "The old man is their leader. At first he wanted Brown here to be delivered up, but I told him I had a Sioux squaw who was still young that I'd trade him instead. He's an honorable old man, and Yellow Grass knows it would be an honor to be his newest wife. She'll go with him. She wants to be back with her own people."

He glared at Brown a moment longer, then shifted his eyes to Abbie, and she wondered if it hurt him to give up Yellow Grass. Surely he had feelings for her now, but if he did, they didn't show. She felt she vaguely understood how it was between them and was certain that if he were to choose a wife of his own free will, like Ellen, he would die a cruel death before he would give her up. But Yellow Grass was more like a good friend, an Indian woman who had understood his Indian blood and who had comforted him in ways the white man considered sinful. Yet Abbie wondered if such things were always sinful in God's eyes, and she wondered at the vast differences in the ways the white man and the Indian looked at life and death, friendship and love.

"If I thought she wouldn't be happier, I'd not take her to him," Zeke told Abbie, as though he felt a need

151

to explain.

"I know that," she replied. She smiled softly for him. "You get yourself back here quick. You're bleeding awfully bad." He nodded and whirled his horse, riding out to the old warrior, who looked very pleased at the sight of Yellow Grass. Abbie walked up to Willis Brown.

"I hope you'll thank Cheyenne Zeke for saving your life just now!" she told him disgustedly. "That warrior would have cut you up like a fresh-killed buffalo if not for Zeke!"

To everyone's surprise, Brown actually grinned. "The man was just doing his job," he replied. "I don't much worry about whether a half-breed lives or dies, Miss Trent, especially one who gives me orders about my own woman and my own animals."

"You're filth!" Abbie shot back angrily, and everyone stared at her. "I wish Zeke had split *you* up the middle!" she added without thinking.

"Abbie!" her father gasped. By the time he had walked up and grabbed her arm, she was crying.

"I *do!*" she whimpered. "How can a man be so ungrateful?"

Trent looked at Willis. "I have to agree with you there," he said.

"So do I," Hanes put in. The rest of the men surrounded Brown. "You'd best be grateful to Zeke when he returns, Brown," Hanes continued, "or we'll kick you off this train and you can go it alone—except for all those Sioux Indians out there who'd like to have your hide!"

Brown swallowed. "All right," he replied scornfully. "I'll thank the man . . . but only for my wife's sake, because she's carrying and I'll not have her out there alone."

"Sure, Brown," Kelsoe spoke up. "We *all* know how brave you are! And we all know how 'considerate' you are of your wife. You're about as considerate of her as you are of a prize cow!"

Brown swung at Kelsoe, but Kelsoe caught the man's arm and came up hard under Brown's chin with his right fist, knocking the man flat. Brown stayed on the ground.

"I expect we'd all be in a heap of trouble if Zeke had lost!" Kelsoe told him. "Those Indians out there seem to think now that Zeke is some kind of great warrior—our leader. That's going to help us stay out of trouble. Right now we owe Zeke Mr. Hanes's life, little Mary's life, and probably *all* our lives! So I don't want to hear any insults from you, Brown!"

"That goes for all of us," Trent put in.

Brown got up and stalked to his wagon, his parents watching. "I'm afraid I have to agree with all of you," the elder Brown told them. "I'm no Indian lover, and especially not of half-breeds; but Zeke did more than his share today and he's wounded because of my son. We won't give him any more trouble."

As he and his wife left to join their son and pregnant daughter-in-law, Zeke was riding back to camp without Yellow Grass, which secretly gladdened Abbie's heart. Perhaps now with his squaw gone, his thoughts would turn to her again, even thought he would fight against them. But no matter how much she had resented Yellow Grass, Abbie could not have been happy about the Indian woman's leaving if she'd thought that Yellow Grass would have been unhappy

153

and mistreated. She looked past Zeke to see Yellow Grass walking behind the old warrior's horse, as the rest of the Sioux were turning to ride away. Some other Sioux women gathered around Yellow Grass, and Abbie could hear laughter. She looked up at Zeke who had ridden close to her.

"She'll be all right?" Abbie asked with genuine concern. She was glad she'd asked, for she could see gratefulness in Zeke's eyes because she cared.

"She will be fine," he replied. "You have an understanding heart."

"Zeke, come to our wagon and let my daughter fix those wounds," Trent told him.

"Thanks for what you did today, Zeke," Kelsoe spoke up.

Zeke looked over at the Brown wagon. "White trash!" he hissed through his gleaming teeth. "He never should have spit on that buck! That Sioux was a hundred times the man somebody like Brown is!"

"You don't have to explain, Zeke," Mrs. Hanes told him. "We all understand—and we agree. Please go get your wounds cleaned. Olin can lead us while you rest. You'll get an infection if you don't let someone clean those cuts."

Zeke looked at the woman with eyes that had now softened. "Did Mary see . . . what I did with the knife?"

"No," Mrs. Hanes replied. "I made her stay in the wagon."

Zeke looked relieved, but he seemed to be weakening. "Good," he replied. "Good." He leaned forward and, calling for Olin, half fell off his horse.

"Right here, Zeke." Olin said, as he rushed forward

to help Zeke dismount.

"Take care of things," Zeke told him, now trembling from loss of blood. "I'll . . . be out riding again . . . after a bit."

"You've lost a lot of blood. You'd best rest till tomorrow at least and stay off that horse." With a supportive arm around Zeke, Olin led him to the Trent wagon.

"I've lost blood before," Zeke objected. "I'm all right."

"No you ain't. Now you do like I say," Olin ordered. Abbie hurried beside them, and they all climbed into the wagon. Zeke fell onto the feather mattress, all his fierce strength now seeming to be drained from him. Olin climbed out and started shouting orders to people so they would get things rolling, while LeeAnn quickly climbed forward, as though she couldn't stand to be near the awful savage who had used his knife so cruelly. She still had a bad taste in her mouth from vomiting, and she looked at Abbie and made a face, unable to understand how Abbie could care about a half-breed who could be so violent. LeeAnn wanted nothing to do with Cheyenne Zeke, for he'd already insulted and threatened Quentin Robards. Now she and Robards planned to run off together and leave the train—when the right time came. LeeAnn knew Zeke would try to stop them if he found out, so she kept her secret, determined that Zeke would not interfere with her plans to go off and marry her handsome, rich lover.

Zeke watched her climb quickly away; then he turned to face Abbie as she unrolled some gauze and the wagon started to roll. "Your sister speaking to you

155

since I cut off her lover's tie?" he asked. Abbie grinned a little.

"Not much. She's changed, Zeke."

"It's that damned gambler that's done it," he replied. "I don't trust him—and I don't trust that Connely either."

"That makes two of us. Now be quiet and let me see what I can do about these cuts." She made a face as she helped him get his vest off.

"Use plenty of whiskey," he told her. "I don't want to be losing any limbs from infection."

"Then lie still and stay that way for a while so the whiskey can get all the way inside," she replied. She uncorked a bottle and hesitated. "This will hurt something fierce," she told him.

He smiled a little. "I've felt it before."

She sighed, studying his provocative frame which seemed to fill the whole wagon. Having seen that vicious fight, as she now looked into his dirty and painted face, she wondered what a child like herself thought she was doing, trying to snag a wild mustang like Cheyenne Zeke.

"Yes, I suppose you have," she replied, studying the thin scar on his cheek and thinking about the scars on his back.

"I'd say there's no other woman with this outfit who'd be as careful with me as you will, though," he added.

She blushed and leaned over, pouring the whiskey into the worst wound, the one in his shoulder. He closed his eyes and tensed up for several seconds, but he made no sound, only clenched his fists as sweat broke out on his face.

"You okay?" Abbie asked, tears in her eyes.

"Put a little more in," he answered. "I don't intend to go around half a man by losing an arm."

She poured again, and this time he grunted a little. "You could never be half a man, Cheyenne Zeke," she told him softly. "Not even with one arm."

Their eyes held a moment, then she leaned over and placed a towel under his left forearm which had also been cut, but less severely. He watched quietly as she poured whiskey over that cut, as well as the cut on his thigh, pouring it right over his buckskins because she was too bashful to touch his leg.

"The cut on your leg . . ." she began, then paused. "I mean . . . I can't do much for it unless you take off your britches." She blushed more deeply he'd ever seen her do before, and he suppressed a laugh.

"It isn't that bad. I'll leave my britches on. Being this close to you, things might be safer that way," he replied.

At his remark her blush darkened even more and her eyes teared. Zeke tugged at a piece of her hair, making her wish she could be casual with this man the way Yellow Grass had been.

"It's all right, Abbie," he told her. "Right now I'm in so much pain, I thought I'd feel better by teasing you a little, that's all. The leg's okay. You just tend to the shoulder. That's the biggest problem. You patch me up quick, and I'll get out of here. I'm filthy, and I'm making a mess of things."

"The bedclothes can be washed," she replied, swallowing. "And you'll stay right here and sleep a while. If you move around too much, you'll start bleeding worse again. It's starting to slow up now." She finally met his eyes.

"I can't stay in here, Abbie girl," he told her. "It wouldn't look good."

"To hell with how it looks!" she replied, surprising herself with her boldness. "You've got my pa's permission, and everybody knows we're just wanting to help you for what you did today. Nobody is going to think a thing of it! Now you lie still, Cheyenne Zeke, and let me wrap those cuts! If you get up, I'll hit you over the head with my skillet and *knock* you out!"

He broke into a chuckle, and his smile made her skin tingle. "I think you'd really do that!" he told her, studying her admiringly.

"I most certainly would!" she replied. "Now sit up just a little so I can wrap your shoulder, then you lay back down and rest."

"Yes, ma'am." He winced a little as he sat up, and she nervously began to wrap his shoulder. She had to reach around him, so they were very close; and he had to fight the desire she brought to his loins.

"Why couldn't you be . . . well . . . not so nice . . . and not so pretty?" he asked quietly as she bandaged his wound. Her heart pounded. "Why couldn't you be an Indian hater or something like that? And why did you have to be on this particular wagon train?"

"Perhaps it's fate," she replied, reddening again, her whole body on fire with her craving for him. "Perhaps there is nothing either of us can do about it after all."

"Don't say that, Abbie," he replied. "Because I don't like thinking about what that could mean for a nice little girl like you." He surprised her when he put

158

his free hand to her waist, than ran it over her stomach. "Such a small thing you are," he said in a near whisper. "I know it cannot be, and then when I am close to you—" He stopped short. "Hurry and finish," he told her, "and then get up front with your sister. I don't want you back here too long. It wouldn't look good."

"That doesn't matter to me."

"Do like I say, Abbie," he told her with pleading eyes.

She blinked back tears, then could not stop herself from leaning forward and kissing his scarred cheek. "You're too lonesome, Cheyenne Zeke."

He moved his hand to her neck, their eyes holding, and then he leaned closer, brushing her cheek with his lips, then meeting her own lips for a beautiful, glorious few seconds in a gentle kiss. His mouth was sweet, and she thought to herself how good and manly he smelled, in spite of just having been in a fight and being covered with dirt. He left her lips and gently kissed her eyes.

"If only you didn't make me think of her," he said softly. "Life can be cruel, Abigail. I've been dealt a good share of hard blows, and I can take another by turning you away. It's just that I don't like seeing you hurt, too, especially when it's my fault. But it's for the best. I'm sorry, Abbie girl, but that's the way it's got to be."

The wagon jolted, and his grip on her neck tightened.

"And when we get to Oregon?" she asked.

"Then we go our own ways. And we always think about each other, and learn to live with a memory. Fact is, you get to me more than you realize, Abbie.

159

There will likely be some good men at Fort Bridger, men who can join up with Olin and take the train from there. I gave my word to take this train to Oregon, but I didn't figure on you. So I'll be leaving at Fort Bridger. We'll be in the Rockies then. With good men you'll do okay from there. I won't take any pay, because I won't finish the trip."

"Oh, but you must go all the way with us!" she whispered desperately, unable to bear the thought of his leaving. She'd hated the hardships and dangers of the trip, but now she didn't care if it lasted forever; for to have it end would mean saying good-bye to him. But at least she thought he'd be with them until they got to Oregon. "Please don't leave the train early!" she whispered.

"No, Abbie girl. See what happens every time I'm close to you? It's not good. I'll be saying good-bye at Fort Bridger and that's that."

"I can't go on without you!" she pleaded.

"Yes you can. Now finish me up and get up front with your sister where people can see you. I'm already disgusted with myself for what I just did."

She sniffed and finished wrapping his shoulder, feeling as though her whole world had come to an end. Neither of them spoke for a while. She thought about how changeable he could be, one moment as vicious as a wild animal and the next as gentle as a kitten. An untamed savage . . . and a quiet Tennessee man.

These different aspects of him tore her heart into pieces, and prompted emotions in her that ranged from fear to admiration, from apprehension to desire. These turbulent feelings were being experienced by a girl trying to change into a woman, and she cursed the fact that she'd been born too late to quite know how to handle such a man. He closed his eyes and lay back as she wrapped his arm.

"Is that Rube Givens behind us?" she asked, not wanting to think about what he'd said about leaving.

"I expect so. If I leave, I'll take care of him. He'll be no bother to you."

"Maybe the Sioux will do him in."

"Not likely. He's too clever at trading with them. He'll give them a couple of rifles or maybe some horses he stole, or some whiskey, and they won't do him any harm."

"That horrible Willis Brown didn't even appreciate what you did for him today," she said disgustedly, tying the gauze. "You should have let him take his due!"

He did not reply right away, and when she finished she realized he'd fallen asleep . . . or had he passed out? She felt his forehead. It was cool, and his breathing was even, so she assumed he was only asleep, and she wondered if he'd been up all night watching for the Indians—and for Rube Givens. She leaned over and kissed him softly, taking advantage of that precious moment and knowing there might not be another like it. Although he was elusive and changeable, his mind was set, and Cheyenne Zeke was a man whose mind was not changed easily.

She sighed and climbed up front where LeeAnn sat, staring straight ahead, a hard look in her eyes.

"How is he?" the girl asked.

"I expect he'll be all right," Abbie replied.

"I can't say as I care. I'm sorry," LeeAnn told her.

"I didn't figure you'd care—no more than I care

161

what happens to Quentin Robards," Abbie answered, her heart breaking because of the resentful feelings between them. "And I don't care that you hurt me, Lee-Ann Trent. But you're hurting pa, and that I do care about."

"Pa is too old to remember what it's like to be in love."

"Is he? He remembers so good that he's running away from familiar things because he loved our ma so much. Don't you even realize that?"

"All I realize is that I hate it out here!" the girl snapped. "And I love Quentin. How dare that savage even suggest that a fine gentleman like Quentin Robards could do me any harm?"

"Zeke knows people good, and he thinks Quentin Robards is a gambler who's taking you for a ride," Abbie replied quietly.

"He's a half-breed Indian! I don't listen to uneducated, backwoods people like that! And you'd best keep your tail away from him before he gets under your skirts like some kind of squaw he can just trade off—like Yellow Grass!"

To Abbie's surprise, she was undaunted by Lee-Ann's remark. "Zeke would never do that to a woman he truly loved," she replied.

LeeAnn sniffed and did not reply. But Abbie hated Robards even more, for she was sure he had done his share of talking Zeke down. She'd lost the companionship she'd once had with her sister, and after Fort Bridger she'd lose Zeke, although she'd never really had him in the first place. She was beginning to feel an odd loneliness. It struck her that what was happening paralleled Zeke's vision, and she was frightened. At

162

the thought of being totally alone, she shuddered and looked out at the prairie that never ended, wondering when she'd see the big mountains Zeke had told them about.

Up ahead, Quentin Robards smiled at the thought of what a lucrative prize LeeAnn would be for Tina's whorehouse. And Morris Connely, growing more concerned that Cheyenne Zeke would discover who he really was and banish him from the train, pondered ways in which he might be able to get rid of their half-breed leader.

Seven

It was nearly the end of June when the weary group of travelers approached Fort Laramie. The six weeks of travel had been hot and tedious. Mile after mile of the same monotonous landscape made them all look forward to seeing new faces at the fort. The horizon still had not changed, but their hearts lightened somewhat at the thought that they at least were getting closer to the great Rockies and higher, cooler land.

Abbie had seen little of Cheyenne Zeke after the day she'd dressed the wounds he'd received in his fight with the Sioux warrior. She could only suppose he was healing well, for he quickly returned to his job of scouting, riding astride the big Appaloosa and acting as though he had no pain at all. She knew he avoided her to prevent hurtful gossip, but she would have gladly suffered the gossip if she could just speak to him and be close to him. Yet she knew it was hopeless to let her thoughts dwell on Cheyenne Zeke, for she could never have him. After Fort Bridger he would be gone, a fact that brought a terrible ache to her heart in the still of the night when she lay awake thinking of him.

She hadn't seen Zeke at all for three full days before they reached the fort, and she often wondered where he slept and what he ate. He seemed as much a part of nature, and as elusive, as a wild animal. But no matter how invisible he was, she felt safe in the thought that he was out there somewhere, protecting her.

Shouts and cheers went up when they spotted the fort, and drivers urged their animals to move a little faster. At first the tired animals balked, but they soon obeyed. Those with only horses, like Quentin Robards, rode on ahead at a fast gallop, and LeeAnn watched Quentin ride by on his fine, black stallion, her eyes lighting up with desire and pride. Kelsoe and his three men broke the line and passed the other wagons, all of them hooting and hollering, while the Brown wagons brought up the rear with what was left of Willis Brown's cattle and the horses he'd nearly got them all killed over. Preacher Graydon rode by on his horse, sitting tall in the saddle and clinging piously to his Bible.

Anxious to go into the fort, where there were new people to meet and where there was considerable activity, Abbie eagerly helped set up camp. All the people from the train were laughing and talking, relieved to finally be at a place where they could rest and stock up on supplies. Even LeeAnn, who had become quiet and distant, was excited and acted more friendly as she walked with Abbie and their father and little brother into the fort, where they spotted Kelsoe already dealing with a trapper.

Abbie's heart raced when she spotted Zeke inside the gates of the fort. He was standing off to the side

166

with Olin Wales and four other men—all of them big, burly trappers dressed in skins. As they were laughing and passing around a bottle of whiskey, one of them spotted Abbie and LeeAnn.

"Hey, now, what do we have here?" the man said with a pleased grin. He started toward the girls but Zeke caught his arm.

"The ladies of the train are to be left alone," he said in a friendly but stern tone.

The man stopped short and backed off, apparently not eager to cross Cheyenne Zeke. "Sure, Zeke," he replied with a nervous grin. "Can't blame a man for lookin' at somethin' that pretty, can you?"

Zeke grinned a little, but eyed the man warningly. "No, I can't," he replied. "But those two aren't for the likes of you or me, that's for sure. Looking is as much as you'll get, Talis."

The men all laughed a little, and Abbie smiled to herself, satisfied that Zeke was looking out for her.

"Just the kind of trash that Zeke would hang out with!" LeeAnn said under her breath.

"He set them straight," Abbie replied smugly.

"Honestly, Abigail, what do you see in that man?"

"I see just that—a *man*. *All* man. He'd die for me in a second—and for you, too, only you don't even know it. He'd give his life for you a whole lot quicker than that Quentin Robards would, I'll bet you that! A woman doesn't have to worry around a man like Zeke."

"Well, you can have him! And stop insulting Quentin! He's a gentleman in every sense, and he would *too* die for me. And you needn't worry about having to put up with him too much longer. We may not go on much farther with the train."

Abbie stopped in her tracks and stared at her sister, as her father and Jeremy walked on, unaware of the statement. "LeeAnn!' she exclaimed. "You know pa would never let you run off with that man! And neither will Zeke! And quit referring to Zeke as mine. A man like that doesn't belong to anyone but himself. There's nothing between us. He's dead set against it. It has something to do with what happened to him back in Tennessee."

LeeAnn looked down and sighed. "Abbie?"

"What?" Abbie replied, folding her arms, surprised at the girl's sudden humbleness. LeeAnn Trent had become as changeable as the skin on a lizard.

"Can we . . . be friends again?" the girl asked, suddenly realizing that if she made her sister mad enough, she might tell Zeke LeeAnn was planning to leave the train. "I mean . . . we've hardly spoken since . . . since Zeke insulted Quentin. I know it was mostly my doing—"

"Oh, LeeAnn, it warms my heart to hear you say that!" Abbie told her, hoping perhaps the girl had not changed as much as she'd thought. "And I'm sorry for the things I've said about Quentin. It's just that . . . I love you. And I wish you wouldn't talk about running off with that man. It would be dangerous. I can't help but think that Quentin couldn't *possibly* love you if he'd consider submitting you to the dangers out there!"

She immediately realized she'd said the wrong thing, because LeeAnn's eyes hardened again.

"Oh, there I go again!" Abbie fretted. "You know what I mean, LeeAnn. It's *you* I'm thinking of."

"Stop mothering me!" the girl spat out. "My God,

168

Abbie, *I'm* the older sister, remember? It's *me* who should be doing the mothering, not you! And I *know* what I'm doing!" She turned to walk away, and Abbie put a hand on her arm.

"LeeAnn, don't do something that stupid!"

The girl whirled. "I belong to Quentin now, and *he's* the only one I listen to!" she pouted. "Not an inexperienced little sister!"

LeeAnn's eyes flashed when she said that, and full knowledge of the situation suddenly hit Abbie. Her eyes teared. "LeeAnn . . . has Quentin . . . has that man laid his claim on you?" she asked quietly. LeeAnn jerked her arm away.

"Yes!" she replied haughtily. "So don't be advising me about men, because I already know all about them! I'm Quentin's woman, and nothing is going to stop me from doing whatever my man *wants* me to do! He hasn't quite made up his mind yet, but whether we go on to Oregon or go back East, he's going to marry me and I'm going to be a fine lady and live in a fine house." She glanced over at Zeke, still standing and drinking with the other men. "That's more than you'll ever get out of Cheyenne Zeke—if you're ever able to capture that coyote. The most you'll get out of *him* is a tepee and sixteen kids!"

"Well, that would be fine with *me!*" Abbie snapped. "There's nothing I would like better than giving that man sixteen kids, and I expect I'd have a lot more fun getting pregnant than *you* ever will!"

LeeAnn's eyes flared, and Abbie wished she'd not said things that would cause hard feelings between them again. But her sister's stupidity irritated her, and she couldn't stop herself from trying to make the

169

girl see what Quentin Robards really was.

"Think what you want of Quentin," she said heatedly, nonetheless keeping her voice down. "But I'll do whatever he asks, and you'd better not tell that Zeke, or you'll regret it! Quentin could probably get him kicked off this train if he wanted. And he could make things bad for you, too!"

Abbie paled. "What are you talking about?"

LeeAnn looked somewhat regretful, but she kept her mouth in a hard line. "*You* figure it out! Folks don't take kindly to a half-breed who moves in on young white girls!" As her sister whirled and walked on to the supply store, Abbie watched, tears stinging her eyes. Apparently there were no limits to what LeeAnn would do for Quentin. Her father and brother, who'd been talking to the blacksmith, walked toward her now.

"Let's go in the supply store, Abbie," Trent said with a cheerful smile. But he sobered when he saw the tears in her eyes. "What's wrong, honey?"

Abbie shrugged and wiped at her eyes.

"Is it LeeAnn?" her father asked, putting an arm around her shoulders.

Abbie swallowed, tempted to tell him LeeAnn might leave the train with Robards, but afraid of what the girl meant about Zeke. Besides, her father had enough worries without adding to them. How could LeeAnn and Robards possibly leave anyway, stuck this far out in the wilderness? Surely they wouldn't be stupid enough to try to go back alone, and it was doubtful there would be anyone at the fort to take them.

"It's nothing, pa," she told the man. "I'm . . . just tired."

"Don't you be fretting over LeeAnn," he told her. "She'll come around. That Robards will show his hand one way or another. Come on inside and I'll buy you some new material. Would you like that?"

She smiled. "Thanks, pa."

He patted her shoulder. "You're a good girl, Abbie. A good girl. I don't know what I'd do without you—or what little Jeremy would do."

Zeke approached them now, obviously in a good mood from his whiskey. "Mr. Trent, I'd like to introduce you to the man who runs the supply store," he told Abbie's father. "He's a personal friend of mine and he'll give you more than a fair deal on whatever you want, especially when I tell him what good people you are." He glanced at Abbie, his heart torn by the obvious tears in her eyes. Having seen LeeAnn storm away, he felt he knew the reason for them. He longed to hold her and tell her not to cry, but that was an impossibility, so he covered up his concern, casually returning his gaze to Trent.

"That's mighty nice of you, Zeke," Trent replied. "But we don't deserve any special favors."

"Oh, but you do," Zeke replied. "And so do the Haneses . . . and Kelsoe. There are good and deserving people in this world, Trent." He glanced over at the preacher, who stood off by himself. "And there are those this world could get along fine without."

"Well, I have to agree with you there, Zeke," Trent replied, as they headed for the supply store.

"Look there!" Jeremy said, tugging at Zeke and pointing to some Indian children standing with some Indian men and women. "Would they play with me, Mr. Zeke? I never played with Indian kids before!"

Zeke grinned softly and knelt down in front of the boy. "Those are Arapahos," he told Jeremy. "And of course you can play with them. I'll take you over, but I doubt they speak English."

"Then how can we play?" the boy asked curiously, pursing his lips. Zeke chuckled and tousled his hair.

"Hell, kids don't need to talk the same language to play together," he told the boy. "I'll tell them in their tongue who you are, and I'll find out their names for you; and in no time at all, they'll be showing you their bows and arrows and their hoop game and—"

"Hoop game?" the boy asked with a smile.

"You'll see," Zeke told him.

"How come they're over there by themselves?" the boy asked. "How come nobody here talks to them?"

Zeke's eyes saddened for a moment. "You know, Jeremy, if adults could sometimes think like children, we'd all be better off," he replied. He took a blue stone necklace from around his neck and held it out to Jeremy. "Here. A gift from Cheyenne Zeke to Jeremy Trent, a young man who might someday help bridge the gap between the Indian and the white man."

The boy's eyes widened. "For me?"

"For you. But only if you promise to always try to remain friends with the Indian."

"Sure I will!" Jeremy answered, taking the stones and placing them carefully around his neck. "A real Indian necklace!" he exclaimed. "Does this make me your friend forever, Mister Zeke?"

Zeke grinned. "Forever," he replied. "You are now officially a friend of the Cheyenne; that's what the necklace means. If a Cheyenne warrior saw it around your neck, he'd not harm you."

172

"Golly!" Jeremy replied, fingering the stones and studying the half-breed he considered the strongest, bravest, and wildest Indian he'd ever known. Zeke just chuckled and shook his head, as he stood up and led the boy over to the Indian children.

Abbie watched them for a moment. Zeke spoke in both tongues in order to help Jeremy get acquainted, while the Indian children stood obedient and quiet, staring at Jeremy with the huge, brown eyes set in their lovely, round, brown faces. She wanted to walk up and hug them. They were beautiful children, and she thought of giving Cheyenne Zeke babies with such large, dark eyes and bright smiles.

Zeke soon rejoined them, assuring Abbie's father that the boy would have a lot more fun playing with the Indian children than standing around in the supply store. Already Jeremy was running with one of the Arapaho boys, both of them rolling hoops and laughing. Abbie, her father, and Zeke went on to the supply store, where Zeke introduced them and the Haneses to the owner, an old man named Gus Clinton, who shook Zeke's hand like a long-lost friend. Abbie felt relieved to see another white man besides Olin Wales who apparently considered Zeke a friend and an equal.

"Now this here is a man who can be trusted as much as you can trust the sun to come up every day," Clinton told them, still shaking hands with Zeke, who laughed. "I'll take Zeke's word any day over most of the whites that come through here," the man went on. "That's all a man is worth out here, you know. His word. It's somethin' for you folks to remember. Zeke here—he's a right good friend to have. But look out if he catches you lying or cheating or aiming at his back!

173

Then he's as vicious as a wolf with rabies!" They all chuckled.

"We've seen a little of that side of him," Trent replied.

"I expect so," Clinton replied. He winked at Zeke. "How have things been going for you, Zeke? Any problems on the way out?'

"Just the usual," Zeke replied, grabbing up a few thin cigars. "Had a little run-in with the Sioux. Had to put a Sioux warrior in his place . . . a little misunderstanding with one of the emigrants."

"Well, if the white folks would learn how to deal with Indians, there wouldn't be any problems," Clinton replied. "I suppose the Sioux warrior is dead?"

Zeke reached into a small pouch on his leather belt and pulled out some coins, laying them on the counter. "You suppose right. I don't generally end a fight any other way if I can help it."

"You got the Cheyenne mean streak in you, Zeke. You watch yourself around civilized parts or you'll be hanging from a tree. It would be a shame to hang a good man like you."

Zeke chuckled and shoved the money across the counter. "Thanks for the cigars. I'll be heading out for the Arapaho camp now. Figured I'd spend a day with Indians instead of whites—gives me a chance to relax and be among people I can trust." He nodded to Jason Trent. "Present company is not included in those I do not trust," he added. "You folks get all you need now and rest up. We'll head out day after tomorrow." His eyes rested on Abbie for a moment, and he thought to himself how pleasant it would be to take her with him and spend some time with her in a tepee. "Good day,

Miss Abbie," he said cordially.

"Good-bye, Zeke," she replied.

He turned and left, giving no visible sign of caring about her any more than he cared about anyone else on the train, and she watched him go, wondering jealously if he had some squaw with whom he'd spend the night at the Arapaho camp.

They spent nearly an hour in the supply store, trying to make up their minds about supplies and then waiting in line to pay for their items. LeeAnn joined them, coldly asking her father if she could buy a necklace she'd found. Her father agreed reluctantly, because he knew the necklace would be worn for Quentin Robards' benefit.

When they finally left the store, their arms full of necessary items, they headed for their camp outside the fort; but as they walked toward the gate, Abbie's heart froze at the sight of five men who were riding in. Even LeeAnn gasped, and they stopped and swallowed as the five men rode up close to them. Abbie looked up into the sneering face of Rube Givens!

"Get out of our way, Givens!" Jason Trent told the man heatedly. "You have a lot of nerve showing your face again! You'd best not let Cheyenne Zeke see it!"

Givens snickered. "I got a right to ride wherever I want. I don't cater to Cheyenne Zeke. But I happen to know he ain't around right now," the man replied haughtily. He eyed Abbie and LeeAnn, remembering their slim thighs and small bottoms revealed in the hollow back at Sapling Grove. "My apologies, ladies. I was drunk back there in Missouri. I never meant to harm anyone."

LeeAnn blushed, and Abbie's eyes glinted. "You're

a lying coward!" she shot back. Trent grasped her arm warningly.

"Hush up, Abbie. Don't even talk to this scum. Come on, girls. Let's put our things away and go find Jeremy."

"Sorry you choose not to accept my humble apologies," Givens told them, spitting out some tobacco through his brown teeth. He eyed Abbie up and down and tipped his worn, leather hat. "See you ladies at the big celebration tonight. There will be lots of dancin' and singin' and feastin' and such. Afternoon, ladies."

Abbie felt undressed, and her heart pounding with hatred and fear, she quickly turned and walked toward camp, while Rube Givens and his men rode on into the fort. She wished Cheyenne Zeke had not left the fort for the Arapaho camp. But then surely a man as cunning and knowledgeable as Zeke knew Rube Givens was about. Perhaps he'd return before the evening's celebrations to guard her against Rube Givens. And just in case he did return, she'd look her prettiest that night—for Cheyenne Zeke. Her heart raced with anticipation.

Givens rode on inside the fort and dismounted, tying his horse and eying a well-dressed man in a gray suit standing near the entrance to the supply store. He nodded to the man and the man nodded back. Givens headed inside, but the man stopped him with his words.

"You're the fellow who had the run-in with Cheyenne Zeke back at Sapling Grove, aren't you?" the man asked. Givens stopped and looked at him suspiciously.

"I am. And you're a part of the wagon train, ain't you?"

"Name's Connely. Morris Connely," the portly, graying man replied. "I . . . uh . . . I believe you and I have similar feelings about Cheyenne Zeke, sir. And so does another man on this train, a man by the name of Quentin Robards. Now that I see you're still with us, I'd like to talk to you about something. I don't like this half-breed scout we have, but I can't do anything about it directly. Perhaps you can help for a little . . . fee?"

Givens smiled. "For a big enough fee I'll do anything, mister."

"I thought so," Connely replied. "I think I've finally figured out who Cheyenne Zeke really is. I spent some time in Tennessee myself, and I've been putting a few things together. If my hunch is right, I can get the man kicked off the train. That would . . . uh . . . leave those girls a little more . . . unprotected, if you know what I mean."

Givens grinned. "I'm listenin'."

"One thing. I'll pay you well, Givens. But only if you leave my name and Quentin Robards' name out of it, understand? I don't want Cheyenne Zeke knowing where the information came from. Understood?"

"You afraid of that big blade of his?" Givens snickered.

"Aren't you?" Connely replied.

"Only when I'm facin' him. But once he's off the train, he's out there alone. I know where he is now. Been lookin' for Zeke for a long time. That's why I stayed behind, waitin' my chance to put a bullet in his back. Trouble is, Cheyenne Zeke ain't the type that's easy to catch. But I will . . . someday."

"Come with me, Givens. Perhaps I can help you toward that goal," Connely replied. He led Givens around the corner of the building to where Quentin Robards stood waiting.

The celebration that night would have been the best time Abbie had ever had, if not for the lurking presence of Rube Givens and his men—and the absence of Cheyenne Zeke. She tried her best to enjoy herself. She wore her hair in curls and put blue ribbons in it that matched her blue cotton dress with the ruffled hem and the bodice that helped make her breasts look a little more womanly. But Zeke was not there to see her, so she danced a few times with Bobby Jones, just to be nice.

Her father and the others, aware of Givens' presence, were prepared, all watching both Givens and the women of the train. Jason Trent kept his rifle beside him as he sat and played the fiddle. David Craig again joined in with his banjo, but he watched LeeAnn and Quentin Robards with both hate and hurt in his eyes. One man from the fort played the fiddle, and another the harmonica, so together they all made music that had everyone dancing and clapping.

Abbie decided that nothing bad could happen in such a large group, so in spite of Zeke's absence, she tried to enjoy herself, for ahead lay more dangers and possible heartache. And she did want to show her gratitude to old Mr. Clinton and others at the fort who had gone out of their way to show the emigrants a good time and to prepare a side of beef, from which everyone ate heartily, over a pit of coals.

The entire group of travelers attended, including the preacher, who stood off to the side talking to Yolanda Brown about how he intended to make Oregon a more "Christian" place for the new settlers by "saving" the savage Indians and the lawless men who were already there. He acted as though he had no guilt feelings whatsoever about what he'd done to Yellow Grass, and apparently Yolanda Brown didn't see anything wrong with his past behavior. That aggravated Abbie. Abbie supposed Yolanda Brown didn't hold it against the man simply because Yellow Grass had been an Indian, and therefore, she didn't count. After all, a man, even a preacher, can't be blamed for trying to get a little manly pleasure out of a squaw; that was the way she'd heard Willis Brown put it once. It sickened Abbie that such people could exist and that they smugly joined decent people and piously talked about being Christian.

The men to whom Abbie had seen Zeke speak earlier were present, and there were even a few Indians there, who apparently hung around the Fort all the time, eager to trade horses and buffalo robes to the whites in exchange for trinkets and mirrors and such.

Old Mr. Clinton called out square dances, and skirts swirled and people laughed, meanwhile complaining that they were dancing too hard on full stomachs. Everyone was eager to let loose; the strain over little Mary's snakebite, the run-in with the Sioux, and all the other problems they had experienced had made them ready to celebrate reaching the fort.

Abbie's disgust with Quentin Robards grew when the man actually stepped up to her and asked her to dance with him. She knew he was doing it simply to smooth-talk her into liking him better, but she suspected there was even more to it. He smiled slyly, as

179

though he knew something she did not know, and she grudgingly consented to dance, intending to let him know through her coldness and through her eyes that she did not like him or trust him. She thought to herself that he smelled more like a woman than a man. It made her long even more for Zeke, who smelled like leather and the out-of-doors; he was always fresh and good-smelling, masculine and naturally sweet, even the day he'd had the fight with the Sioux warrior. His was a smell that brought out the natural desires in a woman, but Quentin Robards' smell made her feel a little sick. It was perfumy and unnatural. She tried to hold her breath as much as she could until the dance was over, concentrating on Zeke and the memory of his sweet lips and breath the couple of times he had kissed her. She wished he could see her tonight, and that she could dance with him, but she knew that he would never allow himself to be seen dancing with a white girl in front of others.

To Abbie's relief, the dance finally ended, and Robards bowed low to her. When she glared back at him, he grinned. Bobby Jones brought her some coffee to drink, and the two of them watched the others for a while. Abbie noticed Morris Connely talking to Rube Givens, and that worried her. It was already obvious the man hated Zeke for some reason, and now he was talking to one of Zeke's most hated enemies. To make matters worse, Quentin Robards joined them, and they all talked like old friends. Abbie's heart raced with apprehension. She tried to piece together why they would be talking, especially Robards, who should by all rights hate Rube Givens for his attack on LeeAnn. How could he possibly act friendly toward the worthless Rube Givens?

The music started again, and the three men nodded as if in agreement and split up. As she danced again with Bobby, Abbie's mind whirled with confusion over what she had just seen. When the dance ended, Bobby left her to speak with Kelsoe, and Abbie walked over to a table of food and picked up a piece of berry pie. She stood there alone for a moment, watching the skirts of the dancing women whirl—and watching the crowd for Zeke. But he was not there. She started to bite into the pie when she felt a hand on her waist.

"How about a dance, pretty girl?" came the hated voice. Her blood ran cold, and she whirled to see Givens behind her, grinning.

"You get away from me!" she hissed. Everyone was so busy having a good time that no one had noticed.

"Some day you're gonna be out there somewhere unprotected, little girl. And I'm gonna finish what I started back there at Sapling Grove—and you're gonna be moanin' and likin' it," he told her with a grin. "I'm gonna be first between them pretty legs, missy."

Far more angry than afraid, she impulsively shoved the berry pie into the man's face, rubbing it in slightly; then running over to her father, she picked up the man's rifle, aiming it at Givens.

"You come near me again, Rube Givens, and I'll blow you in half!" she spouted, not caring who heard. The music stopped, and people quieted. Some started to snicker at the sight of Rube Givens standing there scraping pie off his face, which was now purple with berry stains. Trent stood up and took the gun from his daughter, just as Cheyenne Zeke suddenly loomed

181

into the circle out of the darkness. Abbie's chest tightened; she wondered if Givens had deliberately created the incident, knowing Zeke was out there somewhere and wanting to start something with him. But she was too angry to worry about that. And she was too glad to see Zeke to fear a confrontation. After all, Zeke could easily take care of a man like Rube Givens.

"You people got a problem here?" Zeke asked, calm but hard. His eyes were on Givens, and if looks could kill, Abbie knew Givens would have been sliced up the middle then and there. Her heart fluttered with pleasure because he'd stepped in on her behalf.

"He said a foul thing to me!" she spoke up in a shaky voice, glaring at Givens herself. Trent had been keeping his rifle on Givens, and now he pushed Abbie to the side. Givens wiped his face with the sleeve of his filthy buckskin shirt, and looked back at Zeke with hate-filled eyes.

"I ain't armed, Zeke!" he growled.

"Too bad." Zeke reached over and gently pushed down the barrel of Trent's gun, telling him without words to back off. This was between Cheyenne Zeke and Rube Givens. "What are you doing here, Givens?" he asked. "I thought I told your men back at Sapling Grove that I didn't want to see your face again—else you'd be dead."

Everyone quieted to a deadly silence, backing away slightly. Most knew Zeke's temper and skill, and Abbie was relieved to see that the men he'd been with earlier now stood near Givens' men, warning them by their eyes and their presence that if they intended to join in with Rube Givens against Zeke, they'd better think twice. Olin Wales was with them, his rifle in hand.

"You can't order me around, half-breed!" Givens snarled. "I've got as much right to be here as you do! All I did was ask the girl to dance! She's lyin' about what I said!"

"I don't lie!" Abbie blurted out. "You said a filthy thing!"

Zeke stepped closer to Givens, but Givens just smiled confidently. "You gonna kill a man in cold blood in front of all these people?" he sneered. "I told you before, I ain't armed. I came to this dance real respectable like, and I left my weapons with my gear on account of the ladies present."

Abbie rolled her eyes, and would have laughed at that ridiculous lie if not for the gravity of the situation and her own anger.

"Oh, yes, we all know what a gentleman you are, Givens," Zeke replied. "Some of these folks here have seen firsthand how you treat ladies. You rope them and drag them off! You get yourself out of here, Givens, or I'll kill you—armed or not!"

Givens crossed his arms. "I don't think so. These are Christian folk, and they won't allow you to get away with guttin' out an unarmed man! Besides, I openly admit to these people that I was just drunk that day, and I humbly apologize for what I done." He grinned slyly and bowed to Abbie. "I am most sorry, young lady." He looked around at the others, putting on a grand act of humility. "I am sure you Christian folks can find it in your hearts to forgive a man for one moment of weakness, brought on by the demons of whiskey. I have not touched a drop tonight, and—"

"Cut the act, Givens!" Zeke roared. "You're a murderer and a thief. Olin and I know that firsthand!"

Givens moved his bloodshot eyes back to Zeke. "Well, while we're talkin' about murderers, why don't we talk about *you*, Zeke Monroe!" he replied.

A few people whispered at the mention of Zeke's last name, and Zeke actually backed up a little, looking as though someone had just hit him in the belly. His breathing quickened, and Abbie's heart raced with confusion, while Givens grinned more, looking around at the others.

"See how he reacted to that name?" he gloated. "That's cause that's his *real* name—give to him by his white pa back in Tennessee!" Zeke stood speechless as Givens strutted, cocky and sure of himself now. "Can't say as how I found out, but I done figured out who your half-breed scout *really* is!" he bragged to the others. "You folks ought to find out more about who you pick to lead you!"

"Shut up, Givens!" Zeke snarled, his fists clenching and his jaws flexing with anger.

"Why should I?" Givens shot back. "I'm *right*, ain't I? You're Zeke Monroe. I know by how you reacted to the name. Some of the other folks here from Tennessee might know that name. Because about five years ago, back in Tennessee, a young half-breed by the name of Ezekiel Monroe murdered eight men—one by one! Hung them by their heels and gutted them out like fresh-killed deer while they was still *alive!*"

People gasped, and Yolanda Brown actually fainted. Abbie's heart bled for Zeke, who stood there like a piece of stone. He wasn't denying any of it.

Eight

Zeke glanced around at the quieted crowd of people, his dark eyes searching, as though he expected to be pounced upon and captured like a hunted animal. Abbie watched him with a mixture of love and apprehension, telling herself there had to be a reason for the eight brutal murders of which Rube Givens had accused him. She knew by his eyes that the story must be true, and for the first time she realized a man had the upper hand with Cheyenne Zeke. That could not be gotten with fists or weapons, courage or strength. But it could be done with simple words, and Rube Givens had found the right ones. Zeke had flinched at the name Ezekiel Monroe as though Givens had injured him physically, and now Givens stood grinning at Zeke, feeling victorious. The attention had been drawn away from himself and directed at Cheyenne Zeke.

"Is it true, Zeke?" Kelsoe spoke up quietly. "Did you kill eight men back in Tennessee—in cold blood?"

Zeke slowly turned to face the man, his muscles

185

hardened as though ready to defend himself, his hand resting on the handle of his knife. He stared almost blankly at Kelsoe a moment, then replied in a low, strained voice. "It's true." He offered no explanation, and the tenseness in his statement, along with the fact that he'd like nothing better than to kill Rube Givens for what he'd said, seemed to emanate from his body, making him almost tremble, like a volcano preparing to erupt.

"You wanted by the law back there?" Jason Trent asked. Zeke's eyes darted in the man's direction, then rested on Abbie for a moment, holding her eyes, trying to explain without words. The pain she saw there erased her horror at the thought of what he'd done. Surely there had been a reason, and she had no doubt it had to do with the still-unknown fate of his wife and son.

"I expect the authorities would like to see me step back into the state," he replied. "It's been a few years, but I suppose I'm still a wanted man there."

"You bet he is!" Givens spoke up. "They'd like to string that half-breed's hide from the highest tree! And I say we can do it *for* them, and rid ourselves of a dangerous, murderin' half-breed who likes *white* women! That's what his first wife was, you know. You'd best get rid of this half-breed bastard before one of you men finds his wife or daughter's been violated by—"

Zeke whirled and his knife was out now. "You shut your filthy mouth, Givens! Ellen was my *wife* and I *loved* her," he hissed through gritted teeth.

Givens smiled haughtily. "What are you gonna do, Zeke? You gonna gut me out in front of all these people? Go ahead! Show them the kind of things half-breeds do. Show them how you killed those eight men!"

"That's enough!" Harriet Hanes spoke up, stepping forward. She walked up to Zeke, her chin held high, her eyes showing no fear. "Put the knife away, Zeke," she said, almost pleadingly. Zeke stood there a moment, still glaring at Rube Givens; then slowly he looked down at Mrs. Hanes. "Please," she added calmly. "Mary is watching."

Zeke blinked as though coming out of some kind of trance, and he slid the knife into its sheath. Mrs. Hanes looked around at the people from the train.

"This man saved my husband from infection. He saved my daughter's life from snakebite, and he risked his life to save *all* of us from an Indian attack!" Her eyes moved from person to person. "Do all of you intend to leave it like this—to believe Rube Givens, whom we already know is a far from reputable man? Don't any of you want to know *why* Zeke killed the men? Perhaps it was not justifiable, but neither is what we are doing here justice!"

"Indians don't *get* the same justice as a white man!" Willis Brown sneered. "Everybody knows Indians aren't allowed to have any say. And a half-breed is worth even less! I say since he's admitted to his crimes, we do the Tennessee authorities a favor and hang him—here and now!"

"No!" Abbie cried out, not caring that people stared at her because of her sudden outburst. Her heart raced with panic at the thought of such an end for Cheyenne Zeke. Zeke had already backed up a little, and he had his hand on the knife again, ready to defend himself if someone tried to grab him.

"*You're* the one who ought to be hung!" Kelsoe spoke up. "You almost got us all killed back there by the Sioux! I don't want to hear any more talk about hanging!"

"We have no right even discussing such a thing," Jason Trent added, putting a gentle and reassuring hand on Abbie's shoulder. "We call ourselves Christians. Would a Christian stand here and hang a man just on another man's word, without a chance to defend himself? All I want is a reason, and if it's good enough, then what this man did five years ago is past. He's a damned good scout and he's been honest with us."

"Was it honest of him to leave out the fact that he's a wanted man in Tennessee?" Brown retorted. "That he killed eight men a few years back? He could have told us—"

"Why should he?" Bradley Hanes shot back. "Would *you* go around advertising that you were wanted? Maybe it's something he's already atoned for. Maybe it's just something from his past that he'd rather *keep* there."

"He's a murderer!" Rube Givens growled.

"And so are you, Givens!" Olin Wales roared. "Why don't you tell these folks how you pumped lead into *me* one night, left me for dead, and stole my furs!"

There were a few murmurs and whispers, and the preacher stepped forward.

"Let us not forget the topic of this conversation!" he said piously. "One Cheyenne Zeke. The fact remains he is wanted for killing eight men in cold blood, and he has no business leading a train of innocent, Christian people through the wilderness."

"You would do better to speak like a true minister!" Mrs. Hanes spouted back to him. "I believe Christ taught that he who was without sin could cast the first stone! You should be defending this man through the love of God, not accusing him! And we all know how 'sinless' you are, don't we?" Her eyes blazed. The preacher glared back at her a moment, as though he intended to say more, but he stepped back without speaking. Mrs. Hanes put a hand on Zeke's arm. "Just tell us *why*, Zeke," she asked. "Why did you do such a thing? Not all of us blame you for it. Help us understand."

As she herself waited anxiously for a reply, the tense silence of the crowd felt like a heavy weight on Abbie's shoulders.

Zeke stared at Mrs. Hanes for several long seconds.

"It isn't something a man talks about with ease," he finally spoke up. "You believe what you want. Most folks have their minds made up about half-breeds, so it wouldn't do much good to explain it." He started to walk away, but Mrs. Hanes grasped his arm tighter.

"No, Zeke!" she said sternly. "We hired you believing you to be an honest man and the best guide we could find. You've done your job well, and you've helped us—even saved my little girl's life! We've trusted all our lives and our belongings to you. You owe us an explanation, and you owe it to yourself. Don't let people think things about you that are not true." She searched his eyes, and he looked as though he wanted to speak, but was having trouble getting the words out. She was shocked to see his eyes actually tearing, and he suddenly looked like a lost and frightened boy.

"The men I killed," he managed to say in a choked voice, "they . . . raped my wife. They even . . . tortured her! Cut off her arms and told her she'd never put them around another half-breed again! They cut off her hair and stuffed it in her mouth . . . and they let her lay there and die slow like that! In horrible pain . . . and humiliation . . . bleeding to death!" His breath came in quick gasps, and Abbie's heart screamed with pity. "And before she died . . . she watched them murder our little boy! One year old! They . . . cut off his head!"

People gasped, and tears ran down Abbie's face.

"Animals!" he roared. "They were nothing but animals! They *deserved* to suffer! They *deserved* it! And if I had it to do over, I'd do it again!"

Mrs. Hanes closed her eyes and lowered her head, and Yolanda Brown grasped her stomach, looking ill.

"I *found* her that way! And my son, too!" he went on, his voice choking with both sorrow and rage. "She was still alive when I got there! And she . . . managed to live long enough to give me names. All of them were men she'd known all her life! As children they'd even played together!" He suddenly turned and looked straight at Abbie. "*That's* the kind of hate being a half-breed can bring! They *knew* her, yet they did that to her—just because she'd lain with a half-breed—even though he was legally her *husband!*"

"Zeke—" Abbie choked out, but he whirled and looked at the others again, his voice rising even more, his fury at the memory building.

"I hunted them down—one by one—just like Giv-

190

ens told you!" he shouted. "And I *found* them! They *suffered*—like *she* suffered! One small, helpless young woman against eight men! Eight men, who took turns with her—raping and torturing her! Eight men who murdered a little tiny boy who never hurt anybody and never knew evil! Can anybody here say they deserved to *live?* Ellen was a good woman—a *good* woman!"

"But you took the law into your own hands!" Willis Brown shouted. "A man can't do that!"

"And why not?" Zeke growled. "Do you think the *law* would have done anything to those men? Why should they back up a *half-breed?* They wouldn't do it any more than *you* would! You already said the Indian gets no justice!"

"The fact remains you're a half-breed and a wanted man," Givens sneered. "And you ain't fit to be leadin' no wagon train of decent Christian people."

Zeke turned to face him, and Givens suddenly paled and lost his smile when he saw the look in the Zeke's eyes. Cheyenne Zeke had been forced to think about his wife, and it brought out a thirst for murder that showed vividly now. Givens suddenly wondered if he'd erred in being the one to open up Zeke's past before the others.

"You think you did a clever thing tonight, Givens!" Zeke snarled, stepping closer, his hand on the blade of the knife again. "You know I won't do you in here, you being unarmed and all. But you've stirred something in me that makes me not *give* a damn if I get hung or not! When my wife and son died, a whole lot of *me* died *with* them, so I don't much care! So I'm telling you now to leave—quick. Else I'm going to use this knife on you for what you've done—whether

191

you're armed or not! You get the hell out of here, and this time it's for sure a promise that if and when I see you again, you're a *dead* man! And I'm a man who keeps his word!"

Givens swallowed and glanced over at Robards, who looked away quickly. Connely stepped back into the shadows, and Abbie knew then that both men must have had something to do with the news of Zeke's past. She remembered having seen them talking together earlier, and it all made sense now. Robards would like nothing better than to get Zeke kicked off the train, and for some reason Connely also was against him. Perhaps they'd hoped to get Zeke hung. Givens stepped back even farther, fully aware that Zeke was treading a thin line between control and fury, and knowing what Cheyenne Zeke could do with a knife.

"Threaten me all you want," he told Zeke, swallowing hard. "I'll leave now, Zeke Monroe; but don't think you've seen the last of me! There's a heap of settlin' to be done between us, and it's gonna get done."

"It will be settled when you're *dead!*" Zeke snarled. Givens turned to walk away, but Zeke shouted his name and the man stopped in his tracks. "Where did you get your information?" Zeke asked. "Was it somebody on this train?"

Connely moved back even farther, his heart pounding, and Robards casually put an arm around Lee-Ann, looking innocent and unconcerned.

"No," Givens replied, his back to Zeke. "One of my men—he's from Tennessee. I got to talkin' about your worthless half-breed hide, and he got to rememberin'.

And between us we figured it out, that's all."

The man quickly walked away grinning to himself now at the thought of the five hundred dollars Connely had given him to bring out Zeke's past, and at the idea he and Robards had come up with for LeeAnn Trent. Yes. He would lead Robards back East as he'd agreed earlier in the day. It was a fine idea Robards had: to drug the girl and sell her to a whorehouse. But why go to all the bother? He'd simply kill Robards once they got away and take all the man's money—and also take little Miss LeeAnn Trent for himself. And somehow, some day, he'd find a way to get to her bratty little sister who had shoved the pie into his face. He'd break in Miss Abigail Trent till she begged for mercy.

Zeke stared into the darkness, wanting very much to throw his knife so that it landed square in Rube Givens' back. But he wouldn't do it with everyone present, and Givens knew that. Zeke didn't believe it was one of Rube's own men who'd discovered Zeke's past, but there was no way to prove anything, and now his heart burned with the horrible sorrow of reawakened memories. As he turned to face the others, the terrible pain in his dark eyes tore at Abbie's insides.

"We head out day after tomorrow," he told them. "You folks decide whether you want me along or not. I'll be north of here . . . at an Arapaho Indian camp till then. I'll come back the morning we're to leave . . . and you can give me your decision. I'll understand if you want me to leave the train. Olin can get you to Fort Bridger. You'll likely meet up with another train there or find yourselves another good guide to help Olin take you the rest of the way over the mountains. I'm . . . sorry." His voice weakened. "I

never lied to you . . . at least I never meant to. I just
. . . left out a part of my life that I try not to think
about too much." He vanished into the darkness. For
a few moments everyone remained motionless, and
Abbie heard the sound of a horse's hooves riding off
somewhere in the darkness. She knew this would be a
miserable night of nightmares and painful sorrow for
Cheyenne Zeke. Now she understood it all.

"I say he goes!" Connely spoke up as they all sat
around the campfire the night before their departure
from Fort Laramie, their argument over Cheyenne
Zeke not yet settled. Abbie prayed they would let him
stay with the train, for she'd rather die than go on
without him.

"I can't say as I wouldn't have done the same thing
he did," Jason Trent shot back, "if it had been my
wife and son. Good God in heaven, how can you
blame the man!"

"The point is he's part savage. He just can't be fully
trusted," Connely replied.

"*I* think you've just got *other* reasons for getting rid
of him!" Abbie blurted out. "*Personal* reasons! And
so does Quentin Robards! You schemed with that
Rube Givens to bring up Zeke's past last night!"

"I did no such thing!" Connely shot back at her.
"Givens found out from one of his own men! And
you'd best watch that mouth, young lady. Folks might
get to thinking you're sweet on that murdering half—"

"That's enough!" Jason Trent ordered. "You raise
your voice to my daughter again and I'll knock your
teeth in! Abbie's a good girl, and who she might or
might not care for is none of your business, Connely!

It's *my* business!''

"There, you see?" Willis Brown spoke up. "The man's got us all on edge, knowing what he's capable of doing. Here we are, arguing over a half-breed who's killed eight men we know of—plus that Indian he fought with—and God only knows how many men he's killed over his lifetime. If he stays, there will be more trouble."

"If he hadn't killed that Sioux, *you'd* be the one who was dead!" Hanes growled at Brown. "You can't hang that one on Zeke! He saved your own worthless hide, you idiot!"

"I say we can't go on without Zeke," Kelsoe spoke up. "The man knows everything a body needs to know about this country out here and about Indians. How can we ask for better when it comes to dealing with the redskins? He talks their language. We know for a fact he's good at treating wounds and such, and he's been all the way to California and back—probably more than once. He's never done any of us a stitch of harm, and if not for him we might have the Sioux on our tail, or our wagons might be sitting back there on the trail burned out, with a bunch of dead bodies around them. We have to realize Rube Givens didn't have us in mind when he spouted off about Zeke's past last night. He had *himself* in mind! Now that he's run across Zeke again, he'd just as soon get the man out there on the trail alone so he can sneak up on him and do him in for the beating Zeke gave him back there at Sapling Grove. And Olin Wales has already told us the other things that happened between them. Rube *Givens* is the one who deserves hanging! At least what Zeke did back in Tennessee was for good reason. A man can't let a thing like that go unavenged, and it's crazy for all of us to be sitting here *blaming* him for it."

"I agree," Trent replied. "And I say it's time to take a vote. Let's get it over with."

Robards sighed and rose. "Personally," he said casually, "I think Zeke is trouble, even when he doesn't try to be." He straightened the ruffled cuffs of his shirt. "But I don't want to go against you good people." Abbie almost choked on his words. "I vote that he stays, and I'm tired of all this bickering. I'm going for a walk." He turned to LeeAnn. "Will you walk with me, my dear?"

She smiled prettily and rose, but Jason Trent glowered at his daughter.

"LeeAnn!" Abbie spoke up. The girl turned to look at her sister.

"What?" she answered irritably.

"What's *your* vote?"

Their eyes held a moment, and LeeAnn's smile faded. She was inwardly angry that the plot to get rid of Zeke had failed, for it would make her plans with Robards more difficult. And she wanted to hurt Abbie for her remarks about Quentin.

"I guess I am not as kindhearted as Quentin," she replied. "Mister Zeke Monroe is a murderer—reason or no reason. He frightens me. I vote no." She tossed her head and walked off with Robards as Abbie glared after her in the darkness. Abbie's father sighed and turned to the others.

"All right. We have one for and one against. The rest of you who want Zeke to stay, raise your hands."

He raised his own, along with Abbie and Jeremy. Mr. and Mrs. Hanes and their three children raised theirs, as well as Kelsoe and his three men, and the schoolteacher and his son.

"Kids don't count!" Willis Brown snapped.

"The hell they don't!" Trent shot back. "They're going through this hellish trip with us, making the same sacrifices, suffering the same problems! And they all heard about Zeke last night. They have a right to be part of our decision."

"This is ridiculous!" Connely spoke up.

"Just cast your vote!" Trent replied. "We have fifteen that say yes. How many does that leave against?"

All four of the Browns raised their hands, as did Morris Connely and the preacher.

"That makes seven, counting my eldest daughter's vote," Trent said with a note of bitterness. "Zeke stays and that's that."

Kelsoe rose. "All of you voted me in charge of these civil matters," he told them, lighting a pipe. "So I say it's done, and we'll not bring this up again. If we're going to get to Oregon, we've got to stick together, cooperate, and work things out. Zeke's a good scout, and he'll get us there. Anybody that causes more trouble because of Zeke might find himself lagging behind or looking for a different train to hitch up to, if you all get my meaning."

Hadley Brown sighed disgustedly and rose. "We'll cooperate," he replied. "We all voted, and it's a democratic decision."

"How about you, Connely?" Kelsoe asked warningly.

Connely stood up and waved him off. "You're all crazy," he mumbled. "But I'm keeping my nose out of it from now on. Just don't come to me when Zeke ends

197

up doing one of you in"—his eyes shifted to Abbie—"or ends up losing control and violating one of the young ladies."

"I personally don't want to hear any more such talk!" Mrs. Hanes answered, stepping forward. "I trust Cheyenne Zeke, and so do a lot of others here. And to put it bluntly, Mr. Connely, I'd feel safer if I or my daughter were to spend a *week* alone with Cheyenne Zeke, than with Preacher Graydon!" Yolanda Brown gasped in disbelief, and Preacher Graydon stiffened. "You'd best remember who's already done the violating around here, Mr. Connely!" Mrs. Hanes finished. Abbie felt like clapping her hands, and Connely just turned and stormed to his wagon.

"I will try to forgive you for that remark, Mrs. Hanes!" the preacher said pompously.

"I couldn't care less if you forgive me or not," she replied coldly. "I meant what I said. If I'm not sorry for it, then there is nothing to forgive!"

"Harriet, honey, let it go," her husband spoke up, coming up and putting his hands on her shoulders.

"All I know is I sat and watched Cheyenne Zeke save my little girl!" she replied almost brokenly. "I'll not have these people continue to insult him and abuse him with their words and prejudice!" Her voice choked, and she turned and put her face against her husband's chest.

"Let's all get some sleep," Hanes told the others. "We head out in the morning. Kelsoe, you'll be the one to tell Zeke?"

"I'll tell him," Kelsoe replied.

As the group broke up, Abbie hurried to catch up to Olin Wales and tugged at his sleeve. Wales tried to wave her away.

"I know what you're wantin'," he told her. "I got nothin' to say."

"Please!" she begged. "I just want to know a little bit about her! Please! Was she real young like me?"

Wales sighed and shook his head. "Yes, she was. But Zeke was only eighteen himself when they first hooked up; twenty when she was murdered. He says he knows now how foolish it was to fall for a white girl, but at eighteen a young man thinks he can conquer the world, especially when he's in love. And he was crazy in love with that girl. Her pa was against it, of course, so they run off together. She was sixteen. Her pa searched for them, lookin' to kill Zeke, but a man don't find Zeke if Zeke don't want to be found, so he give up and hired them eight men to do the huntin' for him. Figured with eight against one, Zeke was sure to be found eventually."

"But . . . they ended up killing her!" Abbie exclaimed.

Olin nodded. "The old man didn't plan on that. The way Zeke tells it, they lied to the old man, said Zeke had done it himself—'cause of the savageness in his veins. I guess the old man believed them, 'cause the only one anybody was after was Zeke. But at the same time, Cheyenne Zeke was after them men. And he found them—one by one—just like he said. So he's wanted not just for their murders, but for murderin' his own wife and son. Rumor spread that he was just a crazy man—the Indian in him gone wild. Then he disappeared for good. He's been out here with the Cheyenne ever since."

Abbie blinked back her tears. "Poor Zeke," she

said softly. "And his poor wife! It must have been so hard on her, always running and hiding."

"I expect so. But then she loved Zeke, and I reckon she didn't care as long as she could be with him. Zeke says she lost one baby—almost bled to death. I expect that's why he worries over that Yolanda Brown. But then she had that boy, and they was so happy. Zeke had a son. They finally decided to head West and get the hell out of Tennessee. They almost made it. She was killed the very day Zeke went into the little town they was livin' near to get supplies to head West. He came home and found them. I think what made it harder on him was that she was still alive. I reckon that's a sight that will make him scream in the night for the rest of his life."

Abbie wiped at her eyes. "*Does* he scream in the night?"

"Sometimes. I've heard him yell out. Sometimes he screams her name . . . sometimes he just yells things that don't make sense. But he's mostly at peace when he's been with the Cheyenne for a while. The Indians are very spiritual people, Abbie. They've suffered a lot and have learned to live with the sufferin'—through prayer and sacrifice and a closeness to nature and the spirits. Zeke finds his strength down on the Arkansas with his people, especially when he goes back to his mother."

"What is she like? How did he find her? Did he remember her? How old was he when his father took him away from her?"

"Now hold up there! I done told you everything I'm gonna tell. You want to know anything more, you ask Zeke yourself. But don't do it now, or in the near future. He's gonna be in a mighty bad way when he comes back here in the mornin', and he ain't gonna be wantin' to talk about nothin' from his past."

"I understand," she replied. "Olin, I . . . I love him. You know that, don't you?"

The man patted her head. "That's a road that leads to nowhere," he told her. "You won't do nothin' but get your heart broke, Miss Abbie. And if you push it, you'll just hurt Zeke, too. He's been hurt enough. He ain't about to get into a mess like that again. Now you go on back to your wagon, say a little prayer for him . . . and forget him."

"I'll never forget him," she whispered. "Not ever!" She turned and ran, and taking off his hat, Olin slammed it to the ground.

"God damn all pretty young girls!" he mumbled. "Why'd she have to look so much like his wife! And why'd she end up on *this* train!" He stalked off to unsaddle his horse.

LeeAnn and Quentin Robards lay alone in the grass far to the other side of the fort. LeeAnn, literally worn out from the ecstasy of Quentin Robards' expert hands and lips and tongue, was glorying in all the deliciously naughty things he had taught her, and her insides still ached from their heated intercourse. She curled up next to him, reaching down and caressing his privates, feeling very alive and very mature and very much in love.

"Are you sure we can trust that Rube Givens?" she asked in her girlish voice.

Robards patted her bare bottom. "I'm sure," he told her. "He was just drunk that day back in Sapling

201

Grove. You don't have to be afraid of him, honey. I'm paying him well. He'll get us back East."

"But why can't we leave right now—from Fort Laramie?" she asked, sitting up slightly and kissing the hairs on his chest.

"How many times do I have to explain, you silly child?" he replied. "We have to do it at an unexpected time. That damned Zeke will be watching for us to make a break, believe me. You might *think* he's not around, but he is. Like a hawk. Givens says he has to lay low a few days, that we should keep going like nothing has changed. Then when it's a good time, like maybe when there's big problems with the train and Zeke is wrapped up in them and paying no attention to us, we'll just ride off quietly. Givens won't be far behind. We'll meet up with him. He'll be watching for us. He knows the land as well as Zeke and he'll take us back. Zeke will be too busy with the train to come after us. And before you know it, we'll be in St. Louis, man and wife, living in a grand house and going to all the finest theaters. You'll be wearing beautiful dresses, and all of my business associates will be jealous of me!"

"Oh, Quentin, I love you so!" she replied. "You're so smart!"

He grinned and rolled on top of her. "I am also very much in need tonight, my beautiful flower. You wouldn't mind spreading for Quentin once more, would you? You're so beautiful I can't get enough of you."

"Oh, Quentin! Quentin!" she whispered, parting her legs.

* * *

He approached the train slowly, sitting proud and silent on the big Appaloosa. Abbie saw him in the distance and stood waiting, hoping for a glance when he approached; but he wouldn't even look at her, and she knew why. Not only did she look like Ellen, but he was not about to allow any feelings he might have for Abigail Trent to go any further.

He looked so full of pain that Abbie's eyes teared immediately. Anyone could tell he'd been grieving. His face was strained, his eyes were tired-looking, and his body seemed weary. He rode straight up to Bentley Kelsoe, and Abbie hurried along behind to listen.

"You still want me along?" he asked. "Or shall I keep riding?"

Kelsoe removed his hat. "We want you with us, Zeke."

Their eyes held a moment, and it was obvious Zeke was a little surprised at the decision. Zeke nodded, gratitude in his eyes, while his horse whinnied and scuffed its feet as though it were eager to get going.

"We'll cross the river today," he told Kelsoe, his voice losing a little of its icy ring. "It's high, so we won't have an easy time of it—may not get much more than that done today. In about ten days we'll come upon Independence Rock, maybe fifteen days, depends on how things go. The country gets mighty hilly from here on, and it's pretty rough going between the north fork of the Platte and Independence Rock—dry country, lots of alkali. The animals will have to be watched so they don't poison themselves on the water. But we won't hit that country till we cross the north fork. We'd best get moving." He backed up his horse. "Obliged for your confidence," he added.

"There was twice as many for as against," Kelsoe told him.

Zeke nodded again. "I have a good idea who voted against," he replied, "but I'll do my job, which means everybody gets treated and protected and guided the same—hard feelings or not."

"You're a fair man, Zeke. And we're . . . uh . . . we're sorry about your wife and all that. Not everybody is that way, you know."

Zeke did not reply. He turned his horse, his eyes catching Abbie's against his will. He stared at her a minute, then rode closer.

"You understand a few things a little better now?" he asked her. She hung her head and he rode closer, so that his leg was right in front of her, then he talked quietly. "Stay close to your wagon, Abigail, at all times, you hear? Farther ahead there are more trees and rocks, better cover for anybody with a mind to follow us, if you know what I mean."

It gladdened her heart that he was still watching out for her. She raised her eyes to meet his, trying to use them to express silently how sorry she was about his wife. "I'll stay close," she replied.

Their gaze held a moment, saying everything that needed saying; then he nudged his horse and rode on ahead. She watched him, her heart bursting with love and desire.

"Let's roll!" he shouted, kicking his horse into a faster pace.

Nine

Most of the day was spent just crossing the Platte. If not for the gravity of the situation, Abbie would have laughed at all the cursing and grumbling that took place. Sometimes she did snicker to herself, but she had to feel sorry for the animals, who struggled and strained to drag the wagons through the muddy river bottom. The clearance of the wagon beds was about two and a half feet, but the river was at least three and a half feet deep, which wouldn't have been so bad if there hadn't been that sucking mud beneath the water.

Zeke seemed to be everywhere at once and spent more time in the water than out of it, shouting orders, helping push, carrying people across on his horse. He was soaked to the skin; but Abbie was almost glad for the problems, because they occupied Zeke's mind that day, as he needed it to be.

They took the wagons across one by one, starting with the Haneses'. First, Zeke carried the three Hanes children across the river on his horse, the animal half-swimming but remaining sure-footed. Abbie supposed Zeke must be a fine horse breeder, considering the quality of the mount he rode. Then he signaled Bradley Hanes to start his wagon. It was pulled by Haneses' four oxen plus two of Jason's, as Zeke had ordered. But in spite of all six animals, and Hanes, soaking wet in front of them, tugging, shouting, and cussing, the wagon still became mired in the mud, at which point the stubborn oxen halted in their tracks, refusing to go any further. Hanes began sinking into the mud himself, and the water began to creep up to his shoulders. The wagon shifted, and Harriet Hanes screamed. Zeke warned their children to stay put on the other side; then he rode the big Appaloosa back into the river up to the Hanes wagon.

"Get on my horse behind me!" he ordered Mrs. Hanes. "The wagon might go over!"

"No, I can't!" she screamed. "I'll drown! I can't swim! I'm deathly afraid of water!"

"You don't need to know how to swim, and you don't need to be afraid!" Zeke shouted. "Just hang on to me. My horse won't fail us!"

Three and a half feet of water hadn't sounded like so much to Mrs. Hanes, but when she saw her husband sinking into the mud, with the water rushing fast around him, the river suddenly seemed a hundred feet deep. She stared at the water, frozen, until Zeke reached up and yanked her off the wagon. She screamed and grabbed him around the neck, burying her face against his shoulder and refusing to even look. Her position made it difficult for him to maneuver his horse, and everyone watched, in fear for the both of them. It was a scene they would later laugh about: Mrs. Hanes screaming and clinging to Zeke so tightly she surely was choking him, while Zeke tried to guide the horse across. But they did finally reach the other side, where Zeke had to pry the woman's arms away.

"Oh, dear God!" she exclaimed. "Oh, thank you, Zeke! I'm so sorry, but I'm afraid of water!" She slid down from the horse and ran to her children, hugging them as though they'd just been rescued from the hands of death. Zeke just chuckled and shook his head, turning his horse into the river again. This time, he jumped off the horse and held the animal's reins in one hand while he smacked some of the oxen hard with the other and growled at them to get moving. Eventually, he and Hanes managed to stir the oxen into motion. The wagon lurched, then pulled free, and Hanes took it across.

Again Zeke returned to the river, this time to help the schoolteacher get across. The Brown's two extra oxen were hitched to the teacher's wagon, and by using a different position than the Hanes Wagon, Zeke and Mr. Harrell got Harrell's wagon across with little trouble.

Then it was back into the water for Zeke. The Trent wagon was next. Zeke hoisted Jeremy up in front of him and ordered Abbie to jump on behind him from the wagon seat, which she did eagerly, loving the brief chance to be so close to him. LeeAnn announced she would ride across with Quentin Robards.

"Suit yourself!" Zeke hollered to her above the rushing waters. He headed into the river with Jeremy and Abbie, and Abbie hung on tight, having no fear as long as she was with Zeke.

They made it across, and Zeke lifted her down from

the horse as though she were a mere feather. Without a word he mounted up again and reentered the waters to help Jason Trent with his wagon. LeeAnn and Robards were nearly across themselves, and when they reached the bank of the river they simply kept riding, deciding to use the time they had to be alone while the others were involved with the crossing.

The next two hours were spent getting the rest of the wagons across. Kelsoe's wagons were the biggest problem because of his extensive supplies. The preacher rode across on his own, while Connely, who grudgingly accepted Zeke's help in getting across, was followed by the Browns. The Browns presented the only other problem that day, for Yolanda refused to ride across with Zeke, acting as though she might somehow be "infected" with some mysterious plague if she were near the "half-breed who'd killed all those men."

Zeke didn't argue. He rode back across and ordered Kelsoe to saddle one of his horses and ride back with him to get Yolanda Brown, because it was too dangerous for her to cross in the tipsy wagon. Willis Brown was so absorbed in getting his cattle and horses across that he did not even realize there was any difficulty in getting his wife across. Zeke looked at Yolanda in disgust when he returned with Kelsoe; then he ordered her to get on Kelsoe's horse and go across with the man, which she did willingly. But the minute they got to the middle, the horse stumbled, and Kelsoe and Yolanda both were plunged into the water.

Zeke rode in fast, water flying. Quickly he scooped up Yolanda Brown with one arm. Unable to get her all the way up on the horse, in spite of her pregnant condition, he literally carried her over. She screamed and kicked the whole way, as though she were being kidnapped, calling Zeke names and yelling for him to get his hands off her.

"That's just what I *should* do!" he yelled back at her. "Let you drown! Is *that* what you want?"

But the horse lost its footing just slightly, whereupon Yolanda grabbed Zeke's arm and shut her mouth until they reached the other side of the wide and treacherous river. Zeke set her on her feet and ordered her to get into something dry quickly before she took sick and lost her baby. She cried and carried on that all her clothes were on the other side, so Zeke yelled back to just use someone else's. She stood there, like a wet rat, glaring at Zeke, while Abbie stood watching, amused by the sight.

"You *wanted* me to fall in!" Yolanda screamed at Zeke.

"If you'd gone with *me* in the first place like I told you to do, it wouldn't have happened!" Zeke yelled back. "Now get your clothes changed. Borrow some from Abbie for now, but get them changed."

"Don't give me orders, you half-breed!"

He rode closer to her. "Get them clothes changed, or by God I'll strip you myself!"

Yolanda put her hands on her hips and glared at him. "I *dare* you to strip me, half-breed!"

Zeke jumped down from the horse, and her eyes widened. She started running for the Trent wagon, and everyone started laughing, even her in-laws. Willis Brown never even knew what was happening, because he was still herding his cattle across.

As Abbie giggled and looked up at Zeke, she noticed a grin pass over his lips. She was happy to see it, and to see the mischievous twinkle in his eyes.

"See if you can find something to fit her," he told Abbie, turning to mount up again.

"I'm not sure I want to," Abbie replied with another giggle. "She's not the nicest person I ever met!"

"Well, nice or not, she's carrying, so get her dried off," he replied with a wink. "I know what you mean, though." He tipped his hat, and as water ran from it, they both laughed. Then Zeke headed back across, meeting Kelsoe on the way as the man finally made it out of the river.

It was midafternoon by the time they got across. Everyone was wet and tired and needed to dry out clothes and bedding, so that first day they traveled only a mile from the river and made camp. Abbie tried to forget about the fact that LeeAnn and Quentin Robards were still off alone somewhere. She knew it worried her father; she had seen him constantly glance out into the distance. By now everyone knew the two were carrying on, and it shamed Jason Trent. But there was nothing he could do to stop her without suffering her sharp tongue and total refusal to speak, and those hurt him even more.

They gathered up dead cottonwood for a large fire, around which they all gathered that night to dry out, feeling chilly in spite of the warm night. Abbie worried about Zeke, who must surely have been soaked to the bones and who had gone to scout the trail ahead after getting them across. By nightfall he still had not returned.

Jason Trent dug out his fiddle and played some soft, pretty tunes as they all sat around the campfire talking

210

and drinking coffee. The preacher, refusing to join them, had bedded down already, and Connely sat somewhat apart from the others; but everyone else stayed close, enjoying the heat of the fire and the pretty Tennessee hill songs Trent played on his fiddle.

"How about a hymn?" Abbie's father asked after finishing a song. "We all ought to be glad we got across safely today. Any of you want to sing a hymn?"

"That's a wonderful idea!" Mrs. Hanes replied. "We've done no praying or singing together or had any kind of church service since we started out."

They all looked at each other a moment, realizing they had a preacher along; yet they were thirsty for hymn singing and to hear the Lord's word. Mrs. Hanes actually snickered, aware that none of them, except perhaps the Browns, even cared to hear anything Preacher Graydon might have to say.

"How about Rock of Ages?" Trent asked. "You all know it?"

"I expect so," Hanes replied.

Trent whined out the tune on his fiddle, and they all began to sing:

> "Rock of Ages, cleft for me,
> Let me hide myself in Thee.
> Let the water and the blood,
> From Thy wounded side which flowed,
> Be of sin the double cure,
> Save from wrath and make me pure."

It was then that Zeke stepped into the firelight, silent as a panther as always. Most didn't see him right away; but Abbie did, and her breath left her for a moment.

He'd put on a different pair of buckskin pants and moccasins. His shirt was buckskin also, but it was pure white. The front was beautifully beaded in a multitude of colors shaped like an eagle. It was the most beautiful piece of artwork Abbie had ever seen, if a shirt could be called artwork, and against the white shirt Zeke looked more dark and more handsome than ever. His hair was braided down his back and he was hatless, and that night he smoked a pipe instead of the little cheroots. He stood there, looking to Abbie like the grandest specimen of man ever to walk.

"Zeke! Come join us!" Jason Trent spoke up when he spotted him. "We're just doing a little hymn singing."

"We wondered if we'd see you anymore tonight," Kelsoe put in. "You did a good job getting us across today, and we were a little worried over how wet you got."

"I've been wet before," Zeke said quietly, moving into the circle. Yolanda Brown watched him sullenly. "I laid my skins out to dry," he added. "These are the only other clothes I had along. I don't generally wear this shirt except for special occasions."

"Well, I'd say getting across that river is a special occasion," Kelsoe replied. "Jesus, Zeke, you look like a chief or something. That's one hell of a grand-looking shirt there."

Zeke seemed a little embarrassed. He smiled and sat down on a log beside Trent, while Abbie stared transfixed at the striking man in the beautiful, white-fringed buckskin shirt.

"My Indian mother made it for me," he told them.

212

"That's why I generally keep it with me but save it for special times. It's kind of a ceremonial shirt. You folks go on with your singing. I'll just sit here and listen."

"Do you know the hymn 'Rock of Ages'?" Trent asked.

Zeke puffed the pipe. "I know it. I know lots of hymns. Back in Tennessee—" His face clouded somewhat. "Back in Tennessee . . . when I was little my . . . uh . . . stepmother took me to church. Told me I needed saving more than the average person because of my Indian blood." He puffed the pipe again. "But the people at the church . . . they . . . uh . . . they finally made her stop bringing me—didn't want a half-breed sitting in their pews."

"That's terrible!" Mrs. Hanes spoke up.

Zeke shrugged. "You get used to it."

"Do you truly?" Abbie asked, hardly realizing she'd opened her mouth. Zeke met her eyes.

"No," he answered. "I guess you don't—not really. You just pretend you do." He looked at Trent, forcing a smile. "Well, get going on that fiddle. Let's hear the rest of that song. You folks sing right well together."

Abbie's father played the tune again, and little Mary Hanes, looking drowsy, walked over to Zeke and crawled up onto his lap, putting her arms around his neck and falling asleep right there in his arms while they sang:

> "Could my tears forever flow,
> Could my zeal no languor know,
> These for sin could not atone;
> Thou must save, and Thou alone.

In my hand no price I bring;
Simply to Thy cross I cling."

Zeke stared at the fire, his arms around little Mary, his eyes looking distant and troubled. Abbie wondered if he was remembering being a little boy who was kicked out of church or, perhaps, thinking of his dead wife and son again.

"While I draw this fleeting breath,
When my eyes shall close in death,
When I rise to worlds unknown,
And behold Thee on Thy throne.
Rock of Ages, cleft for me,
Let me hide myself in Thee."

They all sat quietly for a moment when they had finished, Zeke staring at the fire until the spell was broken by Mrs. Hanes coming to gently take Mary from him and put her to bed. Zeke looked up at her and smiled, and Trent cleared his throat.

"You . . . uh . . . you got family then, back in Tennessee, Zeke?" he asked cautiously. "Brothers and sisters maybe?"

Zeke puffed the pipe and stared at the fire again. "I do," he replied. "Got a pa and a stepmother, but I'm not sure if either one is still alive. I have three half brothers. The oldest would be about eighteen now, the youngest eleven. He was only six when I—" He stopped and puffed the pipe, and again no one spoke for several minutes, while Trent repeated the hymn on his fiddle. Yolanda and Willis Brown got up, leaving without saying good night, to join Willis' parents, who were already sleeping.

"Hey, Zeke," Kelsoe spoke up, trying to lighten up the mood. "Tell the rest of us the truth, will you?" He grinned when Zeke met his eyes. "What would you have done today, when you got down off that horse, if Yolanda Brown had stood her ground and refused to go change."

They all waited anxiously while Zeke puffed his pipe thoughtfully. Then he took the pipe out of his mouth and grinned.

"I'd have stripped her naked as a plucked chicken," he replied flatly.

They all burst out laughing, and some laughed so hard they cried, including Abbie, who would have dearly loved to see Zeke humiliate Yolanda Brown that way.

That broke up the tired little group, and they all returned to their wagons with lighter hearts. Abbie watched Zeke's white shirt fade off into the darkness. She was disappointed that she'd not had a chance to speak alone with him, but she knew he'd never allow her that chance either, if he could avoid it. She climbed into the wagon, surprised to see LeeAnn already inside and in bed. The girl had apparently returned quietly, not caring to face her father or anyone else. As Abbie crawled in beside her, she noticed dirt and grass in the girl's hair, and it pained her heart.

She wanted to hate her sister, but in spite of how rotten she might think Quentin Robards was, she realized that LeeAnn truly thought she was in love with him. And Abbie knew that if she herself had a chance to lie in the grass with Cheyenne Zeke, she'd do it. It was Robards she hated, not LeeAnn. The whole situation troubled her, so she turned her thoughts to Zeke, trying to picture him stripping Yolanda Brown right in front of everybody. That made her giggle again, and she snuggled down into the quilt to sleep.

Outside, Zeke watched her wagon longingly.

The journey became more difficult as they veered away from the Platte. Abbie could see why Zeke said they would begin to progress more slowly now. They were in higher country, hilly country. Zeke told them they were in the foothills of the Laramie Mountains. The land here was thick with pine trees, and between the trees and the grades, climbing the hills was difficult and treacherous.

Going down was even more treacherous, because the weight of the wagons pushed against the animals. Keeping the wagons from tipping was a constant problem; they had a high center of gravity, and the animals had to be maneuvered so they didn't go at a sidelong angle down a hill.

Four days into the hills, the mules of the Kelsoe wagon driven by Bobby Jones grew stubborn and were out of control. The more Bobby tried to maneuver them into the right position, the more they balked, until suddenly the wagon started to tip.

"Look out below!" they heard Bobby yell. Luckily, according to Zeke's instructions, most of the wagons were well behind the heavier Kelsoe wagons, but there were two other Kelsoe wagons in front of Bobby's. Abbie screamed as the wagon went all the way over, breaking loose from its hitch, and the rest seemed to happen in slow motion.

The mules went one way, the wagon another, and at

first, no one was sure which way Bobby Jones had gone. The mules, still hitched together, scuttled off into the woods, while the wagon rolled and crashed and bounced past the two in front of it and on past Zeke, who managed to jerk his horse out of the way just in time to avoid flying debris. Dust flew, and the ground in the wagon's downward path was gouged out. It seemed forever before the pieces of the wagon and its cargo all found a resting place at the bottom of the hill. Rocks continued to roll afterward, and at first there was nothing but noise and confusion as the rest of them struggled and whistled and cursed to keep their own animals still, cracking whips and hanging on to keep their teams from doing what Bobby's mules had done.

To Abbie's relief, when the dust cleared she saw Bobby staggering to his feet about halfway down the hill. Zeke was already riding up to the young man. He dismounted and caught hold of the dazed Bobby, who had bent over and held his head a moment before straightening up. Zeke helped him walk to one of the other wagons and spoke with Kelsoe a moment. Then the rest of Kelsoe's wagons began slowly moving to the bottom, while Zeke rode up to the others.

"Is Bobby hurt bad?" Abbie asked anxiously, suddenly realizing how much she liked the young man who had paid quite a bit of attention to her and had always bashfully asked her to dance whenever they were playing music and celebrating. For a moment an odd look passed through Zeke's eyes, one that Abbie did not realize until later was a flicker of jealousy. But it quickly vanished, as Zeke thought to himself that Bobby Jones was the perfect kind of young man for

Abigail Trent to get herself interested in.

"Got quite a bump on the head," he replied. "But I think he'll be all right. He'll have to lie still for a while." He looked upward and shouted. "Let's get the rest of these wagons down—real careful! We'll have to help Kelsoe gather up what's left unbroken and divide it up—share the load for him. All of you can take a little extra in your wagon to help him out."

Most nodded and agreed, but Willis Brown cursed the extra burden.

"Get the women and kids out of the wagons!" Zeke yelled out. "Willis, get your wife out of there. I'll take her down easy on my horse. And I don't want any arguments!" He rode the big Appaloosa up to Willis' wagon, and to everyone's surprise, Yolanda climbed out and onto his horse without a word of objection. Apparently she had learned not to argue with Cheyenne Zeke. She'd been quieter ever since she'd gotten dunked in the river, and Abbie wondered if the girl ever got upset with her husband for his uncaring attitude toward her. Perhaps they had had words, because Willis Brown had seemed to quiet down himself.

Zeke walked his horse down so Yolanda would not be jolted around too much, and the other women and children climbed out and walked down, while the men took the rest of the wagons down with no more problems. They all joined together to gather up Kelsoe's cargo and were able to pack most of it onto the loose mules that Zeke and Olin had rounded up out of the woods. More was tied to the other Kelsoe wagons, so that there was little left to burden the others with.

The wagon that had crashed was practically in splinters, but they saved most of the wood, realizing it

218

could come in handy when they reached places where wood was not available for fires. The cleanup took most of the rest of the day, so they made camp right there, all of them sleeping hard because of the extra work the day had brought.

After witnessing Bobby's wagon crash, everyone was jittery when they set out again the next morning. The going got rougher as they headed for the north fork of the Platte, and they were even more worried because Zeke had informed them that they would again cross the river at a spot where it curved southward across their path.

On their ninth day out of Fort Laramie, tragedy showed its face to Abigail Trent, the beginning of Cheyenne Zeke's vision. How or why it happened was something that would haunt her for the rest of her life, and she would feel forever responsible, for she'd become the only mother little Jeremy had.

Her little brother climbed back into the wagon after it started rolling, yelling that he wanted to find a jacket that was too small for him.

"Jeremy Trent, you know you're not to climb in and out of the wagon when it's rolling!" Abbie scolded.

"I want to give Zeke that jacket!" the boy balked. "It's for one of the Indian kids who might need it, if Zeke wants to give it to him."

"That's a fine thought," Abbie yelled back as she walked along beside the creaking wagon wheel. "But you could have waited till we make camp."

"I want to run and give it to him now!" the boy pouted.

"You'll stay inside that wagon now!" Abbie ordered. "You know the rules!"

The boy ducked his head back inside, rummaging for the jacket until he finally found it. He pondered disobeying his sister, which he seldom did. But he was filled with a child's eagerness to give something to someone, and he'd heard Zeke talk about how cold the Indians got in the winter, especially the old ones and the children. He looked down at the blue stone necklace, wanting only to give Zeke something in return.

Outside Abbie and LeeAnn walked behind their father, both lost in their own thoughts. The only sound Abbie heard was a soft whimper, almost like the sound of a kitten crying. She turned curiously at the sound, and her blood curdled. Jeremy's body lay under the wagon, and the front wheel had apparently already run over him. Before Abbie could scream out, the back wheel also went over him, across one arm and kitty-corner across his chest.

"Pa!" she screamed. "Stop! Stop!"

She stood there frozen, while her father struggled to stop the oxen, unaware yet of the reason. Jason Trent turned to look. He made a strange choking sound when he saw Jeremy.

The Haneses' wagon, which was behind Abbie's, had already stopped.

"Oh, my God!" Mrs. Hanes groaned.

"Jeremy!" Trent screamed, running up to the boy. Bradley Hanes reached Jeremy at the same time.

"You'd best not touch him!" he warned Jeremy's father. "Somebody get Zeke!"

"Get Zeke!" another voice yelled out, as LeeAnn and Abbie knelt beside their shaking father. Jeremy lay there quiet, obviously in shock. He looked up at

220

them but could not speak.

"Oh, God, not my son!" Trent choked out, tears filling his eyes. "Not my son, tóo! I already lost his ma!"

Abbie put her arm around his shoulders. "Don't, pa," she said quietly. "You'll upset Jeremy more."

It was obvious the boy was badly injured, and her mind raced with guilt. Should she have kept a better eye on him? Should she have gotten into the wagon with him to be sure he didn't jump out against her orders? She should have realized how ignorant excited children were of danger and reckless behavior.

Zeke's horse came thundering up, and in the next second he knelt down across from Jason Trent, Olin Wales standing behind him. Trent was weeping, and as Jeremy shifted his frightened gaze to Zeke, his eyes filled with hope, sure that Cheyenne Zeke would know of some miracle to help him, the way he had helped little Mary Hanes. Zeke leaned over the boy and gently unbuttoned Jeremy's shirt.

"*Now* what did you go and do?" he asked, trying to sound casual. But Abbie could see he was deeply concerned. He opened Jeremy's shirt, and already the small chest was purple. LeeAnn gasped and turned away, while Abbie choked back a sob, trying to stay calm. Trent cried openly, thereby causing Abbie to worry about him as well as her brother. He had not taken his wife's death well and was just beginning to recover from it. How would the death of his only son affect him? Would he blame himself for bringing the boy West in the first place?

Zeke ran expert hands gently over Jeremy's ribs and down the injured arm. He moved the arm just slightly, and a bone popped through the skin. Jeremy made no sound, but some of the others gasped and had to turn away.

"He's apparently in deep shock," Zeke said quietly. "He doesn't feel anything now, but he will soon. We'd best get some whiskey down his throat if we can."

"Jesus God! We have to help him! We have to fix him!" Trent sobbed. Zeke looked at the man with pity; then he looked at Abbie. He shook his head, and she understood. She covered her mouth and forced back the tears that tried to surge forth, but she wanted make to scream and tear her hair.

Zeke turned to Olin. "Fetch a flat board over here from that busted wagon," he told the man. "We'll try to get him onto it without disturbing him too much and carry him into the wagon that way. If we pick him up loose, God knows how many more bones will break up. I don't want to handle him too much. He's broke up bad inside, and I think he's bleeding internally."

Olin turned to get the board, and Jason Trent grasped Zeke's shoulders.

"You've got to *do* something for him!" he growled. "There has to be *something* we can do! Maybe . . . maybe you have a remedy of some kind! An Indian remedy!"

Zeke put a hand over Trent's. "Not for something like this, Jason. The best I can do is mix up some herbs with some whiskey that might take away the pain . . . and we can all do a lot of praying. But what we need is a good doctor, and there's not one to be had—not out here. I'll do my best to set what bones I can set, but I can't do much for his insides. Now you'd best calm down. If you collapse, you won't be much good to your son. He needs you."

Trent wiped at his eyes and nodded. "I . . . reckon' so," he replied in a choked voice. "Can't we . . . stay here? At least for the rest of today? I don't want to jostle him around. Maybe by tonight we'll know better . . . how things look."

Abbie knew without being told that her brother would very likely die, and she felt compelled to speak to him before the pain set in and he became delirious and incoherent. She leaned close to the boy, smiling for him.

"I love you, Jeremy," she said softly. "I love you as much as mama did." She kissed his forehead. "You'll be okay, baby. In just a few days you'll get better, you'll see."

The brave little boy looked up at her and actually smiled a little, and his smile hurt her more than if he'd screamed and cried. She looked over at Zeke, picking up the little jacket still gripped in Jeremy's other hand. She handed it to Zeke, wanting Jeremy to see so he'd know Zeke got the jacket.

"He . . . climbed back into the wagon . . . to get this . . . for you," she told Zeke. The man frowned in confusion. "It's . . . an old jacket of his," Abbie went on. "It was too small . . . and he wanted to give it to you . . . for an Indian child. I guess maybe he was so excited about giving you something . . . he jumped out of the wagon when he knew he shouldn't."

Zeke closed his eyes and grasped the jacket.

"I . . . don't mean to make you feel bad, Zeke. It's not your fault. Jeremy thinks the world of you. I just . . . wanted him to see me give you the jacket."

Zeke nodded, and when he opened his eyes they

were full of tears. Olin returned with the board then, and he and Zeke and Kelsoe carefully slid the boy onto it, but already the pain was setting in, and Jeremy was beginning to whimper. Abbie slid her arm around her father's waist and helped support him to the wagon. The men placed Jeremy inside and climbed back out; then Trent, Abbie, and Zeke climbed in, while Lee-Ann rushed over to Quentin Robards to cry against his chest. Abbie could hear Olin Wales quietly ordering the others to circle and make camp. Her head reeled and her stomach sickened when she looked down at Jeremy. But the next thing she knew Zeke had supportive arms around her, and she was quietly weeping against his chest.

Ten

Little Jeremy's suffering was like a horror story for the boy's father and his sisters. The child's agony grew rapidly throughout the day, in spite of Zeke having set as many bones as possible, and in spite of the herbs and whiskey that were forced down his throat. Jeremy's fever rose and his moans turned to louder groans, then finally to intermittent screams mingled with crying. These sounds cut into Abbie like a hatchet. If she could have taken Jeremy's place, she would have. But there was nothing to do but sit and watch helplessly, as his gruesome injuries enveloped him, slowly sucking away his life. His chest and even his stomach grew darker and darker, and it was obvious he was badly injured internally. This was something they could do nothing about, and something that would most definitely kill him eventually—perhaps within hours, perhaps not for days.

Abbie's concern was doubled by the fact that her father just sat crying, drinking, and carrying on about how it was all his fault for coming West in the first place. The man's guilt and suffering were overwhelming, as he carried on about not wanting to live if he lost his little boy. Everyone, including Zeke, tried talking to him to soothe him, but it was obvious that if Jeremy died, nothing could bring happiness to Jason Trent again. His fiddle lay in the corner of the wagon—silent.

Zeke watched Abbie with quiet admiration and agonizing sympathy. She was the only one who remained strong for poor Jeremy, the only one with the stomach to tend his wounds and stay by his side through his terrible suffering, and the only one to talk to him, sing to him, tell him stories, encourage him, and hide her tears from him. LeeAnn was no use at all. She moaned about the blood and the pus, the horrible purple chest, and the screams; and she threw up twice. Abbie told her to go stay with the Hanes until it was over, and of course, Quentin Robards was right there to comfort her.

His injuries tugged and pulled at the life inside Jeremy throughout the rest of that day and into the next, until by nightfall of the second day his arm had swollen to gruesome proportions and pus leaked from the spot where the bone had broken through the skin. His chest and stomach were also swollen, and he'd thrown up blood, a sure sign of grave injury. His fever rose until the boy was delirious. Throughout the night, Abbie slept fitfully beside him, with Zeke camped right outside the wagon, available the moment she might need him. The rest of the train retired grimly to their wagons, saying prayers and trying to block out Jeremy's screams.

Abbie tried desperately to keep the flies off the boy's

226

open wounds, but when she awoke from a short sleep in the early dawn of the third day, she gasped at the sight of maggots on his arm. She choked back vomit and tears as she desperately tried to wipe them away, but touching Jeremy only made the boy scream. She looked into his desperate eyes and wanted to scream herself, just as loud and long as she could, and she wondered if she'd lose her mind before long. She struggled to keep from completely breaking down in front of Jeremy. She needed someone to give her strength, and more than that, she needed an end to her poor little brother's misery. To watch him suffer as he was suffering was asking more than a human being could bear. She longed to talk to her father, thinking to herself how he should be the strong one and not herself, but he was slumped over in the corner of the wagon, completely blacked out from a night of weeping and torturous heartache and a good supply of whiskey. She looked at Jeremy again, and she knew.

"I'll be back real quick, Jeremy," she told the boy reassuringly. She bent over and kissed his forehead lightly, bracing herself against the odor of blood, vomit, and infection. "I love you, Jeremy Trent. I do love you so. And God loves you. Wouldn't it be nice to be with God right now . . . and with mama . . . and to be free of the pain?"

A tear slipped down the side of the boy's face. "Yes," he squeaked. Abbie smiled for him.

"The pain will be gone soon, Jeremy. I promise," she said softly. "I have to talk to Zeke, and I'll be right back. You want Zeke to come inside when we come back?"

"Yes," he whispered. She smiled again and climbed

out of the wagon, thinking to herself that she must look terrible by now in her crumpled dress and with her hair uncombed for the last two days and nights. The sun was not even up yet, but the sky had lightened somewhat. She could see Zeke lying curled up on the ground with only a light blanket beneath him and a dead fire beside him, and she loved him more than ever for his loyalty and attention. Already it was this man from whom she got her strength, and she wondered if it weren't a sign of the future.

But she could not think of such things now. There was only Jeremy to think about. She walked close to Zeke and started to stir him awake, but his eyes opened before she could touch him. In an instant he was on his feet, as though he'd never been asleep. He reminded her of a wild animal that always seemed to know when someone was close by. He glanced at the wagon, then back at Abbie.

"Is he . . . ?"

"No," she replied. "Not yet." She glanced around at the quiet camp, everyone still in their wagons. "I . . . have to talk to you, Zeke," she said quietly, "away from camp . . . so there's no chance of somebody hearing us."

He nodded. "Just a minute." He reached over and, taking his canteen of water, poured a little into his hand and splashed his face with it. Then he took a drink from it and rinsed his mouth. He opened his parfleche, took out a small cloth, wiped his face, and then reached inside again, taking out a peppermint stick he'd bought at Fort Laramie and breaking off two small pieces. He put one into his mouth and handed the other to Abbie.

"Sometimes a body's mouth needs to be kind of woke up in the morning," he said with a grin. The remark surprised her and actually made her smile. Zeke smiled back.

"It's good to see you smile, Abigail. This has been an awful thing for you," he told her, "and I admire your courage and strength."

Her smile faded slightly, and she nodded, putting the peppermint in her mouth. She raised her hand to her hair, which hung long and loose, blowing in the Wyoming wind. "I need more than this peppermint," she remarked. "I'd like a whole bath, a hot one, in a real tub, you know?"

He smiled softly and reached out to touch her hair. "You look just fine. Let's walk out a ways." He put a supportive arm around her, at the moment not caring how it looked, but only caring that this young girl was carrying the weight of three other people on her shoulders at the moment: her useless and worrisome sister, her drunken and guilt-ridden father, and her dying brother. She had no one to turn to herself, and she must be at her wits' end. He walked her a good distance from the train and through some trees to where they could not be seen, then motioned for her to sit down on a fallen log. She took the seat wearily, and he knelt down in front of her. "Well?" he asked. "What do you want to talk about?"

Her eyes teared immediately, and she struggled to get the words out. "Jeremy. There's maggots on his arm now." Zeke closed his eyes and sighed. "He's dying for sure, Zeke, and his pain must be beyond the imagination. I . . . I asked him this morning . . . if it wouldn't be nice to be with God . . . and with his

229

mama . . . and he said yes. I . . . I think he knew what I meant, Zeke. And I think you know what I mean. He's suffered enough. This can't go on."

He opened his eyes and met hers, overwhelmed by the courage it took for her to suggest what she was suggesting. He reached out and put a hand to the side of her face.

"You want me to do it," he stated quietly.

She nodded, tears spilling down her cheeks now. "It's . . . an awful thing I'm asking!" she told him through her tears. "But I . . . can't do it myself, Zeke. It has to be done . . . so there's no noise—so even pa doesn't know he didn't die naturally. And . . . I thought . . . with you being so good with a knife and all . . . I thought maybe . . . you'd know a way to do it quick—so he wouldn't even feel anything. I know it's a terrible, terrible thing I'm asking . . . but it would be so much better for him . . . just to have it end, and . . . ." She could not go on. She broke down into wrenching sobs, and he stood up, pulling her up with him and into his strong arms, holding her tightly and knowing she needed to feel someone else's strength and power. It seemed they stood there a long time. He let her cry until it was all out of her, holding her the whole time as she wept against his chest. He held her until he felt her begin to relax in his arms, and her tears subsided.

"You . . . don't have to do it," she whimpered, pulling away a little. "I don't even have the right to ask—"

"I'll do it," he interrupted.

She raised her face and met his eyes.

"It would be an act of mercy," he went on. "And

it's something you should never feel bad about, Abigail. It took a lot of love for you to even consider it. What about your pa?"

She sniffed and took a handkerchief from her dress pocket and blew her nose. "He's stone drunk and passed out," she replied. "I thought . . . I thought if you could put Jeremy . . . out of his misery . . . we could dress him and make like he just . . . died from the injuries. Nobody needs to know but us."

He reached out and grasped her face in his big hands. "And nobody will. It will be our secret," he told her. "I can do it quick, and I promise little Jeremy won't know what's happened to him."

She searched his eyes, seeing the pain of his own memories. "I'd . . . feel better if . . . if you'd tell me you'd do the same . . . for your own son," she said quietly. His dark eyes held hers for a long time, and his grip tightened on her face.

"I would," he finally answered. "And I did . . . for my wife. She was . . . still alive . . . when I found her. I fixed it so she'd die quick."

Abbie reached up and put her own hands over his. "Then you understand."

"I understand."

"I want you to explain it to Jeremy, so *he* understands, too, Zeke," she replied. "He has that right. And he'll know it's out of love you'll be doing it. I don't expect he'd want to die by any other man's hands but yours. He thinks you're some kind of grand warrior. I wouldn't doubt he'd be proud to have it be you. He won't be afraid, Zeke."

He pulled her into his arms once more. "The Indians believe that to die bravely at the hands of another brave warrior is an honor. A strong and brave heart is something to be respected, and honored in the afterlife. Jeremy has a strong and brave heart. He'll be considered a brave warrior in heaven."

"Just promise me it won't hurt," she told him, her face buried against his broad, strong chest. "It has to be a knife, so no one hears any noise. That's why I figured . . . you'd be the best one to do it."

He squeezed her tightly. "It's all right, Abigail. And I give you my word it won't hurt. And Jeremy will finally be at peace. . . . Then you and your pa can be at peace, too."

"I'm scared, Zeke. I'm scared . . . about what you saw in your vision . . . about me being alone. I'm so scared!"

He kept his arms tight around her and kissed her hair. "Don't you be afraid, Abigail. Don't you ever be afraid. You're a strong girl and will be an even stronger woman, and there is much ahead for you. I feel it. You will have a long life, and you will have many stories to tell your children and grandchildren. You might be alone for a while, but you won't always be alone. And you remember the stones I gave you. Hang on to them, Abigail. And hang on to the strength that is within yourself."

He led her back to the wagon, and she waited outside while Zeke climbed in. He noticed Trent still passed out. Abbie paced restlessly, holding her stomach and quietly begging God to forgive her for what she'd decided to do. Everyone else still slept, except Olin Wales, who was starting a fire, oblivious to what was taking place. Abbie waited for some kind of noise or scream, but the wagon was quiet. Zeke was inside for only about five minutes, but it seemed five hours. Then suddenly he was behind her, putting his hands on her shoulders.

"It's over," he said quietly. "He's not suffering anymore."

She slumped slightly and he grabbed her, then pulled her close, as her terrible sobbing woke the whole camp. Jason Trent had slept through it all and continued to sleep as some of the other men began building a coffin.

They buried him deep, not wanting the wolves or anything else to be able to dig him up. Zeke had dressed the boy himself, in the one and only little woolen suit he had, and it gripped Abbie's heart to see that the sleeves and trouser legs were a little too short. She remembered telling him not long ago that she would have to let them down. Now it would not be necessary.

There was no outward sign that the boy had died other than naturally, and considering the fact that there had been no sound from the wagon, Abbie knew that Cheyenne Zeke had apparently done his job well. She did not, nor would she ever ask him how it had been done. At least now Jeremy lay peacefully at rest. His dark hair blew softly, and Zeke's blue stone beads were still around his neck.

Jason Trent sat near the grave, sobbing uncontrollably, and LeeAnn wept quietly beside Quentin Robards. Abbie stood off alone, not wanting anyone to touch her or even speak to her, except for Zeke. Her face felt dry and stony, but she hadn't even bothered to use the creams she'd brought along to guard her skin against the hot, dry West winds. She felt as desolate as those winds, and was thinking to herself that one day they all would blow away and no one would ever know they'd existed. And others would come, to be greeted by the endless, endless Wyoming winds, to forge against them and move on. And just like the little group she traveled with, some would make it—and some would not. And in a few years little Jeremy's grave would disappear, and no one would even know he lay there beneath the earth.

She held Zeke's crying stones tightly in her fist, squeezing them as she stared at Jeremy in his little coffin. She tried to gear her thoughts to the positive, in order to save her sanity. Jeremy was no longer in pain; he was with their mother. And she realized she should be weeping for her father, rather than her brother, for Jason Trent was a broken man and not likely to mend.

She allowed Preacher Graydon to speak some words over Jeremy, and he did a better job than she expected. Abbie felt that for little Jeremy's sake the Lord would surely overlook the preacher's own sins and accept the man's offering of Jeremy's soul to the Lord. When he finished and stepped back, Abbie swallowed and spoke up.

"I'd like . . . Zeke . . . to say something over my brother's grave," she told the others, not caring whether they liked it or not. The preacher colored slightly, but did not object, and none of the others seemed to mind. Zeke himself was glad for her request, for he'd been prepared to give little Jeremy a tribute of his own.

Zeke stepped forward, dressed in his outstanding white buckskin shirt that looked even more beautiful in the midmorning sunlight. He removed a turquoise handled knife from his belt, not the large one he'd used in the fight with the Sioux, but a slightly smaller one. It was obviously an expensive and beautiful knife, and Abbie knew right away it was the one he'd used on Jeremy. He laid the knife in the coffin beside the boy, and only he and Abbie knew why. She fought against breaking down completely.

"Jeremy Trent was a man, not a boy," Zeke spoke up in a firm, clear voice. "He conducted himself on this train like a man, helped out like a man, and he . . . died . . . like a man. The Cheyenne bury their brave warriors with their weapons, to ward off evil spirits that might try to keep the dead man's spirit from reaching the hunting grounds of the gods, where he is forever happy and at peace."

He walked over and took a blanket from Olin. He opened it up for the others to see, and some of them gasped with pleasure at its beauty. It was a hand-woven blanket made of brilliant colors.

"Jeremy died because he was all excited about giving me a jacket for an Indian child," he told them. "Right toward the end, as I sat beside him, he managed to say enough to tell me that once he was gone to be with God, he wanted me to have *all* his clothes for any Indian boys who might need them to keep from freezing in the winter. Now I give Jeremy a gift in return. This blanket took my mother many hours to weave, and it's special to me. It will keep Jeremy warm in his grave and give him a wrap of bright colors to show his Master in heaven."

As he knelt down and covered Jeremy with the blanket, Jason Trent burst into renewed sobbing. Everyone else was in tears—to Abbie's surprise, even Quentin Robards and Morris Connely and the Browns. A moment later Abbie's father collapsed completely, and Bentley Kelsoe and Bobby Jones helped him back to his wagon. Winston Harrell and Bradley Hanes put the lid over the coffin and began nailing it down. The others watched a moment, then began to leave, the women crying openly now. Abbie felt oddly cold and estranged, yet she stood staring as the men pounded in the nails. Zeke walked over to her, putting a hand on her shoulder.

"You should leave now, Abigail."

She looked up at him with tired eyes. "I . . . want to stay."

"It isn't good. Come away from here . . . please. After he's buried you can come back, and we'll put a marker on his grave." He felt her trembling under his touch as he gently urged her away from the site.

"He . . . didn't feel anything?" she asked quietly, stopping to look up at him again. Her heart ached when she saw tears in Zeke's eyes.

"No," he replied. "He didn't feel a thing. He said . . . he trusted me to do it right. He wasn't scared at all, Abigail. Fact is, he was braver than most grown men I've known. And he . . . told me—" He stopped and cleared his throat, as though to keep from crying. "He said he'd tell God . . . not to hold it against me . . . so that one wouldn't count when I got to Heaven. I think he . . . uh . . . I think he figured he could put in a good word for me—something like that." He smiled nervously, and she could see by his eyes that what he'd done had been harder than she'd thought it would be for him. And she loved him all the more

236

for it.

"If I live to be a hundred, Zeke, I'll never forget what you did for Jeremy today—for me, too. It took a lot of courage . . . a lot more than facing a grizzly or standing up against men like Rube Givens. It took a different kind of courage—the rarest kind."

Their eyes held a moment, and then he suddenly backed away, as though he'd just realized someone might be watching. "There are all kinds of courage, Abigail. You've got courage, too," he replied. "It took courage to even ask me to do it. And it takes courage to face the fact that certain things you might want . . . you can't ever have, Abbie girl."

Her lips trembled and she closed her eyes and nodded. "I know," she whispered.

He led her back to her wagon, and she climbed in and tried to console her father. But he sat sobbing in the corner, and there was no way to get through to him. His eyes were wild, his hair disheveled from running his hands through it over and over, and already an open whiskey bottle sat beside him.

Zeke decided it was best to leave the death site as soon as possible, and that afternoon they got underway to get in a few miles before nightfall. Olin Wales led the oxen for the Trent wagon, as Jason Trent still sat inside crying and drinking. Abbie sat at the back of the wagon, watching the little grave disappear.

"Jeremy Trent—age seven," the market read. "A brave boy, who gave his life on the trail to Oregon." She wondered how long the wooden marker would last.

* * *

Six days later, as they neared the north fork of the Platte, where they would have to cross the river again, Jason Trent had not improved. He'd been drunk most of the time and unable to lead his own oxen. He barely spoke and ate even less often. He'd brought along plenty of whiskey, for medicinal purposes and to trade with, but now he'd drunk up most of it, and by the ninth day after Jeremy's death, the man was on his last bottle.

With Trent too drunk to think straight most of the time, and Abbie wrapped up in tending to him and doing everything by herself, Quentin Robards moved in on LeeAnn almost completely. She rode with him on his horse some of the time and spent all her spare time with him. She had become even colder and more distant toward Abbie since Jeremy's cruel death. Now when Abbie needed her sister more than ever, she was unreachable, and the loneliness Zeke had predicted was becoming a hard reality.

Zeke and others tried to talk Jason Trent into wanting to live again. They reminded him that his daughters needed him; but the man only wailed that they were nearly grown, and that LeeAnn didn't need him at all, for she had Quentin Robards now.

"Abbie, she's the strong one," he whimpered. "She'll always be all right. She knows her way, my Abbie. She knows her way. Soon she'll be gone from me, too. And I'll have nobody—nobody!"

Always he used the same words. Jeremy's death had seemed to affect the man's mind to the extent that there was no reaching him.

They made it to the north fork, where they made camp on the east side. Everyone turned in early to rest up for the crossing in the morning, which Zeke promised would be as bad or worse than their first crossing. Jason Trent bedded down under the wagon, unable to bear being inside near Jeremy's things any longer. Abbie fell asleep to the man's soft sobbing. That sound was to haunt her forever, for it was the last thing she heard out of Jason Trent.

It was a single gunshot, and it startled all of them awake. Abbie sat straight up, as did LeeAnn, and they looked at each other. It was still dark outside, and Abbie's first thought was of Zeke. Had Rube Givens sneaked up on him and shot him in the night? She panicked and grabbed her robe, throwing it on and climbing out of the wagon, followed by LeeAnn. Now others were exiting their wagons.

"What's happening?" Abbie shouted.

"Don't know," Casey Miles replied, buttoning his shirt.

"Who fired that gun?" someone else asked in the confusion.

Abbie turned to check on her father, but he was gone. "Pa?" she called out. "You up, too?" There was no reply, and they all stood looking at each other, feeling an eerie premonition, yet none of them realizing the reality of it yet. "Pa?" Abbie called out.

A chill swept through her, giving her goosebumps on her arms. "Pa? Where are you? Pa?" Her voice was panicky now, as her eyes darted around the small group that had moved closer to the campfire. "Has anybody seen pa?"

Hanes frowned. "He . . . doesn't seem to be about, honey," he replied. They all walked around now,

239

searching and calling, but blackness began to sweep over Abbie as she turned back to the wagon and searched frantically for her father's Spencer carbine. It was not there. The shot they'd heard had been a very loud boom, the kind of sound a Spencer would make. She climbed back out. "Find him!" she screamed. "Find pa! It's gone! His rifle is gone!" She started to run off into the darkness when someone grabbed her arms.

"Don't go out there," came Zeke's voice. He kept a tight grip on her arms. "Your pa is . . . dead, Abigail. He shot himself."

An awful pain grabbed at her stomach, and she wanted to scream that he was lying, but she knew he wasn't. Suddenly her breathing came so hard she thought she might suffocate. LeeAnn let out a strange whimper, and Quentin Robards was immediately at her side.

Abbie could think only of running—somewhere . . . anywhere! She tugged at Zeke's grip, almost getting away in her maniacal sorrow, but he grabbed her again, pulling her around to the other side of the wagon where no one could see.

"Hang on, Abbie!" he pleaded.

"No! No! No!" she screamed. She had to get away! Who cared if she died out there? Who cared if Rube Givens got hold of her and killed her? She had nothing left anyway. LeeAnn would be lost for good now; her father and brother were dead. She could not have Cheyenne Zeke. She had nothing but herself— and her mother's clock, which she'd probably end up having to leave behind when they got to the mountains.

She tugged again to get away, wanting to run! Run! Run! Run until her breath was gone and she could fall down and die from exhaustion. But Zeke would not let go, and in that moment she hated him with a passion. She hated him because he was all that was left that she loved, and she knew he'd never allow anything to come of it. He'd just break her heart more, and she couldn't take any more. Being near him only made everything blacker and more hopeless. If she could have gotten hold of a gun, she'd have shot herself, too. She had to get away! She made animallike grunts as she struggled, and finally she did the only thing she could think of that might startle him enough to make him let go. She rammed her knee hard between his legs, and she timed it right. He grunted and let go for a moment. Abbie ran.

She knew she was running faster than she'd ever run before or ever would again, spurred on by an extra something that gave her more strength and speed. Perhaps it was her terrible need to run from everything familiar: from the horrible memory of little Jeremy's grave and the thought of her own father putting a rifle to his head and pulling the trigger, from her half-witted sister who didn't care about her anymore, from the knowledge that her mother would never again embrace her, and from Zeke. Especially from Zeke, whom she loved with every bone in her body, yet hated just as passionately. She ran! Oh, how she ran! She had no idea where she was going, but she knew her feet were beginning to bleed from stones and rough foliage and hard ground. She literally ran into a couple of trees in her blindness, and she fell twice, but got up and just kept going, heedless of the danger of doing such a foolish thing, heedless of bears or wolves or snakes or rocks, heedless of the possibility of Rube Givens being around. None of it mattered, and if she fell to her death, who would care?

Then she heard someone behind her. Someone running—chasing her! She ran even faster, holding up her nightgown and robe, her hair flying out behind her. But the person behind her came closer, someone big, someone faster than she. She ran until her chest felt as though it would explode, then screamed when a hand grabbed her arm. She started fighting, struggling, screaming louder than she realized.

"Stop it now, Abbie!" came his voice. It was Zeke. For some reason he infuriated her. He had no right to stop her, no right! What should it matter to him if anything happened to her? He didn't want her anyway. She reached up and scratched at him, screaming and crying and telling him she hated him. He jerked her around so her back was to him; then he grasped her wrists and pulled her arms behind her, amazed at the strength her sorrow and anger provoked. He held her arms tightly behind her, yelling at her to calm down. She kicked backward into his lower legs as hard as she could, but it was to no avail, and her angry words turned to whimpers, the sounds of an injured wolf, as exhaustion began to overtake her. She gritted her teeth, furious at not being stronger than the man who held her. She wanted to hurt him. She wanted that more than anything! For he was hurting her, and she didn't want to live. He felt her weakening, so he swung her around. But she bit his hand hard, and the next thing she knew a big hand whacked her across the side of the face.

She gasped and froze for a moment. When Cheyenne Zeke hit a woman, she knew she'd been hit, and reality began swimming in front of her. She felt as though she were coming out of a strange sleep. She realized she'd run very far from the wagon train, for it was nowhere in sight. It was still dark, and she could hear a rushing stream somewhere nearby. Zeke's tall, dark frame loomed over her in the moonlight.

She began shaking from the horror of her situation as she realized that Cheyenne Zeke's prediction was coming true. She was alone—completely alone. He let go of her and she grasped her stomach and slumped to the ground, making odd choking sounds, her body jerking convusively like that of a wounded animal. Then she got up to run again, but Zeke grabbed her and literally tackled her to the ground, jerking her around to face him and pressing tight against her to hold her there.

"Please just kill me!" she sobbed. "Kill me like you did Jeremy! Please, Zeke!"

"Don't talk that way, Abbie girl," he said softly, brushing his lips over her cheek, her hair, her eyes, her lips. His strength seemed to surge through her, calming her, and his words were whispered tenderly. "My poor Abbie!" he groaned. "It will be all right. It will be all right in time."

By then the exhaustion began to set in. She hurt all over, and her sorrow swept over her so that she lay there limp and weeping, her crying sometimes as loud as a little child's. She put her arms around his neck, grasping him tightly, and he stayed there on the ground with her, whispering her name over and over. She cried so hard she thought her insides might erupt, and she ached—her ribs, her stomach, her lungs, her legs—everything ached. Meanwhile he held her there, her back against the thick, soft grass, until finally she had no strength left, not even to cry. Their eyes held in the moonlight, and they both knew what had to be, in spite of what had just happened to her, and in spite of the hopelessness of their future together.

In the next moment his lips were on hers again, this time searching tenderly, forcing her own lips apart, groping hungrily for what he needed and giving her what she needed in return. It seemed an almost apologetic kiss, as though to tell her it was not something that could last forever, and his hands moved up to grasp her hair. Their kiss lingered for a long time, until finally his lips moved to her neck and his hands moved down to her hips, and she felt a hardness against her stomach.

"Just for tonight, Abbie girl," he whispered, "because you're needing to be held and loved, and because I can't bear the thought of any other man being first!" His lips met hers again hungrily as one hand moved up her leg, pulling up her robe and gown, beneath which she wore nothing. He moved a hand gently over that private place no man had ever touched, then up over her flat stomach and on up to open her robe and unbutton her gown, gently reaching inside to caress her breasts. As his lips left hers again and moved down to gently kiss a firm nipple, her breath came in short, resigned gasps. Zeke was touching her!

"It has to be you!" she whimpered. "Even if it can't be forever! I want you to be the one to make a woman out of me, Zeke! Only you! No other man . . . would do it . . . gentle as you would."

Her mind whirled in a terrible mixture of grief, need, and love as his lips met hers again. Then his hand moved back down between her legs, sending fire through her veins and pulsations through her groin she had never felt before. His lips moved to her neck again, and she wanted only to feel alive and loved.

"Make me forget all of it!" she whispered. "Make me forget, Zeke! Just for a little while."

A glorious ecstasy surged through her suddenly as his hand worked some kind of magic with her, and she opened her legs to him willingly, not caring if it might hurt or if it was wrong.

In the next moment everything was forgotten; she was lost in the pain and the wonder of becoming a woman. He surged inside of her, branding her as his own even if they should part and never see each other again. He was a big man, and she wondered how such pain could be so welcome; but she knew that Cheyenne Zeke was as good at making love as he was at fighting.

Eleven

He moved off her and pulled her to him, putting a leg over one of hers and letting her rest her head on his shoulder, his arms enveloping her. For a moment they lay there silent, the only sound being that of the rushing waters of the stream somewhere nearby.

"You all right?" he finally asked.

She swallowed and blinked back tears, her momentary happiness at being made a woman by none other than Cheyenne Zeke darkened by the memory of her father's death as reality now came back to her. "Everything hurts," she replied. "My feet hurt bad. I think they're bleeding."

"I meant . . ." He hesitated and sighed. "Did I hurt you?"

She was glad for the darkness so he could not see the redness she knew came into her cheeks. "Some," she replied.

He kissed her hair. "More than some," he answered. He rose, picking her up and carrying her in the direction of the running water. She was like a babe in his arms, and she did not resist when he removed her robe, pulled her gown over her head, and carried her into the water, setting her down in it to her waist. She shivered and clung to his neck, while he gently rubbed her abdomen.

"I know it's cold, but if you're bleeding, the water will help stop it," he told her. "Besides, you want to be cleaned up when you go back. How about your feet? Does the water make them feel better?"

"Yes," she replied quietly.

He kept her there a moment, still rubbing her stomach and sometimes her hips. "Abbie, I—"

"It's all right," she interrupted. "I wanted it. In fact, I needed it. And I'm woman enough to know you needed it, too."

"I took advantage of the situation."

"Not intentionally. Not with the intent to hurt me."

She could feel him trembling as he moved his hand up to the side of her face. The cool water felt good on her flushed cheek. "I'm so sorry, Abbie girl. I wish I could keep from hurting you other ways," he said softly. "It's a terrible thing I've just done, because I can't take it any farther than tonight. May the Great Spirit curse me for being so damned weak when I'm near to you."

She kissed the palm of his hand. "I already knew the risk. I'd argue with you that it could work, Zeke, because in my heart I feel it can. But you're dead set against it, and God knows the horrible memories you have to live with, so I can't blame you. Perhaps some day I will marry another. But there's not another man I'd have wanted to do this, and I don't care how wrong

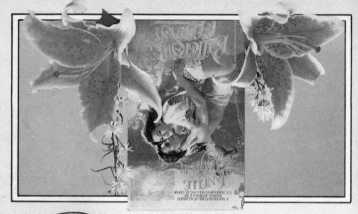

it was or how hopeless it is for you and me. I gave you pleasure, and that makes me happy. You were my first, and that makes me happy, too."

"I took something that didn't really belong to me—probably never will," he answered, kissing her hair again.

"I don't care. There's only one thing that matters, one thing I need to know from you." She turned her face up to meet his dark eyes in the moonlight. "Tell me it wasn't just . . . just you remembering . . . her . . . Ellen. Tell me it was *me* you were wanting."

Their eyes held for a long moment, and he ran his fingers over her lips. "It was you—just Abigail Trent."

She smiled a little. "That's all I needed to know," she told him. "And I love you, Cheyenne Zeke. No matter where we go from here, no matter if I never see you again after Fort Bridger, I love you, and I'll never stop loving you."

He met her lips, and they kissed once more, hungrily, as though to say good-bye. Then his lips moved over her neck and down to kiss her small breasts once more. He picked her up out of the water.

"We can't let on like anything is different after we go back," he was telling her, as he dried her off as best he could with the bandanna he had been wearing around his head. "If anybody suspected, you'd be branded. Word would get around and they'd call you every name in the book for lying with a half-breed." He slipped the gown over her head, then helped her put her robe back on. He grasped her arms firmly. "Abbie, promise me you won't let on. Sometimes . . . sometimes a woman has a way of looking at a man—"

"I understand. I'll try hard not to look at you with

love in my eyes, but it won't be easy."

Their eyes held again, and she was sure there were tears in his, but it was too dark to be certain.

"I'll watch out for you good, Abbie girl, till we get to Fort Bridger," he told her. He sniffed and swallowed. "And . . . uh . . . I'll talk to the Haneses. They're damned good people. Mrs. Hanes is a fine woman. I'm sure they'd be glad to look after you the rest of the way to Oregon—give you a home till you're old enough to . . . marry . . . or whatever." The words seemed to choke in his throat. "You . . . uh . . . you're a good worker and all. You can help out Mrs. Hanes with the kids and—"

"Oh, Zeke!" she cried, bursting into tears. He pulled her close to him, hugging her tightly.

"Damn it, Abbie, don't make it harder!" He breathed deeply, and she could feel the pounding of his heart through his chest. "Your sister—I'll watch out for her, too. But God knows that Robards will probably take her over completely now. She's eighteen and there's not a hell of a lot I can do about it, Abbie. If I try to keep them apart, she'll just hate me—and hate you, too. And right now you need her. It's best to keep things civil between the two of you. The only reason I mention the Haneses is . . . well . . . I expect LeeAnn will run off with that Robards once we get to Oregon. There's no way a flutter-brain like her is going to stay around and help her sister. And there's no way you can be out in the world alone, not in this untamed land and at your age and all. You must promise me that you won't go off alone, not till you have a man to look after you. Promise me, Abbie."

"I don't want any man but you!"

"Promise me!" he answered, squeezing her harder. "I can't bear the thought of some terrible thing happening to you! God knows I want to be the one holding you in the night, protecting you, but that can't be. If you really love me, Abbie girl, promise me you won't go off alone. Let me have that much to ease my mind."

She cried, clinging to his buckskin shirt, drinking in the manly scent of him. "I promise," she finally whimpered.

They heard the sound of an approaching horse, and he quickly let go of her.

"I'll not treat you any different once we get back, Abbie girl," he whispered. "What happened tonight —that's all of it. God in heaven, tell me you understand! Tell me you forgive me!"

"There's nothing to forgive," she sobbed.

"Zeke?" someone hollered. He relaxed slightly, recognizing Olin's voice.

"Over here!" he shouted in reply. He quickly kissed her cheek. "God be with you, Abigail," he said softly.

"I'll always pray for you, Zeke," she whimpered in reply. Olin approached.

"You found her?" he asked, dismounting.

"The kid can run like a deer," Zeke answered.

"She all right?"

"She's scraped up pretty bad, especially her feet, She took off barefoot. You take her back with you on the horse, Olin, and I'll walk back."

Olin reached out and touched her hair. "I'm damned sorry about your pa, honey. It's damned cruel what life's been handin' you these last few days. But we'll all look out for you."

He put his arm around her and led her to his horse, lifting her up into the saddle.

"Olin," Zeke spoke up hesitantly. "When you get back, put something around her—a blanket if you've got one on your saddle there. There might be something on the back of her gown. I wouldn't want anyone to see."

Clinging to the saddle horn, Abbie reddened. Her whole body screamed now with pain and exhaustion. Olin frowned as he looked from Zeke to Abbie and back to Zeke.

"Your own heart is already tore to pieces," he told Zeke sympathetically. "Did you have to go and add her to the mess it's *already* in? What about *her?*"

"What's done is done!" Zeke replied almost angrily. "It's between me and Abbie. And don't think I'm not considering the fact that I'd be better off to shoot myself right now for what I've done!" He turned away. "Just take her back," he said dejectedly. "Tell the others . . . tell them you found her . . . alone. Tell them you didn't see me anywhere, that I must still be out here searching for her. I don't want any of them to suspect I was the one who found her first. Do you understand?"

Olin sighed and shook his head. "I understand, Zeke." He put a hand on Zeke's shoulder. "You'll be all right?"

Zeke actually snickered, but it was a bitter laugh. "Sure. Get going. I'll turn up later."

Olin turned and mounted up behind Abbie, putting one arm around her for support. "You okay to ride, honey?"

She hung her head. "Yes, sir," she answered quietly.

He gave her a squeeze. "Things always look better in the daylight, Miss Abbie," he told her. "Everything is gonna be okay. Ain't none of us gonna let anything bad happen to you. You're a good girl." He kicked his horse into a walk. "No. I guess I should say you're a good woman—a damned good woman." They rode back toward camp, leaving Zeke beside the stream where he knelt down and wept in the privacy of the darkness.

Because Jason Trent had shot himself in the head, the other men put a lid on his burial box right away, so that Abbie and LeeAnn would not see the ugly wound. The morning broke bright and sunny, and Abbie walked with Bradley Hanes to pick out a burial spot. She chose a grassy hill that faced the rising sun, and the others quickly dug a hole, Zeke included, while Abbie and LeeAnn waited in their wagon, cleaning up and fixing their hair.

"Thank God for Quentin," LeeAnn kept whimpering. "Oh, Abbie, what will *you* do now?" She dabbed at her tears, but Abbie knew what her remark meant. Abigail was not to count on joining up with LeeAnn and her lover, nor was LeeAnn about to abandon Quentin to care for her sister.

"I haven't thought about it much," Abbie replied quietly. "I expect I'll stay with the Haneses. They're nice folks. They'd keep me till I know what I'm going to do."

"It's a man you'll be needing," LeeAnn replied, tying a bow in the lovely blond hair. "God knows that wild half-breed you have eyes for isn't about to settle down again. Perhaps you'll find some nice man in Oregon. And what about Bobby Jones? He's got eyes for you, that's a fact. Of course he isn't rich and educated like Quentin, but he's an honest boy and sweet. And you keep saying being rich and educated doesn't matter to you."

Abbie's heart ached so badly that she could almost cry out from the pain. Zeke! He was all she could think about! Zeke! She'd lain beneath him just hours earlier, taken him inside herself, let him make a woman of her while giving him pleasure at the same time! For one short, beautiful moment she'd been Cheyenne Zeke's woman, and it had been everything she'd expected and more! How gentle and sweet he'd been! Yet how full of sorrow and remorse he'd been afterward. To have to treat him casually now, as though nothing had changed, would be an overwhelming task. But she had promised. She entertained the thought of ending her life the way her father had, but she discarded that idea because of the one thin thread of hope she held. As long as she was alive, and as long as Cheyenne Zeke was alive, there was a chance, especially now that he'd put his brand on her.

She watched LeeAnn primp, finding it hard to believe that the girl had recovered so quickly and seemed so little disturbed by their father's death. Perhaps Lee-Ann was relieved. The one major obstacle to her romance with Quentin Robards was her father's interference and disapproval. Now LeeAnn's responsibility to her family was gone. Abbie could fend for herself. How LeeAnn had changed since meeting that smooth-talking gambler from the East!

When they climbed out of the wagon, Quentin was waiting to take LeeAnn's arm, and he patted her hand consolingly. Mrs. Hanes waited for Abbie.

"I want you to put your mind completely at ease," Mrs. Hanes told Abbie right away as they walked to the grave site. "Zeke has spoken with us and asked us to look after you. We will gladly do so, for we had already considered speaking to you about it before Zeke said a word. I just want you to know it's with open hearts we will take you into our home once we settle in Oregon—that it was really our own idea and not because someone else asked us."

"Thank you very much, Mrs. Hanes," Abbie replied. "I'll help all I can. I can sew and cook. I know how to can food and tend a garden, make butter, milk a cow—everything."

Mrs. Hanes smiled and put an arm about her waist. "That's fine, Abbie, but we aren't taking you because we want a servant! We'll treat you like our own." She gave Abbie a light squeeze. "Come now. Remember you have friends in us. And try to keep in mind that your mother and brother and father are all happy now, at peace, and together with God. I prayed so hard for you last night after you ran off, child. I felt so sorry for you. I'm glad Olin found you and that you're all right."

Abbie wished she could tell the woman about her love for Zeke. Surely a nice woman like Mrs. Hanes would understand. But what if she didn't? She might change her mind about giving Abbie a home, and at the moment, the thought frightened her. Besides, she had promised Zeke to keep the secret. It might spoil everything and create a host of trouble if she opened her mouth to Mrs. Hanes, but it was so hard to keep so much love inside.

255

They walked the rest of the way to the grave site, and Abbie's chest hurt at the sight of Zeke standing there in his beautiful, white, beaded shirt. Such a handsome specimen of a man he was, standing there in the bright sunlight! Could God mold a more beautifully carved face and body? Surely not. And he'd been her first man—just hours earlier. That was all like a dream now. For she must face the reality that she could never have him for good. She must pretend what had happened earlier had not really happened at all. She tried to catch his eyes, but he would not look at her, and then Preacher Graydon began the services. His words were a blur in her mind. But she dared to glance at Zeke several more times, being careful not to stare for too long. Bradley Hanes brought her some mountain flowers to throw on top of the box before it was buried beneath the earth. When he did, it hit her full force that Jason Trent was dead, and his fiddle was forever silenced. Gone! She could see him playing the fiddle, while her mother laughed and danced and little Jeremy clapped his hands to the music. Now all three were gone! And she could not even have Zeke. She knelt down and threw the flowers onto the box. Was it her voice screaming, "Papa"? Of course it was, and yet it sounded like someone else's—far away. The wrenching sobs came now, with the awful reality. Zeke's vision had indeed come true! Now someone was dragging her away from the grave. Zeke stared after her, longing to comfort her himself; but the vision of his raped and bloodied wife flashed into his mind and he turned away to help the others fill in the hole that held Jason Trent.

* * *

Zeke waited two hours after the burial before beginning the crossing of the north fork of the Platte. He wanted to give Abbie time to feel "near" her father before leaving the spot she would probably never see again. Abbie sat alone in the wagon, preferring it that way, holding her father's fiddle in her hands and caressing it lovingly. LeeAnn, in the meantime, was consoled by Quentin Robards in some secluded spot; and when she returned to the wagon, her face was tear-stained, but her eyes were hard and determined. By then Zeke had started the crossing, and he was busy helping the Haneses' ford the river when LeeAnn climbed into the Trent wagon. The girl immediately began throwing clothes into a carpetbag. Abbie watched her a moment, her heart heavy, for she knew what LeeAnn intended to do.

"You'd really leave me, LeeAnn?" she spoke up quietly, realizing she'd miss her sister more than ever, now that LeeAnn was all the family she really had. "Now? With pa gone, and Jeremy, too?"

LeeAnn stopped packing a moment to face her sister, looking a little bit apologetic, but very sure of herself. "We're going no farther!" she said decidedly. "Quentin and I are going back. I'm not passing up this chance, Abbie. *I can't!* If I don't go with him, he'll go without me, for he doesn't intend to go on to Oregon. He wants me to go with him, to be his wife. Somehow I . . . I'll get word to you as to where I am. I . . . we'd . . . take you with us, but right now it would be too much of a burden for Quentin to be looking after two women and—"

"Don't lie to me, LeeAnn," Abbie said disgustedly. "Quentin doesn't give a *damn* about me! And you'll find out soon enough he doesn't give a damn about you either! He'll use you till he gets back East, then dump you!"

The girl's eyes blazed, and she returned to her packing.

"Don't go, LeeAnn! Please!" Abbie urged. "Come to Oregon with me!"

The girl snickered. "And do what? We'd be dirt poor. Pa didn't leave us anything but the few belongings in this wagon. I do not intend to be a maid for somebody else when I have a man who can make me rich enough so *I'm* the one with a maid! I'll not go on to a strange land and clean up *other* people's messes! I never wanted to make this trip in the first place, but I had no choice. Now I *have* a choice. Quentin said he was going to Oregon just for the adventure, but now that he's fallen in love with me, he wants nice things for me—and civilization. He loves me enough that he doesn't want me subjected to any more of this barbaric life! Maybe you can live like the wolves and the bears, but I can't. I have to have people around me, things to do, nice clothes and all. Quentin can give me those, and he loves me besides. I'm only happy when I'm with him."

"LeeAnn, it's *dangerous* to go back all alone! Rube Givens might be out there, for one thing!"

LeeAnn thought for a moment about telling her Rube Givens was the very man who was to meet up with them and guide them back. But if Abbie told Zeke that, Zeke would come after them for certain. That was one thing they wanted to avoid at all costs.

"Quentin has guns and knows how to use them," she answered coolly, packing more items. "I'm not

258

afraid. It isn't that far back to Fort Laramie."

"Please don't go, LeeAnn!" Abbie pleaded, now starting to cry. "Don't you even care that I'll be alone? How can you *do* this?"

The girl smiled almost wickedly, and Abbie wondered if Quentin was giving her some kind of potion that was changing her personality. "I highly doubt you'll be alone, Abigail," she replied. "You have your precious half-breed, and some day you'll have that tepee and your sixteen kids, remember?"

The words hurt even more because of what had happened between Abbie and Zeke the night before. It was something she could have shared with her sister at one time, and she longed to share it now. A girl's first intercourse can be a traumatic and painful experience, both physically and emotionally, but Abigail had to keep it all buried inside. LeeAnn was no longer someone with whom she could share secrets.

"You know that can't ever be," she replied despondently. "I'll have nobody, and you don't even care!"

The girl zipped the bag. "Why should I? You've insulted Quentin time and time again. You don't care anything about my feelings for him, nor do you appreciate what a wonderful man he is. I *love* him, and I'm going back with him. That's that! And I'm taking one of the horses. I have the right."

Abbie wiped at her tears. "Zeke won't let you go!" she reminded her. "He'll come after you!"

The girl turned, her eyes boring into Abbie's. "I don't think so," she replied with a sneer. "You'd best warn him not to make a fuss. Because if he tries to stop us, or if he comes after us and drags us back, I'll put on the biggest show you ever saw! I'll carry on about how he *raped* me farther back there on the trail—that I never said anything because I feared for my life. I'll tell them I left with Quentin because I was afraid he'd rape me again and hold that big knife against my throat like he did the first time!"

Abbie sat there dumbstruck, her eyes widening in disbelief.

"I'll do it, Abigail, believe me. I can get Zeke in all kinds of trouble. I'll tell them the only reason he wouldn't let us go is because he wants me for *himself*, that he told me he loved white girls with blond hair the best. Rube Givens already planted the idea in their heads back there at Fort Laramie that he likes white girls. He about got in trouble then, Abbie, so don't stand in my way, because it wouldn't take much to get him into even more trouble. He's already a wanted man. If he stops us, I'll make a scene like you never saw in your life, and you know I can make them all believe me. If you want to keep your half-breed out of trouble, you keep him *away* from us!"

Abbie's tears spilled down her cheeks, mostly from disappointment that her sister could be so cruel. It was obvious she meant every word.

"Go on then," she said in a choked voice. "I don't know you anymore. Somewhere back on the trail the *real* LeeAnn got left behind. I prefer to remember you the way you used to be."

"That's when I was stupid and going nowhere. Now I've *got* something—a way to live like I've always dreamed of living! And if it isn't enough to tell them all that Zeke raped me, I might add that I can make something up about Zeke and *you!* Zeke would hate that more than anything. He'd not want you slandered. I expect he'd be almighty devastated if I made up a story about catching him and you going at it one night."

Abbie angrily wiped at her tears. "Well, maybe that wouldn't *be* a lie!" she spit back at her sister. "And maybe I wouldn't *care* if you told such a story!"

LeeAnn's eyebrows went up. "You mean . . . you've actually lain down for that half-breed?"

"Not the way *you* make it sound! I . . . needed him . . . and he needed me. And it was special . . . beautiful."

LeeAnn chuckled. "With a man who wears buckskins and probably never washes?" She made a face. "Well, if you can pull up your skirts for a worthless, wandering Indian, then don't be putting me down for wanting to go off with a proper gentleman like Quentin!" she said haughtily. "And it doesn't matter that *you* wouldn't care if I told. *Zeke* would care. So don't make me have to make him look bad and maybe get kicked off the train or even *hung!*"

Abbie turned away, picking up their father's fiddle. "I'm glad pa isn't here to see this or hear the way you're talking," she said quietly. "Good-bye, LeeAnn."

LeeAnn surprised her by putting a hand on her shoulder. "I'm not all that bad, Abbie. I . . . I *do* love you. But my love for Quentin is so deep, so wonderful, I just *can't* let him go without me, Abbie! And I have to get away from this horrible West: the bugs, the heat, and the awful ugliness of it all—and the danger and the dust. I *hate* it, Abbie! I *hate* it out here! The only thing that kept me this long was the fear of what

261

Zeke would do, and pa. But now pa is gone. And once Zeke sees how much trouble I could get him in, he'll leave us alone. And I promise that somehow I'll get in touch with you again. Perhaps you'll even want to go back yourself some day, and you can look me up. I'll have a fine big home by then, maybe in Chicago or St. Louis and you can live with—"

"Just go, LeeAnn. I'll never live under the same roof with Quentin Robards!" She felt like a stone as LeeAnn sighed disgustedly and climbed out of the wagon. Abbie could hear Robards' voice as he helped her saddle up, calling her "darling" and "lovely one" and other silly names. In the distance she could hear whistles and curses, as Zeke helped get the Haneses' wagon across the river. Everyone was so busy, they paid no heed to LeeAnn and Quentin riding back in the wrong direction, figuring the two were off to some private place again and would return.

The crossing took as long or longer than the first one at Fort Laramie. It was an all-day affair that left them wet and exhausted, and early in the evening Abbie pulled from the wagon a few of things things that had gotten wet in order to hang them out to dry. For the first time that day Cheyenne Zeke spoke to her, approaching her on the big Appaloosa.

"You doing okay?" he asked, looking off in the distance and trying to appear casual in his conversation.

"I'll make it," she replied, keeping her back to him.

"Where's your sister? I haven't seen her and that Robards all day. They should be showing up by now."

Abbie swallowed. "They . . . left . . . back in the other direction. They're going back East . . . headed for Fort Laramie where I expect they'll find a guide.

262

With pa gone, LeeAnn just . . . didn't want to go on."

He made no reply at first. As she turned to face him, his dark eyes flashed with disgust and his jaw twitched with obvious anger. He moved his horse closer and looked down at her.

"Why didn't you *tell* me?" he hissed. "I'd have stopped them! It's dangerous! *Much* too dangerous! Besides that, I'd never have let her go off and leave you alone like this! What the hell kind of sister *is* she? I expected her to at *least* go on to Oregon!"

"Zeke, it's best this way!" she replied, her eyes tearing. "Please, *please* don't try to stop them! I *beg* you, Zeke. She . . . she said she'd say all kinds of awful things about you if you did! She'll say you raped her back there somewhere, and she'll say you've been carrying on with *me*. She's *changed*, Zeke. I can't let myself worry about her anymore. And I won't let two people like that make more trouble for you! I tried to warn her; but she's made her bed, Zeke, and now she's got to lie in it. Let it *go*, Zeke! It will be bad for you if you go after them! *Real* bad!"

He yanked his horse's reins, causing the animal to whirl in a circle as he tried to gather his angry thoughts. The girl probably would do exactly what she'd told Abbie she'd do if he went after them. The worst part was she'd slander Abbie's name, and that was the last thing he wanted. He rode closer to Abbie again. "Abbie, I'll go after them if you want. It's too damned dangerous for her out there. I'll do whatever you ask me to do, Abbie."

"I don't want you to do anything but keep this train going," she replied in a determined voice. "Just keep us going. I don't know my sister anymore. She *chose* to do this, Zeke. We can't do anything more for her. All I can do is pray she makes it safely."

"But what about you . . . what about—"

"I'm okay. I have the wagon and the rest of the animals, pa's fiddle and my mama's clock—all our belongings. And I'll have Mr. and Mrs. Hanes when I get to Oregon. I don't want you to worry about me, Zeke. It would be bad for both of us if you brought her back here. She's so different now, it just isn't worth it. Just go and tell the others that she wanted to go . . . and that I let her because she was so terribly unhappy out here and wanted to go back with Mr. Robards and marry him."

He swung the horse around again, then stopped and looked out over the horizon. "Are you sure, Abbie girl?"

"I'm sure."

He sighed. "All right, Abbie. I'm against it. But I'll not let that bastard Robards drag you down in the dirt along with your sister. And I'll not let her hurt you, either."

"Zeke, I wouldn't consider being linked with you as being dragged down in the dirt," she answered. "I consider it beautiful and wonderful . . . an honor."

He backed up the horse. "It isn't how *you* consider it that counts. It's how *others* consider it. And nobody knows better than I do what most whites think about one of their own kind who lies with a half-breed." The thought brought pain to his loins. She could see the desire in his eyes, but he instantly replaced it with a look of stern warning. "Nothing has changed from what I said before," he told her. "Get inside now and get some rest. I'll tell the others."

He turned his horse and she watched him lovingly as he rode away. Perhaps it would be better if he *did* leave the train at Fort Bridger. To go all the way to Oregon with him under these conditions would be unbearable.

Twelve

The next three days were like a living hell, not just mentally for Abbie, but physically for everyone. They passed through a canyon that wound for miles toward Independence Rock. It was unbearably hot, and all the water was poisoned by alkali. Wearied by the terrible heat, everyone's strength was stretched to the limit by having to lose sleep for three nights in a row to chase after the animals and keep them from drinking bad water.

Zeke had warned them about what it would be like, and they'd stocked up on fresh water from the Platte, but there were always animals that would try to get to the salty beds of water in the canyon. In many spots these were simply big white beds of pure alkali, where small lakes had dried up completely. Abbie thought it a terrible, desolate place, and knew how much Lee-Ann would have hated it. Being there only accented Abbie's own lonely, desolate feeling, until she felt that the empty, vacant land epitomized her soul. She wondered if she'd ever be a whole and happy person again.

She longed to hear her father's fiddle, to hear Jeremy's laughter, to be held in her mother's arms.

For three days they dragged through the canyon, and Abbie lost her two spare oxen to the poison water. Willis Brown lost one of his cows also. Abbie cried intermittently as she walked along beside her oxen, missing the two that had died because they'd become like pets to her, the only living things left that she could care for and call her own. Others had offered to help her guide the oxen, but she'd stubbornly refused, insisting on doing it herself. She'd helped her father plenty of times and knew what to do. Zeke stayed ahead of the train, but she sensed that his thoughts were of her and that he was watching out for her, even though he was not obvious about it. She was aware that he probably did not like her leading the oxen alone, but he had to keep from appearing too concerned. Besides that, Abigail Trent had made up her mind to somehow convince Cheyenne Zeke that it was indeed possible for them to be together. She would show him how strong she was, how she could endure and that she wasn't afraid of work. She'd show him she could live just like an Indian squaw, if that was what it would take to be with him. The thought of proving something to him gave her a stubborn strength, and the slim hope that there could yet be something between them was all that kept her going mentally, the only thing that helped mitigate her pain from the death of her father and brother, and the desertion of her sister. And so she ignored the horrible heat as she plodded along beside the oxen through the hellish canyon, passing the bleached bones of animals that had come this way before them and had not made it.

By the fourth day they reached Independence Rock and the Sweetwater River, an occasion of great relief and rejoicing for the weary, sunburned travelers. They all carved their names in the great, giant monolith of stone, and found enjoyment in studying the names of others who had carved their names there before them. Abbie wondered if the names would still all be there a hundred years later, and if, in the future, people would remember and appreciate those who went first and suffered so terribly.

By that evening, Abbie had recovered enough emotionally to begin thinking practically. She sorted through the things in her wagon, selling most of her father's clothes to Bentley Kelsoe for a fair price. There was no sense in holding onto them, except for one of his favorite shirts that she kept in his memory, as well as his cherished fiddle. But she kept Jeremy's clothes, remembering the boy's desire to give them to Indian children. When they reached Fort Bridger, she would make some kind of arrangement with Mr. Jim Bridger to see that Indian children got the clothes.

For the first time since her father's death, Abbie joined the others around the campfire that night, and to her great pleasure, Zeke also joined them, his mandolin in his hands. He played some soft, haunting Tennessee mountain songs, the wonderful music of the mandolin strings floating out over the night air. She knew it was his way of indirectly soothing her heart, of taking her back for a little while to Tennessee and the days when she still had a family. He again sang the song about a Tennessee mountain morning, and she thought of Tennessee, while she gazed out at the snow-capped peaks of the Rocky Mountains that loomed ahead of them. They were far off on the western horizon, and she could tell already how mighty and magnificent they must be. It helped to have them in sight, for it stirred an excitement in that part of her heart where the child still dwelled. They were approaching something new, something she had never seen before. A whole different world lay ahead of them, and, perhaps, somewhere ahead lay some kind of happiness for Abigail Trent.

But she knew that her real happiness lay in the man sitting across the fire from her—in Cheyenne Zeke. He'd picked up the tempo now, and had everyone clapping to "She'll Be Comin' 'Round the Mountain". Again he was all Tennessee man instead of Indian. In fact, he was everything when she thought about it—mountain man; scout; Indian fighter, although himself an Indian; and a down-home Tennessee man, too. How could she not love him or not want him? And how was she to forget him once he left them?

The music picked up even more, and before she knew it, Abbie was singing with the rest of them. She even laughed once. Zeke glanced in her direction when he heard her laugh, and he smiled. That provocative grin of his white, even teeth created a stir in her groin, and she thought about how sweet his kisses were. Their eyes held a moment, then both quickly looked away.

They headed out the next day, in better country now, following the Sweetwater. There was more grass for the animals, and the water was good. But as if someone were out to torture Abbie, at midafternoon, they were greeted by a horrible sight, The train came to a halt for seemingly no reason. Abbie strained to see what was up ahead, and to her horror she could see a man tied to a post. She ran to the sight before anyone could stop her, and her blood froze and she made a choking sound when she saw it was Quentin Robards, his wrists tied over his head to the post, his body stripped to his long johns and horribly mutilated, apparently with a knife, but there were also bullet holes in his chest. A deck of cards lay at his feet, and a note was stuck in his underwear. Others had already seen and turned away, but some of the men circled the scene, shaking their heads and discussing what could have happened. Zeke stood staring rigidly at the body, already figuring out the answer. It could be none other than Rube Givens. He reached for the note now, while Abbie stood paralyzed with fear. Zeke scanned the note, then handed it to Olin and glanced at Abbie with terrible pain in his eyes.

"LeeAnn! Where's LeeAnn?" Abbie screamed desperately.

Their eyes held. "Givens has her," he replied in a strained voice.

Her mind raced, whirling with confusion and desperate fear for her sister. "I . . . what do you mean? Why did they kill Robards?"

Zeke sighed and looked down at the note, his heart aching to make things better for Abbie. But things would not get better, and she had to know and face the truth. He read the awkward scrawling on the note.

"Robards gambled for his life—with the pretty blond as his stake." Abbie shuddered and grasped her stomach. "He lost. And we won the girl. He got

271

mad—planned to sell her to a whorehouse. We decided to leave him for"—Zeke hesitated and cleared his throat—"for the blond's bratty sister to find. We have her uppity sister with us now. Having a mighty good time with her."

"Oh, my God!" Mrs. Hanes gasped. "Poor Lee-Ann!"

Zeke watched Abbie closely, expecting her to scream and faint. But she only held his eyes with her own determined ones.

"You have to find her!" she said in a shaking voice. "You have to try to find her before they kill her!"

"Abbie, they *will* kill her," he replied gently. "And if I *do* find her first, she'll . . . she'll be crazy from what they've done to her. I know those men."

"But you have to *try*!"

Zeke nodded. "I know that. I intend to."

"Wait a minute!" Olin spoke up. "Givens has another angle to this! Don't you see? He *wants* you to come after her, Zeke! He wants to get you out there alone. He'll be waiting for you!"

Abbie's heart pounded with dread, for she realized Olin was right.

"I know that, too," Zeke replied. "I can handle it. LeeAnn Trent might have been selfish and flighty, but she doesn't deserve what they'll do to her. Rube Givens has made his last mistake by goading me into going after him. He'll pay *dearly* this time!"

Zeke's eyes were again dark and vengeful, filled with a frightening animallike hatred. He wadded up the note and threw it down, then looked around at the others.

"I don't think any of you would disagree. I have to
272

go after them," he told them all. "There's a slim chance I can get to them before they kill LeeAnn, which they most certainly will do eventually! I have to try to get to her first."

"It's all right, Zeke," Kelsoe replied. "We can get along without you for a few days. You just point the way and we'll keep going and wait for you to catch up."

Morris Connely listened attentively, surprised at what Givens had done to Quentin Robards, but pleased that it would draw Zeke away from the train and perhaps even lead the man to his death. He'd been worried all along that Cheyenne Zeke would discover his own background and, perhaps, make him leave the wagon train, but, luckily, so many things had gone wrong that Zeke had been too wrapped in the problems of others to think any more about Connely. Connely turned away from the gruesome sight of Robards' dead body, thinking to himself how little it resembled the smooth, handsome, well-dressed man who had ridden off with LeeAnn Trent.

Abbie's mind whirled as the men gathered together with Zeke to discuss how they would go ahead without Zeke and Olin, because Olin had already told Zeke he'd go along to help hunt LeeAnn and would not take no for an answer. She stared at Robards, feeling no remorse when she realized what the man had intended to do with her sister when he got her back East. If only LeeAnn had listened! What a horrible ending to her sister's big dreams of a lovely home in Chicago or St. Louis! What awful things would Givens and his men do to her? It was too gruesome to dwell on without wanting to scream and scream until she had no breath

273

left in her.

"LeeAnn!" she whispered. "Oh, God, my poor LeeAnn! Why didn't you listen to me! I knew it! I knew Robards was bad!"

Mrs. Hanes came up and put her arm around Abbie, urging her to come away from the horrible remains, around which buzzards already circled. But when Abbie turned to face the woman, Mrs. Hanes saw a new strength and womanly determination she had never before seen in the girl's eyes, and she was surprised at her calm attitude.

"Mrs. Hanes, I'm going with Zeke—if he'll let me."

"Abbie! That's impossible, and you know it!"

"I'm going!" Abbie replied firmly, as the men dispersed and some began cutting down Quentin Robards.

"The bastard deserved it for what he intended to do with that poor, stupid girl," Casey Miles mumbled.

"I hope Zeke guts Rube Givens out like the pig he is!" David Craig added, his heart crying for LeeAnn, the girl he'd loved since he'd first seen her, but who had spurned him badly. He had wanted her to regret that, but not this way; and he felt crazy with the thought of Givens putting his hands on her. Zeke walked toward Abbie when he noticed Mrs. Hanes arguing with the girl. She faced Zeke.

"This child wants to go with you!" Mrs. Hanes exclaimed to Zeke. "I've been trying to tell her it's a ridiculous thought."

Zeke looked down at Abbie and shook his head. "It *is* ridiculous. What makes you think I'd let you go out there with us? You get that thought right out of your head, Abigail Trent." He started to walk past her, but she grabbed the sleeve of his buckskin shirt, surprising him with the firmness in her voice.

"I'm going, and you can't stop me!" she shouted. "If you don't let me go with you, then I'll run off and follow behind! LeeAnn is the only family I have left, and she's in trouble. You *have* to let me go, Zeke! If she's still alive, she'll *need* me! I'm her only kin and the only one left to love her and help her! She'll be needing a woman when you find her. God knows what they've done to her! Please, Zeke! She's all I have left! *Please!*"

Tears began to fill her eyes against her will. She wanted to appear strong and determined, but the calmness to her voice had begun to rise to hysteria. Zeke studied her a moment, then shook his head again.

"Do you have *any* idea how dangerous it would be?"

Olin Wales and David Craig were both approaching them now.

"Of course I do!" Abbie answered. "But I'd be with *you* and Mr. Wales. How could I be in danger if I'm with you?"

Zeke rolled his eyes. "I can't make guarantees, Miss Trent. It's too dangerous, and that's all there is to it." He turned to walk away.

"No, that's *not* it!" she screamed at him. "You have to understand, she's all I've *got!* Maybe she didn't care about me, but I care about her, and I owe it to pa to help her!" Zeke looked back at her again, and tears streamed down her face. "Don't you understand? If I stay here with the train, after all I've been through already, I'll go *crazy* with wondering about her, wondering if she needs me—if you found her alive! Please, please let me go, too, Zeke. I can ride and I can shoot pa's Spencer rifle real good. And I don't"——her voice began to break—"I don't have . . . anything left . . . nothing . . . except LeeAnn! I want to help her if you find her! I mean it! If you don't take me with you, I'll follow! I swear I'll follow! Isn't it better that I'm with you than out there alone?"

He studied her eyes, realizing she meant every word of it. Abigail Trent was going to be stubborn about this. And she was right. She'd suffered greatly the last several days, and part of the blame was his own. He was tired of going against what she wanted, of always telling her no.

"She's right, Zeke—about LeeAnn maybe needin' her if we find the girl," Olin spoke up. "I'll be along, too. If things get bad, or we find LeeAnn dead before we catch up with Givens, I'll bring Abbie back here for you and then catch up. We both know the woods. You track them and I'll track you."

Zeke sighed indecisively and glanced at Mrs. Hanes. "I don't know what to tell you," the woman spoke up. "It seems ridiculous and dangerous, yet we all know what poor Abbie has been through. If it will soothe her tortured mind to be able to go along, perhaps she *should* go. All of us are confident of your abilities, Zeke. And as Mr. Wales said, he'll be along, too. He can bring her back as soon as you find LeeAnn, and then LeeAnn will have Abbie with her the whole time. The poor girl will surely need that."

Zeke's eyes shifted to Abbie again. "You realize, of course, that we just might find LeeAnn the way we found Robards? Do you think you could bear such a sight?"

She wiped at her tears and kept her chin up. "I could bear it better, knowing I was there myself to help bury her and pray over her, than staying here . . . not knowing till later . . . and never being able to see her again—even dead. But there's always the hope she's alive, and I have to be with her if she is. Please! I won't get in the way . . . I promise. I'll do everything you say! Everything!"

"To the letter? Even if I tell you to go back?"

"Yes, sir," she replied, her eyes lighting up with hope. In the back of her mind she realized that Zeke himself might be needing her also. What if he were wounded? She couldn't bear the thought of his being hurt without her there to tend to him.

"I'll be blunt, Miss Trent," he told her, trying not to sound too familiar with her by using her first name. "If things go wrong, and we get trapped, if I think Givens might get his hands on you, I'll put a bullet between your eyes myself. You understand me? You'll not live to suffer at his hands."

That statement brought silence to the others, who were a little surprised at the remark. But Abbie knew what he meant, and she knew it meant he did love her. She struggled not to allow her love for him to show through.

"I understand," she replied. "I'd want it that way."

He emitted a disgusted sigh. "This is crazy, but if you want to take the risk, you can go—but only until we find LeeAnn. After that, Olin brings you back. The only reason I'm agreeing is that I think they'll dump her someplace when they're through with her. They know I'll still come after them because it's the way I'm

277

made. This is going to be the last showdown, and he knows it."

"I want to go, too," David Craig spoke up, moving to stand beside Abbie. "You'll need all the help you can get, and I'm good with a rifle. And LeeAnn was . . . important to me. I cared for her a lot, and I need some revenge of my own, Zeke. If we find her and she's still with them, you'll be needing the extra gun. But if they dump her, like you say they will, I can bring her and Abbie back. That'll leave Olin free to go on with you and help you. You shouldn't go after them all alone. They'll lay a trap, sure as fire. And the train needs you. They understand why you have to go, but they all want you to come back. Please, let me help. I need to—just like Abbie does. Surely you understand that kind of need. You felt it when you went after those men who killed your wife."

Zeke almost flinched at the remark, and a terrifying hatred came back into his dark, Cheyenne eyes. He nodded. "All right. But the same goes for you, David. You do every damned thing I tell you to do!"

"Yes, sir. I will."

Zeke turned and glared at Olin. "This is all ridiculous! I must be losing my mind!"

"Maybe," the man replied. "But part of what they say makes sense, Zeke."

Zeke scowled at him. "You're as ignorant as they are!" he growled. He turned to Abbie and David. "Go saddle your horses and pack a few things!" he barked. "And neither one of you had better slow me down!"

Abbie wanted to hug him. As she ran off with David, she could hear Zeke, obviously irritated at this sudden change of plans, barking orders to Kelsoe.

278

"Just keep the train moving," he told the man. "Follow the Sweetwater, like I said. It's about ten days to the South Pass. If you get there before we get back, hold up there a couple of days. If we don't get back by then, go on southwest, and in about ten more days you'll reach Fort Bridger. If we haven't caught up by then, we're all dead. At Fort Bridger you can get help to lead you the rest of the way. I'm damned sorry for this mess."

"You have to try to find her, Zeke," Kelsoe replied. "All of us understand. It's just too bad that Rube Givens chose to plague this train all along. I hope you find him and get rid of him for good."

"No worry there," Zeke hissed. "His life is nearing an end! And remember what I said about the Indians. If you meet up with them, keep Willis Brown and the preacher out of their way, and just talk civil to them! They'll be mostly southern Cheyenne, some Shoshoni —and mostly friendly—wanting just to trade. Relax and stay calm and you won't have any trouble."

Abbie climbed into her wagon and quickly began to pack, taking only a change of underclothes, one extra dress, some soap and a heavy woolen jacket. She rolled up two blankets for a bedroll and stuffed some jerky, beans and coffee onto her saddle bags, along with a few biscuits she'd made the day before.

Olin walked over and began saddling her horse for her, chuckling inside at the helpless position into which Abbie had managed to put Zeke, but also worried—especially for Zeke. Rube Givens would try to be very clever about this.

Kelsoe shouted orders, telling the preacher to lead Abbie's wagon and oxen for her while she was gone.

Losing David Craig wouldn't put them back any, because Kelsoe had already lost one supply wagon when it crashed down the hill. Abbie finished packing her saddlebags and climbed out, glad to have something to occupy her tortured mind. Surely Zeke understood that. That was why he'd said she could go. If he would just say he loved her and wanted to marry her, she'd stay behind and protect herself for him. But he was determined not to have a place in her future, and without him, as far as Abbie was concerned, there was no future. So, she had nothing to lose by going along, for even if she lost her life, it didn't seem to matter anymore. Perhaps he realized that. Perhaps somehow it would make him change his mind about her, especially once he realized how strong she was, how good with a gun, and how brave—as brave as any Cheyenne squaw, maybe braver.

She mounted up on her horse, thanking Olin for saddling it for her. She looked over at the post, where Robards' body now lay on the ground after being cut down. She thought about the man's fine, black horse. Rube Givens had surely kept it, and she realized he'd keep LeeAnn's horse, too. She decided she'd get the horse back, if they found it. It belonged to her, Abigail Trent, and if LeeAnn was dead, she would have to protect everything she owned, because she didn't have much, and she might need these things for trading and surviving. Besides, Givens had no right to steal that horse! It was a fine, sturdy quarter horse and worth good money.

She was surprised at her own cold and practical thinking, but supposed a person got that way when he or she was all alone and had nothing but himself or herself to fall back on. She had to be very practical now if she was to survive in this new and dangerous land all alone. She adjusted her skirts and trotted her horse over to where Zeke was standing next to his big Appaloosa. She could see he was getting mentally prepared to face Rube Givens and do the man in. He was stonily silent, but the storm inside him rumbled loud and clear. He checked his two rifles, one an extra-fancy Spencer with a fine, carved butt. He wore the menacing knife on his belt in a beaded sheath, and she didn't doubt that he had one or two more knives on his person, hidden inside that wide, leather belt, or perhaps in a moccasin. With the gun he wore on his hip, plus the extra one he'd shoved into his belt, he looked prepared to go to war. She felt apprehensive, not for herself, but for Zeke. Rube Givens would surely be expecting the man. She had faith in Zeke's skill and ability, but when a man was expected, it was a strike against him.

Her heart rested easier when she realized that anyone with his wits about him would think twice about getting Cheyenne Zeke riled. Zeke was as fearsome looking as a ten-foot, hungry grizzly, and she could not help but take secret pride in the fact that she'd broken down that strong-willed, fearsome man one night. She'd caught the wild mustang in him and briefly tamed it, and in that moment she'd been wild herself, wild and free just like Cheyenne Zeke, giving herself to an untamed stallion and knowing the joy of it.

But the man she watched now was not the gentle, subdued man who'd made a woman out of her. He was a stalker, a hunter, a killer—probably much the way he'd been when he'd gone after his wife's killers. If she didn't know him so well, she'd have been afraid of him because of the way he looked now. He turned his horse and spoke to Kelsoe again.

"You think you'll be all right?"

"We're pretty seasoned now, Zeke, and into good country. We'll be fine. You just find that poor girl and get her back here."

Zeke turned to Bradley Hanes. "You'll keep your promise about looking after Miss Trent when she returns?"

"You know we will. And if LeeAnn is with her, she has a home with us, too, until she's recovered."

Zeke nodded. "You're good people," he told the man. "But I don't expect to find LeeAnn alive." He turned to Abbie, trying to discourage her with the words. "You ought to stay here."

"She might be alive," Abbie replied firmly. "I'm going to be with her, whether you like it or not! I'll not change my mind!"

"You're stubborn and stupid!" Zeke barked.

"Call me what you will! I'm still going!"

He wanted to hit her and kiss her at the same time, wanted to shout at her and smile at her. He looked her over, suddenly having to suppress laughter. She wore her father's leather hat, which was too big for her, and a jacket that was also too big.

"One of my first orders is that you eat, hungry or not!" he ordered. "You look like a damned, starved bird! You'll blow away in the Wyoming winds. I'm not packing along a half-starved kid who doesn't have the strength to pick up a rifle when she might need it. I'm supposed to depend on you to back me up, remember?"

She puckered her lips in a pout, "I'll eat," she replied. She sat there, all of five feet and two inches and perhaps a hundred pounds, and he suddenly wondered with a terrible ache in his groin how he had been able to make love to her without killing her, he was so big. But the memory of the one lovely night with her that he was trying to forget stirred a fire in his blood. He whirled his horse disgustedly, wondering what had ever possessed him to let her go along. He put a cheroot in his mouth and lit it.

"All set, Zeke?" Olin asked, as David Craig rode up to them on his own mount. Zeke turned and looked Abbie over again, scowling and puffing on the cheroot.

"Let's ride," he mumbled. He took off on his Appaloosa, and how he knew which way to go, Abbie could not imagine. Apparently the Indian in him could smell a rat like Rube Givens from miles away. He merely glanced at the ground occasionally and rode hard, and she rode hard to keep up, determined to do everything right so he'd have no excuse to leave her behind. They headed into thick pine trees, and the wagon train was soon lost from sight. She knew Cheyenne Zeke was doing this for her sake, to give her a little hope, a little adventure, something to steer her mind away from the horrors the last several days had handed to her. She needed something to live for, some purpose, some way to vent her terrible sorrow. And he owed her this wish. For he felt an indebtedness to her for stealing her virginity when he knew it did not rightfully belong to him.

* * *

They headed northeast into wooded hills, Zeke following a trail that seemed obvious to him, but one Abbie could not see at all. She took it for granted he knew what he was doing and followed, trying to decide as she rode just what she could do or say for her sister once they found the girl. It seemed ironic, after the nasty things LeeAnn had said about Zeke, that it was now Zeke who was risking his life to go after her, but that was the kind of man Cheyenne Zeke was—a man who would defend a girl's honor, no matter how that girl might treat him. And Abbie did not doubt that what was happening brought back memories of his own wife and a new thirst for vengeance.

Within a day, they came upon a spot where several men had obviously made camp. There was evidence of a large fire not long extinguished, and the foilage all around was trampled and scattered with horse dung. LeeAnn's carpetbag lay on the ground near the fire, ripped open, its contents scattered.

"Oh, God!" Abbie gasped, putting her hand to her mouth. She started to dismount; but Zeke ordered her to stay put, and she'd promised to do everything he asked. Only Zeke dismounted, while the others waited, watching him prowl around the campsite like a bobcat. Abbie watched in fascination as he studied the trampled earth and the remains of the campfire. He walked around for several minutes, not speaking, seeming as alert as a wild animal, listening, studying the dirt and the grass and the trees, kneeling down and studying hoofprints and bootprints.

"I figure at least six, maybe seven," he finally spoke up to Olin. "One of them is Rube for sure. Here's that funny print he leaves. Them boots of his must be full of holes by now because he's still wearing that pair with the run-down heels. I tracked those boots that first time I went after him when he'd shot you up."

"Must figure they're his lucky boots or somethin'," Olin said sarcastically. "Where do we go from here?"

Zeke stood up and seemed to be sniffing the very air. He walked off into the woods a ways, then came back. "West," he replied. "They're keeping to the hills and the land gets too flat east of here."

"How did they get ahead of us in the first place?" Abbie asked. "Robards and LeeAnn headed back the other way."

Zeke walked over to his horse. "The way I figure it, Givens had an idea Robards would turn back before we crossed the Platte. Apparently, he and Robards had had an agreement to begin with—probably for Givens to guide them back East. Only Robards didn't know Givens had no intention of getting them there because he planned on taking LeeAnn for himself."

He mounted up. "At any rate, I figure they planned to make the break at a time and in a way that would make it hard for me to go after them and stop them, and they succeeded in doing that. Givens figured Robards would do it before we entered that hellish canyon between the Platte and Independence Rock, so my guess is Givens waited somewhere around the north fork of the Platte, right where Robards rode off with LeeAnn like Givens expected he'd do. He probably met up with them pretty quick, then Givens headed West, too, only north from us and out of our sight. They got to the other side of the canyon before we did because they were on horseback and not slowed down by wagons and not confined to the route they could take. Then they killed Robards and staked him out for us to find—to get back at Abbie for shoving that pie in his face and to goad me into coming after him."

It was all like a nightmare, to think of LeeAnn being with Givens and his men. They'd all have their turn at her, that was certain, and, shuddering at the thought, Abbie literally shook her head to try to get rid of it.

"You all right?" Zeke asked her. "You have plenty of time to go back, Abigail."

"I'm . . . fine," she replied, holding her chin up.

Zeke turned away, not believing what she'd said but admiring her courage. "Those tracks were made sometime yesterday—late. So, they aren't all that far ahead of us. In fact, they'll probably deliberately go slow, let us catch up, maybe lay a trap. We have to be awful careful." He looked at Olin and David. "I don't want Abigail to be part of their catch. If anybody sees any movement in the bushes—anything—shoot first and ask questions later. And we'll build no big fires. Maybe I don't know for sure where Givens is, but I don't want him knowing where we are either. We'll make a small fire, just enough to heat some coffee and beans, but not big enough for much warmth. Let's go."

He nudged his horse into motion, and the others followed. Soon they were into even thicker pines, and in spite of the danger involved and the purpose of the trip, Abbie could feel herself becoming attached to the beautiful country through which they rode. Everything was big: the sky, the woods, and the beautiful mountains west of them that stood stalwart and strong. The smell of pine was all around them, penetrating their nostrils with a lovely, soft aroma. Squirrels and chipmunks dashed here and there, but Abbie dwelled on the glorious hues of the forest wild flowers. Their maze of colors and their lovely designs helped ease her mind, for each time Zeke stopped to dismount and study the trail, she concentrated on the flowers, blocking out the ugliness of what could have happened to her sister.

They rode through lovely meadows and past small lakes, through more fragrant forest and past cascading waterfalls, always with the jagged peaks and spires in the distance. She was beginning to see why men had come West and why most who did stayed. And Cheyenne Zeke fit this country. It was obvious he loved it. He was as much a part of it as the trees and the animals, and if she could ever be his woman, she would have to be a part of it also. She knew in her heart that it would not be difficult to love this land and call it home. But she also knew how harsh it could be, how cruel and demanding. Yet, with Zeke at her side, she could bear all things. Of that she was sure.

Zeke drove them hard for two days, and at night the three men took turns keeping watch, while Abbie was allowed to sleep. Concerned that she'd get too cold, Zeke gave her all his blankets except one, and she loved him for it. But she worried about him, for he had just one thin Indian blanket, and he never even lay down at night. He just sat, even when it was supposed to be his turn to sleep. She would wake up, and there he'd be, sitting near her, his knees drawn up with his arms wrapped around them and the blanket about his shoulders. She was sure he couldn't possibly be asleep in that position, and she wondered how he could keep going like he did. But Zeke was a disciplined man, who always seemed to be in control of himself and his body—except for the one night she'd broken through that wall of discipline. The thought of it made her smile. She snuggled under her blankets, relaxed in the knowledge that if one twig snapped or one pine needle fell out of place, Zeke would be up and shooting.

On the second night Abbie woke up with a start, a nightmare about Givens making LeeAnn scream forcing her suddenly awake. Her breathing quickened, and she blinked back tears.

"What is it?" she heard Zeke's voice ask nearby. She turned her eyes to see him sitting there, as usual, keeping watch and quietly smoking.

"Nothing. I had a bad dream," she replied in a near whisper.

Their eyes held in the moonlight, and he changed his position. "I never should have let you come along," he told her quietly. "I don't feel right about it. Something's amiss."

"I'd have followed you if you hadn't let me come," she replied.

"I knew that. That's the only reason I gave in. You're a single-minded girl, Abigail Trent."

"No more than you," she replied. "And I don't scare easily not from dark forests nor from men like Givens. I'm more scared of being all alone than of those things. A person can be alone even with a hundred people around her."

"That's a fact," he replied. "I surely do understand that. I'm just sorry you're learning such things so hard and so fast."

"It isn't your fault. It's a fact of life."

"I haven't helped matters any," he answered. He puffed the cheroot and picked up a leather-covered shaft with something hanging from its end, also covered with leather. Abbie could see well now in the bright moonlight. He dangled the strange instrument and seemed to be testing the strength of the leather thong that was tied between the shaft and the round object that hung from it.

"What's that?" she asked. He moved a little closer, the cheroot dangling from the corner of his provocative lips.

"This, Miss Trent, is a paggamoggon. It's an old Indian weapon—works pretty damned good, too. I've used it a few times."

"How does it work?"

"Well, you see this leather strap on this other end?" She sat up a little. "Yes, sir."

"A man ties that strap around his wrist and then gets a good, firm grip on the shaft here. Then he just uses it to swing the heavy rock on the other end here. It's a good horseback weapon. Your enemy rides up on you and you take a swing and . . ."

Swiftly he swung the paggamoggon and took a chunk right out of the bark of a tree. She jumped a little at this sudden movement and realized the damage that could be done to a man's head with the weapon.

"I see," she replied with raised eyebrows. Zeke smiled a little. He handed the weapon to her, and she studied it. "The Indians and their ways fascinate me," she told him. "They're so . . . so independent . . . self-reliant. They live completely off the land, whereas

289

we have to shop at stores and all."

"Speak for yourself, Abigail," he replied. She smiled a little now herself. "See what I mean . . . about you and me?" he said quietly. "We're worlds apart, Abigail Trent. Don't ever forget it."

"But I could—" He put his fingers against her lips. "Not another word, little girl."

She sighed and lay back down. "Zeke?"

"What now?"

"LeeAnn. Will they . . . will they really kill her? Do you think perhaps she's already dead?"

He picked up the paggamoggon. "If she's lucky," he replied. "I know Givens, and if she isn't dead, she's wishing she was."

Abbie swallowed to keep from bursting into tears.

"They'll get their fun out of her and then get rid of her," he went on bluntly, "because she'll slow them down and only be in the way when the time comes for a showdown with me. This whole thing was just a way to get me out here. I know that. And you're only along on the slim hope that she's alive. You just remember that as soon as we find her, you go back."

She nodded silently, then choked on a sob. "Will they . . . kill her quickly?" she whimpered.

He reached out and touched her hair. "Stop torturing yourself, Abigail." She cried harder, and he touched her face with his big hand. "There was a time when I, too, thought that life just wasn't worth living. But life goes on, Abigail, and it's going to be a good life for you. I see it in the stars." He leaned over her, wanting more than anything to crawl under tha blankets with her and comfort her as a man would comfort the woman he loved. But he merely tucked the blankets around her. "You get back to sleep. We have some hard riding to do tomorrow."

She sniffled and wiped at her eyes, forcing them closed. But sleep would not come right away.

"Zeke?" she asked.

"Yes, girl?"

"Would you just . . . hold my hand? Please? It's not the dark I'm afraid of . . . just the loneliness." She reached out from under the blanket, and she felt his big, warm hand close around her own. Soon she was asleep again.

Thirteen

It had been a long time since Abbie had ridden a horse at such a constant pace, and by the third day she was getting stiff and sore. But she kept her complaints to herself, realizing she'd asked to come along and not wanting to be a burden on the three men. By that afternoon, Zeke slowed his horse's pace, suspecting they were getting closer to something or someone. They rode through an open area, where buttes and mesas rose from the ground in great cones with nothing around them except stark, isolated hills that seemed to be there for no reason. They made their way up an escarpment between two steep hills, a treacherous ride over loose rock, then rode down the other side and into some thick woods again, Zeke in the lead like a wildcat after its prey. He suddenly stopped and put his hand up for them to do the same. Then he just sat there, smelling the air.

"What is it, Zeke?" David asked.

He turned his horse, and Abbie could see the sorrow in his eyes.

"There's a dead body up ahead," he replied quietly, looking at David. Abbie's heart throbbed, and she prayed desperately it would not be LeeAnn. "All of you stay here. This could be a trap." He turned the horse and rode on ahead. They waited until he finally came riding back at a moderate gallop.

"Get Abigail out of here fast!" he told David. "They've picked up more men and they can't be more than a half day to a day West of here! I smell a trap."

"What's up there?" Abbie demanded to know. "Is it LeeAnn?"

He rode up to her, pulling at her horse's bridle and turning her horse in the other direction. "Your sister's dead, Abigail. It's like I told you it would be. Get her out of here, David!"

"No!" Abbie screamed. "We have to bury her!"

"There's no time!" Zeke growled. "You made me a promise that once we found her you'd go back right away if she was dead. You can't do her any good now, Abbie! Now quit your fussing and get the hell out of here!"

Her mind spun from the shock of it. Dead! Pretty LeeAnn! Worthless as she was, she was still her sister. She couldn't just leave her that way. Zeke yanked on her horse, pulling it away from the thick cluster of trees, and David and Olin Wales were riding on either side of him. All Abbie could think of was her sister lying dead in the woods, and in her anger and frustration she pulled her Spencer from its holder and cocked it.

All three men whirled automatically at the sound, but Zeke's gun was out first. His eyes widened with disbelief when Abbie sat there with her rifle pointed at them. He'd nearly fired his gun when he heard hers click. Now he eased his own gun back into his belt.

"What the hell do you think you're doing?" he asked her.

"I'm not leaving this place until my sister is *buried!*" she replied in a determined voice. Tears spilled down her cheeks, but she sat firmly astride her horse and held the Spencer like a person who knew how to use one. "I don't care that David knows, or that Olin already knows about *us,*" she went on angrily. "And I'm telling you right now, Cheyenne Zeke, that I can't take any more! My pa is dead, I watched Jeremy die a horrible death, and I love you and can't have you! Now my *sister* is dead too! I've got so many ugly things racing through my mind I'm not even sure I'm still sane, and by God I'm going to have this one little thing to help ease my mind! We're going back there and we're going to bury my sister! I swear to God if you yank on my horse again I'll shoot! What do I have left to lose?"

All three of them gaped at her, trying to determine whether she would really shoot Zeke if he made her leave. Zeke decided that if it came right down to it, that wasn't likely, but then he realized what she was trying to tell him, and she was right. How could he say no to the pretty woman-child whose virginity he'd robbed and whose heart he'd broken? The least he could do was to let her bury her sister. It angered him to see her so strong and sure, sitting there holding the Spencer as good as any man, yet it made him love her even more. Abigail Trent would be a fine, strong woman some day, the kind of woman a man like him would need. What a tragedy it was that he was a half-breed, and she was white.

"Put the rifle away," he said resignedly. "We'll go bury her. But I warn you I smell something awry, so everybody keep your eyes and ears open." He turned to Olin. "You kind of ride around the edge of that bunch of trees," he told him. "Keep a lookout. David and I will bury her quick as we can."

He turned to David, who sat rigidly on his horse, his lips pressed tight and tears quietly sliding down his cheeks. He quickly wiped at them and turned away, and it was only then that Zeke realized how hard this had to be on David. It tore at Abbie's heart to look at the young man, for he'd truly cared for LeeAnn. How different things could have been for her if she had let David love her and had stayed with the train and gone on to Oregon!

Zeke rode past Abbie, and she and David followed him into the thicket. Zeke slowed his horse and turned to her. "You stay here till we get her wrapped in a blanket," he told her. "She's . . . not dressed, and it's not a pretty sight, Abbie."

She closed her eyes and breathed deeply. "How'd they kill her?" she asked.

"One bullet in the forehead. I don't expect she felt a thing, if that's what you're asking, but she was sore abused before that."

Abbie hung her head. "Why? I'd think they'd keep her alive to lure us on into a trap."

"Givens knows I won't give up now. Even if I find her dead, I'll come after him. He knows that. He's been easy to trail—too easy. He *wants* me to find him."

He dismounted and signaled David to follow him.

David removed a blanket from his saddle pack, and Abbie's heart was torn when she heard David break down into loud sobbing after he entered the thicket with Zeke. The boy cried intermittently, amid the sounds of shoveling, and then Zeke came for Abbie. "She's wrapped and in the hole," he told her, reaching up for her. "You want to say some words over her?"

She bit her lip and nodded, and he lifted her down. Their eyes held; then he hugged her tightly for a moment and led her to the grave. David sat slumped next to it.

"I should have killed him!" he sobbed. "I should have killed Robards, even if she'd have hated me and I'd have hung for it! Jesus Christ, how can a man gamble away a woman—like nothing but a cheap piece of jewelry!"

Abbie knelt down across from him, staring down at the once-beautiful LeeAnn Trent, her blond hair now dirty and disheveled, a small, ugly hole in the middle of her forehead.

She took a small, golden cross from the pocket of her dress and handed it to Zeke. "This was . . . our mother's," she told him. "Can you . . . climb down there and put it on her? Would you mind?"

He took the cross and scooted down into the hole, bending down and clasping it around LeeAnn's stiffened neck. It was obvious her body had already started to bloat; her face looked puffy and out of proportion, and the odor was sickening. Again she thought of how much Zeke must care for her to have done the difficult and repulsive things she had requested. She thought of how horrible it must have been for him to have had to end little Jeremy's life.

He climbed back out and stood behind her, putting his hands at her waist and helping her to stand up.

"I'm sorry, Abbie, but you'll have to say your words fast. We have to get you out of here!"

She nodded. "Thank you . . . for doing this," she answered. She swallowed and stared at LeeAnn. "Dear Lord," she spoke up louder in a shaking voice. "Please accept LeeAnn into your tender care. She wasn't really bad, Lord—just mixed up and scared. She had big dreams is all. Most of us have dreams like that, of things we want so bad we do crazy things to get them. Please don't blame her. Just . . . take her into your arms and comfort her . . . and bless her and mama, and pa and Jeremy. Let them all be happy again. And Lord—"

A shot suddenly rang out, and David Craig's body jerked sideways, then fell over. Abbie's horse reared and she heard a scream, not realizing it was her own. Everything happened in a split second, and the next thing she knew Zeke had tackled her to the ground and placed his body protectively over hers. They lay there for a moment; then there were more shots.

"Stay right here and lie down flat!" Zeke ordered in a low growl. The next moment, he was gone; as more shots rang out, and Abbie knew Olin was being fired at also. She heard a rustling but dared not look up to see Zeke dodge for his horse and quickly remove his rifle, and she prayed with desperate tears that he'd not get hit. Suddenly his leather hat flew off as another shot was fired. She screamed and got up to run to him, but seconds later he grabbed her en route and knocked her down.

"I told you to stay flat!" he growled. A trickle of

298

blood ran down the side of his face from a crease in his scalp.

"Zeke, you're hurt!" she whispered.

"I'm all right," he told her, his eyes darting around the perimeter like a bobcat's. He raised up and crouched on one knee, then took aim and fired. Abbie could not imagine how he'd known someone was there, but a man cried out somewhere in the trees. Then Zeke whirled and fired again, and there was a grunting sound. David Craig was up now and limping to his horse, bleeding badly from his left side. He'd been badly wounded, but he was so full of hate for what had happened to LeeAnn that he was determined to get some kind of revenge before he passed out. He got to his rifle, and another shot rang out. He cried out, blood now oozing from his shoulder, but he whisked his rifle from its holder before he fell. Then he got up again, aiming at something, and fired. A man fell from a tree not far away.

"I got you, you son of a bitch!" he yelled. Then he fell over, and Abbie feared the boy was dead. In the distance there was more shooting, and Zeke fired twice more. Then they heard a horse galloping off.

"Goddamn it, one's getting away!" Zeke growled. He fired once more, but the horse kept going. "Crow!" he mumbled. "Must have been renegade Crow Indians—planted here to see who'd come! No white man could have been around here without me knowing it! Damned Crows! I *knew* something wasn't right! Olin!" he called out.

"Right here!" came the reply. "You okay, Zeke?"

"Got a crease in my scalp is all! They got David, damn it! They're Crows—probably renegades!"

"I know! I got three myself. Didn't even know they was there till they started shootin' at me!" Olin came closer now, stomping through the underbrush, while Zeke helped Abbie to her feet, then hurried over to David's body, rolling it over. He bent over it a moment, then rose, removing a small tomahawk from his belt and slamming it violently into a tree.

"Damn!" he swore again. "I *knew* we should have kept riding! Now they know we have a *woman* with us!" He yanked the tomahawk back out of the tree trunk vigorously, and stalked back to Olin and Abbie.

"They left them Crow behind to spy and see if you was alone or comin' with help," Olin told him. "I expect they aimed to eliminate the help so's you'd be sure to come on ahead alone."

"I *will* be going on alone, because you're taking Abbie back," Zeke replied irritably, pushing the tomahawk back into his belt. "Let's bury David with Lee-Ann and get Abbie the hell out of here!"

"But they'll be waiting for you!" Abbie whimpered. "They'll kill you, Zeke!"

"Not considering the mood *I'm* in!" he answered through gritted teeth. He rubbed the crease on his scalp where a scab was starting to form. "Somebody's aim was off. I expect they intended to wound me and take me to Givens"—his eyes scanned her— "along with you, no doubt—once they'd killed David and Olin. Only the plan kind of backfired." He grinned a little. "Rube would have been real pissed if the bastard who shot at me had killed me. He'd want me alive."

"Zeke, I'm scared for you," Abbie choked out, wringing her hands.

He took her arm. "It's *you* that's in the most danger, Abbie. Now I want you to help Olin fill in this grave. I have something to do. And as soon as David and LeeAnn are buried, you get out of here with Olin!"

He walked off to his horse, and despite her tears Abbie helped with the burial, thinking how fitting it was for poor David to be buried next to LeeAnn. If he couldn't be with her in life, at least he was with her now. Olin carried the boy's body over to the hole and put him down into it beside LeeAnn. Then Abbie tried not to vomit as she helped fill the hole, but she cried even harder as the dirt fell over her pretty sister's face.

She concentrated on flowers and sweet memories, singing a hymn softly until the bodies were finally covered. When they were nearly through she glanced over at Zeke. He'd brushed out his braids, and his hair hung long and flowing as it had when he'd prayed over little Mary and when he'd fought the Sioux warrior. He reached into his parfleche and took out the little pouches of colored powders, mixing them with a little water from his canteen and then smearing them onto his face with his fingers, drawing fierce-looking lines in black and yellow from just under his eyes down over his cheeks and neck. She began patting the dirt over the top of the grave when she noticed him put the powders away, then raise his arms and throw back his head. He said nothing, but she knew he must be praying.

"What's he doing?" she asked Olin.

"Gettin' ready for battle," Olin replied. "He's prayin' for speed and strength and accuracy—and to die honorably, if he's to die at all."

Her heart pounded. "He can't die!" she whispered. Olin met her eyes in sympathy.

"Miss Abbie, he's only human, in spite of you thinkin' he can do anything. I admit, it will take a hell of a lot to put Cheyenne Zeke in his grave, but there's a lot of them and only one of him. Still, he'll go after them anyway 'cause that's how he's made."

She thought about the rift between the Cheyenne and the Crow that Olin had told her about earlier, and the scar on Zeke's face, put there by a Crow Indian. Not only was he going after a white man who hated him and who did not fight fair, but Givens had Crows with him to help. The odds were squarely against Zeke, and it was her fault he'd have to go on alone. If she'd not insisted on coming along, Olin could have stayed with him. Now Zeke approached them, again the Indian, savage and frightening to look at.

"Leave now," he told Olin, not even looking at Abbie. "They'll ride hard to tell them the girl is with us. Givens will want her if he can get her. Get her back to the train as fast as you can. Don't stop to sleep for more than a couple of hours at a time."

"I understand," Olin replied. "I'll try to get back to you, Zeke."

"Just watch out for yourself. Givens wouldn't mind having your hide either." He turned to leave, but Abbie grasped his arm.

"Zeke!" He looked down at her, his body tense and prepared for a fight. "I . . . I'm sorry. It's my fault you have to go on alone!" she sobbed.

His eyes softened, and he reached out to take some of her hair in his hand. "Makes no difference," he told her. "This day has been a long time coming, Abbie girl. But it will be easier for me if I know you're safe. So just leave now—quickly.' He hurried toward his horse.

"I love you!" she called out to him. "I love you, Zeke!" Tears spilled down her face. He turned and glanced at her for just a moment, then leaped upon the Appaloosa in one quick, smooth movement without answering her. He rode off, his long, black hair flying.

Olin took her arm, urging her to hurry and mount up.

"We have to mark the grave!" she sobbed.

"No time. Don't argue with me or I'll knock you senseless," Olin warned. "Zeke said to get you back and you're goin'—now!" He forced her up on her horse, and taking the reins in one hand, he mounted his own horse and they rode off at a fast gallop in the opposite direction from that which Zeke had taken.

Abbie glanced back, but Zeke had already disappeared. She turned her eyes ahead, unable to look at the thicket that hid the rough grave where her sister and David Craig now lay quietly together beneath the earth. She wondered why God had chosen to allow so many terrible things to happen to her. Her only hope was that perhaps God had a reason for taking away her entire family. Perhaps He meant Abigail Trent to be alone, to have nothing left to her name but the land . . . and Cheyenne Zeke. But then it was very possible she would also lose her Zeke to death.

They had ridden hard. Abbie wasn't sure how much longer she could even stay on the horse. Everything ached, and she felt dizzy and weary, but finally, after the sun had been set for more than an hour, Olin agreed to stop and let her eat and rest. She all but fell out of her saddle, and Olin had to hold on to her and help her sit down. He told her to stay put while he fixed a place for her to bed down.

"I'm sorry to ride you so hard," he told her, working up a spot in the earth with his hands until the dirt was softened. "But I had to get you far away from that spot quick. You should be safer now, but don't bet too much on it. Givens is a scheming man, and you can bet that after you shoved pie in that man's face back there at Fort Laramie, he's gonna be wantin' to give you what for. Whoever got away back there has told Givens by now that you was with us." He spread out a blanket. "But I'll look out for you, Miss Abbie."

She shook dust from her hair, thinking to herself what a nice man Olin Wales had been, and what a good friend he was to Zeke. "I'm sorry I got you and Zeke into this mess," she answered. "You should be with him. How can he possibly go up against those men all alone?"

"You'd be surprised what Zeke can do," he answered, now picking up some sticks to start a small fire. "That man is smart—and wily as a fox. He can climb like a mountain goat and run like a bobcat, and when he's cornered, he's like a bear just comin' out of hibernation, all snarly and mean."

Abbie could not help but smile at the thought. "I'll bet he's just like that," she answered, moving over to the blanket and stretching out her legs.

"Well, he's a real disciplined man, Miss Abbie. He can take a lot before he goes down, and mentally, he can make himself do the impossible sometimes, just 'cause he knows he has to do it. With you the one in

304

danger, you can bet he'll go himself one better if it means keepin' you from harm."

She sighed and stared at the little fire he had started, her eyes now tearing again. If Cheyenne Zeke died, it would be partly for her. This realization brought back the ache to her heart, and made her love him even more. She swallowed and watched Olin add some pieces of dry pine to the fire.

"Olin . . . does Zeke love me? I mean . . . does he *really* love me? He wouldn't have . . . used me, would he?" She blushed and looked down, toying with a piece of thread that stuck out from the seam of her dress.

"You're pretty ignorant about men if you don't know a man like Zeke would never use a pretty little thing like you. 'Course he loves you." He moved over closer to her with another blanket, opening it and putting it over her legs. "Why do you think I'm breakin' my neck to get you back safe? Zeke's set on not lettin' anything come of the love he's got for you, but that's beside the point. He'd die before he let any harm come to you, and he's dependin' on me now to get you back. Zeke's my friend, but I won't want to be lookin' him in the eyes if somethin' happens to you."

"But he never really said it out . . . that he loves me."

"Why should he? It would just make things harder on you. Besides, he's never told a woman that since his wife died, so it ain't an easy thing for him to say again. Now lay down there. I'll fix some coffee and beans; then you can sleep a while."

She lay back and pulled the blanket over her shoulders, still watching the burly mountain man with the scraggly, shoulder-length hair and rough beard. If a woman came upon Olin Wales in a place like this alone and didn't know him, she'd likely be frightened for her person and her life. But there was nothing about the man that frightened Abbie. She knew that if she was stark naked before him he'd not touch her, for he had a proper respect for women—and besides that, in a sense Abigail Trent belonged to Cheyenne Zeke, at least for a while. Olin Wales was not a man to take what belonged to another.

"Have you ever been married, Olin?" she asked.

He gave her a frown. "You ask a lot of questions."

"I'm sorry."

He grinned a little. "Once—long time ago. I was married to a Shoshoni woman. She died from smallpox."

"I'm sorry about that, too. Real sorry."

He shrugged. "A man can take more sufferin' than he thinks, I guess. Look at Zeke. At least my woman didn't die like that."

"You should marry again. Every man needs a good woman."

He chuckled. "When did you get to know so much about men? What are you—fifteen?"

"I'll be sixteen in a few months."

He laughed harder. "I see." He shook his head. "Well, I'm a wanderin' man, Miss Abbie. Not many women want an agin', wanderin' man. I find plenty of loose squaws to take my pleasure with."

"That's not the same."

He sobered. "You're right there." He sighed and handed her a plate of beans. "You eat, and quit askin' so many questions. We ain't got time for small talk.

306

You eat and rest, and then we'll be out again 'fore the sun rises."

Abbie was sleeping hard due to her state of exhaustion, and she did not hear the enemy approach. She awoke to the click of a gun and the feel of cold steel against her temple. They startled her, and before she realized what had happened, she had jumped and wiggled back; but a second gun greeted her, this time at her neck. When her eyes focused, she stared up at two men, both obviously Indians, but not clean and beautiful like Zeke. They wore white man's pants, topped with leather vests over bare chests and were loaded down with weapons of various sorts. Their hair was long and dark, but dirty and tangled. One of them grinned, displaying an absence of front teeth, and the other reached down and grasped her hair so tightly that she screamed out with the pain. He laughed and let go, yanking as he did so, so that her head slammed to the ground.

The other man shoved his gun in his belt and grabbed her wrists, jerking them over her head as she began to struggle, still not certain what had gone wrong. She kicked out at the other man as he lifted her dress, and he promptly landed a fist across the side of her face. The blow drew blood inside her mouth and stunned her momentarily. She wanted to struggle and scream, but her body would not respond. She was nauseated by the smell of the men who held her, and she was sure the one holding her wrists was breaking them.

She heard the men grunt something back and forth to each other, then laugh. They put her dress back

307

down and yanked her to her feet. Through blurred vision she finally spotted Olin, slumped over nearby.

"Olin!" she screamed out, now beginning to cry at the thought that he might be dead. "Olin! Olin!"

Another stunning blow was directed at her face. "Woman be quiet!" someone ordered.

The sun was just beginning to rise, so she tried to see the men better. But at the moment they were just ugly images to her; dark, menacing, smelly, and loaded with numerous weapons, any one of which could end her life quite promptly if they so chose. A strong arm grasped her about the waist, and she felt herself being lifted by one of the men as he mounted a horse and perched her in front of him. She vaguely wondered why they had not raped her. Surely these were some of the hated Crow who rode with Givens. Perhaps they were saving her for him.

She shuddered at the thought and convulsed into vomiting because her stomach had become filled with blood from her mouth. The man holding her let out a grunt of disgust and threw her to the ground. She landed face down in the dirt. He waited for her vomiting to end, then turned her over and threw a canteen of water in her face to rinse it. He grimaced and bent down, planting a knee in her abdomen to hold her still while he used some more water to rinse her hair. She coughed and choked and cried and struggled, but to no avail.

"Do that again and Wolf Man will forget he is to save you for *Givens*!" he snarled. He jerked her close to his ugly face. "You are young and tight! It will not be easy saving you until later! But I *will* get my turn, bitch—after Givens has had *his*!"

She grunted with terrible pain as he again jerked her to her feet and lifted her back onto the horse, mounting up behind her. He ripped open the front of her dress and reached inside, pinching her painfully; then he got his horse into motion. Her mind reeled with pain, fright, and horror. Was her life to end as Lee-Ann's had ended? Vomit came to her throat again at the thought of what LeeAnn must have suffered before her death, but she forced it down, afraid he'd beat her.

Leaving Olin's body behind them, they rode northwest, in the very direction from which they'd come; and to keep her sanity, she closed her eyes and concentrated on Zeke. But her blood chilled. Had they already killed him? Was that how they'd gotten through to her? She had to know, for if Zeke was dead, too, she'd grab her abductor's gun somehow and shoot herself before she'd suffer what her sister had suffered. Without Zeke, there was no reason to go on living.

"You'll die by Cheyenne Zeke's hands for this!" she choked out. Her abductor looked over at the other man, and they both laughed.

"It is Cheyenne Zeke who will die, bitch!" the man holding her answered. "And *you* will be the bait!"

Relieved, she closed her eyes, feeling a strange peace and a new strength flow through her veins. With Zeke alive—out there somewhere—there was hope after all.

"Zeke!" she whispered to herself.

Fourteen

It was probably the longest day and the most difficult ride Abigail Trent would ever experience. They fed her nothing, and gave her only trickles of water to drink. Nausea, partly caused by the hard blow she had sustained and partly by her fright, continued to move over her in ugly waves. She knew that if Zeke did not happen to get to her in time, she was headed for rape and things worse than rape, most certainly to be followed by death. Her abductors rode hard, giving her no time to rest. Whenever they stopped, it was just to grab a biscuit for themselves, to give her a splash of water, and to let her urinate; but she only urinated once out of sheer need, for every time she tried, they watched with smiles on their faces, so she could not go. The sun beat down on her as the horse jostled her tired, sore body, and her head ached fiercely.

The landscape had changed from a lush green to harsh brown and was now mostly rock with some thin forests on the hillsides. It seemed a hotter than usual day. Even the late afternoon brought no relief, because as the sun dropped lower, it glared into her face. The man she rode with suddenly stopped, jerking her around so that her left leg swung over to the right side of the horse. Then he forced her face-down across his lap.

"We will be there soon," he told her, his yellowish eyes glowing with excitement. He looked over at his companion. "If I did not fear Givens would shoot me, I would sink myself into this one right now," he told the man. The other man laughed and nodded.

"She is a young one, and she is wild when she is mad!" he answered. "But we will tame her!" They both laughed then and rode a little faster.

Abbie hung limp over her abductor's lap, as they entered what appeared to be a rocky canyon. She had no strength left to fight and knew they would only hurt her more if she did. Her only hope was that Zeke would show up before they all began having their way with her. Her head pounded harder now, for the blood rushed into it because of her position; and she could not help vomiting again from the jostling horse against her stomach. She could hear other voices now, along with hoots and whistles and growls, and soon she was dumped onto the ground and surrounded by men, a few more Crow renegades and a few white men, including none other than Rube Givens.

"Well, well," the man said with a grin. "If it ain't the little bitch that shoved pie in my face." He bent down and jerked her up by the hair of the head, making a face.

"She puked again!" her abductor exclaimed. "She puked on me once before, boss. I told her she'd better not do it again!" Givens threw her back down, at the

312

same time staring at Wolf Man.

"Did you have at her?" he growled.

"Hell no! You said to save her." He rubbed himself between the legs. "But don't take too long."

Givens sneered down at Abbie. "You're a mess," he told her through curled lips. She tried to struggle as he pulled her to her feet again and ripped off her clothes, but every time she staggered away from him, some strange man caught her and threw her back, until finally she was naked and bruised. Givens dragged her to a nearby stream that was nearly dried up. He threw her into it, pushing her face down in the water to wash it off. She choked and gagged on the water, which was mixed with sand, trying to drink some in her desperate thirst, but getting more sand than water in her mouth. She could hear their ugly laughter, as over and over again Givens dunked her, holding her face down just long enough to make her think he was going to drown her.

Finally he pulled her away from the stream, dragging her over to where stakes were pounded into the ground. He and three other men each took a limb and tied her spread-eagled to the stakes. The ropes scraped her wrists and ankles, and the earth was hot and rough beneath her back. Givens stood straddled over her and Abbie looked away, closing her eyes.

"Closin' your eyes ain't gonna stop it, bitch!" Givens sneered. "But I'm gonna let you lay there and think about it a few minutes, while you dry off some. Then I'm gonna have a real good time with you—and so are my men." He laughed, and to her it sounded like Satan laughing. "We'll see if you're as good as your sister!"

She forced back her tears, refusing to cry in front of him, sure he'd enjoy it immensely. Instead she opened her eyes to look straight up at him, and she attempted to spit at him, except that her mouth was too dry. But the gesture was obvious enough, and the smile left his face.

"Tell you what, bitch. I'm gonna let you think about a couple of things. First is, with you here, Cheyenne Zeke is sure to come by tomorrow, and we'll be ready for him. That man is gonna die 'cause of *you!* But by then *you'll* be dead. And I'll let you think about that, too—about *how* you'll die. It won't be as quick as your sister. When me and the boys are through with you, I'm gonna play a little Russian Roulette—with my gun. And just guess where it will be." He chuckled. "You think about that, bitch!"

The men all laughed.

"This has been a mighty fine few days, hasn't it, men?" Givens told them with a broad smile. "I got rid of that swindler, Robards. We all got a damned good piece of his blond bitch. Olin Wales is dead. We'll all get our share of this little girl here. And by tomorrow this time, Cheyenne Zeke will be dead, too—only he'll die real slow!"

They all laughed heartily—all big, dark, ugly men whose vicious mentalities made their behavior far beneath that of animals.

"Cheyenne Zeke won't *be* coming!" she choked out as Givens turned. "He's already here!"

They all sobered, a few of them looking up into the hills.

"We sent him on a wild-goose chase," Givens said calmly. "We have a little time with you before he fig-

314

ures out he's been led astray. We had to get him off the track so's we could get you here. Do you think if he was around he'd have let my men get you to my camp?"

She gritted her teeth, anger helping ease her horror. "Why not?" she sneered back. "What *better* way to find you all together in one spot?"

She enjoyed the hesitant look on Givens' face. Then he grinned again. "It won't work, bitch! You think you can keep us busy searchin' the hills to keep us from rapin' you. But it won't work." He looked at the one called Wolf Man who had brought her to the camp and nodded. Wolf Man smiled and walked over to her, then bent down and ran rough hands over her body.

"It will not be long, bitch," the toothless Indian told her, as he touched her private places. She grimaced and turned her face away. He pinched her breast again, and they all laughed heartily before they walked away to leave her there in the setting sun that was still hot. She felt it burning her, in spite of its angle, and after lying there nearly an hour, her skin was becoming red and raw.

She tried to watch the hills, but her dizziness and thirst combined with the blinding sun to prohibit her from seeing much. She silently begged God to send Zeke, telling herself over and over that he must be out there somewhere.

"Zeke! Zeke!" she whispered, agonizing over the thought of what they would all do to her. She prayed that if Zeke was not there to help her that at least she would die quickly at their hands, just from brutality and exposure, before Givens put a gun inside of her

315

and pulled the trigger. Then she heard crunching footsteps near her and looked up at the hated Givens again.

"Time for fun and games, bitch," he told her through his yellow teeth. "We done searched those hills, and there's no Cheyenne Zeke up there to help you. You're all alone, little girl."

He reached down, quickly cut the ropes that held her, and jerked her up. Wolf Man threw a bucket of water into her face, startling her to a more alert stance. She grabbed her hair and sucked on some of it, desperately needing to get some moisture into her mouth; then she folded her arms around herself as Givens began circling her.

"You can run if you want, bitch. Makes it more exciting that way. A good struggle pleases me greatly."

Her anger returned again. If she was to die this day, she'd be brave about it and not give this man any more satisfaction than he was already getting.

"Far be it from me to please you," she said weakly. "Go ahead and have me." She turned to face him. "But if you think you'll be the first, you *won't!*" she spit out at him. His face darkened, and he stepped closer, grabbing her chin in his hand.

"Did Wolf Man have at you?" he growled. "Truth!"

She actually smiled. "Not Wolf Man," she sneered back. "My first man and my only man was Cheyenne Zeke himself!"

His eyes widened in slight shock, then narrowed in anger. "Zeke! You lay with that half-breed?"

She glared back at him. "He's every bit as good with a woman as he is with that knife!" she shot back at him. "And there's not a man in this camp can

316

match him—especially not you, you fat, ugly piece of filth!"

He jerked her close, forcing her arms behind her back painfully. "We'll see about that!" he snarled. "And it's pleasin' to know it's Cheyenne Zeke's woman I'll be taken!" He shoved her to the ground, and she grunted from the fall, his grimy body now on top of her. He bent down to slobber at her lips when one of the Crow renegades suddenly cried out and fell forward, an arrow in his back.

The others suddenly quieted, and Givens jumped up off of Abbie. She rolled to her side, then sat up, staring at the man with the arrow in his back.

"What the hell?" someone said. Then there was a singing, whirring sound, and another man fell, again with an arrow in his back. Givens' men looked around, studying the hills, stunned and momentarily confused. They could see no one. One of the Crow renegades knelt down and yanked the arrow from his friend's back.

"Cheyenne!" he hissed.

Abbie's heart pounded with joy. "Zeke!" she said defiantly. "It's Cheyenne Zeke! He's out there, and you're all going to die!"

Another arrow sang through the air, and another renegade Indian screamed out and fell. It finally struck the others that someone was most certainly out there and after them, and as though slapped awake from a dream, they suddenly began to move, running for cover. Rube Givens dragged Abbie with him, but she wasn't afraid now. Zeke was out there!

"I thought you men combed those hills!" Givens snarled.

"We did!" Wolf Man answered. "It is true, boss; no one was there!"

"Well apparently someone *is* there, you bastard!" Givens growled.

"But it is *impossible!* How could he get here so quickly?"

"Who knows?" Givens shot back, obviously frightened. "All I know is it was *us* who was supposed to be one up on *him*, not the other way around!"

"I don't like this!" another man mumbled.

"We're safe!" Givens said, trying to sound assured. "We've got his woman, remember?" He jerked at Abbie, pulling her hair unmercifully.

"Sure. But if he manages to get to us, you know what Cheyenne Zeke does to his enemies if they're still alive—especially if they've hurt his woman!" another shot back.

"Shut up!" Givens snarled. "I'm here to get Cheyenne Zeke, and I *will!* Everything else worked out so far, and this will, too. The girl is perfect bait! We can use her somehow—especially if we keep her alive! He has to come right down here after her eventually! He can't stay up in those hills forever!"

Abbie smiled. "You'll end up with your insides hanging out for the buzzards to eat!" she said haughtily. He yanked her again and slapped her hard.

"Shut up, you bitch!" he snarled. Then he yelled out louder from behind the large boulder where they hid. "Zeke! Cheyenne Zeke! I know it's you out there!" There was no reply. "Show yourself . . . or this little girl dies real slow!" The hills remained silent, but for the soft moan of the wind.

Givens turned to his men and talked softly. "We

know he's up on that side someplace. Cane, Dorey, you two circle up and behind that side of the canyon. Comb it good. Maybe you can flush him forward."

The two men looked at each other apprehensively, then nodded and left reluctantly, hustling to their horses as quietly as possible and leading them through a narrow crevice that led out the side of the canyon.

"I've got your woman here, Zeke!" Givens called out. "You'd best show yourself soon! My men are all gettin' anxious to have their turn at her!" He stood up and daringly dragged Abbie out from behind the large boulder. "Here she is, half-breed! Come and get her or we'll all take her and then kill her!"

A shot rang out, and Givens' hat flew off. His eyes widened and he yanked her back behind the boulder. "Why doesn't he show himself?" he snarled. "He must not think much of you, bitch!"

"He knows you won't do anything!" Abbie said confidently. "If he comes down here, you'll kill him for sure, and me, too! Your only hope is to keep me alive, Givens! But he'll probably get you anyway!"

"He could have killed me then and there!" the man growled, yanking at her hair again. She smiled, enjoying the apprehension in his eyes.

"He's just saving you," she sneered. "For *later*!"

For a moment he looked like a little boy about to cry; then he pushed her down to the ground. "Shut up!" he grumbled. Another shot rang out, and a spot on top of the big boulder flew into pieces with a zinging sound. One chip flew off and hit Wolf Man in the face.

"Ouch! Goddamn it!" the man swore. He put a hand to his face where blood had immediately appeared. "What the hell will we do, boss? I don't know how he got there! The man is like a shadow!"

"Cane and Dorey will flush him out!" Givens shot back. "And we can help by lettin' him know she's bein' raped right now! I say we all start havin' at it with her."

The other men just looked at each other. "Like hell!" one of them finally spoke up. "You want to have at it, go ahead. If you can get yourself up while somebody's shootin' at you and maybe sneakin' up on you to skin you alive, then you're some kind of man! Far as I'm concerned, every one of us needs to have our eyes and our ears open and our guns leveled and ready!"

"I'm for cuttin' out!" another spoke up.

"Zeke sees you, you're dead!" one of the renegades replied.

"We can cut out through the crevice where Cane and Dorey went."

"First man that leaves me will get shot in the back!" Givens barked, cocking his gun. "You bunch of yellow cowards! Just wait here till Cane and Dorey flush him out! It won't be long now!"

"You'll never see them alive again!" Abbie warned, enjoying their dilemma. Givens yanked at her hair.

"Then you won't live long either, bitch!" he snarled.

"You can kill me now and run, you pig!" she returned in a firm, brave voice. "But you'd be best to stick it out here and now! Because if you harm me and run off, there won't be a place on earth where you can hide from Cheyenne Zeke, and you know it! You'll always be wondering if he's around the next corner, waiting to slit you up the middle with that knife! And

320

he'll *do* it! So you might as well stay right here and have it out."

The man grinned and nodded. "You have a lot of confidence in your half-breed," he sneered. "But he's only one man. If you want to sit here and watch us torture him once we've caught him, that's your choice, bitch."

One of the men suddenly turned and ran for his horse, but Givens took aim and fired. The man's body jerked forward, a bloody hole in his back. Then he sprawled to the ground. Givens waved his gun at the rest of them. "One more of you runs out on me, and that's how he'll die! Now there's plenty of us and only *one* of him, and he'll come down from that hill soon! So stay put and we'll have us some fun right soon!"

The others settled down uneasily, watching the opposite hill like caged animals, and for the next few moments there was no sound but the wind. Then there was a horrible scream. Wolf Man's eyes widened.

"Who was that?"

"Sounded like Cane to me," another answered.

"Probably Zeke himself," Givens shot back. "I expect Cane and Dorey got to him. I just wish they'd have left him for me."

They watched the hillside a moment longer, and finally a horse began making its way through the sparse pine trees. Abbie's eyes widened.

"That's Zeke's horse!" she spoke up, afraid now that perhaps Givens had been right. "That's his Appaloosa!"

Givens smiled. "What did I tell you?"

The horse came into the clearing then, and his smile faded. The horse was dragging two bodies, and Givens and the others rose from their positions, straining to look as the horse came closer.

"Jesus, it's them!" one of the men spoke up in a thoroughly frightened voice. "They . . . they're split open!"

Abbie had to turn away before they got any closer. Their insides were hanging out, dragging along the ground with the bodies, and even she was horrified at the sight.

"God in heaven!" somebody yelled. "I'm gettin' out of here!"

Just then there was a bloodcurdling scream, like nothing Abbie had ever heard before, and four shots were fired. Bam! Bam! Bam! Bam! Four men fell dead, one of them Wolf Man. One after another their bodies slumped to the ground before the others could gather their wits and take action. Then Zeke was there, charging down the hill behind them and diving into the bunch of them, catching them off guard. He fired twice more as Abbie ran to her own horse to get the Spencer that was still on it. Her captors had brought her horse along when they'd taken her, as well as Olin's horse, horse theft being another one of their many "occupations."

Zeke was swinging the butt of his rifle now, smashing it into two more men, his long hair flying and his screams and painted face putting fear into the others. When Abbie turned with her rifle, Givens got off a shot and Zeke flew backward. Abbie screamed in horror. Zeke hit the ground, but immediately had his handgun out and fired a shot back at Givens, who fell backward and lay still.

Up again Zeke whirled and rammed his elbow into

the gut of one of the renegades who'd dropped his gun and charged at Zeke with a knife. The blow from Zeke's elbow made the man double over, and Zeke grabbed the man's knife hand and pushed, plunging the knife into the man's own body. The renegade made a horrible grunting sound and fell forward, and Zeke turned, blood pouring from his own side now. One of the men Zeke had hit with his rifle butt was getting up, so Abbie quickly cocked her Spencer and took aim. She fired, and to her own amazement, the man fell. Zeke whirled, staring at her in surprise. It was not until later, when she had time to think, that Abbie wondered what a sight she must have been at that moment, standing there naked, bleeding, filthy, and sunburned; her hair matted and her lips puffed, holding a smoking Spencer in her hands.

It was only about fifteen seconds after Zeke's charge, yet all Givens men seemed to be down. When one of them started to get up again, Zeke pulled his own wicked blade from its sheath, and sliced it across the man's throat before he could gather his senses. Blood gushed out and Abbie felt sick. Zeke staggered back, and there was not a Givens man left standing or even alive, except for Givens himself, who lay badly wounded from Zeke's gunshot. Zeke turned and looked at Abbie again. His wound bled badly, and his breath came in short pants. His face still painted in black and yellow, he looked vicious and wicked.

"Find something . . . to put on," he grunted to her. "Stay here. . . . I'll . . . tend to you . . . soon."

"Zeke, you're hurt bad!" she cried out to him.

"Doesn't matter. I have . . . something to do."

He walked over to Givens and grasped the man by

the neck of his shirt, dragging him off into some bushes. Too wounded to fight back, yet alive enough to know what Zeke intended to do with him, Givens started crying and begging for Zeke to let him go. He struggled some, but Zeke punched him once, then dragged him the rest of the way into the bushes. Abbie went to her horse and took out her spare dress, trying to ignore the awful screams she heard coming from Givens. But it was impossible. She shuddered, yet when she pictured LeeAnn's beaten and bloated body and the hole in her forehead, his screams weren't so disturbing.

She started to put on her clean underwear, then decided not to soil it until she could wash. She was filthy, and she smelled of her own vomit. She put all her clean clothes back into her carpetbag and took a blanket from her horse, wrapping it around her shoulders.

Shame began to envelop her now, shame and humiliation, because of what Givens and his men had done to her: at the thought of their looking upon her nakedness, at the horrible memory of their hands touching her, and worse than any of it, at knowing Zeke had seen her as he had. How different this was from the night he'd taken her so gently in the darkness!

She closed her eyes and wept quietly as Givens' screams grew worse. She held her stomach and sat down to wait, covering her ears, thinking what a strange and mysterious man Cheyenne Zeke was—a man of compassion, gentleness . . . and ruthless savagery. There had been at least twelve Givens men, if not more. She never did get a proper count. Now there were none.

The screaming finally ended. Cheyenne Zeke had

finished the job with his knife, and now the whole canyon was suddenly quiet. Only a soft, whining wind moaned through it. She could hear birds singing somewhere, and she realized it was the first time she'd noticed birds singing since she'd been brought there.

Suddenly the canyon seemed eerie to her because of the wind moaning and whistling, and the dead bodies sprawled grotesquely about. Now that everything was over, the wind sounded mournful and lonely, just as Abbie felt. The horror of her losses and of the day's events overwhelmed her, and she broke down into heaving sobs that only made her body ache more. She held her head, hardly able to breathe because of her violent weeping.

Then she felt a presence beside her, and she knew it was Zeke. Kneeling in front of her and putting his arms around her, he said her name softly. She buried her face in his neck and cried, while he stroked her hair.

"I'd have . . . taken my life," he said hoarsely, "if I'd found you as we found LeeAnn." He held her tightly in his strong, sure arms, letting her cry. She was lost in her pain and sorrow until, finally, he whispered to her.

"You . . . have to . . . help me, Abigail. . . . I'm bleeding."

Her heart pounded with fear and shame as she pulled away. The blanket she'd had around her was now stained with his blood, and his pants were soaked with it as it ran from the wound in his side.

"Oh, God, Zeke!" she gasped, wiping at her nose and eyes. "I'm so sorry! I should be helping you!"

She heard thunder then, as black clouds rolled over

the canyon, and she felt a sprinkle of rain on her face.

"A cave . . ." he told her, looking ready to pass out. "Up . . . there." He pointed to the side of the hill where he'd hidden when he shot the arrows. "We'd . . . be dry. I think I can ride . . . that far. Come."

He stood up, leaning on her for support, and managed to get to his horse. He took out his knife again, cutting loose the two bodies still tied to his horse. He groaned as he moved himself up onto the Appaloosa's back. Abbie got LeeAnn's horse, as well as her own and Olin's and leading the other two horses by the reins, she climbed up onto her own mount. Determined not to lose her own animal or LeeAnn's, her seemingly cold, but practical, side showed itself. This was a rugged land, and one's animals could mean survival. She rode up to Zeke.

"What about all their animals?" she asked Zeke.

"Leave them. They'll wander off," he replied, nudging his horse into motion. "Indians will . . . take them . . . take the supplies and weapons. They can . . . have them. And the buzzards . . . can have the bodies!" He slumped forward slightly as he hissed the words, and Abbie prayed he'd be able to stay on the horse until they got to the cave. It seemed to take forever to get the horses up the rocky and treacherous hill, and when they reached the cave entrance, Zeke was hunched over even further. Rain burst from the dark clouds just as they arrived, drenching everything below, including Zeke and Abbie.

Abbie hurriedly led the horses inside. Then Zeke half fell off his horse, as Abbie helped ease him to the floor. She quickly spread out a blanket laying it out on a spot that was mostly dirt so it would be soft, and she managed to help Zeke crawl over to it.

Inside the cave, there was a trickle of a waterfall that ran down the rocky side into a little trench, then disappeared someplace beneath the earth. She sighed with relief that there would be water in which to bathe Zeke's wounds and her own body, as well as water for the horses. Her own horse immediately walked up to the little stream and drank from it.

Zeke groaned, and Abbie ran outside to collect as much wood as possible before it got thoroughly soaked by the rain. She ran back inside and piled the wood near Zeke. Hoping the draft in the cave would draw out the smoke from the fire rather than fill their hiding place and choke them out of it, she dug some flint from her saddle bag and lit the kindling, blowing on it until the flames took hold. She was relieved when the smoke wafted upward, then headed into deeper parts of the cave to places unknown.

"Abbie!" Zeke said in a near whisper. She bent down close to him, suddenly frightened by his ugly wound and the dying look on his face.

"Don't you go and die on me!" she whimpered desperately. "I love you, Zeke! I love you! Don't you die!"

"You . . . have to take the bullet out," he moaned. "Or . . . I *will* die."

Her heart felt as though it had stopped beating. "I can't!" she said, appalled. "I've never done such a thing, Zeke! I'd kill you for sure!"

"I'll . . . die anyway . . . if you don't get it out, Abbie girl," he groaned. "You can . . . do it."

"No!"

"Got no . . . choice. You want to sit there . . . and

327

watch me die? Just . . . cut me open enough . . . so you can reach inside . . . find the lead. You . . . have to do it, Abbie."

"Oh, God, I can't do that to you! I can't!"

"I can . . . take it. Just . . . get me some . . . whiskey . . . in my parfleche. Please . . . Abigail. Please . . . take it out!"

She knew he was right. If there were another way to help him, she'd do it. But the fact remained there was a bullet in him that had to come out or he'd die. The thought of putting a knife to his skin and reaching inside him was horrifying. She'd been through so much already she wasn't sure she was strong enough to do it. But their eyes held and she nodded. She had to be strong now more than ever—or she'd lose Zeke.

"I'll try," she whispered.

"You're . . . a good girl, Abbie."

She went to his horse, her whole body aching and screaming for food and water and rest, her nerves making her shake with fear. She wondered what she would she do if he did die? She had no idea where she was or how she'd ever get back to the train. Maybe she'd just end her life with his. She reached into his parfleche, took out the flask of whiskey, and, walking back, handed it to him.

"There's more . . . in Olin's saddle bags," he told her. "Get . . . a big bottle. You'll . . . need it." He took a drink of his own whiskey. "Get something . . . to bandage me . . . and some leather . . . to hold between my teeth while you're cutting me."

She shuddered at the thought, but did everything he told her. She took her own clean slip from her bag and tore it into strips for bandages; then she took Zeke's

328

knife from his belt. She felt strange holding the knife, knowing what he must have done to Rube Givens with it. But now it was wiped clean. She walked over and cut off a piece of leather that hung from her horse's cinch, the big blade sliding smoothly and easily through the thick leather. When she walked back over to Zeke, his own flask of whiskey lay next to him, already empty.

"Pour whiskey . . . on the wound," he said, "and on your hands. Hold . . . the blade of the knife . . . over the fire to clean it."

Feeling numb, she removed his belt and weapons as carefully as possible and laid them aside. Then she pushed his bloodied buckskins down to his hip bones and moved his leather vest aside. Having exposed his wound fully, she poured whiskey into it. His whole body jerked, but he did not cry out. She balanced the knife on stones so that the blade end was in the flames; then she poured more whiskey over her own hands. She held out the piece of leather she had cut for him to bite on, and their eyes held for a moment. He actually managed to smile for her. When he opened his mouth, she put the leather into it. He clamped his teeth down tightly on the piece of cinch, and with his fists, he grasped the sides of the blanket on which he lay.

As she took the knife from the flames, she hesitated a moment, telling him with her eyes that she was sorry. She said a silent prayer, then started cutting. Although she wanted to scream and cry and throw up, somehow she stayed calm, even though Zeke bit harder into the leather and his fists turned white where they gripped the blanket. He let out a terrible moan, and little beads of sweat broke out on his forehead.

Abbie decided that if she managed to do a proper job of getting out the bullet, then she would have experienced just about everything that could happen to a girl her age. She didn't feel like a little girl anymore. She'd grown up fast, starting from the first time she'd set eyes on Cheyenne Zeke back in Independence, Missouri.

Fifteen

She wasn't sure if Zeke was merely sleeping, or if he'd passed out. She washed the blood from her hands and removed her bloody blanket; then she walked back to him, lifting the blood-stained slip material from the wound to peek at it. She had no idea how to take stitches in someone, and the only thing she could think of doing was to wrap his midsection tightly and hope the bleeding would stop and the skin would somehow heal by itself. She threw aside the stained patch and began wrapping him with the rest of the strips from her slip, a difficult task, because she had to reach under his heavy body and could get no help from Zeke himself, who lay very still. He looked almost lifeless, and she begged Jesus not to let him die as she continued wrapping. Blood was already spotting the new bandaging, but there was nothing she could do about it. She'd poured whiskey into the wound when she'd finished, and now she felt whether Zeke lived or not depended on God and Zeke's own strength.

She had finished bandaging him, but still he did not

move or speak. His buckskin pants were stiff with dried blood, so she pulled at them to get them off. She tore off a piece of the torn and bloodied dress she'd salvaged and wet it; then she soaped it up with the bar she'd packed in her carpetbag. Gently she washed the dried blood from his thighs, feeling a warmth deep in her own belly because his magnificent body had made love to her. That night had been dark, and she'd never seen him this way, with his long, muscled legs bare and only a loincloth covering the part of him that was most manly. His body was lean, dark, and sinewy; and she thought to herself what a horrible waste it would be for such a strong and virile man like Cheyenne Zeke to die at only twenty-five years of age. He seemed much older in wisdom and experience, and she thought to herself that he had lived through and had experienced much more than most men do in a lifetime.

She finished washing him, then covered him with the blankets that were left on the four horses she was keeping in the cave with them. After she'd crawled in naked beside him and snuggled close to keep him warm, she fell asleep to her own whispered prayers as the rain fell softly outside the cave entrance.

She did not know how long she'd slept, but when she awoke, it was morning. She sat up quickly and studied Zeke. Her first thought was that his body was warm, so at least he was not dead. His breathing was even, and the blood stain on his bandages had not grown to any great extent since she'd wrapped him the night before. Apparently the wound had stopped bleeding, and she could only pray it was not still bleeding on the inside.

She crawled out from under the blankets; then, bending down to kiss his scarred cheek, she tucked them around his neck. "I love you," she whispered. She rose and studied his still-painted face, smiling to herself at how vicious and frightening he'd looked the day before, while now he lay asleep, the paint still there but somehow very different. She decided she would have to wash it off when he awoke.

She stood up, removed one blanket from him to wrap around herself, and walked out of the cave to get more wood. The rain had stopped, and the morning sun was bright. Birds were singing. It was a pleasant day. She forced herself to think about the sunshine, the flowers, and the birds, rather than the ugliness of her sister's death and her own abduction. Her mind was not strong enough at the moment to dwell on such things, and she had no choice but to put them out of her mind as much as possible and to pretend that life was still good and happy. At least she and Zeke were still alive, and that was something.

A squirrel scurried nearby as she picked up wood and hummed "Rock of Ages." She took the wood inside and built the fire near Zeke again. The cave was damp and chilly, in spite of the sunshine outside, and she feared it would make him ill. She led the horses outside, removed their gear, and tied them where they could get to grass; then she brought the saddles and gear back into the cave. Taking some food from the saddle bags, she started to make coffee, already having decided she would wash while the coffee cooked over the fire.

She was glad now that she'd saved her one clean dress and the clean underwear. Picking up the soap, she took a small towel from her carpetbag and walked over to the little waterfall in the cave. She splashed herself with the cold water and wet and soaped her hair. How marvelous it felt to wash herself clean again—to be rid of the filth of Rube Givens and his men! She actually smiled as she bathed, and again she sang "Rock of Ages" softly to herself. Raising her arms and letting the water run down over her naked body, she felt like a new person. The sun was shining and Zeke was alive and nearby. Just the smell of the coffee seemed wonderful! As she turned to pick up her towel, she saw that Zeke's eyes were open and he was watching her. She blushed deeply and grabbed up the towel, holding it in front of her.

"How long have you been awake?" she asked.

A faint smile passed over his lips. "Long enough to know it's a damned shame I'm laid up with this wound."

She scowled at him. "You could have spoke up!" she chided.

"Why should I? Watching you is the best medicine a man could ask for," he replied, grinning more. "Kind of puts the life back into a man."

Their eyes held a moment, and she couldn't help smiling herself. "I'll thank you to shut those eyes and give me your Indian's word of honor you won't open them again until I tell you to!" she demanded, her eyes playfully gleaming.

"How about if I give you a white man's promise? I *am* half white, you know."

"That's not good enough. White men speak with forked tongues."

He started to laugh but winced with pain. "All

334

right," he answered in a strained voice, managing to smile again as beads of sweat broke out on his face. "I give you my Indian's word of honor." He closed his eyes. "I have to say, though, it's nice to get a look at something I've already had the pleasure of knowing. The only thing bad about that night was it was so dark. I couldn't see how pretty . . . you really are."

She watched him closely, reddening again as she quickly dried off, slipped her clean dress over her head, and pulled on some underwear. She was warmed by his compliment, and she thought to herself how strange it was that she would rather have died than to let Rube Givens or any of his men touch her, when now she felt she might die if Cheyenne Zeke could *not* touch her. "You may open your eyes now," she told him, as she moved over to the boiling coffee, rubbing her hair with the towel.

"What a disappointment," he told her.

She looked at him slyly, as she spread the towel over her saddle. "It's best for you this way," she answered. "A man who's just had a bullet dug out of him shouldn't get too excited." He grinned and watched as she wet another piece of her discarded dress and soaped it up. Then, grabbing up the towel again, she came to sit down next to him. Gently she began to wash the paint from his face.

"You won't be needing this now," she said quietly, growing more serious. "How do you feel, Zeke—truly?"

"I don't feel like doing any war dances, if that's what you mean."

"You're feverish. That scares me." She wiped his face dry. "I did the best I could, but I've never done

335

anything like that before. I probably messed things up good. I couldn't even stitch you up." Tears filled her eyes as he reached up and grasped her wrist.

"You did just fine, Abbie. Maybe it wasn't a professional job, but I'd have died without it. Now a little fever never hurt anybody, and I'm strong. I'll be all right in a few days. I owe my life to you."

She met his eyes. "Then we're even. I owe mine to you—and more than that, after saving me from those . . . animals!"

His grip on her wrist tightened. "What did they do to you?" he whispered.

She looked away. "Just . . . vile, ugly things. But they . . . didn't rape me, and that's the truth, Zeke. You got there first."

He brought her hand down and kissed the back of it. "They almost threw me off their trail, but I figured out pretty quick what they were trying to do. So I doubled back, thank God. Are you hurt . . . physically?"

She shook her head and brushed away tears with her other hand. "Just some bruises. My face and teeth hurt some." Her voice broke and she stayed turned away as she covered her mouth and cried. He kept a firm grip on her wrist.

"Abbie!" he whispered. "I'm sorry, Abbie girl. I got there as quick as I could once I figured out what they'd probably done."

She breathed deeply to stop her tears. "I don't blame you. You could have died, and it's all my fault for forcing you to take me along in the first place. If they'd killed you—"

"Don't dwell on it, Abigail. It's not good for you to dwell on ugly things right now."

336

She nodded. "At least . . . at least none of them touched me like you've touched me," she replied. "I don't want anybody else to touch me like that."

He sighed. "You will, someday, Abbie girl."

His remark reminded her that he still thought they could not belong to each other. But she was too tired to argue.

"At least you know not all men are like Rube Givens," he went on.

She turned to face him. "They aren't all like you, either," she answered. "Fact is, there's only one Cheyenne Zeke, and that's the hell of it!"

He reached up and touched her bruised face, smiling sadly. "Did you ever stop to think I feel the same way, that there's only one Abbie—only one woman-child who brings out all the passion in me?"

She blushed then and took his hand, kissing his palm. Then she met his eyes again. "I'm afraid Olin's . . . dead, Zeke," she told him cautiously. He closed his eyes and tensed up. "I'm so sorry! He was your friend. When those men took me, we left Olin behind, all slumped over. They took off with me so fast, I never had time to know if he was alive or not, but it's not likely such men would spare him."

"No," he whispered. "It's not likely." He put a hand over his eyes. "I'll . . . try to find his body," he told her in a strained voice. He rubbed a hand over his closed eyes and breathed deeply. "Damn! Damn!" he swore through gritted teeth. His body tensed. "Olin was a good man! A good man! One of the few white men I trusted enough to call friend."

"I'm so sorry, Zeke," she repeated. "I feel like so much of this is my fault!"

337

When he opened his eyes, they were red and watery. "Don't blame yourself, Abbie girl. It's that Quentin Robards' fault and that Rube Givens'. Nobody else's."

He squeezed her hand and wiped at his eyes again.

"Would you like some coffee?" she asked, taking his hand from her lips and gently laying it down beside him. "I have a couple of biscuits in my bag. Lord knows they're not worth much by now, but it's nourishment."

"That's fine. I'm not ready to each much anyway."

She nodded and got up to pour some coffee into a tin cup.

"I admire your skill with that Spencer, by the way," he told her, wanting to get her mind off Olin. "You saved my hide yesterday, little lady. A man like me has a strong respect for a woman as brave and strong as you are."

She'd forgotten about shooting a man the day before, and although she was glad to have been able to show him the stuff of which she was made, the fact remained she'd killed a man. She frowned as she handed him the coffee and moved beside him to lift his head so he could drink.

"I forgot about that," she said quietly. "Do you think God will hold me responsible for that?"

He almost laughed, but he knew she was serious. He sipped some of the coffee, then lay back down, wincing with pain again. "I highly doubt it, Abbie girl. I'd say it's more likely it was God himself who made sure that shot went straight and true. He'd not hold you guilty for shooting a man like that." He waved away the coffee. "One sip and I know I can't drink any more—or eat either. I've got to rest, Abbie." His voice was growing weaker again. "Come lay down beside me. I want to hold you and know you're really alive. For the next few days I'll get to have you to myself."

She put the coffee down and, crawling in beside him opposite his wounded side, she snuggled close into his shoulder. They lay there quietly a few minutes; then it hit her that for miles around they were probably the only living humans. She had seen so much death in the last few days that she felt dead herself, and she broke down into tears.

"Oh, Zeke, they're dead! Papa . . . Jeremy . . . LeeAnn . . . poor David . . . and even Olin! Gone! All . . . gone! I can't stand to think about it!"

"Hush, Abbie," he told her softly, turning to kiss her still-damp hair. "I told you *not* to think about it—not now—if you can help it."

She cried, and he held her; and soon they were both asleep again.

They stayed there five days. By the third day, against Abbie's wishes, Zeke was up and walking around, insisting it was the only way to get his strength back. His resiliency amazed her. She chided him and begged him to rest more, but to no avail.

In spite of the ugliness that had brought them to the cave, their stay there was to remain forever beautiful in Abbie's heart and memory. They did not make love, Zeke because of his outer wound, and Abbie because of her inner emotional wounds. But they didn't need to make love physically. In those few days a new and special love grew between them, a deep bond that gave them both strength and helped them face the fact that some day they must part. Yet Abbie could not believe that day would come. She wanted to pretend their parting would never take place. She almost wished Zeke wouldn't heal completely. She wanted to stay there forever with him, and he knew it. He tried telling her in different ways not to think about it, but secretly he wanted it that way himself. Although he knew that as soon as he was able to get up onto a horse, they must leave quickly, or he would never be able to leave at all. To be alone with her was agony. Their long talks and her tears only made him love her more, and he must not love her. Yet how sweet and wonderful those five days were. They slept together, holding each other, relishing what little time they had, talking, crying, regaining their strength in different ways.

"Where do you think the train is about now?" she asked him on the fifth night.

"South Pass, I expect," he replied, pulling her closer. "I know a shortcut from here. We can catch up."

Her heart pounded with dread.

"I don't want to leave here, Zeke," she whispered.

"Nor do I, Abbie girl. That's why we *have* to leave—in the morning."

She pushed herself closer. "You . . . can't ride."

"I can ride. It's best, Abbie. It's best we get the hell out of here and get back to living our own separate lives."

"I could live anywhere with you. I've proved that."

"A person can do anything . . . for a while. But the day would come when you'd regret it, child. And you'd long for all the finer things—for a white woman's life. It's built into you—just like being an Indian is built into me. And I love you too much to ruin you."

"But you wouldn't—"

He put a hand over her mouth. "Don't, Abbie!" he pleaded in a strained voice. "Please, please don't keep ripping at my insides!" He pulled her close, and she wept against his chest. She cried herself to sleep, and when she awoke the morning sun had risen, and it was time to leave their little hideaway.

They hardly spoke, as she made breakfast and he saddled up the horses and repacked the gear. He put on the only other pair of buckskins he had along. He'd worn only a leather vest the day of his attack on Givens and his men, so his buckskin shirt was not stained. He put that on, along with his wide leather belt and many weapons, and again he was Zeke the half-breed scout, ready for battle or whatever else might come along. He brushed out his hair, then sat down and let her braid it down his back, and for those few moments she pretended she was his wife, waiting on him like a good squaw. She thought to herself how beautiful his hair was, clean and black and shining. She tied it at the end with a little leather string.

Too soon it was time to leave. Zeke put out the fire and walked quietly out into the sunlight. Abbie looked around the cave, her heart aching from the terrible pain of parting. So many things she'd left behind! So many things, and now this! She walked out of the cave with her head hanging, unable to even look at Zeke. She went to her own horse and mounted up, and he put the reins of LeeAnn's horse in her hand, squeezing her hand when he did so.

341

"I'll never forget either, Abbie girl," he said quietly. "But some things just have to be faced. You follow me down now, and don't look back, Abbie."

He went to his horse, wincing slightly when he moved up onto the big Appaloosa. He led Olin's horse and headed down the embankment. Luckily they were upwind of the dead and bloated bodies left by Zeke's massacre. He was careful to lead Abbie away from the scene so that she would not have to look at them and remember. He hoped that some or most of them had been picked by wolves and buzzards by now.

They headed East, Zeke wanting to try to find Olin's body. Abbie was of little help, for she'd had no idea where she was when she'd been abducted. That first day she didn't even care. All she could think about was the cave and how badly she wanted to go back. Never would she have Cheyenne Zeke all to herself like that again! Never! The thought tortured her and made her feel desperate, and she couldn't even speak without bursting into tears. It seemed every nerve in her body had been severed. They were headed back to the train, but what was waiting there for her? Nothing but loneliness and emptiness. All she wanted was to have Zeke to herself in the cave. But that could not be, and that night he made her sleep alone while he kept guard. So, the lovely closeness was over. Back to reality.

"How did you come across Rube and his men when you did?" she asked Zeke the next morning, trying to act casual and pretend she could go on with normal living. Zeke sat on his horse ahead of her, scanning the horizon.

342

"I headed northwest after Olin and you left, following the tracks of the one who got away," he replied. He nudged his horse forward and she followed. "Then I saw they were heading back southeast once I got to the place where they'd been camped. Signs told me they were riding hard. Then they split up, and I had to make a choice as to what trail to follow. I took the wrong one for a time, caught up with those men and killed them, then headed back fast, figuring I'd been duped for a good reason. By that time the others had gotten to you and Olin and had taken you back to the main camp again. When I got there you were already tied to those stakes. I wanted to come right in and get you; but I had to do some planning first, or I'd have got myself killed and been no help to you at all."

"I was so scared we'd get there, and I'd find out they'd already killed *you*," she answered. "I had my mind made up that somehow I'd kill myself before they could touch me. I don't know how I'd have done it, but if they'd caught you first—"

"Catching me is like trying to catch the wind," he replied.

She watched the fringe of his buckskins dance to the rhythm of his horse's gait. "I know," she answered sadly. He glanced back at her, then urged his horse into a faster trot.

They rode all day, and toward dusk they were in a big valley where they could see far into the distance. Zeke spotted a lone figure riding toward them on a horse. He halted his horse and pointed.

"I see him," Abbie replied, shading her eyes.

"Let's ride out and meet him," he told her. "Maybe whoever it is has seen the wagon train or something.

At any rate, I'd just as soon meet a stranger head on as to wonder where and who he is." They urged their horses into a slow walk, Zeke taking out his rifle and cocking it as a precaution. "Look around you, Abigail. Could be a renegade or outlaw. Could be more around. You'd best take out your rifle, too."

She obeyed, and they kept heading toward the lone man on a horse. Abbie saw no one else around. Suddenly, Zeke let out a yelp and put his rifle back into its holder. He dropped the reins of Olin's horse and galloped forward, leaving Abbie behind, and as she watched in surprise, she realized the other man was Olin Wales!

"Oh, sweet Jesus!" she exclaimed, tears filling her eyes. For once something good had happened.

The two men rode hard toward each other now, and she could hear Zeke laugh and give out a holler. When he reached Olin, Olin sat rigid on his horse at first, and the two of them talked. Abbie realized Olin must have wondered what had happened to Abbie and worried about whether Zeke would rather kill him than shake his hand. Perhaps Zeke's cry of joy had sounded more like a war cry to Olin. Then she saw Zeke put out his hand, and Olin shook it. Zeke reached out with his other hand and slapped Olin on the shoulder, and the two men leaned over their horses and hugged briefly. As the two men headed toward her, Abbie wondered where Olin had got the horse. And her joy at seeing Olin Wales alive was dimmed when she realized that now that they had found him, Zeke would head for the wagon train as quickly as possible. Her time with him was growing shorter.

* * *

"They stuck that knife in me, and I was out for a couple of days," Olin told them as they rode. "Next thing I know, I wake up and I'm in a bed in some cabin, a squaw bendin' over me and a white man standin' beside her. I tried to move but just about passed out again from the pain in my back. The white man—his name turned out to be Jim Baggett—said as how I missed bein' dead by about a quarter of an inch."

"I always knew it would take a lot to finish you off, you old buzzard," Zeke answered. They rode through high grass looking for a good place to camp as the sun sank lower.

Olin had come close to tears when he'd first ridden up to Abbie, his face showing guilt and shame at having failed her.

"And I call myself a hunter and trapper—a mountain man!" he'd spat out. "Nobody has ever snuck up on me that bad—not when I had somethin' like you to look out for. If it had just been me, like that first time Givens got me, it wouldn't have been so bad. But I should have been more—"

"I'm all right, Olin," Abbie had assured him. "I'm just so glad to see that *you're* all right."

"I can't tell you enough how ashamed and sorry I am, Miss Abbie," he answered, blinking back tears. "I guess we just rode so hard that day, well I just couldn't stop myself from fallin' asleep. I was just gonna shut my eyes for a minute—just for a minute."

"Zeke got there in time," she told him, reddening and looking down.

"Maybe so. But that don't erase the foul words and the humiliation," Olin replied bitterly. "You got every

345

right not to even speak to me, Miss Abbie—or Zeke, for that matter. I failed both of you, and I'll not forget it—ever! I owe you. If there's anything you need me for—anything—you tell me. If the two of you had died—if you had ended up like your sister—I'd have put a gun to my head."

"Olin, stop blaming yourself," Zeke told him. "It just went wrong, that's all. I should have known better than to split up in the first place. I'd trust your skills any day. If I had it to do over, I'd still trust Abbie to you. You're a damned good man, and I couldn't ride with a better one."

Olin waved him off and urged his horse forward. "I could have cost her somethin' worse than death!" he mumbled. Zeke just shook his head and sighed, and Abbie wished there were something she could do to make him feel better. There were several long minutes of silence before they started talking again, about how Olin had survived and about the people who had found and saved him.

"They was nice folks," Olin was telling them now. "The man was a trapper who'd decided to settle in one spot. Him and that squaw had six kids, and they lived in that cabin out there in the middle of nowhere. Said they was out huntin' when they found me. Sold me this here horse when I got better. I was headed out to find out what had happened to you and Abbie when there you came - across that valley. Goddamn, I sure did feel good seein' you two alive."

They headed south-southwest now, to catch up with the wagon train. Abbie wondered what Kelsoe would think when they returned without David Craig—and without LeeAnn.

346

That first night they all slept hard, Olin and Zeke keeping Abbie between them for warmth. She smiled to herself at what people in the civilized world would think of a fifteen-year-old girl sleeping between a half-breed and a wild mountain man. But it didn't matter. In this land all that counted was being practical, and she knew she couldn't be safer than with these two men. In the morning she awoke with Zeke's arms around her. She opened her eyes to see him watching her, a hunger in his eyes that she could not help but notice. He quickly rose and walked away to tend to the horses while Olin cooked breakfast and watched the two of them, aware of the pain both of them suffered.

The next day was very hot, and Abbie was grateful when the sun went down. Zeke had seemed lost in thought as they rode, and she had wondered if he'd been thinking about how difficult it would be to go on without her. That evening she helped Olin with supper, and afterward Zeke went down the side of a little hill to a spot where Abbie couldn't see him. She watched him vanish, then returned to helping Olin clean up. But Olin grasped her arm to get her attention.

"Go on, Abbie," he told her quietly. "Go and talk to him."

She looked at him curiously. "What do you mean? He must want to be alone."

He shook his head. "He's waitin' for you. I expect we'll catch up with the train tomorrow. We've been ridin' hard and takin' a lot shorter route to the pass than that wagon train could do. So this is probably your last night alone together. Me—I don't count. Zeke's healed now—good enough to know there's somethin' that's got to be done before you go back."

She reddened deeply and turned away.

"Ain't nothin' to be ashamed of," Olin added. "It's the law of nature, and I can't think of a better way for two people to say good-bye."

He got up and went to tend to the horses, and she turned and looked toward the embankment where Zeke had disappeared. What if Olin was wrong? She'd make a fool of herself. But then no one knew Zeke much better than Olin, if anyone could know the man at all. Her heart pounded with apprehension. How could she go and make love to a man she knew she could not have? But her body was on fire for him. That first night had been too quick, and too painful. There had been no time to truly enjoy each other and to make love slowly and deliberately. It had been more of an accident than anything else. And ever since she had longed to know him again—just once more. At the cave he had been in too much pain, and they'd left as soon as he was better because he knew if they stayed and he made love to her there, it would be next to impossible to leave. But now they were closer to the wagon train, and Olin was along. In spite of all the voices that told her this was wrong, she walked to the edge of the embankment and made her way hesitantly down the hill. Zeke sat at the bottom, watching the last flickers of the sun on a rippling brook, smoking quietly. He felt her walking up behind him, and he turned to look at her. Their eyes held, and she reddened.

"I . . . Olin said . . ." She swallowed. "I thought we could . . . talk . . . before we get with all those people tomorrow."

He threw down his smoke and stood up, walking up close to her. He enveloped her in his arms and bent down, covering her mouth with his own, groaning lightly as he kissed her, and pressing his hardness against her belly. She returned his kiss just as hungrily, reaching her arms up around his neck as his hands moved over her hips, pulling her up. She wrapped her legs around his waist and his lips moved to her neck.

"God, Abbie!" he whispered.

"I must be crazy!" she whimpered. "You must think me so bad!"

"Never!" he whispered. "Never! I have to have you just once more, Abbie girl. God, forgive me! After seeing those men . . . abuse you . . . I couldn't stand them . . . looking at you . . . touching you! You're so small and so full of sorrow . . . and after tomorrow . . ."

As their lips met again he knelt onto a blanket he already had spread out, drawing her down with him. It was easy for her to lose herself in his arms, to be hypnotized by his dark eyes and spellbound by his hungry kisses. Her clothes were coming off, and it didn't matter. His lips moved over her body, caressing her bruises, reclaiming the private places that Givens' men had touched. She lay in ecstasy, allowing him to do whatever he wanted with her, wanting only to please him as good as, or better than, any squaw had ever done, and wanting in turn to enjoy a man as she never had before. His hands and lips worked magic with her until a lovely explosion rippled through her insides, then his broad, dark shoulders hovered over her and he was inside of her surging, groaning, claiming. It didn't seem wrong, just natural—something they both took for granted had to be done, like breathing or eating. He had to have her, and she had to have him. It didn't even seem wrong that they shared intercourse twice before the night was over, sleeping naked together beneath the blankets, then making love once more in the morning. It was all beautiful and delicious and wonderful, and there was no doubt Abigail Trent was no longer a child. Far too much had happened to her now, and she'd been loved by Cheyenne Zeke.

The next morning, she screamed and laughed when he arose, picked her up, carried her to the nearby stream, and jumped in with her. They frolicked under a waterfall, dunked each other, and kissed and touched; then suddenly they hugged each other tightly, both crying, while the water roared nearby. They didn't talk as they walked back to shore, dried off, and dressed. It was done.

Zeke kept an arm about her waist and helped her up the steep embankment to where Olin already had coffee made and most of the gear packed.

"Sit down and have somethin' to eat," he told them, going on about his business as though nothing had happened. Zeke gave her one last hug and helped her sit down, pouring her coffee himself. Then the two men started talking, Olin never once looking at Abbie as though she had done something wrong. In fact, he said nothing at all and asked no questions. It was Zeke's business.

"I've been out this mornin'," he told Zeke, sipping his coffee and lighting a pipe. "Saw signs of Indians—a lot of them—probably more Crow, but not renegades like Givens had along."

350

Zeke lit up one of the cheroots he usually smoked, and Abbie's heart pounded with fear. "Goin' in our direction?" Zeke asked.

"Mmmm-hmmm. Headin' south. Some of their scouts might have seen the train and told the others. Probably figure on doin' some tradin'."

"I hope there's no trouble. Crow and Cheyenne haven't always been the best of friends, and I'd hate to have to be the one in the middle."

"What do you mean?" Abbie asked, her eyes wide.

He looked at her, his eyes giving her the once-over and making her blush. Then he winked. "The Crow and Cheyenne warred bitterly for generations, Abbie. A couple of years ago we came to a peaceful agreement, and things have been better. But if there's any kind of trouble, like, for instance, if Willis Brown or that preacher creates a problem, I won't be able to do much to help them because I'm Cheyenne. They'll figure me to be an enemy, too, so they won't be much inclined to listen to anything I have to say. And if they look at me as a white man, that won't help matters much either. They've got as much use for a white man as they do for a Cheyenne."

"Zeke, I don't think I could take anything more happening—anything bad, I mean. It was a Crow who put that scar on your face, wasn't it?"

He actually chuckled. "Don't get all worked up. I licked that one and I can lick any other Crow—just like those renegades back there."

"Being against a whole tribe is different!"

He smiled and stood up, walking over to pat her head. "Don't worry about it. Long as I'm around, you're not to worry about anything."

"You two ready to head out?" Olin asked.

"Soon," Zeke replied. "I want Abbie to eat good first."

"I'm not hungry," she replied, her heart heavy and her eyes on the verge of tears. She did not want to go back.

"Eat. That's an order," Zeke told her. He handed her a biscuit and some jerky. "It isn't much, but eat it down. I mean it, Abbie."

She took the food, and he bent down to kiss her hair, then stood up and patted her shoulder. Those were his last gestures before they mounted up to leave.

They continued on a southwest course, following the trail of Indians most of the way, Zeke pointing out the tracks of the travois. "Must be a whole village," he told them. "If they're dragging travois, then they're carrying supplies, and they've got women and kids along. A hunting party would travel much faster and they wouldn't be packing along so many supplies."

"They ought to be pretty peaceful then," Olin replied.

"Ought to," Zeke answered, seeming to be lost in thought.

By late afternoon the three of them rode carefully through thick forest as they headed for the South Pass. Zeke had advised them to keep to cover, not caring to run into the Crow just in case they were a bad lot. A few Crow still dealt in buying and selling women, and he did not care to be caught alone against a whole tribe with Abbie along.

Larks fluttered about, as well as butterflies. The delicate and pretty butterflies reminded Abbie of Lee-

Ann. Her aching heart was full of gentle memories of her mother and her home back in Tennessee, and of herself and LeeAnn when they were small, playing with dolls. The whole way of life that had been so dear to her had been torn from her in a matter of a few weeks. Soon Cheyenne Zeke would also be gone, for the next stop was Fort Bridger; and she thought she might die of heartache.

As they crested a hill, below them lay a broad, flat stretch of land that seemed to go on for miles, right through the middle of majestic peaks—mountains that Abbie wondered how they'd ever cross—and there below them was the pathway. Zeke halted his horse.

"There she is," he announced. "The South Pass. Damned pretty sight to a weary traveler."

Abbie smiled. "It's as though God himself put it there to aid people to get through," she replied, fascinated.

"Some say that piece was smoothed out by a big glacier millions of years ago," Olin spoke up. "It just shoved its way through and gouged out the pass."

"Makes a person feel small and insignificant," Abbie replied softly.

"That it does," Olin replied.

Abbie stared in awe at the pass and the surrounding purple peaks. "What a beautiful land this is!" she exclaimed. "I've never seen such a place! I don't think I could ever go back to Tennessee now. It's like . . . like I left a different person back there. I feel like I belong out here now."

Zeke turned to look at her strangely, almost angrily. Then he looked at Olin.

"The train is up ahead," he stated, turning and

pointing. "See it? See them little white dots way out there?"

Olin and Abbie both strained to see. "By God, that *is* the train!" Olin replied.

"Ride on ahead, Olin. Tell them we're on our way. I want to talk to Abigail. Just tell them I'm riding in slow with her because I don't want her riding too hard since we both were wounded—whatever you can tell them. Just so they don't suspect there's any other reason we'd lag behind alone."

"I understand," Olin replied, nudging his horse into motion.

"And tell them . . . tell them you and me *both* took on the Givens men. Tell them they attacked us, killing David, and we fought back. That's how we all got wounded. But we got them all. That way they won't know she got caught alone with them. I don't want them thinking the worse happened to her and asking a lot of embarrassing questions. And I don't want them to know it was me, alone, who found her or that we spent those five or so days in that cave. I don't want them to know any of that."

"I'll tell them. You and Abbie just be sure to keep your stories straight."

Zeke nodded. "We will. Get going."

Olin rode off, and Zeke watched him as man and horse became smaller. Then he spoke up, his back still to Abbie.

"I'll flat out say it, Abbie girl, just so you know for sure. I love you. Don't you ever feel ashamed for what happened. I respect and . . . honor you. You're courageous . . . and beautiful and strong. You're everything a man needs—except this man can't have you

354

because you're white. But I love you, and I want you to always know it. I'm sorry I've hurt you so much. When I'm near you, you create a need in me that drives me crazy. I should be ashamed, taking advantage of a mere child like I've done. A man of my age and experience should have better control. But . . . you're different. It's damned rotten of me to fool with your heart like I have, and I'm sorry."

"There's nothing to be sorry for. Everything that happened was because I wanted it to happen. And . . ." She sat staring at his broad shoulders and the long, thick braid down his back, loving him . . . aching for him. "And if you leave me . . . at Fort Bridger . . . then go with the knowledge that wherever you ride from then on, somebody loves you. Whatever happens to you, you're loved and in you're in my prayers. I . . . I don't think I will ever marry, Zeke. But if I do—Oh, Zeke, it doesn't have to be this way! I can't stand the thought of you being with another woman, and how can you stand the thought of me being with another man!"

He whirled his horse. "Stop it!" he growled.

"I can't help it! My God, Zeke, *why? Why* do we have to part? I've proved to you how strong I am! I *can* live with you, Zeke! I *can* live with your people! I can take whatever—"

"No!" He said it so loudly and so suddenly that she jumped. "No!" he repeated, his eyes full of pain and sorrow. "Never again, Abbie! Never again will I put a woman through what Ellen went through!"

Her eyes hardened slightly in anger. "I never thought you'd be one to be *afraid*, Cheyenne Zeke— Zeke Monroe or whatever you call yourself!" she said boldly. "You can go against men like Givens or a whole tribe of Indians, but you're scared to death to love a fifteen-year-old girl! And you're scared to death of your own memories! It can be *different* out here, Zeke! Out here people *accept* Indian and white marriages!"

"Sure! If the *man* is white and the *woman* is Indian! But not the other way around! How often do you hear about white women running off with Indians? Never! People put *labels* on women like that, Abbie! The only white women who sleep with Indians are the *prostitutes! Whores!* I'll not let you be branded that way. Even if you were my *wife*, they'd brand you!"

"You're wrong, Zeke! This is the *West*. It's *different* out here! People come out here to be *free*—to leave all of those social barriers behind and to live a whole different way! Out here a man or a woman can do whatever he or she wants to do!"

"Can they?" He let out a disgusted sigh and removed his hat, wiping his brow. He looked out over the pass again. "You're a young dreamer, Abbie girl. Moving from one side of the country to another doesn't change human nature. It doesn't change the way people were brought up to believe. People don't change with location."

"And there are always those who have to prove the others wrong," she replied softly. "Those who are strong enough to prove it *can* be different. *You're* that strong, and so am I."

He slumped slightly on the horse. "I'm not as strong as you think, Abbie. I don't doubt maybe *you* are strong enough. But I've got that memory . . . of my

356

wife and little boy laying in pools of blood . . . suffering horribly. I still wake up at night sometimes, screaming their names. Ellen, naked on that bed, her arms cut off, her head shaved . . ." His whole body shuddered. "You're right, Abbie girl. I *am* afraid . . . of seeing something like that again. God knows a man like me doesn't like to admit to a weakness, but that's mine. I just can't risk something like that happening again, no matter how much I love you."

She rode closer and reached out to touch his arm. "But if I lived with the Cheyenne, away from whites, it would be easier—not as likely to happen, Zeke. For you I'd give it all up—a house, wood floors, windows, a fireplace with a clock on the mantle. I'd give up pretty dresses and fourposter beds. What good would a fourposter bed be to me if I was in it with a man I didn't love? I could live anyplace with you, Zeke. I could learn the ways of the Indian. I'd do anything to be with you—*anything!*" The tears came then, streaming down her face. "God, Zeke, I love you so much!"

He turned and reached out to brush at her tears.

"It's easy to talk like that when you're only fifteen, Abbie. But after a while you'd hate me. You'd hate that kind of life, and you'd be longing for all those things. And besides that, Abbie girl, I see an ill wind for the Cheyenne—for all Indians. There are a lot of bad things to come, and they'll get chased from here to the Pacific Ocean. The settlement of this land that's just started can only mean the end of the Indian eventually, as more and more land gets fenced in and there's no place for them to go—nothing for them to eat. Life will get mighty hard for them, Abbie. I see

357

starvation ahead, deprivations, massacres. It's in the wind, Abbie girl. And you'd be right in the middle of it." He shook his head. "It would never work. Never. And I've done a terrible thing to you! Forgive me, Abbie."

She choked in a sob and covered her mouth, turning away. How was she going to live without Cheyenne Zeke?

"There's nothing to forgive!" she sobbed. Then she whirled on him. "I won't let you go out of my life, Zeke! Do you hear me! I won't let it happen! I *belong* to you! And I know it was *you* that you saw standing beside me in that vision you had! It *was*, wasn't it? *Tell* me!"

He jerked his reins, looking angry. "No! I know what's best, Abigail! Now let's get going! The sooner we get to Fort Bridger, the better!" He whirled his horse around in a circle, then started down the hill. She watched him for a minute.

"Zeke!" she called out. "I can't go down! *I can't!*" Tears poured out of her eyes. "It means . . . saying good-bye!" she choked out, as her panic began to build. She could not let it be over! But he just kept riding. "Zeke!"

"Come on!" he ordered. "Those Crow might be around close!"

"Zeke!" She just sat there frozen until finally he realized he'd gone a little too far away and turned to look up at her.

"You're a *woman* now!" he shouted. "And you say you *love* me! This is no easier for me than it is for you, Abbie! Don't you understand that? Please come down! Don't make this so hard on me! I'm doing this *because* I love you! And if you love me, then get down here right now and show me the kind of woman you are, Abigail Trent! *Show* me you're a woman of strength and courage, not a sniffling little girl!"

"I . . . love you," she whispered. He was trying hard to be practical and give her the courage she needed. Why had she picked such a man to love? Why couldn't she love a simple boy like Bobby Jones? It seemed everything that happened to her was destined to turn bad and to bring heartache. She wished a Crow Indian would come along and put an arrow through her heart.

She nudged her horse forward, but that trip to the wagon train was the longest and hardest journey of her life. They rode the rest of the way without saying another word, Zeke staying ahead of her deliberately to keep from talking to her. His stubborn mind was made up.

They reached the wagon train and he went about his business, answering questions from the men while Mrs. Hanes whisked Abbie away, fussing about the awful experience they'd all had and carrying on about poor David and LeeAnn. She insisted that Abbie change into a nightgown right away and lie down to rest from the terrible journey.

Abbie blindly obeyed, feeling numb and weary, yet she could not sleep, for her heart was heavy with awful loneliness. She kept thinking about the cave and remembering those quiet days with Zeke. The cave was far away now, and she'd never see it again—ju~ she'd never see her family again, or even th~ She was filled with desperation and b~ was all over now. Everything was o~

Sixteen

Abbie awoke to hear Willis Brown shout, "Indians!" She was not sure what time it was or how long she had slept after finally managing to get her restless mind to settle down. Now she awoke reluctantly, realizing just how worn out she truly was from that horrible encounter with Givens and his men and the aching loneliness brought on by her family tragedy and by her love for Zeke. She started to drift off again when she realized people were rushing around outside and guns were being cocked. She stretched, rubbed her eyes, and moved to the back of the wagon. The sun's position told her it was late afternoon. She'd slept all the night before, and on Mrs. Hanes's insistence, she'd stayed inside the wagon and slept most of the day, while Olin led her oxen. She had seen nothing of Zeke since they'd gotten back, and she surmised he would make sure she continued to see little of him as they headed for Fort Bridger, where he was to leave them. That recurring thought brought back the awful ache to her heart, but it was dimmed somewhat by the excitement of the moment.

The wagons were circling, and people were bustling about, pulling the stock inside the circle. Mr. Hanes was shoving his children inside their wagon, and Mrs. Hanes was hurrying over to Abbie's wagon.

"What's wrong?" Abbie asked, as the woman came closer.

"Indians are coming—quite a lot of them," the woman replied. "Zeke says they're Crow, and he doesn't completely trust them. Crow like to make war. He said you were to stay inside the wagon, Abigail. All the women are to stay inside."

"But Zeke will be right in the middle of things!" Abbie protested without thinking. She searched her trunk for a clean dress. "I want to be out there! I want to see! What if he gets hurt?"

Mrs. Hanes grabbed her arm. "Abbie, the orders are for the women to stay inside. You know how important it is to do what Zeke and Olin say. They know what's best."

Abbie's heart pounded with apprehension. All she could think of was Zeke. It was as though she had an obligation to be at his side. After all, she loved him, and until they reached Fort Bridger, she still considered that she belonged to him, and he to her, even though he continued to insist they must not think that way. Her eyes teared as she heard the men's voices; but she pulled her arm away and removed her gown, revealing the scratches and faint bruises still left from Givens' men. Mrs. Hanes noticed them and looked away, as Abbie pulled on a slip, insisting she had to go. She picked up her dress, but Mrs. Hanes grabbed it from her.

"No, Abbie!"

"But, he's all alone!"

"And how would it look for you to go running out there, dashing up to his side?" the woman asked gently.

Abbie blushed, suddenly realizing how revealing she'd been about her feelings. Her eyes teared more, and she turned away. Mrs. Hanes touched her shoulder.

"Abbie, I'm a woman, too. Did you really think I don't know that you love him?"

Abbie swallowed and sniffed. "Nobody . . . is supposed to know. He doesn't want anyone to know . . . for fear of me getting a bad name. But he loves me, too. He truly does, and I don't care who knows it!" She burst into tears, and Mrs. Hanes put her arms around her. Abbie cried against her shoulder, longing for her own mother.

"But Zeke *does* care, Abbie. And if you truly love him, you have to let it be *his* way, because he's older and he's been through more, and he knows what's best. He's just looking out for you. That's all."

"But if . . . if you know, then everybody must know!" Abbie sobbed.

"Oh, I'm not so sure about that. Perhaps a few just suspect. No one has said anything as far as I know." She stroked the girl's hair. "And what is the truth about what happened out there, Abbie? I saw your bruises. Did Givens' men get hold of you?"

The girl just cried harder for a moment, and Mrs. Hanes held her tightly. "You poor child! Did they . . . rape you?"

"No," the girl choked out. "Zeke got there first." She pulled away from the woman. "Oh, you should have seen him, Mrs. Hanes!" she added, grabbing a

363

handkerchief to blow her nose. "He got them all—all of them! He was magnificent—everywhere at once! I never saw a man like Cheyenne Zeke! Not ever! He's the most wonderful, strongest, bravest, and yet the kindest and gentlest and—" Their eyes met and Abbie blush deepened before she looked away. "I don't care what you think," Abbie added in a near whisper. "I would never have wanted it to be any other man but him. And I'll never love another man or let another man touch me—not ever!" When she bent over and cried more, Mrs. Hanes touched her head.

"Oh, Abbie, Abbie! You've let yourself in for a terrible, terrible hurt. And so has Zeke. It's such a shame the circumstances are what they are."

"It's for sure . . . an awful ache, Mrs. Hanes," the girl sobbed. "I hurt . . . so bad! So many awful things have happened. But . . . it feels good to tell somebody. It's so hard . . . to keep it inside."

"Of course it is."

Abbie's body jerked in quiet sobs for a few minutes, while Mrs. Hanes just sat stroking her hair, aching for this half-woman, half-child whose mind and heart were so torn. What a terrible trip this had been for her! Abbie blew her nose again and sat up, wiping at her eyes.

"You don't . . . think I'm bad?" she whimpered.

Mrs. Hanes smiled softly. "What a woman does when she's in love is never bad, Abbie. And I'm very sure Zeke knows that, too. But after what he's been through, he's so afraid of what others *would* think. If he's asked you to keep it hidden, then that's what you must do."

Abbie sniffed and pulled on her dress. "He's . . .

leaving the train . . . when we get to Fort Bridger," she told the woman. "He said he could find good scouts there to finish the trip. He thinks it's best . . . to leave before we get to Oregon . . . be on his way and never . . . see me again." She pressed her lips together, a new wave of tears wanting to come.

"Oh, Abbie, I'm so sorry," the woman said with sincere sympathy. "But we'll take good care of you. You'll have a home with us, and in time your heart and mind will heal. You'll grow into a woman and you'll meet another man. Life will be good for you."

Abbie shook her head. "It will never be good for me, not without Zeke. And I *am* a woman. *He* made me that. Besides that I even killed one of Givens' men myself, and I dug a bullet out of Zeke and nursed him back to life. We have something special. Something I'll never have with another man." She breathed deeply to stop the tears. "It . . . feels good to tell somebody. I thank you for listening and not condemning me, ma'am. I need a friend I can talk to."

The woman leaned forward and kissed her cheek. "I'll be your friend, Abbie. And I agree. You've been through too much to be called a child any longer. I'm very sorry—about you and Zeke. Whatever happens, we will support you, Abigail. And for now I'll keep the secret, too." She squeezed the girl's hand. "I must get back to my own children, Abbie. Please promise you'll stay inside the wagon like Zeke asked. He'd be very upset if you got out. You wouldn't want to upset him at a time when he needs to concentrate on those Crow Indians, would you?"

Abbie sighed. "I guess not. I can peek, though, can't I?"

The woman smiled. "I suppose. Just don't let those Crow see you!"

"Yes, ma'am."

Mrs. Hanes patted her arm and left the wagon, and Abbie scurried to the front, folding back the canvas and staring out to the place where the men had gathered outside the circle of wagons. She spotted Zeke right away, standing out ahead of the others and waiting as a large band of Crow men approached; the rest of the tribe had halted far in the distance. This time Zeke did not paint himself or brush out his hair, and Abbie suspected to do so was a sign of respect and that he felt little of that for the Crow. He appeared to be determined to simply act relaxed and unafraid. He leaned on his rifle and lit a cheroot, smoking casually as the Crow warriors came closer. Her heart pounded with pride and fear.

Perhaps the Crow did not put fear into Zeke's heart, but they put fear into the hearts of the rest of the travelers. They wore paint: black on their faces, white around their eyes, and yellow and black over their chests and arms. Abbie watched Morris Connely, who stood a little behind the others, wipe his brow. Apparently Zeke had ordered all the men to walk out and greet the Crow, but Connely was not too happy about the decision. Willis Brown stood staring with his arms folded in front of him, and the preacher stood next to him. Abbie prayed both of them would keep their mouths shut and let Zeke do the talking.

The apparent leader of the band of Crow men rode forward, sitting proudly on his mount in front of Zeke. He looked Zeke over, while Zeke glared back at him. Then the Crow grinned.

"You are tall, and your moccasins are fringed with square designs on the toe." The man spoke in a deep voice. "You have the look of a Cheyenne about you."

Zeke shifted his feet. "Perhaps that's because my mother *is* Cheyenne," he replied.

"And your father?" the Crow asked.

"Hugh Monroe, from Tennessee."

The Crow burst into laughter and his Pinto pony whinnied and tossed its head.

"A half-breed," the Crow sneered. He raised his chin a little. "I am called Iron Hand, and I am *all* Indian! *Crow* Indian! A true Cheyenne would not be afraid to do battle with a Crow, were it not for some of the yellow, white man's blood that runs in his veins!"

Zeke shifted again, taking the rifle and slowly handing it back to Kelsoe, then throwing down his cheroot. "Why don't you climb down off that horse and we'll find out just how much Cheyenne blood I've got in me," he replied calmly. The Crow eyed the big blade he wore on his belt.

"I do not fight with a man whose name I do not know," he replied proudly.

"Glad to oblige," Zeke replied. "I'm called Cheyenne Zeke." The Crow seemed to flinch a little and a flash of fear shone in his eyes for a fraction of a second, but he quickly forced it away. He nodded.

"I have heard of you among my people," he answered, still sitting straight and proud.

"Then maybe you know how I got the scar on my cheek, and what happened to the Crow Indian who put it there," he answered. "I'd be glad to give you a demonstration if you like."

The Crow grinned slightly, obviously struggling to

figure a way out of the predicament into which he'd put himself.

"Let it be known that the Crow and the Cheyenne have come to peace," he finally answered. "I did not come here to fight you, Cheyenne, only to test you out. We are here to trade." He rode the Pinto in a circle around Zeke.

"And just what do you have to trade?" Zeke asked. "And what do you want in return?"

The Crow scanned the wagons and grinned evilly. "You have . . . women perhaps?"

"Not to trade," Zeke answered. "We can give you food—maybe a couple of horses."

The Crow chuckled. "We need no food or horses. But we can trade some horses to you . . . for rifles and whiskey."

Now Zeke grinned a little. "No way. Food's all we'll bargain with—and a few horses. It's all we have to offer."

Iron Hand's grin faded. "You are in no position to argue!" he said haughtily, as another Indian who had remained farther back with the rest of the tribe began riding forward.

"We all shoot straight," Zeke answered, watching the rider in the distance. "But we've done you no harm, and you've no reason to do us harm. I was of the opinion that the Crow wanted peace now. Do you intend to dishonor the Crow name?"

The Crow smiled a little again. "You speak with a clever tongue. Will you trade for tobacco?"

"We can give you some."

The Crow backed his horse. "I will discuss it with my warriors." The approaching Indian came closer, and it was obvious to Abbie that he was not a Crow. He was dressed differently, especially to the fact that he wore a turban. She'd seen few Cherokee in Tennessee, as most had already been run out by the time she was old enough to think about Indians, but she knew by the turban that this odd-looking Indian did not belong on the Plains. He belonged in the Smoky mountains of Tennessee and Kentucky. He was Cherokee. She frowned with curiosity and her heart pounded with fear at the ensuing few seconds and events. At first, no one was sure why the Cherokee was with the Crow or why he had suddenly ridden forward; but as he came closer, scanning the settlers, his eyes rested on Connely. There was a brief moment of almost stunned recognition between the two men, then Connely paled and turned, fleeing to the inside of the circle of wagons and ducking down behind his own wagon wheel, panting and sweating as though greatly afraid.

Zeke frowned with curiosity himself, totally confused at this sudden turn of events. The Cherokee began ranting and raving at Iron Hand in the Crow tongue, while Zeke kept looking from them to the spot where Connely had disappeared inside the circle, his expression changing from confusion to anger as the Crow and the Cherokee argued heatedly. He apparently knew what they were saying, and it most definitely had something to do with Connely, as Zeke continued to look back, his own eyes growing angrier and more disgusted by the minute.

"Cheyenne Zeke!" Iron Hand barked. Zeke turned back to face the man. "It is no longer tobacco we want!" the Crow hissed. "My Cherokee friend here will trade anything—women, precious stones, horses, *anything* of

369

value—in return for the man who just ran!"

The other men looked back and forth at one another in total confusion, and Zeke lit another cheroot.

"I heard him," he answered. "I understand Crow. What's this Cherokee doing living with you?"

"He was chased out of the East by white men!" the Crow spat back, while the Cherokee sat next to him with a bitter sneer on his lips. "You have heard of the Trail of Tears?"

Abbie put a hand to her mouth.

"I've heard," Zeke replied. "I know of it firsthand. I walked it myself with some of the Cherokee. I know how they suffered. I was only thirteen at the time—joined the Cherokee so I wouldn't be found too easy. I was running away from home—headed for the West to find my Indian mother. It was on the Trail of Tears I learned firsthand about suffering and starvation and disease—and real sorrow."

The Crow nodded. "My Cherokee friend says it is that fat white man's fault that he walked the Trail of Tears. It is that white man's fault that he now lives in exile from his *true* homeland!"

"Can he name the man?" Zeke asked.

Now the Cherokee spoke up, obviously understanding English but at first not caring to oblige the others with it. "He is called Morris Connely, is he not?" the man spat out.

Abbie's eyes widened, as did those of the others on the train, with complete surprise that the Cherokee, so many hundreds of miles from home, knew Connely. The Cherokee gritted his teeth and spat at Zeke.

"If you are friend of such white men, then you are not a true Cheyenne!" he growled. Then he turned, said something angrily to Iron Hand in the Crow tongue, and rode off, screaming like a wounded hawk and planting fear in the hearts of the emigrants.

"It is done!" Iron Hand sneered at Zeke. "You have nothing else we want—only that fat white man called Connely!"

"We don't trade for human lives," Zeke replied.

"You have no choice!" Iron Hand snarled. "It is either his life—just one life—or the lives of *all* of you! For if we must go through all of you to get him, we shall do so! *Bring* him to us by sunrise tomorrow, or we will make war on you! There are many of us—and few of you! It would be best if you acted wisely— especially if you have white women with you!"

Iron Hand turned his horse and thundered off, and the other Crow warriors followed him. Zeke watched them ride away, then he turned and stormed toward the wagons, his own face black with anger.

"What is it, Zeke?" Kelsoe asked. "What the hell is going on?"

"I'd suggest we ask Connely!" Zeke growled. "That man has us in big trouble, and I aim to find out why!"

Now Abbie and the other two women scrambled out of their wagons and stood back to watch as the men approached the cowering Connely, whose eyes darted about with fright.

"But we *can't* give them Connely!" the schoolteacher spoke up. "Can't you talk to them, Zeke?"

Zeke whirled on him. "Those are *Crow*, Harrell!" he snapped. "Crow and Cheyenne don't exactly get along. Now if those Indians are all heated up over something about Connely, it isn't likely they're about to listen to anything *I* might have to say! If I go out there, they'll use me for bait to get what they *really* want. I know what the Crow can do to make a man holler, not that I *would* accommodate them by hollering; but I'll be damned if I'll do it for a squirrel like Connely. For you—yes! For the women—yes! But not for *him*—not if he's done what I think he's done! And if he *has*, then my advice is to give him over to them and be on your way! I highly doubt it would be a great loss."

"That's—that's unchristian!" Willis Brown protested, his eyes wide with horror at the suggestion. Connely just clung tighter to his wagon wheel. Zeke stepped closer to Brown.

"Mister, out here you do what's *practical* and *hope* that God will *forgive* you for it! I can tell you right now, them Crow are *mad*, and it's not likely you'll leave this pass alive unless you hand them what they *want!*"

"All right now, wait a minute!" Hanes spoke up. "Let's hear Connely's side of the story! We gave you that option once, Zeke, if you'll remember."

Zeke sighed and nodded. He turned toward Connely, who grabbed up his rifle and pointed it at the men.

"You aren't turning me over to *anybody!*" he warned, getting to his knees. "Especially not that Cherokee!"

"Put that gun down!" Zeke ordered.

"You!" the man snarled back. "You goddamned half-breed! I might have known somebody with filthy Indian blood in him would vote to turn me over to his own kind to be tortured! You stinking, dark-skinned, ignorant savage! You're just like the *rest* of them!"

372

Everyone stared in surprise at Connely, who had never shown any great liking for Zeke, or anyone for that matter, but whose sudden outburst amazed them. Whatever Connely's feelings or background or reasons for coming West had been, he'd been a quiet man and had never shown quite so much emotion.

"Why don't you tell us why it is the Cherokee wants you in the first place," Casey Miles spoke up. Connely's eyes continued to dart back and forth, and he held the gun nervously.

"What have you been hiding?" Zeke asked, undaunted by the man's insults. "Why are you out here?"

"It's none of your business!" the man sneered. "It's *no* one's business!"

"It is, if it means the lives of all these people and something worse than death for the women!" Zeke growled. "Now speak up, Connely, or I'll drag you out there with my own two hands right now and kill any man who tries to stop me! A lot of Cherokees got swindled back East on crooked land deals! Is *that* what happened? You out here looking to set up a business on money you swindled from the government and Cherokee Indians? Is *that* it, Connely?"

Connely raised the rifle slightly, and Zeke took advantage of the man's nervous hesitancy. Before anyone realized what was happening, Zeke's knife was out and he'd brought it down, grazing Connely's forearm. The man had not even thought to cock his rifle when he'd raised it, and by the time he'd remembered, Zeke's knife had sliced through his coat, shirt, and skin, taking a small hunk out of his arm. Connely screamed and cried out, dropping the rifle, and Zeke lunged at him, jerking the panting and moaning Connely to his feet. Zeke held him by his lapels.

"You owe these good people here the *truth*, Connely!" Zeke ordered. He shoved Connely against his wagon. "Now spill it, or you and I will take a little walk outside this circle of wagons!"

Connely shook badly, as he grasped his injured arm and went limp in Zeke's hands. When Zeke let go of him, he slumped to the ground, the sleeve of his gray suitcoat saturated with blood. Zeke bent down and picked up his blade, wiping it and shoving it into its sheath while Connely hung his head.

"Damned, stinking Indians!" Connely mumbled. "And I hate half-breeds even worse! You represent white mixing with Indian—as low as a white man can get!" He raised his head. "*Or* a white *woman!*" When his eyes darted toward Abbie, Zeke's foot came up, slamming into the man's chin and sending him flying backward. The man landed with a grunt, and Zeke jerked him back up again.

"I was *married* to a white woman—one of the finest!" Zeke growled. "You're damned lucky you're *alive*, Connely! But that might not last much longer if you don't give us a straight story! For a remark like that, I'd like to carve you up myself and present you to the Crow in little pieces! Now *talk*, Connely!"

He threw the man back down, and Connely just sat there a moment, swallowing blood and rubbing at his jaw. He coughed, got to his knees, brushed at his hair and clothes, and then grasped his still-bleeding arm. His hair hung in thin, white strands over his forehead now, and he quickly pushed it back with his good hand. Then he grasped his injured arm again, and glowered at the rest of the men, none of whom seemed to feel too sorry for him at the moment.

"All right," he grumbled, looking down at his arm and grimacing at the blood on his coatsleeve. He looked back up at them. "I knew the Cherokee . . . back in Tennessee." He swallowed. "I was a government representative . . . and it was my duty to inform all Cherokees in my territory that if they renounced their tribe and heritage, they would be allowed to remain in Tennessee and would be given several acres of their own. Otherwise, under an act passed in Congress in 1834, they would be rounded up with the other Eastern Indians and put into prison camps—to be sent out here past the ninety-fifth Meridian to the newly established Indian Territory."

Abbie inched closer, watching Zeke, who walked around behind Connely, glaring at the man, while the others listened.

"My father broke my mother's heart by taking up with a whoring Cherokee squaw when I was a boy!" Connely went on. "So I always hated Indians anyway! I deliberately worked myself into a position where I could do them harm. When I got that job, it infuriated me that Indians should be allowed any land at all, no matter what they promised in return for it!" He stood and glanced at Zeke out of the corner of his eye as Zeke came around to his side now, pacing nervously and listening. "Indians are nothing but ignorant vermin!" Connely growled as he continued. "But the government, for some reason, decided they could be made civilized. A few of the Indians actually thought they *could* make it the white man's way. They agreed to stay and work the land, in return for promising allegiance to the United States Government, renouncing

375

their own people, and promising not to cause trouble for their white neighbors."

"The only reason they agreed was because they loved the land where they lived and knew it was the only way to *keep* it!" Zeke barked. "They had little choice. They didn't *want* to go to a strange land!"

"As far as I'm concerned, they shouldn't have been allowed any choice at all!" Connely shot back. Zeke's fists clenched.

"Hold it!" Kelsoe spoke up quickly. "Let's hear the rest of Connely's story." Zeke shifted his eyes to Kelsoe, but he wanted very much to put his hands around Connely's neck and squeeze. Then he turned away, his breathing hard and quick. "Go on, Connely," Kelsoe told the man.

"It was my job to draw up papers for those that wanted to stay," Connely continued. "I only took the job because I wanted to do my part to make damned sure those that stayed got the least amount of land they could be allowed—at least in the territory I covered—and to swindle them out of as much of it as I could. Indians don't have any *right* owning land! I knew how ignorant they were of white men's dealings. It was *easy* to fool them!" He grinned a little. "One of those who stayed was Tall Tree, the Cherokee you saw today. He and the others—they signed the papers I gave them, most just putting strange little marks on them that stood for their names. But I saw to it that in some cases, where the land was extra good, the papers didn't deed the land to the Indians. They deeded the land to *me!* And rightly so! I'm not ashamed of it and I never will be! Why should an ignorant, dirty Indian be allowed that land! *Good* land, it was! Worth a lot

376

of money to a white man! So they ignorantly signed it away to *me!*"

The others looked at him with disgust, and Zeke still stood with his back turned to Connely. His rage radiated from his body.

"So what brought you out here?" the schoolteacher asked.

"The government began to catch on," Connely replied. "Just enough for me to know it was time to finish selling off what I'd got from the Indians and get the hell out with my money! By then I had a lot of land to sell! Each time, after an Indian family would sign the papers that unknowingly deeded the land to me, I sent soldiers to their farms the next day to arrest them for trespassing!" He laughed lightly, haughtily. "The soldiers would have the papers to prove the Indians no longer owned the land, and the Indians were helpless to argue about it! They hadn't the knowledge or the power to reason with the soldiers or prove anything to the contrary! The soldiers would round them up and put them into camps with the rest of their kind! Family by family I got them off the land. Now I've sold it, and I'm going West to found a bank and make some land deals there. I'll be rich! *Rich!* And none of you backwoods farmers is going to *stop* me!" He smiled more broadly. "Nor will you turn me over to those Indians out there! Like Brown said, it's unchristian! I'm still your own kind. You *can't* hand me over to that Cherokee! It would be *blood* on your hands!"

"And there's no blood on *yours?*" Mrs. Hanes spoke up, now moving closer herself. "How could you *do* such a thing, Mr. Connely? And why hasn't the government come searching for you?"

Connely breathed deeply, feeling more confident all the time. "The government doesn't *care* enough about the Indians to really do anything about it. As long as I've left the area and left their service, they'll let it go at that. And all of you ought to be *glad* the government has ways of getting rid of the Indians! It will make this land a better and safer place to live in! This land *ought* to belong to people like us—*civilized* people, with education and a desire to work the land, to farm it and build cities and railroads—bring progress! That's the word! *Progress!* Men like Cheyenne Zeke and those redskins out there don't understand that! Just listen! Listen to the drums those Crow are already beating! Savages! Ruthless savages is all they are!"

He stopped a moment, and they all could hear drums, their rhythmic pattern putting fear in their hearts. The Crow were working themselves up for battle.

"They'll never change!" Connely hissed. "Animals and savages—that's all they are! After my father started mixing with them he turned into a drunk and a wife-beater. And finally one night that slut of a Cherokee woman he slept with came to our house and threatened my mother with a knife, telling her to leave or die! My mother took me and left, and she was never happy again!"

"That's just one incident!" Zeke spoke up. "And it sounds to me like it was your *father's* fault! You can't blame a whole class of people for that! Just like *I* try not to blame all whites for what happened to my wife!" He whirled on Connely. "You call the *Indian* savage! Let's talk about the *white* man! The Indian never *knew* the kind of deceit and savagery the white

378

man can deal out until he began moving in on *Indian* lands, with all his greed and lust for more and more and more! It's the *white* man who has started all the problems—men like *you!* And prejudiced, hateful men like those who killed my wife!" He looked around at the others. "Stick up for him if you want! But Connely represents the worst kind of white man, the kind the Indian hates the most, because his tongue is split and he can't tell the truth! He has helped drive the Cherokee out of the southeast. Do any of you know what those marches were like? I was along on one of them! Civilized, educated, wealthy Cherokees were robbed of everything they had worked for, and herded into filthy barracks on hot, treeless temporary prison grounds until they could be disposed of. I saw *true*, unmerciful savagery! Men and women and little kids being treated no better than *pigs!* I was with some Cherokee and Choctaws back in thirty-eight. They were made to walk—even the old and sick ones! Sometimes they *crawled!* We ran into blizzards that winter, and half the Indians were practically naked because the government had stripped them of everything they owned! They traveled with what they had, most of them sick from already being in prison after being robbed of the land that belonged to them! And hundreds and hundreds of them died on that trail: frozen to death, starved to death, or dying of white men's diseases. Little kids, old people, women—dying off like flies! And nobody helped and nobody cared! I carried a little girl in my own arms for six days, and that's where she died—right there in my arms! The ground was so frozen they couldn't dig to bury her, so we had to just leave her. The soldiers wouldn't even let us take the time to build her a platform to keep her up and away from animals and such. So she was just left behind on the *ground!* You've all heard about it! You know about the Trail of Tears! And that's just what it was! It's a fitting label! And a shameful one for the government!"

"Not everyone had a hand in that, Zeke," Kelsoe spoke up, while Abbie watched Zeke with an aching heart. "A lot of us didn't know they were being treated like that until later, when the stories started leaking out about it. Some of us really thought the government was doing the Indians a favor, giving them land farther West where they could live peacefully farther away from white civilization and that those who remained got the chance to own and farm land and mix in with the white settlers."

Zeke closed his eyes and sighed. "That's where the *white* man's ignorance comes in," he replied resignedly. He glanced at Abbie, then turned back to Kelsoe. "The white man just doesn't understand that the Indian can't live like the white man. The Indian has to be *free!* He can't be confined by fences and wood walls. Most of them aren't farmers; they're *hunters.* And those that were banished didn't *want* the land farther West, no matter how they would be allowed to use it. The Indian has a deep relationship with the land he's always known. Removing him from it is like—like removing a piece of his heart. Those southeast Indians who were removed will never be happy again—*never.* And those who stayed were willing to compromise and at least to try to live like their white neighbors. But the white man won't give them a chance! They got cheated and lied to, but they got no real help from their neighbors or the government - and then men like Connely came along and completely destroyed whatever trust they might have had in the whites. It's men like *Connely* who will never let the Indians rest! Men like him will continue to round them up as the white man moves westward. Indians will be hounded and hunted and murdered and cheated until they're driven to the edge of the land and into the Pacific Ocean!"

"But you're helping *us* settle some of that very land, Zeke!" Hanes spoke up. So far Willis Brown had said little, and the preacher had said nothing at all. Both had learned not to argue too much with Zeke.

"Sure, I've helped a few wagon trains," Zeke replied. "I'm not stupid enough to think that one man can stop thousands from doing what they've got a mind to do. I may be Indian, but I have enough white in me to know the white man won't stop—that this is just the beginning of a migration that will run over the Indians like a herd of unstoppable buffalo. Leading these wagon trains is just my small attempt to seeing that at least some of the whites get through Indian territory without making too much trouble for the Indians—and to see that things go smoothly so that whites don't start something up and then go back with tales about Indian cruelty and uprisings. There's trouble coming—*lots* of it. If I can do some little thing to stop some of it, some small thing to help bring some understanding between Indians and whites while all this moving and settling is going on, then at least I've *tried*. I have the blood of *both* races in my veins, Mr. Hanes. I have enough knowledge of white man's thinking to know *nothing* can stop the movement, and enough Indian in me to want to weep *because* of it!

381

Don't think I don't wish to hell I was all one or the other! It would make life a whole lot easier for me! But I *can* tell you where my heart lies—especially after what happened to my wife. It lies with the Indian. However, I'm here as your guide and scout, and I'm here to help because I *do* understand both sides. And I can tell you right now I understand the Indian enough to know those Crow out there won't rest until they have Connely in their hands—and that's one area of their thinking with which I have to agree!"

"You can't turn me over to them!" Connely shouted, backing up now. "It's murder! Murder!"

"You don't deserve any more than that!" Zeke growled.

"You half-breed scum!"

"Stop it!" Mrs. Hanes shouted. Abbie watched helplessly, wanting to drag the cowardly, cheating Connely out to the Crow herself and wanting to run to Zeke's side. But she could do neither. "There *must* be a solution to this without turning over Mr. Connely!" Mrs. Hanes continued, turning her eyes to Zeke. "I know the man has done wrong—a terrible wrong! But we're Christian people. It goes against everything we believe in to just turn the man over to those Indians, knowing what they'll do to him! Can't you do *something*, Zeke? Can't you talk to them at all? Perhaps you could offer the Cherokee some or all of Mr. Connely's money as recompense."

"You'll do no such thing!" Connely shouted in outrage.

"You've no say in whatever we do!" Kelsoe snapped. "You got us into this mess, Connely!"

"How did I know that damned Cherokee would run

382

across me out here? I never dreamed such a thing could happen!"

Zeke still stood looking at Mrs. Hanes. "That Cherokee doesn't want the money, ma'am," he told her. "Think how you would feel if a man came and told you you had to get off your own land, land promised to you, land you were forced to renounce your own people to keep, land you love more than your own life—especially after you'd decided to stay on it rather than to subject your little children to the horrors of prison and starvation and deportation to a new and strange land. Then you find out you've been cheated by the very government that promised you could stay put and settle and be happy. You find out that in spite of your hard work and sacrifice, you still have to leave and to subject your family to the very things you promised them would not happen. You've been tricked and made a fool of, and soldiers come and haul you out of your home. You have to leave behind all your worldly goods. You're taken to a prison camp where you are forced to live in starvation and filth. Maybe your wife or daughter is raped by the soldiers. Then in the dead of winter you're forced to go to a strange land, forced to *walk* the whole way without shoes or the right clothing for warmth. Some of your family, maybe your *whole* family, dies on the way." He shook his head sadly. "No, Mrs. Hanes. That Cherokee doesn't want money. He has his pride and honor to think about. He needs revenge, and all the money in the world can't change that! I understand the need for revenge, Mrs. Hanes!"

Mrs. Hanes just sighed and nodded, blinking back tears of resignation and experiencing a growing fright for herself, her little daughter, and her young sons. Zeke glanced at Abbie again. He wanted to run off with her to keep her from harm. But he had a duty to this small group of people who had hired him in good faith and who had remained loyal to him after discovering his past. He moved his eyes to Kelsoe.

"You've always voted on these things," he told the man. "I suggest that's what you do now. I say you have no choice but to turn Connely over to them. But that's not my say. It's up to you."

"What are our chances if we stand and fight?" the man asked.

Zeke smiled sarcastically. "Next to none," he replied. He paced silently for a moment, stopping to look disgustedly at Connely. Then he turned to the others. "Would you really risk your life and the lives of the women and children for a man like Connely?"

Kelsoe closed his eyes and shook his head. "My God, man, we can't just . . . turn him over! It's barbaric!"

"What the Crow will do with the women is also barbaric!" Zeke snapped. "And what Connely did to Tall Tree was barbaric! It's a cruel, barbaric world, Mr. Kelsoe!"

"A half-breed ought to understand about barbaric things!" Connely snarled. "Don't listen to that animal!"

"Shut up, Connely!" Kelsoe growled, turning on the man. "You're treading on very thin ground!"

"You can't hand him over like Christians to the lions!" the preacher spoke up haughtily. "Now perhaps all of you understand what heathens these Indians really are!"

384

"And doesn't what Mr. Connely did matter?" Abbie spoke up, unable to hold her tongue any longer. "What he did can be tolerated—just because he's *white*! Does the color of his skin mean he should be allowed to get away with his crimes, and that all of *us* should *suffer* for them? Why is it so wrong for that Cherokee to want his revenge? Why is it wrong for the Indian and not for the white man?"

Zeke shot her a warning look, afraid to have her sticking up for the Indians.

"You *would* talk that way," Connely sneered. "You've been around the half-breed too much. You've been brainwashed." He looked her up and down. "How do any of us know what went on out there while you were alone with him?"

Zeke moved so quickly Connely had no time to move away. In the next second the man's vest and shirt were split open by Zeke's blade, his bared chest and fat stomach popping out. Zeke's blade was flat against the side of his face by then, and Zeke held the thin hair on the back of Connely's head grasped in his fist and pulled painfully tight.

"That could have been your whole midsection—guts and all!" Zeke hissed, moving the blade over the man's face enough to tingle Connely with pain but not cut him. "You apologize to Miss Trent for that remark, or the next swipe of my knife will go deeper—*much* deeper— and I'll save that Cherokee a lot of trouble!"

Connely's eyes widened, and his whole body shivered.

"*Apologize*, Connely!" Zeke growled. "My patience is growing short! You're only alive because of these other people here, but I'm likely to forget about them any minute!"

"I'm . . . sorry," the man mumbled.

"Louder!" Zeke roared.

"I'm sorry!" Connely shouted. Zeke let go and pushed him viciously to the ground. He turned to the others and shoved the big blade back into its sheath.

"As for Connely," he told the others, "I say he gets delivered to that Cherokee. You go ahead and take your vote. If you intend to keep him here and defend his life with your own, I'll help you do battle. But you're all fools! *All* of you! I know how the Crow think! That Cherokee isn't going to let this go, and the Crow are his friends now. They all want Connely, and they'll come for him! I'll tell you right now that when it looks like they're winning, you men had best kill off your womenfolk and your kids before they get through!"

He walked toward his horse, and the others looked at each other in terrible indecision.

"Go ahead and make camp!" Zeke ordered them. "It's getting on to dark. They won't do anything more today or tonight. They'll dance themselves up into a war mood first."

Everyone began to move, slowly, their hearts sick at the sound of the war drums in the distance. All of them wondered what else could go wrong. Their journey had been plagued with tragedy and death. Still, up until now Zeke had been able to help them. But now even Cheyenne Zeke could not make things right. Connely crawled into his wagon to nurse his wounds.

Seventeen

The decision was made. They could not bring themselves to turn Connely over to the Indians. They would stay and fight. Abbie had to sit by and watch quietly, while Zeke seemed to be everywhere at once, giving orders, checking out rifles, riding out and back again several times, trying to decide just how the Crow would come at them, and trying to explain a few things to the farmers who had had no experience in fighting Indians. She worried about his health, for surely the gunshot wound he'd suffered from Givens was not yet fully healed, and Zeke looked tired. She knew he worried about the women more than anything, and he especially worried about Abbie herself. Yet he would not come close to her or speak to her, for he'd made up his mind to end all rumors and never speak of his love for her again. To be held up in the pass by the Indians would only prolong the inevitable, his departure at Fort Bridger—if they ever got there.

"They'll tease us first," he was telling the men now. "They won't give us their all in the first attack. They'll just try to scare us into handing Connely over, show their force, come at us without really doing a hell of a lot of damage. They aren't as bloodthirsty as you think, but they'll get worse if we don't give up Connely."

He was obviously perturbed that they had decided to risk their lives for Connely, yet he respected their decision and their Christian feelings. Abbie was certain that Connely did not appreciate what these people were doing for him. She had never liked the man in the first place, and she had reluctantly voted not to turn him over to the Indians, only because of her own fear of God's punishment if she voted otherwise. But in her heart she had no desire to suffer at the hands of the Crow for a cheating, lying, prejudiced man like Morris Connely.

Night came, and they could do nothing but try to sleep, something that did not come easily to any of them. Abbie lay awake well into the night, thinking about how Connely had not even thanked them for their decision and wondering if Zeke would sleep at all. It was early morning before she dozed off lightly, and it seemed she'd only slept an hour or so before she heard a light tapping at the back of her wagon. She opened her eyes to see the sky just beginning to lighten with dawn.

"Abbie?" It was Zeke's voice. She sat up quickly and moved to the back of the wagon, quickly running her fingers through her hair to straighten it a little; then she opened the canvas flap. Their eyes held a moment, then his darted around to be sure no one was looking. She reached out to touch his face, but he pulled back. "Don't do that!" he said quietly. She pulled her hand away.

"You look so tired, Zeke," she said lovingly. "How about that wound in your side?"

"I'm all right," he replied. He looked around again, then back at her. "I just . . . I wanted you to know I'll be watching out for you when they come."

She smiled softly. "I didn't doubt it." Their eyes held again, and then he turned away.

"You . . . uh . . . you stay under the wagon, not in it. It's hard to shoot underneath a wagon, whether it's arrows or guns. Understand?"

"Yes, sir. And you watch yourself. I'm scared for you."

"If you want the truth, I kind of look forward to shooting a few Crows. It's just the women and children I'm worried about. If not for them, the situation wouldn't be so bad. I still say they should just hand Connely over and be on their way."

"I agree. But I voted to keep him. I guess I have too much Christian white in me. Keeps a person from being practical sometimes."

He smiled a little. "That's true." Bradley Hanes climbed out of his wagon and Zeke stepped farther back. "Load your Spencer and get under the wagon," he said quietly. "They'll come soon as the sun is full up."

She nodded, wanting to hug him and stay close to him, but he quickly disappeared. Her heart ached with love and worry as she quickly rinsed her mouth, splashed water on her face, and checked out her gun. She climbed out of the wagon, grabbing a stale biscuit to soothe her growling stomach. People were moving about now, and Mrs. Hanes was quickly and quietly feeding her children while the men congregated to make last-minute plans. Connely did not join them. He stayed beside his wagon, his face pale with fright, holding his rifle tightly in his hand and waiting.

All too soon they could hear the thunder of horses and the distant hoots of Indians. Mrs. Hanes crawled under her wagon with little Mary, while ten-year-old Jeff loaded a rifle of his own. Abbie kept six-year-old Mike Hanes under the wagon with her, pulling the little boy close and crouching behind two barrels that sat just alongside the wagon.

When the Indians came closer, none of them were ready for what happened next. The men positioned themselves at various places around the circle of wagons, and the yelps and war cries of the Crow chilled Abbie's blood as she prayed for Zeke and the others. Then suddenly Bradley Hanes yelled out.

"What the hell! What's that crazy son of a bitch doing?"

Abbie peered through the crack between the barrels to see the Indians coming, and Preacher Graydon running out to meet them, waving his arms and holding a Bible.

"Repent!" he yelled. "Repent, you heathen sinners! Come to Jesus, and He will cleanse you and make you as pure as the white man! God is my protection! Come to Jesus, you lost people."

"Sweet Jesus, he's lost his mind!" Abbie whispered to Mike.

"Will the Indians kill him?" the boy asked her.

"Most likely," she replied. "You'd best not look." He closed his eyes and covered his face and she hugged him close.

"Get back here, you crazy hypocrite!" she heard Zeke holler. The preacher turned to look back as the Indians came closer.

"You'll burn in hell with the rest of them!" he roared. "I've come out here to do what I can to save the souls of these heathens, and I—"

He did not finish the sentence. In the next moment an arrow pierced his back, and he fell forward. Abbie closed her eyes, yet could not quite feel badly about the man's death. He had been a hypocritical and sorry excuse for a preacher, and he'd even raped Yellow Grass. Soon there was not time to worry about him anyway, for the Indians were upon them. She heard the sharp report of Zeke's rifle, and one of the warriors riding in front fell dead. Then they were circling, around and around, yelping and screeching. She heard someone cry out somewhere, and she hoped no one had been hurt too badly.

She jumped as Zeke's rifle fired again near her, and a Crow warrior screamed and fell from his horse, rolling right toward her and Mike. When he landed no more than six inches from the barrels, Abbie screamed and scooted back. The Indian's hand twitched a couple of times, then stopped.

"Abbie?" Zeke hollered out anxiously.

"We're all right!" she shouted back. The firing continued for several more minutes, but it was obvious the Crow were doing just what Zeke said they would do. They were making more noise and show than actually shooting and killing, and soon they rode off with a couple of Willis Brown's cattle and a few horses. Dust rolled for a minute or two, and when it settled, the Crow were gone.

It seemed the fighting had ended as quickly as it had begun. At first they all stared at each other, not sure if they could relax. A lot of dead Indians lay outside the circle, a gruesome sight.

"Anybody hurt?" Zeke called out, as the women and children crawled out from under the wagons.

"I think just me," Kelsoe replied. "Grazed my arm. Nothing serious."

"Come here and let me have a look," Zeke told him.

"Looks like we lost our preacher," Kelsoe told him as he walked up to where Zeke stood.

"No great loss as far as I'm concerned," Zeke answered bluntly. He looked past Kelsoe at the others. "Two of you men go on out and get his body. Bury it quick. They won't be back for a while—maybe not even until tomorrow." The men left and Zeke tore open Kelsoe's shirtsleeve to study the wound. "Not real bad." He looked over at Abbie. "Put some whiskey on it for him, will you? And bandage him up." He looked around the circle. "Where in hell is Connely?" he asked. They all searched around, at first thinking the Crow had somehow got hold of the man; but then Connely came crawling out from under his wagon, and it was obvious to them he'd not even joined in helping with the fight.

"You yellow-bellied skunk!" Willis Brown blurted out. "Here all these people are risking their lives for you, and you cower under your wagon like a woman!"

Connely swallowed and looked around. "I . . . I had to stay low," he tried to explain. "If they see my face, they'll ride inside the circle and take me. Surely you all realize I couldn't let them see me!"

Zeke's jaw flexed in anger. He stormed over to the

392

man and backhanded him hard, making Connely's body spin around and fall flat. Zeke turned to the rest of them.

"I say I take him to them right now!" he growled.

Kelsoe frowned, holding his wounded arm. "I have half a mind to myself, Zeke. But we took a vote. And we still have to do the Christian thing. Let's wait it out. Maybe they won't come back."

"They'll be back, all right! And they'll be thirsty for blood! And if one person—just one person—gets hurt bad, I'm taking Morris Connely out there to them, and that's my final word! I don't give a damn what *any* of you think! You were supposed to take my advice on these things. And I'm telling you it's Morris Connely or *all* of us! They deliberately let us think we have the upper hand. The second time around will be worse. Then they'll come at us harder and harder! And you'd best go easy on the water! If they can't drive us out by fighting, they'll starve us out and keep us from getting fresh water. Before long you'll understand that out here all that counts is being practical. The word is *survival*, people! *Survival!* That's all that matters! You've come West, and now you're going to have to learn to live by a different set of rules!"

He stalked off to help bury the preacher, and Connely picked himself up and climbed sullenly into his wagon.

The day lingered for what seemed an eternity to the frightened and anxious settlers. Occasionally each would glance out at the grave of Preacher Graydon with mixed emotions. He had been a hard man to like, and a foolish one for exposing himself as he had, pompously believing that God would protect him from the "heathens." And there had been his shameful attack on Yellow Grass. Still, the man was dead, and some of them could not help but be sorry for him. But all knew that what bothered them most about the grave was their own fear that they, too, would soon be dead.

The rising sun brought a warmer than usual day to the high mountain pass, and there was little movement or talking—only endless waiting for the hated sound of renewed Crow war cries.

Bradley Hanes had suggested they just pick up and move on, but Zeke warned them that breaking up the circle would leave them too vulnerable.

"They *want* you to think they aren't coming," he told them. "They want you to start moving and break into a straight line. You'd be playing right into their hands."

"But this could go on and on!" Willis Brown complained. "They could keep us here until we all—" He stopped short, not finishing the sentence.

Zeke nodded. "That's right. But you folks made the decision. Apparently you think Morris Connely is worth dying for."

Connely remained inside his wagon, unwilling to face the others and afraid to be out in the open at all. Yolanda Brown lay weeping and fretting in her own wagon, occasionally becoming hysterical and screaming that the Crow were going to cut her baby out of her stomach. Zeke ordered Willis Brown to pour some whiskey down his wife's throat to quiet her down.

The day melted into afternoon, and now Zeke slept beneath the shade of the Hanes wagon. Only Abbie and Olin knew just how badly the man was probably hurting. Abbie had noticed him occasionally rub his side as he rested. She was sure he had not slept at all the night before, and she worried about his still-healing wound, longing to go to him, to hold him, and to assure herself that he was all right. It was torture to watch him and not be able to care for him. She wondered if violence was something that would always follow someone like Cheyenne Zeke. Surely to live with him would entail always fearing for his life; yet the worry and fear would be worth it if she could be his wife. She tried to imagine what his mother and half brothers must be like. Full-blooded Cheyennes. How well would they accept a white woman into their clan? That question sent shivers through her blood. Were the Cheyenne any different from the hated Crow who lurked out there in the hills now?

She sighed and walked a few feet from her wagon to gaze out at the green foothills. Perhaps he was right. To think she could live among a people so different was just the daydream of a foolish young girl. And yet, to live without him . . .

She stared at the gray, snow-capped peaks of the Rockies, standing silent and magnificent, always far off and untouchable. She wished life could be as sure and dependable as those mountains. They had probably been there for millions of years and would still be there thousands of years after her own small self was dead. No matter what happened to the Indians, no matter how the white man's progress affected the West, the mountains would never change. She decided this land was probably the most beautiful place God had ever designed. It was splendid and immense, painted in beautiful colors. Yet it could fool a person. For it was also dangerous and threatening. It beckoned a person on, like a witch beckoning children into her home so she could eat them. Abbie felt that it was eating her, piece by painful piece. Yet she knew that no matter what this land did to her, she could not leave it. Tennessee would never be the same.

"You're straying a little too far," Bobby Jones stated from behind her. She jumped and turned, startled by his voice, and surprised to see that she had absent-mindedly wandered away from the wagons as she stared at the Rockies. Bobby Jones had spotted her and hurried up behind her with his rifle.

"Oh!" Abbie replied, blushing slightly. "I . . . the mountains are so beautiful . . . I guess I just kind of lost myself." She glanced back at the train to see Zeke still asleep, then looked around at the distant foothills. "There's nothing out here but a few rocks anyway," she went on. "If those Indians come again, we'll hear them in plenty of time."

"Zeke says they're tricky. They can sneak up on you right easy, Abigail."

She glanced around again, crossing her arms in front of her nervously, then looked back at Bobby. "You scared, Bobby?"

He shrugged. "Some. I guess all of us are—except maybe Zeke."

She smiled a little and blushed. "I think he just acts first and gets scared later," she answered. "Sometimes there just isn't time to be scared. You just dive in and do what needs to be done and don't think about being scared."

"I guess." Bobby sighed, watching her closely.

"I've been meaning to tell you, Abigail . . . well . . . we might not live through this . . . and just in case we don't, I want you to know . . . I watch you all the time and I . . . like you a lot, Abigail. You're awful pretty, and I'm damned sorry for the terrible things you've suffered on this trip."

Her stomach felt fluttery at his compliment, and she blushed more, unaware he'd had such feelings for her. She smiled nervously. "Thank you, Bobby."

"I . . . uh . . ." He sighed again. "I thought maybe, once we get to Oregon . . . *if* we get to Oregon . . . maybe I could . . . see you?"

She glanced at Zeke again. It would be foolish to say no to Bobby Jones. What kind of future was there for her if she didn't at least consider someone else? Cheyenne Zeke had apparently said his last word on the subject. There was no future with him. Yet how could a boy like Bobby Jones compare to the man who had been first to make love to her?

"I guess that would be . . . fine," she replied, turning away to hide the tears in her eyes. Her heart ached for Zeke. And she knew that to take another man to her bed would be to deceive him, for in her mind and heart she would be lying with Zeke. "Oregon . . . is still far off, Bobby. A lot could happen."

"I know that." He put a hand to her waist and urged her a little farther away. "I just . . . well . . . it helps a man fight better when he knows he has something to fight *for*, something he can think about in the future to stay alive for."

She turned to face him, a tear slipping down her cheek. "Bobby, I can't promise—"

"Hell, I know that," he answered with a smile.

"And I've seen . . . how you look at him." Her eyes widened in surprise, and he caught her hand. "It's all right, Abigail. I understand. I just . . . just wanted you to know I care . . . and that if— Well, Cheyenne Zeke is wild and half Indian. It's not likely he'll keep you with him. I know I'm not much by comparison, but I don't want you to be alone, Abigail. So I just want you to know that if things don't work out, if you get to Oregon and you're alone, I'll stay around. I won't go back East. I care about you and I want to be with you."

She hung her head. "That's very nice, Bobby. I appreciate that. I truly do. I'd be . . . honored to see you, if things happen like you say. But I . . . care very much for him, Bobby. And you must know, I'm hoping things will work out differently, although Zeke is determined they won't."

"He's a wise man."

She looked up at him, unable to deceive his goodness. "Bobby, you . . . you might not *want* to see me. I mean I . . . I kind of belong to Zeke." He frowned a little, and then a rather sorrowful disappointment flashed through his eyes. But she saw no anger. "Do you know what I mean?" she asked boldly, her face reddening.

"It's something I already suspected," he replied. "Fact is, some of the others probably do, too."

She turned away. "I don't hide my feelings too well, I guess," she answered. "And Zeke is so determined nobody should know. Seems kind of silly, doesn't it? Trying so hard to hide something everybody already knows. But that Zeke, he's stubborn and immovable as those mountains out there. And I guess nothing will change his mind. He's determined it could never work with another white girl, and when we get to Fort Bridger, he's . . . he's leaving the train." Her voice broke slightly. "He's going back . . . to his people on the Arkansas River, and I expect that's the last . . . I'll see of him."

She sniffed and her shoulders shook. Bobby grasped her shoulders in his hands. "Don't cry, Abbie," he said softly. "And don't be ashamed. I understand. A girl so young and so lonely, she's bound to turn to a man who's older and strong and sure of himself. A man like him would be easy for a girl to . . . to love, but I expect he'd be hard to live with, Abigail."

She nodded, wiping at her eyes and blowing her nose. Bobby turned her around.

"Abigail?"

She looked up at him.

"In case we all . . . die right here, I wonder if . . . you'd let me kiss you."

She smiled bashfully and looked down. "Bobby, I can't kiss somebody I don't love, I mean . . . not that way."

"Oh, I don't mean anything disrespectful, and I don't even mean it has to be any kind of promise. I just . . . want to kiss you. Sometimes *friends* kiss, Abbie. And I'm *your* friend. I just want you to know . . . how sorry I am about all you've been through. Lots of times I just wanted to hold you and tell you not to worry."

She sniffed again and looked up into his handsome but boyish face. Their eyes held a moment, and then he hesitantly bent down, meeting her lips and kissing her sweetly. But suddenly his body jerked, his grip on her shoulders tightened for a moment, and he pulled back a little.

"I . . . love you, Abbie," he said in a strained voice. "Run! My God, run, Abbie!" He slumped to the ground, and she stood there frozen for a moment, staring down at Bobby, who had an arrow in his back. A cold shiver passed through her.

"Bobby!" she screamed. "No! No! No!" She looked up to see a black-faced, white-eyed Crow looking back at her as he moved out from behind a large boulder where he'd been hiding. He was grinning. She quickly picked up Bobby's rifle, but the Indian just stood there, still grinning, apparently sure that the white woman would not know how to use a gun. Abbie quickly cocked and fired the rifle, and the Indian jerked backward, looking wide-eyed and stunned as blood poured from the center of his chest. Then he fell backward. Abbie looked down at Bobby again, turning him on his side.

"Bobby!" she screamed. "Bobby! Bobby!" She knew he was dead. For some reason his death hit her as hard or harder than those in her own family, for it was like seeing all hope for her future die with him. Here lay the nice boy who had quietly loved her. In him there had been a chance she could be happy without Zeke. Now everything would end for her at Fort Bridger. She screamed his name again desperately, shocked and somewhat maddened by the thought of sweet Bobby's lips on her own at his death.

She felt a darkness swimming around her, but a bloodcurdling screech from another Crow Indian brought her back to reality. As she stood up, she saw Zeke running toward her from the wagon train. She wondered how she and Bobby could have been so foolish as to wander so far from it, and she suddenly realized her own danger. She whirled to see that the second Indian who had screamed was running toward her, hatchet raised. She tried to fire Bobby's rifle again, but it jammed. So she threw it down and started running, keeping her eyes on Zeke, who was headed toward her, yelling at her now to run and run fast.

"Zeke!" she screamed. "They killed Bobby! They killed Bobby!"

She ran hard, but when she got within a few feet of Zeke, a horrible pain ripped through her left shoulder, all the way through her and to just above her left breast. As she gasped and staggered, she saw Zeke pull out his side arm and start firing. Then she could hear the Indian behind her cry out. There was the sound of distant horses, their hooves thundering; of Indians hooting and hollering, and then of guns being fired from both sides. Zeke and Abbie were caught in the middle of the cross fire, and he grabbed her and pulled her down to the ground. Glancing down at her painful shoulder, she saw an arrowhead sticking out of the left side of her chest.

"Zeke! Zeke! Zeke!" she screamed, gunfire all around them. "Oh, God, help me!"

"Hang on, Abbie girl," she heard him say lovingly as blackness began to envelop her. She felt herself being lifted and knew he was running with her in one arm, while shooting with his other hand. She hated herself for getting into such a mess and for putting Zeke in such danger. She clung to his buckskins while he dragged her back.

401

Soon she sensed they were inside the circle of wagons. She felt herself lying on the ground, and the horror and agony of the ugly arrow in her body overwhelmed and frightened her.

"Get it out! Get it out!" she screamed. "God, help me, Zeke! Get it out of me!"

"Calm down, Abbie!" he replied in a shaking voice. It was the first time she had ever detected fear in the man. "What in God's name were you *doing* out there?"

"Get it out!" she screamed again. She tried to tug at it herself, but it only made the pain worse.

"Jesus Christ, Abbie, you've got to calm down!" Zeke was ordering her. "Come on, now, where's my brave Abbie?"

He kept her on her right side, now pulling her wrists behind her to keep her still. He couldn't lay her on her back or her stomach, as the arrow stuck out of both sides. All around her she could hear a volley of rifle fire, men shouting orders, Indians screaming, horses thundering around the train.

"Help me, Zeke!" she sobbed. "I'm scared! I'm scared! Get it out of me!"

He put a hand under the side of her face that rested against the ground, hollering above the gunfire for Mrs. Hanes to bring a pillow and blanket. He had not had time to get her into a wagon, but she lay almost underneath her wagon where she would be relatively safe.

"Abbie, I have to help with the fighting," he told her, bending down close to her ear. "But I'm the only one who can take that arrow out of you. You've got to be brave for me and hang on until the Indians leave again."

"No! Take it out now! Now!"

"Damn it, Abbie, I *can't!* I'll help you just as soon as I can, girl. Please, please just lay still, Abbie! Still as a rock. It's very important that you don't move at all. If you lay still, honey, the pain won't be as bad, and there won't be so much bleeding."

"I can't! I can't lay here with this thing in me!" she screamed hysterically.

"You've *got* to!"

"Oh, Zeke, help me!"

"You've got to help *me,* too, Abbie, if I'm to help you later! You've got to stay calm and do like I say!"

Mrs. Hanes came with the blanket and pillow, and Zeke put the pillow under Abbie's head and covered her with the blanket. "Keep her propped this way!" he ordered. "Don't let her move!"

"Dear God, what more can happen!" Mrs. Hanes fretted, tears in her eyes.

"Nothing more!" Zeke growled. "Soon as I get this arrow out of Abigail, I'm taking Connely to the Crow, and nobody here is going to stop me! This is *his* fault! And they've killed Bobby Jones! If Abigail dies, I'll *help* the Crow torture Connely!"

"Zeke, we didn't think it could really go this far," Mrs. Hanes tried to explain.

"Just keep her still!" Zeke replied.

Their conversation seemed far away to Abbie and had an echolike quality. Her head swam from pain and fear. She heard more shooting and cursing, horses whinnying, children crying, Indians screaming. She breathed dust and felt her body shaking violently, uncontrollably. She knew she was in shock, knew the arrow was still in her, and she tried hard not to think about that, but it was impossible. Then she sensed someone at her side.

"Drink this, Miss Abbie," came Olin's distant voice. "It tastes bad, but you'd best drink plenty of it and get numbed up now so Zeke can take that arrow out just as soon as this is over."

Someone raised her head, and she coughed and choked on the whiskey. She swallowed as much as she could, her insides in flames, and then things quickly began to swim and fade before her eyes. She was still aware of the pain, only it had become more of a dull throb that burned into her with every heartbeat. She wondered if she was dying and she called for Zeke, thinking she was screaming when she was actually barely audible.

Then it seemed to be quieter again. She could smell smoke, and she felt herself being lifted.

"Won't be much left of Connely's wagon," she heard someone say.

"And nothing left of Connely himself when that Cherokee finishes with him," came the reply from the man who lifted her.

"Zeke?" she whispered.

There were more voices, and she knew she was screaming as someone laid her down again, but at least now she lay on something soft and cool.

"Abbie? Can you hear me, Abbie girl?" Zeke asked. "Don't you go and die on me, Abbie!" Someone kissed her cheek. "Hold her arm up a little, Olin," the voice continued. "I've got to cut off this dress. There's no other way to get it off."

"How are you fixin' to get that arrow out?" came a

man's voice in reply.

"I'll have to break it first, and that won't help her pain any. But with a head and a tail on it, I can't do it any other way. I just hope the arrowhead wasn't poisonous."

"Zeke!" she sobbed, coming around a little.

"I'm right here, Abigail. You lay still and be a good girl for me, and I'll have this damned thing out of you in no time."

"It . . . hurts! It hurts!" she moaned.

"I damned well know it hurts, honey," he answered. "I've felt it before myself."

She was vaguely aware of her dress being stripped off to her waist, but she didn't care. She just wanted the arrow out of her chest and the pain diminished. She felt a gentle hand on her back, and then it moved around to her chest and breast. Someone else was holding her left arm up and stroking her hair while her head rested on a pillow.

"I don't think any vital organs are damaged," she heard Zeke say. "But she's going to be one sick and sore little girl. The dangerous part could be infection." She felt the arrow move a little, and in agony, she screamed.

"Don't touch it! Don't touch it!" she shrieked, terrified.

"Abbie honey, I've got to get it out," came Zeke's voice. "Now a while ago you were screaming for me to get it out of you. I can't do that without touching it, Abbie girl. I'm damned sorry, but I've got to hurt you before I can help you."

She just lay there, crying, and his heart ached for her.

"This goddamned thing is made of buffalo bone," she heard him say. "There's no way I can break it, and it would be too painful to have her lay here while we saw it."

"How about a hatchet?" she heard Olin reply. "That would be quick. Brace somethin' underneath it and give it one chop. That wouldn't even move the shaft much."

Zeke sighed. "Damn!"

"Calm down, Zeke," Olin replied. "She needs you. Nobody else here can take that arrow out—except maybe me. You want me to do it?"

Abbie heard an odd, choking sound. She sensed it was Zeke crying, but she was too lost in her own pain to be sure.

"I'll do it," came his strained reply. "Go get the hatchet."

"She'll be all right, Zeke."

"The kid's been through hell!" she heard Zeke groan in reply, "It's not fair!"

She sensed that Olin had left the wagon for a moment, and although she could hear Zeke breathing deeply, he said nothing. But he kept her still, gently stroking her hair until Olin reentered the wagon. She heard some scraping sounds; then something was pushed up against her back. She screamed again before she heard Mrs. Hanes' voice outside saying she had some hot water. There were more voices, and Abbie floated in and out of consciousness as a great deal of commotion seemed to be going on around her. Then she heard a thud, and the arrow jerked some; and she screamed again.

"I've cut off the tail of the arrow, Abbie," Zeke told

406

her. "Now you'll have to be real, real brave, because I've got to pull this thing out of you. They don't come out easy, Abigail."

Her only reply was to cry harder.

"Hang on to her," Zeke told Olin. "Kelsoe, you keep hold of her ankles."

Abbie felt embarrassed because Kelsoe was there; she was aware that she was naked from the waist up. But their voices were gentle, and the grasp of their hands was gentle, until Zeke straddled her body and pressed his thighs tightly against her stomach and back to hold her firmly, then told the men to tighten their grips. When their hands tightened on her, her fear mounted and her body shook.

Then came the horrible, black pain, as Zeke tugged at the arrow, finding it difficult to get out despite his own strength. Abbie's shrieks filled the pass, and she let out with a volley of cursing and swearing. She screamed that she hated them all for hurting her, that she hated Indians and the West, hated mountains and wagon trains, and she screamed at Zeke because he hadn't just let her die.

Then there was one last jerk, and one last, long scream out of Abbie. After that, she felt her senses fading fast.

"She's bleedin' bad, Zeke," came Olin's voice.

"Get some whiskey on there and let's bandage it tight!"

She felt hands quickly working on her and a terrible sting in her wound, then bandages coming around her breast and back.

"That's the hardest thing I've ever done," she heard Zeke saying, his voice actually shaking.

"She'll make it, Zeke," Olin replied. "She's a fighter."

"I . . . shot one." Abigail recognized her own voice. She wondered who had moved her mouth.

"What?" Zeke asked.

"I . . . killed . . . one of those . . . black-faced . . . goddamned Crows!" Abbie groaned.

She heard Olin chuckle.

"Jesus Christ, she's a regular Cheyenne at that," Zeke commented.

Those were the last words she heard before she passed out.

Eighteen

The first time she opened her eyes again, Abbie saw Mrs. Hanes sitting near her feet, reading the Bible. The wagon was moving, and Abbie winced with pain when it bumped over a rock.

"Where are we?" she asked weakly.

Mrs. Hanes looked up and smiled. "Abbie!" She moved closer. "Do you know me, child?"

"Sure I do," she replied, frowning.

"You've been delirious for two whole days," the woman replied. "We've been so worried about you. How do you feel now, Abigail?"

She tried to move her left arm, but the moment she even wiggled her fingers pain shot through her shoulder and chest and she suddenly felt sick to her stomach. "Not . . . very good, ma'am," she replied.

"Perhaps it would help you to eat," the woman told her. "As soon as we stop, I'll fix you some hot broth."

A tear slipped down the side of Abbie's face. "I hurt awful bad," she whimpered. "I don't want to be . . . a baby about it, but I never . . . hurt like this be-

409

fore!"

"Stay calm, Abigail," Mrs. Hanes said soothingly, stroking her hair back from her face. "Of course you hurt. You have a very bad wound, and Zeke says it will hurt for quite some time. He figures you can rest up good at Fort Bridger, and he's hurrying to get you there to a solid bed that doesn't move. But it will be a rough ride and could be another seven or eight days."

"Where are we?" she asked again. "Where's Zeke? Was it him that took the arrow out?"

"Yes, it was, and a hard thing for him to do, I'll say. I've never seen that man so shaken. Right now we're headed out of the South Pass. Soon we'll be at a place called Little Sandy Creek. Zeke says the trail forks there, going south to Fort Bridger, or west through a cutoff. But the cutoff is a rough route, and Zeke says it isn't worth the time saved. We've been through enough, so he's not taking any chances. Hopefully we've seen the last of our bad luck."

"I want to see Zeke."

"We'll stop soon. You can see him then."

Abbie closed her eyes and sniffled. "What happened . . . about the Indians . . . and Mr. Connely?"

Mrs. Hanes frowned, wetting a rag and gently washing Abbie's face as she spoke. "Some of the Crow broke through," she replied quietly. "Then they burned Mr. Connely's wagon and dragged the man off, and I'm afraid we all just . . . watched." Her voice faded and her eyes filled with tears.

"You shouldn't feel bad, ma'am," Abbie told her, feeling sorry for this kindhearted woman. "It would have been foolish . . . to interfere. Just think about

410

your children . . . them getting hurt or killed. You couldn't have stopped all those Crow Indians. It's like Zeke . . . says. Out here a person has to . . . be practical."

"Yes. And that's the hell of it," the woman replied, surprising Abbie by using the word hell. She dabbed at her eyes. "Sometimes practical means going against what's really right to do. I hope God can forgive us. I can see what a hard life it will be out here. Lord knows I'd not have come if not for my husband's big dreams."

"You must . . . love him a lot," Abbie replied, wincing with pain again.

"Bradley is a good man. A man is always dreaming, Abbie. You remember that. If a woman stifles those dreams, she stifles him, and their marriage isn't any good anymore. But if she lets him grow and stretch out and be free, he'll always be at her side. If a woman is clever enough, she can have a man tied to her apron strings without his even knowing it."

Abbie's heart seemed to pain her as much as her wound, and she wondered which was wounded more. "There's no tying down . . . a man like Zeke," she replied.

Mrs. Hanes sighed and sponged around Abbie's neck. "If not for his past haunts, that man would let you tie him down in a minute," she replied. "I've never seen someone so worried as he's been about you. He's going to be glad you're awake and coherent." She felt Abbie's forehead. "But he won't be happy about this fever. You feel awfully warm, Abbie."

"I'm . . . burning up," Abbie answered, closing her eyes and already feeling tired from their little bit of talk. "Is everyone . . . all right?"

411

"Yes, My husband has a deep scratch on his cheek from a wood chip that flew when a bullet hit near our wagon. Willis Brown got a laceration in his leg from an arrow, but it isn't serious. And so far Yolanda is still hanging on to her baby. But, of course, we lost Bobby."

Abbie's eyes rapidly filled with new tears. She thought of the sweet words he had spoken to her just before he died, and of his tender kiss. "Oh, poor Bobby!" she sobbed. "Oh, God, I feel so alone!"

"Please don't cry, Abbie. I'm sorry I mentioned him. Crying will just make your wound hurt more, darling. It makes your body jerk. Please stay calm."

"I want to see . . . Zeke," the girl sobbed. "I don't want . . . to wait! I want to see him now!"

She could not stop her crying, even though it did make the pain worse, as Mrs. Hanes had said it would. The pain, the memory of Bobby, and the realization that the time was drawing near when Zeke would leave her, all combined to drive her into near hysterical crying that could not be stopped. Mrs. Hanes tried to calm her to no avail, so finally she crawled to the front of the wagon and called out to Olin, who was leading Abbie's oxen.

"Yes, ma'am?"

"See if you can get a signal to Zeke! Abbie's awake and she's getting almost hysterical. She's feverish, Olin, and she's asking for Zeke."

"Whoa! Whoa there!" Olin's voice boomed at the oxen. "Slow down, you damned stupid animals!" It took a moment for the wagon to slow to a halt. "Hold on up the line there!" Olin hollered out. "Somebody get Zeke back here!"

There were more shouts, and Abbie could hear cursing as others pulled their wagons to a halt. Abbie's crying continued, her emotions fed by heartache, loss, pain, and weakness. Nothing could make her feel better except Cheyenne Zeke's face, his voice, and his touch. Her sorrow was compounded by a fear of dying from some horrible infection, for she had a fever, which usually meant only one thing. She remembered how poor little Jeremy had died and wondered if she would suffer the same way. A moment later Olin Wales was climbing into the wagon beside her.

"Hey, Abbie girl! What's an Indian killer and a brave little girl like you doin' cryin'?"

Her tears continued, and she could not answer him.

"Please try to calm down, Abbie!" Mrs. Hanes said anxiously.

"Hey, Miss Abbie, everything is gonna be okay," Olin assured her. She could hear a horse thundering up then, and she knew whose mount it was. Only a moment later Zeke climbed into the wagon from the front, and Mrs. Hanes moved to a back corner to make room for his big frame, shutting the canvas so no one else could look inside.

"Hey, Abbie girl, are you really awake? What's with the tears?" Zeke asked as he took hold of her good hand. "And here I was bragging about what a brave girl you are—brave and strong as any Cheyenne squaw."

"Am I . . . really?" she responded, wanting to die from the pain. She felt his big hand at the side of her face.

"Sure you are. You know I never lie."

"I'm scared, Zeke!" she sobbed. "It hurts . . . so

413

bad! I'll die out . . . here, like pa . . . and Jeremy
. . . and LeeAnn! I'll die out here . . . all alone . . .
and be buried . . . where nobody will ever know! I'll
die all alone!"

He bent down and kissed her forehead. "That's not
so, Abbie. I won't let you die, and you sure as hell
aren't alone." He brushed at her tears with his thumb.
"Please don't cry, Abbie. It breaks my heart to see
you cry."

"I can . . . stop . . . if you . . . stay here," she
choked out. "Don't go away . . . Zeke!"

He sighed. "All right. We'll camp right here. It's
getting close to dusk." He looked at Olin. "Go tell the
others." Olin nodded and left, and Zeke asked Mrs.
Hanes to help him change Abbie's bandages. "I don't
like this fever," he said with concern. "I want to check
the wound. She feels mighty hot to me." He bent
down close to her. "Hang on, Abbie. I said I wouldn't
let you die. You can't make a liar out of me, Abbie
girl."

"Don't go away!" she pleaded again.

"I'm right here. Now you calm down." He pulled
the blankets down to her waist, and she realized she
wore no clothes beneath the blankets. She tried to see
her bandages, but she couldn't even bend her head
down.

"Don't make me move my arm!" she screamed as
soon as he touched her.

"I'll try not to move you too much, Abbie, but I
can't help but move you some." He looked at Mrs.
Hanes. "She been urinating?"

"Yes. All her functions seem to be working nor-
mally. And there's been no vomiting."

414

"Good."

Abbie reddened at the casual conversation about her bodily functions. She could tell by the feel of things that her bottom was wrapped in some kind of rags or towels. She felt humiliated and embarrassed.

"I'm a baby!" she whimpered. "I'm just a big baby!"

"Like hell!" Zeke answered. "You can't help yourself, Abbie. It's important for you to lie very still. You can't get up for anything. If you try to, I'll tie you down. I don't want any complications. And as soon as I'm done here, I want you to eat something. All you've gotten into your stomach for two days is water and whiskey."

"I'm sorry I'm . . . such a burden," she sobbed.

"Don't be silly," Mrs. Hanes answered. "You're badly wounded and we all want to help you."

"Go get Olin back in here," Zeke told the woman. "He's got to hold her up a little, while I cut off these bandages and check for infection."

Mrs. Hanes summoned Olin, and Abbie looked up at Zeke, who was taking out his knife. Their eyes met.

"Promise me . . . you won't let me suffer . . . like Jeremy did," she whispered. "Use that knife on me, like you did on Jeremy . . . if I'm bad infected and you know I'll die anyway. Promise me!"

His eyes filled with tears and he nodded. "I promise," he told her. She knew he meant it.

"I'm sorry . . . for all the things I said . . . when you were taking out the arrow," she whimpered. "I don't hate you . . . or even the Indians. I love this land, Zeke."

"A man would be crazy to believe what a person

415

says when he's in pain."

"I love you," she whispered. "Please . . . tell me again . . . that you love me, Zeke!"

He touched her hair. "You know I love you, Abbie girl."

Just then, Mrs. Hanes was came back inside with Olin, so Zeke withdrew his hand and grew cooler again.

"She knows, Zeke," Abbie said quietly. "Mrs. Hanes . . . guessed. You can talk to me . . . freely in front of her."

Zeke frowned and looked at Mrs. Hanes.

"It's all right, Zeke," the woman said kindly. "I won't say anything to anyone. I understand. And Abbie needs you right now. You say whatever you need to say." Their eyes held a moment.

"You're a kind and good woman, Mrs. Hanes."

"You saved my little girl's life. That isn't something I can forget. You're a fine man—a truthful and honest man. You've risked your life for us more than once. And you have a right to love whomever you choose. Everyone has that right."

Zeke sighed. "I wish it was that simple, ma'am. But there are some of us who have no rights." He changed his position beside Abbie, while Olin moved around to the other side of the girl. "Please have somebody find some moss, Mrs. Hanes," he continued, wanting to change the subject. "Then get some water boiling and get a fire going, with good, hot coals—hot as you can get them."

Abbie's heart pounded with fear at the request, and Mrs. Hanes frowned. "Why?" she asked. Zeke reached out and touched the woman's arm.

"Just do it," he said quietly. Their eyes held, and Mrs. Hanes' eyes filled with tears at the realization of what he was telling her. She nodded and started out of the wagon.

"Mrs. Hanes," Zeke spoke up. She turned to look at him. "Thank you," he told her. "For everything."

"You're welcome, Zeke." The woman left, and Abbie's breathing quickened.

"What are you going to do?" she asked, shaking.

"Calm down, Abbie," he replied softly.

"You're going to *burn* me!" she screamed.

"Damn it, Abbie, I don't know *what* I'm going to do yet! I haven't even seen the wound. Now just relax and let's have a look. And trust me, Abbie girl. You must know that whatever I do, it will be to help you and make you feel better in the long run."

"I'm scared!" she whimpered again.

"Well, so am I," Zeke replied. "Olin, get a hand under her ribs and her neck, and lift her, real gentle, so I can slip off the bandages."

"Sure, Zeke." Olin did as he was told, and Abbie cried out when he lifted her, grasping Olin's forearm with her good hand. "It's gonna be okay, Abigail," Olin reassured her. Zeke took his knife and quickly slit the bandages in one quick movement, not even touching her skin with the knife. He gently unwrapped the gauze.

"I don't want . . . everybody seeing me!" she sobbed.

"Nobody's here but me and Olin—and Mrs. Hanes has been helping, but she's a woman anyway," Zeke replied. "Olin—he's not seeing anything he hasn't seen before, and most likely he's seen a lot more of it,"

417

he added, trying to make her laugh. "Besides, he's my friend and yours. Friends have a way of fast forgetting things that are best forgotten."

He slipped the bandages from under her arm, then looked at Olin with concern.

"What's wrong?" Abbie asked.

Olin gently released her, so that her head was on the pillow again.

"I have to raise your arm some, Abbie," Zeke told her.

"No! It will hurt too much!" she protested.

He leaned closer. "Abbie, look straight at me."

She met his eyes and saw love, tenderness, and deep concern. "Don't you trust me, Abigail?"

"You know I do," she squeaked.

"I won't let you die, Abbie. No matter what it takes, or how much I might have to hurt you at first, I won't let you die. Do you understand me?"

"But . . . you promised—"

"Only if I know it's hopeless. But it *isn't* hopeless, Abigail, and I intend to keep it that way."

"Stay with me!" she whispered.

"I'm not going anywhere. Now let me have a look at you."

She sniffled and closed her eyes. When Olin raised her arm some, she groaned and gritted her teeth against the pain. Then Zeke touched her ribs, and when his hands moved to her breast, she recoiled because of the pain.

"Real bad there?" he asked.

"Yes, yes!" she yelled, breaking into a sweat. He moved his hand to her shoulder and along the top of it.

"How about here?"

418

"It doesn't hurt there."

He moved to her back and shoulder blade, his hand as gentle as a kitten's. "Any pain back here?"

"Just a little."

He touched her upper arm. "Here?"

"No. It's not the arm that hurts when you move it. It's . . . all the muscles around it . . . in my chest."

He touched her side near the breast again, and she screamed, fearing she'd pass out from the pain. Zeke looked at Olin again and Olin gently laid her arm back down. Zeke covered her with the blanket and they gently rolled her onto her back. Zeke bent closer again.

"Abbie girl."

She opened her eyes to stare into his, his gaze dark, hypnotic, and full of love mixed with sorrow for what he would have to do.

"I'm looking at the bravest woman I ever knew. Hell, you've killed yourself two Crows, that renegade who worked for Givens and that one you killed a couple of days ago." He smiled a little, but she knew he was leading up to something bad. "I've never known a girl as brave as you, and that's part of what I love about you."

"You're going to burn me!" she whispered. choking back fresh tears.

"I have to, Abbie. I won't let you die. It's a fact you're full of infection, but I think we can lick it if we move fast. Otherwise you'll end up like Jeremy, and I won't let that happen. But I can't lie to you, Abbie. It will be bad. And I'm asking you to let me do it—not just for you, but for me. Don't make me sit and watch you die like Jeremy did. And don't make me do what you know would be a terrible thing for me. I'll kill myself if I have to do that to you, of all people."

"What will you do?" she asked. "How?"

He kissed her forehead. "I'll have to cut you first, along the side and a little bit around the breast, then I'll force out the pus. Just that much will actually feel better once I'm through, honey. And I'll make it clean as a whistle, so there will be hardly any scar at all. You trust me with this big blade of mine, don't you?"

"I do," she whimpered. "But . . . I don't know, Zeke. It'll hurt . . . so bad!"

"That's a fact, Abbie girl. But you know I'm good with a blade, and I'll do it fast as I can—get it over quickly." Their eyes held, and she began to calm down.

"What if . . . the infection . . . comes back?"

"I doubt that it will, not if I . . . cauterize it good." He swallowed. "I . . . I'll have to burn the infection out of there, Abbie. I have to . . . drive a hot iron through that wound, honey."

Her eyes widened. "N-no!" she finally choked out. "I won't let you! I didn't think . . . you meant to go that far! Don't do that to me, Zeke!"

"It *has* to be done, Abbie. My God, do you think I *want* to do it?"

"No! I'd rather die!"

"You've got no choice. It's the only answer, and if there's a chance of saving you, I intend to do it."

"Please, don't, Zeke!" she sobbed, her fear building to terror. "I'll be all right! Just drain it!"

"No, you *won't* be all right. I'd have to cut you—again and again. It's best to get it burned out of there right now."

"I have to agree with him, Miss Abbie," Olin told her. "Zeke knows what he's doing. He sure as hell doesn't want to do it, honey, but you can make it a lot easier on him if you just accept it. Someday you'll wonder why in hell you wanted to die. You'll be all better—just like new."

She looked back at Zeke and caught him wiping at his eyes. And she knew what a horrible thing it would be for him to hurt her the way he would have to hurt her.

"Stay with me—through everything," she told him, now calmer.

"You know I will," he answered. "Hell, I'm the one who'll be doing it."

"I mean . . . afterward," she pleaded.

He nodded. "I'll be with you, Abbie girl." He bent down and kissed her again. "I'll be with you."

He looked at Olin. "Let's get some more whiskey down her."

He smiled at Abbie. "You'll be able to drink me under the table before this is all over," he teased. But his remark did little to quell her fear and apprehension. He ran a hand over her thighs and belly, and up to her face. "It'll be all right, Abbie girl."

"I'll . . . uh . . . I'll go see what I can find to use for a rod and get it heated up," Olin told Zeke, his own eyes tearing. "You just stay here and keep talkin' to her." As he climbed out of the wagon, Zeke took a hanky Abbie had wadded up in her good hand and wiped tears from her cheeks with it.

"Did you . . . really mean it . . . about me being a real Cheyenne?" she asked him.

"Sure I did. Hell, the Cheyenne men would honor

421

you for killing two Crow. And now you've lived through a Crow arrow. That's mighty strong medicine, Abbie girl."

"Strong enough . . . for you . . . to keep me with you? Let me live . . . with the Cheyenne?"

She felt him tense up, and he moved his hand away from her face. He looked away. "Don't talk about those things right now, Abbie," he answered.

"But . . . I don't care . . . if I live or die . . . if you're still going to leave . . . at Fort Bridger," she whimpered, new tears coming. "I can't . . . take anymore, Zeke! I . . . can't go on! I just . . . can't!"

"Abbie!" he said sternly, grasping her face between his hands. "Not now, Abbie. We'll talk about it . . . when you're better. All right?"

"You mean . . . you'd reconsider?"

Their eyes held for several seconds. "I don't know *what* I mean," he told her. "All I know right now is I don't want you to die, honey. Please hang on for me."

Mrs. Hanes climbed into the wagon with some moss and clean bandages, and their conversation ended. "How are we going?" the woman asked with reassuring smile. Zeke took a long drink of whiskey himself, then started gently forcing some down Abbie's throat.

"I've got to cut her, Mrs. Hanes," he told the woman, as Abbie coughed and grimaced with pain. "Drain the infection. Then I'll cauterize the wound—drive a hot rod through it."

Mrs. Hanes's eyes widened and she grasped her stomach. "You . . . can't do such a thing!"

"I can and I will," he replied, quietly but sternly. "I just got *her* talked into it, Mrs. Hanes, so don't go getting her to change her mind. It's the only way to save her life. If I don't do it, the infection will only get worse and she'll die, and I won't let that happen. I'd rather slit my own throat than do it, but there's no choice. It's the practical thing to do."

There was the word again. "Practical." Abbie wondered how often it was used in this strange, wild land. No matter how painful, or perhaps even sinful it was to do so, like when they'd let the Indians take Connely, one had to be practical in this cruel land to survive. Mrs. Hanes nodded.

"I understand. What do you want me to do?"

"I need a pan for draining the infection," Zeke replied matter-of-factly. "And I need hot water to wash it afterward, and some needle and thread to sew her up. Boil the needle and thread. We already have moss and clean bandages. I'll pack her up good when it's done. Then all we can do is wait. When I'm through, we'll lift her and let you change the bedclothes."

"I'll be right here to do whatever you ask."

Zeke met her eyes and smiled. "I figured you would be. I'm glad I have you to help instead of that worthless Yolanda Brown. How about your kids?"

"Bradley will look after them. He understands. He's as concerned as I am." She pushed a strand of hair behind her ear. "I already have some water heating. I'll go and get a needle and thread and boil it."

When Mrs. Hanes left again, Abbie turned her face away, fighting her awful fear of what was about to be done to her, her only consolation being that it was Zeke himself who would do the work.

"I think I'd rather . . . face Rube Givens again . . . than this!" she whispered. "I'd rather . . . face those . . . renegades."

"Hush, Abigail," he replied softly, while he gently rubbed her forehead and temples. "You know what's out there around us?" he asked.

"What?" she whimpered.

"The Wind River Mountains. They're awful pretty, Abbie girl, and you've got to get well quick so you can see them. There's a lot of snow way up there on those peaks. It's a damned pretty sight. We're high now—real high. We'll have to wrap you up good tonight, because it gets mighty cold here after dark—cold enough to put ice on top of the water barrels."

"In July?" she asked, turning back to face him.

"It's the first of August. But, yes, even in August. It might be summer down on the prairies, but up here it's never summer."

She turned away again. "It will never . . . be summer in my heart again," she told him.

"Don't talk like that, honey."

"It's true. You know . . . why I was . . . out there . . . with Bobby?"

He didn't answer right away, but he kept rubbing her head. "I have a suspicion," he finally answered. She detected a vague ring of jealousy.

"We were . . . just talking," she told him. "Then Bobby . . . he flat out . . . told me he . . . loved me . . . wanted to see more of me . . . when we got to Oregon. . . . He said he . . . suspected and understood . . . about you . . . that it didn't . . . matter." Her voice choked up again. "I saw a chance . . . to maybe just . . . be happy without you, Zeke. But it . . . wouldn't have been . . . what I really wanted. I knew that even . . . if I married Bobby . . . or anybody else . . . it wouldn't be that man . . . in my bed at night."

"Abbie, don't—"

"I . . . can't help it!" she sobbed. "You know . . . what else?"

"What else, Abbie girl?"

"He wanted to . . . kiss me . . . just as a friend. He was so sweet . . . the way he looked at me . . . the things he . . . said to me. . . . And I knew I had to do . . . like you said . . . and be thinking about . . . somebody else. So I . . . let him kiss me. And right when . . . he touched my lips . . . he . . . died! He died! Right then!" Her voice rose to a near scream. "He died! He died! Everybody is dead! Everybody! I want to die, too, Zeke! Just let me die!"

He grasped her face tightly again. "No, Abbie!" he growled. "Now hang on! Hang on for *me!* For *Zeke!*"

"I'm scared! I'm . . . so scared! Stay with me!"

"I said I would." He kissed her forehead and her eyes, keeping her face tight between his hands. "Come on, Abbie girl, you can do it! Make me proud of you."

She choked on a sob. "Do you . . . think I'm bad . . . for kissing Bobby?"

He smiled a little. "No," he replied softly. "You were just being practical."

Now she actually smiled just a little herself, her eyes held by his dark ones. "Practical . . . isn't as . . . exciting," she answered. He bent down and kissed her eyes again.

"It seldom is, Abbie girl. But fewer people get hurt."

"Maybe . . . physically. But . . . what about . . . emotionally?" Her eyes dropped slightly, and her words were slightly slurred. The whiskey was taking effect, and he was glad, for he wasn't quite sure how to answer her last question.

Abbie's head swam and her mind began to drift. Someone poured more whiskey into her mouth, and she was vaguely aware that Mrs. Hanes and Olin had returned. But when she heard Zeke giving orders, she felt her panic building, in spite of her whiskey dulled sensations.

"I wish we had some laudanum along," Zeke said disgustedly. "Whiskey doesn't work near as good."

"Let's hope it's at least almost as good," Kelsoe spoke up. Abbie remembered being upset that Kelsoe was there again; but she had no strength to object, and she knew the man was good-hearted and only there to help. However, if he was there, they must be ready. Her heart pounded and her breathing grew more difficult. She thought she might suffocate; it was so hard to breathe. She heard whimperings and groans as someone moved her, but was not even aware they came from her own lips.

"Stay calm, Abbie," she heard Zeke's gentle voice telling her. That was all she had to still the terrible fear in her heart. Someone had hold of her ankles again, and Olin pulled her arm up. She screamed with pain at the movement, but that was nothing compared to Zeke's knife cutting into her. Then she screamed again, and didn't seem to be able to stop. Her screams were more from fear and horror than from pain; for Cheyenne Zeke was adept with a knife, and he worked cleanly and quickly. The real pain came when she was rolled to her side, and Zeke forced a considerable amount of pus and infection from around her breast and under her arm. She screamed so much that it left her weary, but her screams dwindled to sobs as they washed the cuts and Zeke sewed up the wounds.

Then came the worst part—the pain she would not forget for the rest of her life. Nor would Zeke forget her terrible shriek as he took the red-hot rod and with one quick thrust, using all his strength in order to be quick, forced it through the arrow wound. It was then that Abbie finally passed out.

Nineteen

For the next two days Abbie was aware only of pain and darkness. She lay in a delirious fever as horrible visions floated through her mind: LeeAnn's bloated body with the bullet hole in its forehead; little Jeremy's ugly, infected arm covered with maggots; her father holding a gun to his head; and Rube Givens' leering face. All of the visions were blown out of proportion, and the experience was like one long, never-ending nightmare. At times she was aware of voices, but she was unable to speak or respond. Sometimes she recognized Zeke's voice, urgent, frightened, growling orders; yet she could never really remember actual words—just voices that seemed miles away. Sometimes she heard screams and wondered where they came from, not realizing they came from her own throat.

The first time her mind truly roused again to reality, she opened her eyes to a dimly lit lantern and sensed that it was dark and cold outside. She was warmly packed in quilts, but her nose was cold, and she lay there looking straight up for a moment, wondering if she was truly still alive. At least, she thought, if she was dead, she was not in hell. It was too cold.

As her eyes and mind focused, she realized someone was in the wagon with her. She moved her eyes only, afraid to move her head or any other part of her body, and she saw Zeke. He'd kept his promise to be there when she awoke. He looked much the same as he had when he'd sat and prayed for little Mary Hanes. His hair, unbraided, hung long and shining over his shoulders. He sat cross-legged, his eyes closed, his back straight, and his whole body rigid and concentrating. She knew he was praying for her, and she smiled, her eyes tearing. She wondered how he could possibly be warm, for in spite of the cold night he wore only a leather vest, rather than his usual buckskin shirt. But then a man like Zeke was hardened and tough. The scar on his cheek showed whiter than usual in the lamplight, yet the rest of him seemed darker than usual. She studied his handsome, finely carved face, his strong jawline, and high cheekbones. Her eyes took in his broad shoulders, and the lean, hard muscles of his arms. Once again she found it difficult to believe that she had lain beneath the man at whom she was now looking and had given him pleasure. Her memories of him were gentle and sweet; they always would be—except for those horrible moments when he had shoved the awful hot rod through her wound. At that moment she had hated him with a passion. But she had known why he was doing it.

She tried to swallow, but felt herself choking from the dryness in her mouth and throat. Her slight movement made his eyes instantly open, and he looked at her, surprise and pleasure showing on his face as he realized that she was truly back with the living. She moved her tongue over her lips to try to wet them.

"I . . . need . . . a drink," she managed to choke out. He said nothing, but very quickly moved to a bucket inside the wagon, dipped a ladle into it, and brought her water. Gently he placed a hand under her neck and held the ladle to her mouth.

"Try not to move too much, Abbie girl," he said in a near whisper. "I'll clean you up if it spills." He tipped the ladle slightly, and she drank the water eagerly.

"I . . . want more," she said when she was through.

He put the ladle back. "Let that one settle. See how it sets in your stomach," he replied. "You lost a hell of a lot of blood. That's why you're so thirsty. I'll give you more after a few minutes." He came back beside her and, leaning down close, touched her forehead. "How do you feel, Abbie girl? I think your fever is finally down."

"I don't . . . really know yet," she answered, looking up into his tired, bloodshot eyes. "I have a feeling you look and feel worse . . . than me," she told him, trying to smile.

He grinned a little. "Could be. You've put me through quite a scare the last couple of days. I figured we'd lose you." He pulled the blankets off her shoulder and arm, making sure nothing had bled any further. "Can you bend your arm at all? Move your hand?"

She swallowed. "No!" she answered, afraid to try, sure she could not bear any more pain.

"I'll help you," he told her, touching her forearm. She cried out in fear.

431

"No! Don't touch me!" she whimpered. "I don't want to feel any more pain!"

His eyes filled with sorrow. "I had to do it, Abbie girl. I'd rather have cut out my own heart, and you know it. Please, try to move your arm—for me. If the infection is mostly gone, it won't hurt that much, I promise. It won't be the kind of pain you had before. We have to know, Abbie."

She swallowed again. "Let me try it . . . by myself."

He nodded and held his hands out to his sides. "Be my guest. I won't touch you."

She closed her eyes, took a deep breath, and slowly bent her arm, grinning broadly when she realized it didn't hurt nearly as badly as she had thought it would.

"Good!" he said, moving closer again. He blinked rapidly, as though to hide tears. "You bent your arm, Abbie! Damn, that's a good sign. See if you can lift it straight up, honey."

She smiled with pride at her minor accomplishment, unbending her arm and keeping it straight beside her. Then she raised it slightly, only about four inches, before it began to pain her enough to frighten her. She put it back down quickly.

"It . . . hurts too much . . . that way," she answered, her eyes filling with fear.

"That's okay, Abigail," he told her, leaning closer again. "It takes more chest muscles to move it that way, that's all. They've been cut into and they're just sore." He stroked her hair. "It will be a long time before you're completely healed. When we get to Fort Bridger, I want you to remain there for the winter.

You're going no farther. You've been through too much, and you need a good, long rest. Enough is enough, Abbie girl. Your body and mind are just about spent, and you're way too thin. It would be better if you could just stay put awhile, but we've got to get to Fort Bridger. We've got no choice."

"What will happen to me . . . if you leave me there?"

"You'll be watched good, and I'll take the train on to Oregon—come back in the spring."

"For what? To take me on to Oregon?"

Their eyes held, then he leaned over and pressed his hand gently against her bandaged breast. "Does it hurt bad around here?" he asked, avoiding her question. Abbie decided not to press the subject of what would happen to her in the spring. To think that he might be considering coming back for her permanently was enough hope to go on for the moment, and she needed that hope. "Not like before," she answered. "It's . . . different. It hurts, but it's not that awful kind of hurt that the very air seemed to bring on before."

"Good!" he replied with relief. "Before it was the infection that made the pain so bad. Now you're just plain sore, from the cutting and stitches and all." He moved his hand gently over her shoulder, then along her side under her arm. "Better?"

"Yes."

"The only thing I still have to do is take that thread out of you in a few more days. That will sting some and maybe bleed a little."

She looked down as best she could, and it seemed she was all bandages.

433

"Will I . . . be ugly?" she asked.

He smiled. "You'll be pretty as ever."

Her face fell. "No I won't. Besides, it doesn't matter. Who cares - if no man wants me. There's . . . no man I'd want anyway."

He sighed, and when she met his eyes, it looked as though he wanted to say something but was keeping it to himself.

"Don't talk that way, Abbie girl. You *will* be just as pretty. I'm good with a knife, remember? I did a right neat job, if I must say so myself." He kept stroking her hair. "I don't think the breast is damaged, Abbie. And the scars will fade in time."

She blinked back tears. "Will you . . . stay with me the rest of the night?" she asked. "And would you . . . sing to me?"

He grinned. *"Sing* to you! *Now?"*

"Please?"

He chuckled. "People would think it was mighty strange, me sitting in here singing to you. They'd get to thinking things I don't want them to think."

She sighed. "Why fight it?" she replied. "They all know it anyway, Zeke. Mrs. Hanes guessed. Bobby guessed. Mr. Connely knew. They all know."

He turned away, rubbing a hand over his face and looking weary. "Then I've done a terrible thing," he answered. "The sooner I'm out of your life the better."

"I don't think you really want that. And it's not terrible to love somebody, Zeke. Now, please, sing to me. It would help me go back to sleep. I love the sound of that mandolin, and I'd sure like to hear that song about Tennessee mountain mornings. I want to hear about Tennessee, Zeke."

He smiled resignedly. "You're something. You've got more power over me than ten men, Abigail Trent, and I'm a damned fool. When I thought I was losing you to death—" He stopped short, again looking as though there was more he needed to say. "All right," he went on. "I'll play and sing for you if it will make you rest better. That's what's important." He reached over and picked up a biscuit. "You eat this while I go get my instrument."

She watched his catlike movements as he climbed out of the wagon quietly, and she bit into the biscuit, realizing that she had a true appetite for the first time in weeks. Perhaps the arrow injury had been a godsend, for there was a different look in his eyes. Perhaps nearly losing her to death had made him think about what it would be like to live without her. Now he would have to come back for her at Fort Bridger in the spring. Maybe he would come back before that and spend the winter with her there; then it would be even more difficult for him to leave her.

When he returned, he gave her another drink of water. He'd put on his buckskin shirt and tied his hair at the back of his neck.

"Aren't you cold, Zeke?" she asked. "Don't you want a jacket or something?"

He sat down beside her, crossing his legs and setting the mandolin on his lap. "Indians get used to being cold," he replied. "The winters are mighty long out here, and pretty barren sometimes. I'm all right." He strummed the mandolin and seemed lost in thought for a moment. "Abbie?" He spoke quietly.

"Yes, sir?"

435

"The Crow . . ." He met her eyes. "The Indians aren't all like that, you know."

"I know."

"Even the Crow aren't all a bad lot. Those back there, they were just determined to get what they were after. The Indians are proud and vengeful, Abigail. They believe in proper justice, and they knew the white men had not dealt Connely the kind of justice he had coming."

"I understand Zeke. Like when you avenged your wife's death.'

He looked down at his mandolin. "Like that," he answered. Then he sighed. "Abbie, the Cheyenne, they're mighty warriors," he went on, seeming to be trying suddenly to make her understand Indians better. She wondered why it was suddenly so important to him, and her heart pounded with hope. "But they're also peace-loving, like the Arapaho and the Sioux and the Shoshoni and most others. But they won't be tread on. They have their pride. But they can be a very gentle, beautiful people if a man doesn't push them. They're very spiritual. They have an inner strength and a close contact with the spirit world that most white men will never have."

"Zeke, why are you saying these things to me?"

He met her eyes. "Because their blood runs in my veins, Abbie girl, and because I *love* them! I love them more than anything I've ever loved besides my wife—and you. And anybody that I might . . . bring into my life, he or she would also have to love them. Are you understanding me?"

"I . . . think so," she answered, afraid to take on the full meaning of the question for fear her heart

436

would be broken again.

"Could *you* love them, Abbie? People like the ones who put that arrow in you?"

She swallowed, realizing there was no lying to Cheyenne Zeke. "I honestly don't know . . . right now," she answered. "The ones like you, I could love. And I remember looking at those beautiful little Indian children, back at Fort Laramie, and I could have scooped them up, took them in, and loved them. I would dearly love to have a child like that, fat and brown and sweet. I guess I love the gentle side of you, Zeke, and their gentle side. But the rest of it—their customs and all, their fierceness and rigid pride, their way of life and its difficulties—I'd be lying to jump up and say for sure I could take it all."

"But that's half of what *I* am, Abbie. And I see so much ahead for the Indians, but none of it good. If it comes down to choosing, there is only one way I can go. I know the white man, and I know the Indian; and of the two, the Indian is most times the better human being. Things will get a lot worse, Abbie. But I'll do all in my power to protect and defend my people. They have no one to help them. No one. Some day the government will come through this land like a giant roller; it will crush the Indians right into the earth. And I'll be crushed right along with them, Abbie girl, as will anybody who stands by my side . . . and my children, too, most likely."

Their eyes held for a long, quiet moment. "I understand, Zeke," she finally said. He closed his eyes and sighed. She knew the struggle she would be in for if she walked by his side. He wanted her to see and understand it, wanted her to consider whether or not her love for him and her own constitution were strong enough to bear what they would have to face together in life if they were to marry. To him there was no choice but to live among the Cheyenne.

"I can hear them . . . screaming . . . sometimes, Abbie," he said in a broken voice, his face showing pain and inner struggle. "My people. I see women, children, old people shot to pieces, cut down with no mercy. Sometimes I ride alone, and I hear the rocks talking, telling me someday there will be no more Indians roaming free on the land, no more buffalo, no more wildlife, no more quiet places. And I'm so . . . torn, Abbie!"

His voice choked, and her heart bled for him. It was not an easy thing for a man like Zeke to sit there and spill out his feelings; and she knew he did it only because he knew she loved him, because he'd come so close to losing her that perhaps he knew he could not make it alone anymore. Yet he knew it was important that she understand him.

"I'm torn," he went on, taking a deep breath, "because . . . I want to be with you, Abbie. Only I don't know if I can do both . . . because I don't want to take someone I love and put her through what I know is coming. I don't want to watch . . . someone I love suffer, because I've already been down that road. Living with the whites, my woman would suffer terrible gossip and be shunned, - perhaps even physically abused like my first wife. But living among the Cheyenne could end up badly, too. For there is a rough road ahead for my people."

She reached over and touched his arm. "Tell me about your Cheyenne mother, Zeke."

438

He leaned back, his eyes closed. "She is very beautiful—even now. I loved my father until he took me from her. Then I hated him!" His jaw flexed, and he breathed deeply. "He turned out to be like most whites, thinking Indians weren't worth any more than animals. Seven years! Seven years he lived with my Indian mother, and then, when I was only four, he up and sold her like a slave—took me back to Tennessee. The day we left my mother ran after us, crying, begging pa not to take her son from her, but he just kept riding, with me on the horse in front of him, going faster and faster until finally she fell and couldn't keep up anymore. The Crow man he'd sold her to came and got her and started hitting her." His voice choked again. "And pa, he just kept riding and left her back there with him. That's when I first knew I hated the Crow and I hated my pa!

"Eventually she was recaptured by the Cheyenne during a fight they had with the Crow, and she married a Cheyenne man. But I had no way of knowing it right then. It wasn't until years later, when I went searching for her, that I found to my great relief she was back with the Cheyenne and had had three more sons."

"It must have been wonderful for her," Abbie said quietly, "to see you again."

He nodded. "It was quite a reunion. I love my Cheyenne mother very much, Abbie. She's my true blood."

"What about . . . Tennessee? I guess it must have been real bad for you."

"It's bad for a half-breed anywhere, Abbie girl. My pa, he loved me just because I was his son. He tried to

439

help—got in a couple of fist fights himself over me. But people continued to shun me, and I continued to get in fights at school until they kicked me out for good. Then, like I told you earlier, they wouldn't let me come to the church anymore. But it didn't matter, because I didn't think much of their religion anyway. I remembered what my mother had taught me about the Cheyenne religion, and that made a lot more sense. My pa, he'd remarried, and his new wife never liked me—liked me even less once she had three sons of her own. It's kind of ironic: I have three white half brothers and three red. Their ages aren't even a whole lot different. At any rate, I hated it there—tried to run away once. That's when I walked the Trail of Tears with the Cherokee. But somehow the soldiers discovered I wasn't one of them, and they shipped me back. Then I met Ellen." He sighed and hesitated. "God, I loved her, Abbie!" he whispered. He cleared his throat. "I thought then that I could stay in Tennessee and make it . . . because I had Ellen. Then the white man showed his stuff real good . . . and I lost her . . . and my little son. Then I knew for sure that I belong with the Cheyenne, and so will my children, if I have any more. I came out here and found my mother . . . and I stayed."

He opened his eyes and stared at Abbie. "It's a hard life, Abbie girl. Don't kid yourself that it's anything else. And I'm telling you right now that I've not decided on anything for sure. You've put me in a bad fix, little girl. Me—a grown man—all confused and crazy over a woman-child. I've given you things to think about, and I want you to think real hard."

She squeezed his hand. "I know what you're trying

440

to tell me, Zeke, and I . . . appreciate it." She closed her eyes. "I'm tired . . . Zeke. I don't want you to worry . . . about all that now. Just sing to me. . . . I need to sleep. When we . . . get to Ford Bridger . . . we'll talk again. We'll make a decision . . . and abide by it. At least, I had you for a . . . while."

He leaned closer again, kissing her cheek. "I love you, Abbie," he whispered. His lips moved to her mouth, and he kissed her lightly, then sat back and strummed the mandolin, its haunting music drifting through her groggy mind and making her smile. Faintly, she heard the words of the song about Tennessee mountain mornings, and she decided Zeke was a lot like the mandolin music, mystical and out of reach, a man who drifted over the mountains like his music. She fell asleep dreaming about herself and Zeke floating together over the mountains to a secret place that was just their own, one in which they could live together with no one to tell them it was wrong, one with no white men and no Indians—just the two of them.

Eight days later, on the eleventh of August, they rolled into Fort Bridger. Zeke had not returned to her, once he'd realized she would get better. Mrs. Hanes told her Zeke would be taking out her stitches when they got to the fort, but when Abbie asked why he did not come to see her, the woman only shrugged. "He's been very busy, way up ahead of us most of the time," the woman replied.

Abbie turned away, hiding tears of disappointment. She knew he was allowing her time to think without him around, and he was doing the same for himself.

But her heart pounded with fear that, not being around her, it would be easier for him to decide to take the practical route. And she was more and more certain that at Fort Bridger he would not bring her the answer she wanted.

She healed slowly, but when they reached the fort, she could raise her arm, although not all the way without considerable pain; and she was still much too thin. They limped into the fort with nine men instead of their original fourteen, and seven wagons instead of ten. Kelsoe had lost both David and Bobby, and of course all of Abbie's family was gone, as were Quentin Robards and Morris Connely. Willis Brown had lost five head of cattle and a couple of horses, which greatly upset him; but Abbie thought to herself that he should be grateful it wasn't his own life, his wife's, or his parents' lives that had been lost. She wished that a few animals were all that she had lost.

Abbie was carried by Olin Wales into a small log cabin at the unfinished fort. "Jim Bridger has been workin' on this place slow but sure," he told her on the way. "Figures there will be lots more wagon trains comin' through here over the years and he's gonna be here to keep them supplied."

"Where's Zeke?" Abbie asked him with a heavy heart.

"Don't rightly know, Abbie girl. He's been lost in thought and hardly around ever since you got wounded. I reckon he has a lot on his mind, and you know why. But he's told me nothin', Abbie, so I've nothin' to tell you. I reckon he'll do the tellin' himself before this train heads out again."

Inside the cabin they were greeted by a short, stocky

man, all in buckskins like most of the men in that part of the country. His face was framed by thick, graying hair that hung long, and he smiled at Abbie through a grizzly beard and mustache. He seemed rather unkempt, but not dirty, like a man who was simply too busy to bother shaving and combing his hair all the time. From head to toe he was "outdoors"; every bit of him looked like a man who'd almost never slept under a roof.

"Well, now, you must be Miss Abigail Trent!" the man said in a kindly voice. "Bring her over here to this cot, Olin. Nice and comfy and warm here."

"Thanks, Jim," Olin replied. He layed Abbie on the cot, and the other man put an extra blanket over her, a colorful Indian blanket. Then he knelt down beside her a moment.

"I'm Jim Bridger, ma'am, and this here—Wind River Range, the Green River, the South Pass—it's all my stompin' grounds. This is Jim Bridger territory, Miss Trent, and you don't have a thing to worry about. Between me and Olin Wales, you'll be safe and snug right here for the winter while you get yourself well. Cheyenne Zeke is a damned good friend of mine, and I have a hunch you're pretty special to him, so I aim to take good care of you."

Abbie blushed slightly and glanced at Olin, who just winked. "I'm obliged, Mr. Bridger," she told the man, looking back at him. "And I'm honored to meet you."

He patted her hand and stood up, pulling up a chair by the fireplace and gesturing to Olin to sit in another chair across from him.

"One of your men outside tells me there have been

some Crow and Blackfoot raidin' these parts," Olin told Bridger, removing his hat and hanging it on the back post of the chair. "That worries me some. I expect Zeke told you we already run into some Crow a few days back. That's when Miss Abbie took that arrow."

Bridger got up and threw a few more logs on the fire. "Nothin' to fret about," he replied. "Me and my men can handle the damned Crow. They don't bother the fort much, and I've got good men here—straight shooters and not a coward among them. And you know I've been around Indians most of my life. Been around them so much I might as well *be* one!"

Both men chuckled, and Bridger sat back down, stretching and putting his hands behind his head.

"What about along the Bear River and up to Fort Hall?" Olin asked. "Any more danger for the wagon train? Them folks has been through a lot."

"Once they get past the Bear River, I don't expect they'll have any more Indian trouble, Olin. Their big problem now will be to get the hell to Oregon before the snow sets in. I feel an early winter comin' on. The sooner Zeke gets goin', the better."

Her words pierced Abbie's heart, making her realize that it would not be long before she knew whether Zeke would come back for her or if he would make arrangements for someone else to get her to Oregon in the spring. In the latter case, she would never see him again.

"A couple of my men are gettin' itchy to be on a horse again," Bridger went on, "so I expect Zeke will have some good help with him, now that you'll stay on here with Miss Trent. Me—I've got plenty here to trade to the Indians, keep them calmed down. I just wish the Crow and Blackfoot were as easy-goin' as the Arapaho and the Cheyenne. Not that the Cheyenne aren't capable of making plenty of trouble if somebody makes trouble for *them!*" he added with a chuckle. "No better warriors ever rode the plains." The man lit a pipe.

"Zeke . . . uh . . . he thinks highly of Miss Trent," Olin told the man. "He won't be wantin' anything to happen to her."

"And nothin' will," Bridger replied. "What about her wound? Does it still need attention?"

"It's healin' good, but she'll be mighty sore for a long time and still can't move her arm much. It's more a matter of time than anything else now. She's still got stitches in her. I expect Zeke will be takin' them out before he leaves. But she's been through so much more than just the arrow wound, I expect she's got as much healin' to do mentally as physically. Zeke says if a doctor happens to pass through, he wants us to be sure to have the man take a look at her. Maybe he'd have along some kind of tonic for her."

"Maybe so. In the meantime we'll see she's fed good, get some meat back on her bones," Bridger replied, puffing on the pipe.

Abbie felt embarrassed and strange, lying there listening to the two men talk about her as though she wasn't present. She toyed with the designs on the Indian blanket, thinking of Zeke. So, he would take the stitches out before he left. At least she knew she would see him once more. Her eyes dropped from fatigue again, and she wondered how she could possibly be so tired from just from being carried from the wagon to

445

the cabin. She was aware of more conversation, but she heard little of it until she opened her eyes to a hand on her forehead. It was Jim Bridger's.

"We're gonna go out and let you rest now, ma'am," the man told her. "We'll be by later with some supper for you. I've got a good fire goin', so you'll be warm." When he patted her head and walked out, Olin came close.

"You need anything just now, Miss Abbie?" he asked.

"No," she replied in a tired voice. Then from nowhere the tears came. "Where is he, Olin? I want to see Zeke!"

"Now, now. You rest," he replied, patting her cheek. "He'll be around when he's ready to be."

"I . . . love him, Olin!" she whimpered. "But he won't keep me with him, will he?"

"I can't answer that, honey," Olin told her. "If it was me, I'd sure as hell keep a woman like you. But Zeke is Zeke, and he's got that terrible memory that keeps him from bein' happy. But you gotta try to rest right now, Miss Abbie."

He stroked her hair back from her face, and that, combined with her weariness and the warmth of the fire and the comfort of a real bed, lulled her back to sleep. She woke up in the middle of the night when Olin and Mrs. Hanes came to check her wound and change the gauze; but then she cried herself to sleep again, for it had not been Zeke who came, nor did he come at all that night. Time was growing short before she would have to say good-bye to him forever.

Twenty

Abbie sat in an old, stuffed chair that some of Jim Bridger's men had brought out to the campfire for her. It was their second night at Fort Bridger, a night of celebration before moving on to Fort Hall, and Abbie had cried and begged until Mrs. Hanes had acquiesced and allowed her to join the others, but only if she wore her warmest coat and was covered with a quilt against the chilly, night mountain air. Two of the scouts from the fort sat playing fiddles, a third tooted a beat out with a ceramic jug, and yet another sang humorous folk songs, while the listeners sat, clapping their hands and laughing at the ridiculous words. Abbie tried to participate in the joy of the evening, celebrating with the others the fact that their trip was more than half over. She hoped all their troubles were behind them. But a cold, dark mist lay heavy on her heart, for she still had not seen Zeke since their arrival. Apparently he intended to see her only long enough to remove her stitches before he left, which could mean only one thing—he had made his decision.

When he left for Oregon, it would be the last she would see of him, and by his absence, he hoped to make it easier for them both.

Everyone, even Yolanda Brown, came to tell Abbie good-bye, to wish her a speedy recovery, and to expressing sympathy for her terrible losses on their trail West. Mrs. Hanes stayed close to Abbie, knowing inside her own heart just how unhappy she must be, and she frequently assured her that when she came the rest of the way to Oregon the next spring, the Hanes family would still have a home ready and welcome for her. Even Mrs. Hanes could see what Zeke was doing, and she understood why; but she was worried about Abbie's spirits, and her heart ached for this lonely young woman who would be left behind while the rest of them went on to Oregon without her.

Several of the men from the fort came to speak to Abbie, taking off their beaver-skin hats and bowing low to her as they introduced themselves. All of them expressed praise for the fact that she'd shot a Crow before she took the arrow, and their respect and admiration was obviously genuine. Abbie could not help but feel a tinge of personal pride and satisfaction in her feat, noticing that a woman of courage and determination was well thought of in this wild and untamed land. It was obvious that any one of the men would have gladly pursued further conversation with her, but she sensed a certain hesitance, even in their short conversations. She wondered if the rumor had spread among them that she belonged to Cheyenne Zeke. If so, she did not detect any of the disrespect Zeke seemed to think these white men would show her if they knew, nor were there any leering or suggestive looks. It could be different out here; of that she was certain. There would certainly be those who would deplore such a relationship; but surely it could not be as bad for them in this new and freer land as it had been for Zeke and Ellen back in Tennessee, where society was more civilized and more judgmental.

She could understand why Zeke would want her to stay at Fort Bridger, for Jim Bridger was himself an honest and dependable man; and the other men who worked for him at the fort all appeared to be experienced and strong. She knew her stay there would be safe and protected, yet she could never feel as safe and protected as she would if she belonged to Zeke.

She watched the others from the train, as they sang and laughed and danced, realizing how much she would miss them, even Willis and Yolanda Brown. She decided she would start a diary while she recuperated at the fort. She would write down everything she could remember about the trip, these people whom she had come to know so well, and those who had been lost on the way. In spite of the fact that she did not want to think of a future without Cheyenne Zeke, she knew she had no choice in the matter. And perhaps, after all, someday she would have children and grandchildren and her trip West should be preserved in writing so that nothing would be forgotten—least of all, Cheyenne Zeke. Because of him, and because of all her sufferings, the Abigail Trent who sat at campfire that night at Fort Bridger was incredibly different from the bashful, innocent child who had left Tennessee. She was a woman now, in spite of her age, and her whole world had been turned upside down. She felt as though she were another person, and the new Abbie had never even lived in Tennessee, or had a mother and father, a sister and a brother. All were gone now. There was only herself; and already she was drawing on some secret, inner strength that she had just begun to learn dwelled within her small frame.

"Are you warm enough, Abbie?" Mrs. Hanes asked, interrupting the girl's thoughts.

"Yes, ma'am," she replied. She sighed. "Do you think he'll be here tonight?"

The woman patted her hand. "I wouldn't know, dear. I'm so sorry it has turned out this way. But surely you knew how Zeke felt. Surely you knew—"

"Hey, Olin!" one of the men from the fort called out loudly, interrupting Mrs. Hanes's conversation. "Where's that half-breed friend of ours? I seen him come ridin' in here just before the train arrived, and I ain't seen him since," the man went on jovially.

"You know Zeke," Olin replied. "He might be standin' right behind you and you wouldn't even know it. He's got things on his mind, Dooley. I expect he's out there somewhere doin' some heavy thinkin'."

"If it's that heavy, then it must be over a woman!" the man called Dooley replied, slapping his knee and laughing. Some of the others laughed good-heartedly with him, while Abbie blushed and the one called Dooley took a long swallow of whiskey. "I sure wish Zeke would show up," he continued loudly. "Him and me have shared a lot of whiskey together. Ain't seen the half-breed for a hell of a long time."

"I expect he'll be around eventually," Olin assured the man, glancing at Abbie with troubled eyes.

"Ain't nobody on God's earth better with a blade than the half-breed," Dooley added, looking around at the others now and standing up. "Like I say, me and Zeke have drunk a lot of whiskey together. Why, I remember the time we walked into a saloon down in Cheyenne country by the Arkansas River. The white settlers around those parts—they don't have much use for Indians, if you know what I mean, and they especially don't like Indians comin' into the white men's saloons." Everyone quieted, realizing the man was building up to something. Dooley took another drink of whiskey. "But Zeke, he never let them things bother him much. So he just walked into that saloon and mosied up to the bar and flat-out asked for a whiskey." The man, who was feeling his own whiskey and loved to tell a good story, began walking around the small group of travelers. "And then," he went on, "about six—maybe seven or eight men—they came up and told the bartender not to serve Zeke. Hell, I expect they didn't even know he was a half-breed. That would have made matters even worse. But bein' a Cheyenne was bad enough, and ol' Zeke, he looks *all* Cheyenne." He took another swallow of whiskey and wiped his lips. "Me—I backed off, figurin' Zeke would do the same on account of there was so many of them and they had murder in their eyes. But when Zeke just told the bartender again to give him some whiskey, my blood run cold with fear for what would happen next."

The man chuckled, and everyone listened attentively, even the little Hanes children, and especially Abbie, whose heart felt again her awful loneliness.

"Well, dang it, Dooley, finish the story!" one of the other men spoke up. Dooley smiled, pleased by his listeners' excitement.

"Well, one of the men, he made a remark to the bartender about not givin' whiskey to a no-good, stinkin' Indian," Dooley went on, his own eyes widening with excitement. "Zeke, he just turned and looked at that man. And I'll bet most of you who have traveled with him know how he can look at a man when he's mad. Sometimes just his look can do a man in, you know?"

"We know," Mr. Hanes replied with a little grin, and Abbie could feel the tenseness of the listeners as all waited to find out what happened next.

"Well, them two men stared at each other a minute, and then the one who made the remark, he pulled a knife. A *knife!*" Dooley accented the word, his voice low and raspy with intrigue. "Can you *believe* it? Lord God, that man sure didn't know what he was doin'—pullin' a *knife* on Cheyenne Zeke!"

Everyone grinned, but Abbie felt her eyes tearing at the thought of what Zeke had gone through just because of prejudice against his race. Dooley lowered his voice even more as he continued, walking around the small group of people and looking at them one by one as he spoke.

"The half-breed, he backed up some, and I stayed out of the way, 'cause I knew Zeke knowed what he was doin'. Then he whipped out that big blade of his. 'We're gonna do you in, Indian!' one of them other men says. And a couple *more* of them pulled knives! Zeke, he just crouched down, wavin' that blade of his, ready to pounce on them all like a bobcat! And next thing, they were all on him at once!" He stopped to drink more whiskey, and everyone waited.

"Well?" Kelsoe finally asked anxiously. "What happened then?"

"Well, sir, they all went at it," Dooley finally replied. "Oh, it was a terrible thing to see. Zeke, he was like a roarin' grizzly; right mad, he was! Tables spilled and drinks crashed to the floor and chairs went flyin', and Zeke let out some warhoops like you never heard before—slashin' here, slashin' there! When it was over, four men lay dead on the floor, and another three took off through the windows, leavin' a trail of blood like a river! That there tavern was *covered* with blood, from ceilin' to wall to floor! But you know what?" The man grinned and chuckled, taking one more swallow of whiskey.

"What? What?" the schoolteacher's son asked, wide-eyed with excitement. Dooley stepped close to the boy and replied slowly.

"Not . . . one . . . drop . . . of that blood . . . was *Zeke's*!"

The crowd sat quietly for a moment, as they began to comprehend what the man was telling them.

"Is that the real truth?" Hanes asked.

"As God is my witness!" Dooley answered. "Ask Olin there. He knows what Zeke can do with that knife."

All eyes turned to Olin, and the man grinned a little. "I seen a man draw a gun on Zeke once," he told them. "And before he could fire, Zeke had his blade out and give it a throw—landed in the man's chest before he even pulled the trigger."

Abbie shivered, not sure if it was from the cold, or from the pictures Dooley and Olin had conjured up in her mind. It was difficult to comprehend the vast difference in the two men Cheyenne Zeke could be; for the one who handled the blade as they said he did

453

seemed a far cry from the one who had made love to her so gently.

Everyone actually seemed to jump when Zeke himself suddenly stepped into the light of the fire and glared at Dooley with a rather dissatisfied look.

"You telling stories again, Dooley?" he asked sternly. Dooley's smile faded.

"Just the truth, Zeke," the man replied, walking up to the man and putting out his hand.

"Spreading those stories about me doesn't make my life any easier, Dooley," Zeke told him. Dooley pulled his hand back and rubbed it nervously on his trouser leg.

"Well, Zeke, I . . . just tell them because I'm . . . proud to know you, that's all," the man answered, looking worried. "Ain't many men can share their whiskey with another man who's practically famous for the way he uses a blade." Dooley held his whiskey bottle out to Zeke as though it were a peace offering, and Zeke's anger faded slightly, replaced by a faint smile that passed over his lips. He took the bottle from Dooley.

"Do me a favor, Dooley, and don't be so free with my life's stories. There're some things maybe a man don't want told." He took a swallow of the whiskey.

"Sure, Zeke," Dooley replied, obviously a little worried that he had upset the man. The others just stared, as though Zeke were something to be revered, but also feared. Zeke frowned and looked over at the musicians.

"Well, get busy and give these nice people some more music!" he said in a rather perturbed voice. "I heard a lot of playing and singing a few minutes ago,

454

and these folks have a lot to celebrate for just being alive!"

The fiddlers dived into another song; and the tension was broken, as several of the mountain men gathered around Zeke, offering him more whiskey and slapping him on the back, while some of the men from the train joined them, thanking him for getting them this far and asking him how he thought the rest of the trip would go.

Abbie just watched. He had not even looked at her yet, and her heart pounded with dread at what he would say when he did speak to her—if he spoke to her at all. Yet as she watched him, she was even more sure she could not live without him now. They had been through too much together: laughed together, cried together, suffered together, even fought together. And most wonderful of all, they had made love. He knew her intimately, and he had brought forth from her passion and an almost wicked abandonment of her inhibitions and common sense.

She stared at his broad, strong physique. He wore his white beaded shirt, and his hair was tied near each ear and hung in two plaits over the front of his shoulders. The white headband he wore contrasted provocatively with the dark skin of his stirringly handsome face. His smile flashed bright and beautiful as he spoke and drank with the other men, and she could not imagine anything more wonderful than to be called Cheyenne Zeke's woman.

She watched hopefully until finally his eyes glanced her way and held her own for a moment as though seeking her answer. And there was only one answer she could give him as she looked back lovingly. She would suffer anything to be at his side. He looked away again as little Mary Hanes approached him and pleaded with him to sing and play the "pretty mandolin." Zeke had never been able to say no to the child, so he left for a moment and, returning with the instrument, sat down on a stump. He hoisted little Mary to his lap, reaching around her to play the mandolin, and Abbie found it difficult to believe he was the same man who handled a blade the way Dooley and Olin had said he did. But she knew it was true, for she had seen some of what he could do with her own two eyes.

Zeke strummed on the instrument for a few minutes, while the rest of them quieted, and then he sang a song about a bumblebee for little Mary. The child put her arms around his neck and her head on his shoulder, falling asleep before the song was even finished.

Mrs. Hanes took the child from him then, chuckling and shaking her head at the contrast between the big, dark half-breed and the tiny, blond-haired girl who had learned to love and trust him.

"Sing us another one!" Dooley spoke up, seeming to be anxious to get on Zeke's good side and to reassure himself that they were still friends. Some of the others insisted also, and Zeke strummed on the mandolin softly, letting its haunting music flow forth into the night air, while he sat with his eyes closed, humming a tune Abbie had never heard before. When he opened his eyes, the crowd quieted, and he looked straight at Abbie as he sang.

"She walked into my life like a shadow;
And I watched her move across the meadow bright.
I ran out there to catch her,

But she slipped right through my fingers;
And now she's just a whisper in the night."

Everyone listened quietly to the lovely song that he had apparently made up, for none of them had ever heard it before. He continued to look at Abbie as he sang, and her heart pounded and her eyes filled with tears as she realized the song was meant for her.

"I'm a man without a home, nor a woman.
I suppose that's just the way it has to be.
I was born to be lonely,
To belong to myself only,
And that girl I saw could not belong to me."

Her heart sank at the message he was giving her.

"I watched her walk away in the twilight.
She smiled as she passed, and beckoned me.
But I knew I could not go.
For my soul is not my own;
And that pretty girl and I could never—"

He stopped suddenly and stood up, walking closer to Abbie, his eyes holding hers like those of a hypnotist, while the others watched curiously. Tears slipped down Abbie's cheeks at the thought that this could be the last time she saw him this way, the last time he would sing to her—the last time for everything. Then he reached out and gently touched her cheek with the back of his hand. He closed his eyes and sighed resignedly, then turned to the others.

"Dooley told you a story tonight," he said quietly.

"It was true." His eyes scanned the crowd, as though ready to defend his next words against whatever someone might have to say against them. "I've fought a lot of men," he went on, "and led a violent life because of what I am. I've not asked for most of those fights. But they come to me anyway, and I usually win. But there's one fight I guess I've lost. Some of you folks already know I have . . . strong feelings for Miss Trent here. I've been fighting those feelings—for obvious reasons. I intended tonight to be the end of it for myself and Miss Trent. But a vision I once had tells me different—and almost losing her to death told me even more. Now, tonight, looking at her and knowing what's in her own heart, knowing what she has suffered, I must admit that I've lost this fight." He turned back to Abbie. "I want to marry Miss Trent . . . if she'll have me," he went on. "And I'll kill every last man who dares to insult her for loving a half-breed."

Mrs. Hanes gasped with pleasure, and the others stared quietly as Zeke held Abbie's eyes. Abbie's heart pounded wildly, and her face felt flushed. Zeke reached out his hand, and she took it with her usable arm, putting his hand to her face and bursting into all-out crying as incredible joy and relief flowed through her veins. Zeke stroked her hair with his other hand and looked at Mrs. Hanes.

"Now what's a man supposed to think when he asks a woman to marry him and she starts bawling her head off?" he asked with a grin. Mrs. Hanes laughed.

"I think it means yes," she answered.

"Yahoo!" Dooley shouted, slugging down some more whiskey. The fiddlers broke into the wedding march, but with a fast beat, and the others laughed and came up to Zeke, congratulating him with genuine joy.

"Hell, all of us knew how you felt about her, Zeke," Kelsoe told him.

"You made the right decision, Zeke," Hanes added. "That little girl loves you and she's all alone now. She needs you."

"You got yourself one perty young lady there, Zeke!" one of Bridger's men told him, slapping Zeke on the back.

Jim Bridger himself came up to him then, and Zeke pulled his hand away from the still-crying Abbie to shake the man's hand. "Congratulations!" Bridger told him. "And out here in these parts, we have to make do. So if you want to marry her tonight, I'll perform the marriage myself. I don't reckon God cares much who does it, just so's it's done and it's wrote down on paper legallike. You should be with her tonight, since you'll be leavin' out for Oregon tomorrow."

"That's what I was hoping for," Zeke replied. "I'll be back for her in early spring or sooner—soon as I can get here, Jim."

"With a pretty young thing like that waiting for me, I'd ride hard to get back too!" the man replied with a chuckle. "You get her calmed down, and we'll have us a wedding yet tonight! I'll leave my cabin to the two of you tonight."

The beautiful words swam in Abbie's head, and she wondered if she was dreaming as she felt Zeke lifting her in his arms. She put her good arm around his neck, crying on his shoulder as he carried her away from the

459

crowd and sat down on a log alone with her.

"Come on now, woman, quit your crying," he told her, kissing her hair and eyes. He touched her left breast gently. "How are you healing, Abbie girl?"

"Good," she sniffled. "I'm . . . healing good." She buried her face in his neck again. "Oh, Zeke, do you truly mean it? You'll really . . . marry me?"

"I'd better. I just asked you in front of all those people."

"Oh, I love you! I love you, Zeke! I'll be good to you. I won't ever complain . . . or turn you away in the night. I'll be the best wife a man could ever want!"

"I know all that," he replied softly, moving his lips over her cheek and then to her own lips, kissing her hungrily. The kiss lingered, sweet and hot and searching, as his hands moved over her thighs and abdomen. He left her lips, moving his mouth to her neck. "I know you aren't well, Abbie—"

"It's all right. You'll be gentle, and I can lie still. You'll just have to be careful of the wound. I might not be well, but I'll not let you go tomorrow without being your woman tonight," she whispered.

They kissed again. "I must be crazy to do this!" he whispered. "I see so much suffering ahead, Abbie girl."

"We'll get through it together."

"There will be wars, Abbie—bloody battles."

"Then we'll just fight side by side. We've done it already."

"But it will be white against Indian."

"I'm your woman. Whoever you do battle with, I do battle with. The Cheyenne will be my family. I'll learn their ways, and I'll learn to love them. I'm young, Zeke. I bend easy."

"It's such a hard life."

"I've never had an easy one."

"There won't be a permanent house."

"My home is with you. Wherever we are together, we'll be home."

"You'd be leaving everything familiar to you behind."

"I'll keep a few things: pa's fiddle, mama's necklace—little things. I'll leave Jeremy's clothes here for Mr. Bridger to give to Indian children. And I'll give my ma's clock to Mrs. Hanes. She'd like to have it, and I'll always know it will be taken care of. I have no family left. There is no past for me anymore, Zeke. Only a future—with you."

"What about Tennessee?"

They kissed hungrily again.

"That's behind me, too," she replied when his lips left hers. "I don't belong there anymore. I belong out here, with the mountains and the prairies—and you."

"God, I love you, Abbie," he whispered. "That's the only thing I know. When you took me inside of you, you took my soul, damn you! I don't belong to myself anymore. I've got no strength to fight when I'm near you. I wanted to go on without you, but I can't do it. I'm so tired of being alone, Abbie. I want a wife—children again."

"I'll give you all the children you want," she answered, her body on fire for him. "It's going to be a long winter without you, Zeke."

He searched her eyes lovingly. "That's a fact. But when I come back, you'll be rested and healed, and we can go on down to the Arkansas - and the Cheyenne."

461

She took a deep breath. "It's kind of scary. Do you think they'll accept me?"

He grinned. "You've killed two Crow. They might make you a *chief* for that!"

She smiled. "Oh, Zeke, I'll try real hard to make you proud of me. I'll be as good a squaw as the best Cheyenne woman."

"I know you will." He kissed her again. "I'll do my best to protect you from all harm, Abbie girl."

"I know you will."

"It will be so hard for you."

"Not as hard as living without you."

"It was you in the vision, Abbie. It was you all along."

"I knew."

"But there's more, Abbie girl." His eyes filled with sorrow. "I see great personal loss ahead, things we will be able to bear only because of our love for each other."

She nodded. "I'm prepared, Zeke. I've already known great personal loss and suffered through it alone."

"But someday you'll be alone again. I see that, too. It's far in the future, Abbie girl, but I saw you in a dream. You were older, your hair graying. You stood on top of a mountain alone. I came to you, only I was an eagle. My spirit was in the eagle. My people call me Lone Eagle, Abbie. I know what the vision means. It means I'll go before you."

Tears trickled down her cheeks, and she touched his face. "You said my hair was gray. That means we have a lot of years together first, Zeke. I'll take those years—and whatever comes after. I'd rather have you

462

for a while than to never have you at all. Whatever lies ahead, you'll be with me forever, if not in body, then in spirit. And you'll live with me through our children." She studied his dark eyes. "Let's go get married, Zeke," she whispered. "Tonight we're alive and in love. I want to sleep with you and be your woman. The future belongs to someone else. Today belongs to us."

He picked her up and carried her back, while high above them on a mountain peak an eagle sat, keeping its babies warm. And no one knew that in time, both the eagle and the Indian would be all but extinct. The white man had invaded the Indian's last hunting grounds, and great challenges lay ahead for Cheyenne Zeke and his woman.

* * *

I will stay with you, my love,
I will bear the hardships life brings us.
For life would be so much more unbearable
Without you.
We will follow the uncaught wind,
And range with the eagle and all wild things—
Wild and free . . . like you, my darling . . .
And like the love we share . . . wild and free.
Wild and free.

EXPERIENCE THE SENSUOUS MAGIC
OF JANELLE TAYLOR!